Acclaim

"*Fractured* grips readers from the very first page and won't release its hold until the last. Anderson is a master of prose and has created a compelling world of power and the consequences that come with it. The story is filled with characters who will make you laugh out loud one moment and tug on your heartstrings the next—characters with real depth and struggles to overcome. Each page is woven with supernatural mystery and danger that will have readers racing through chapter after chapter to learn what happens next. I am more than eager to have the next book in my hands!"

—ASHLEY BUSTAMANTE, author of the Color Theory trilogy

"A delicious, gripping thrill of a read! I was alternately on the edge of my seat and laughing out loud. A truly masterful combination."

—AJ SKELLY, author of The Wolves of Rock Falls series and *Of Flame & Frost*

"*Fractured* has all the elements of *X-Men* mixed into a boiling vat of teenage angst, unnerving powers, and nefarious villains. Written in a snappy style with unapologetic snark and wit, the characters Anderson has created are guaranteed to plant themselves in your mind and stay there. I am eagerly awaiting book two!"

—AMANDA WRIGHT, author of *Darkfell*

"Filled with action, snark, and special powers, *Fractured* is a blast—literally. While exploring what it takes to truly to deal with emotions, this book takes you deep while also keeping things light with a fun cast of characters as unique as their powers and an intricate backstory that unravels at just the right pace. Watch out for this one, it'll keep you up at night!"

—E. A. HENDRYX, award-winning author of *Suspended in the Stars*

FRACTURED

SARA K. ANDERSON

FRACTURED

Quill & Flame
PUBLISHING HOUSE

Quill & Flame
PUBLISHING HOUSE

Fractured

To my sweet husband, who somehow gets written into my stories in one way or another. I guess it's because you are my world, and therefore a part of every world I create.

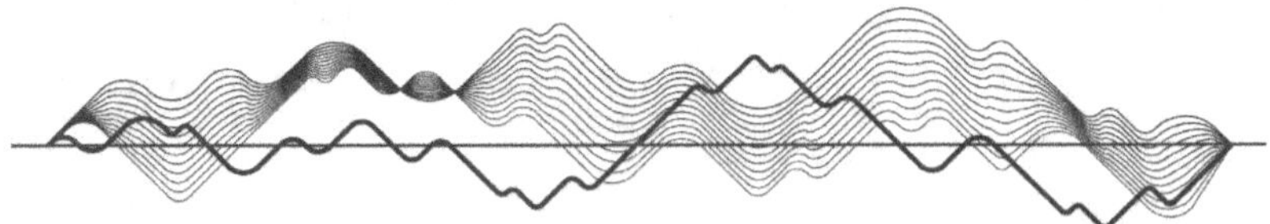

Chapter 1: Ryan

It's time. To anyone else, the text would seem harmless enough, but for Ryan, the two words had his spine seizing as if encased in ice.

Get over it, Ryan, he told himself. *The zombie will take over, and you won't even remember what happened.*

Hunting down fellow Psychics never got easier, but then, he didn't deserve easy. Not after what he'd done.

Ryan pulled up his hood, casting his face in shadow. Moonlight spilled over his hands as he crouched on the sill and flicked the latch with a soft click. When he leapt to the fire escape, his jacket snagged on the window latch. He cursed, his balance thrown off. The rusted railing bit into his back before it snapped in two. Open air embraced him, folding around his body with phantom arms.

Ryan grabbed the broken railing with one hand, the frosty black metal stinging his fingers. He tightened his grip—shoulder throbbing—and glanced down.

I'm such an idiot. His vision blurred. All he saw were oily shimmers glinting off the asphalt almost one hundred feet below. Such a height would definitely crack his head open, splattering the contents like a piñata laid waste by some snotty kid with a bat.

The metal screeched, protesting against his weight. Mrs. Pishta's miniature psycho-doodle wheezed out frantic, pathetic barks from the apartment below like a squeeze toy on its last leg.

Shut up! He mentally shouted at the dog.

Is this it? Done at sixteen? Dying an idiotic death would be the ultimate coda to the rotten symphony that was his life.

Ryan gritted his teeth and kicked, trying to find some sort of footing. Gravity held him down like someone had strapped ankle weights to his legs. His fingers loosened—arm straining, threatening to pop right out of its socket.

Ligaments stretched taut, and his breath hissed out through gritted teeth. *You could just...let go. It would be easier.* He almost relaxed his muscles—almost let his fingers slip.

An image flashed across his mind. His older sister crouched in a corner, black hair tangled and wild, her pale-blue eyes darting until they found his—desperate and accusing.

Dying doesn't keep Jory safe. Pull yourself up!

With a growl, he swung his other arm up and grabbed the rail.

He kicked out and this time his feet met brick. He braced himself there, sucking in a few short breaths. The hinge moaned, and psycho-pup sent out another peal of raspy barks. A few grunts later, he lay on his back, panting on the slim platform of the fire escape. His shoulder burned and his breath puffed above him. The barking finally stopped. Maybe the dog had wheezed its last.

Ryan glanced at the broken railing—at the bowed metal he'd clung to moments before.

That was too close.

He stood, rolled his shoulder, and shook out sore, damp hands before closing his bedroom window. Thankfully, his sister hadn't come to investigate the noise. He ran down the rest of the escape—nerves singing from the rush of adrenaline and breath coming out fast and hard. *I almost died.* The thought chased him, filling his head with gory images of what could have been. When his feet hit the asphalt, he placed a pair of chunky black headphones over his ears.

All right, my man Beethoven. Let's do this. Not only was his music dope, Ryan had always felt a kinship to the old composer. The long-dead musician was the only other guy he knew who shared his five-foot-three-inch stature.

Ryan pulled out his phone, hands still shaking, as he tried to scroll through his music. He stopped on *Allegretto.* While the first chords and long ascending scales played, he let out a long sigh.

You're gonna be late. Stop putting it off.

Back streets around his building were quiet this time of night, but a few alleyways over, the lights and bustle of the city were still in full swing. He moved at a swift jog, squeezing between buildings. His slim frame came in handy for shortcuts through the city, which was pretty much the only thing it was good for.

He knew South Bres, California like he knew the wrinkled lines of anxiety ingrained on his sister's face. He highly preferred it to North Bres—the thriving, business-driven, rich pit of egocentric snobs—even if the South was full of gangs and Mind Hunters.

Leaving the cramped alleyway, Ryan slipped onto the narrow sidewalk. People rushed past as if it were midday, the neon lights from the city casting an unnatural glow on their faces. When shoulders bumped his, various body odors wafted by, along with the skunky smell of drugs and heady perfume. His nose crinkled, and he held back the urge to sneeze.

After a ten-minute, brisk walk, almost the length of Vivaldi's *Summer*, Ryan arrived at the corner of Fifth and Brea. His hands had finally stopped shaking, but hanging nine stories from a broken railing was cheese puffs compared to what Bram had put him through.

It was far more deserted here. Shadows crisscrossed under the flickering yellow lights of ancient streetlamps. Deep into the dregs now, dark figures huddled around burn barrels under every overpass and back alley. The scent of pot and cigarette smoke was thick. He waited at the intersection, huffing out a few hot breaths into his cupped hands.

Ryan pulled his hood down lower, then blinked and activated his abilities, his irises glowing a pale green. His world immediately dissolved into blackness, except for the white hair-like strands outlining the city like a 3D blueprint. Swirling lines lit up the bodies within his sight like tangled strands of white Christmas lights. Each bunch of bright threads represented someone's nervous system, every strand a tangible manifestation of each physical nerve.

All those people wove around each other, completely unaware that if he wanted to, Ryan could lay waste to them all. A wave of his hand and he could Slice through any nerve he chose, cutting off its path to the brain.

One tangle of nerves sat huddled against a wall—the line connecting to his heart throbbing weakly. Ryan blinked, deactivating his ability to get a better look. The man was super old, great-great grandpa status, with a weathered face and patchy beard. Gnarled hands lifted a tin cup, but no one stopped to drop any cash or coin. The old man stared out into the crowd—eyes foggy, gummy mouth moving constantly. Probably muttering to himself.

Ryan could end his suffering, could sever that faint pulsing nerve that controlled the heart.

No. Never again. Not even if it would be a mercy.

He dismissed the old man and blinked—eyes flaring to life once more. The nerves within his own body flowed down from his brain like an old spindly tree, all branches and twisting roots. Lifting his hand, he could see the thin fluorescent lines tracing his fingers. The lines clustered at his palms and shot down his wrist and forearm like bunched copper wire in a cable. They glowed softly, pulsing with every beat of his heart.

Laced among the bright-white lines were multicolored strands, threading and weaving around the physical nerves. Emotional nerves. They were harder for him to see and looked almost invisible in the humanoid tangles of light passing him by. But if he concentrated enough, he could bring them into focus. He worked through the colored strands, ridding himself of emotion. Of pain.

Ryan was careful with each cut—he'd worked out a timer of sorts. It was all about intention. A sort of mental pressure that worked into the Slice to give himself roughly over an hour of no emotion. That should be plenty of time. As a zombie, he wouldn't remember much of what happened tonight. Maybe some patches of conversation accompanied by a few fleeting images. It may be the coward's way out, but keeping his sister away from nut jobs like Bram was worth it.

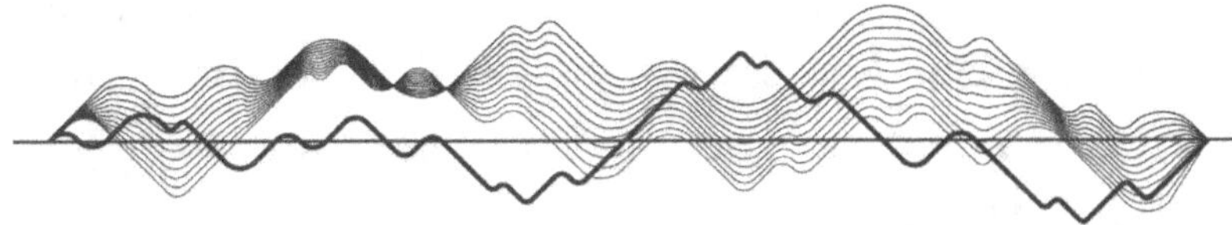

Chapter 2: Amadeus

Amadeus rolled his head from side to side.

Ryan thought cutting off his nerves turned him into a zombie-ish version of himself—turned his brain into a machine.

Dead. Robotic. Unaccountable.

He was wrong. Ryan was still unaware that his mind had split two years ago—unaware that Amadeus emerged every time Ryan rid himself of emotion.

I am far from a machine.

But he locked that thought away behind one of the many doors in Ryan's mind. Amadeus switched the music from Vivaldi to Mozart. Composers such as Beethoven and Vivaldi had lived in Mozart's shadow, never quite reaching his brilliance. Mozart's notes were precise, almost mathematical.

Minutes later, his employer pulled up. Amadeus tugged the headphones down to his neck and shrugged into the deep hood of Ryan's jacket. The black suburban stood out on the cracked and littered street like a cowboy in an opera.

An opaque window rolled down, and Amadeus was met with the orange, heavy-lidded stare Bram was so famous for. People found his strange eyes and slicked-back raven hair intimidating, but Bram didn't phase Amadeus. Ryan, on the other hand...

His employer eyed him up and down—a hunting cat examining its prey.

"I see you're ready to work. It's too bad the effects of your abilities aren't permanent." A slow grin crept across Bram's face. "I could always keep you on full time."

Bram was trying to bait him, but it was pointless.

After a pause, Bram tilted his head. "But that would be a mistake. The thing that's kept me in business this long is that I know precisely how far to push people. And I plan to keep you in working condition."

His smile stretched further.

When Bram held out an earpiece, Amadeus took it, fitting it into his ear canal. Once the back door slid open, he glided into the black leather seat.

Kala sat at the far end, flashing Amadeus a rude gesture before turning away, forehead pressed against the tinted window. She was two years Ryan's senior and had long, boxy platinum braids—a stark contrast to her ebony skin.

"I don't see why I have to sit next to the midget-zombie," Kala grumbled.

Ryan would have snapped back at that comment—too concerned about his short stature to keep his emotions in check. But Amadeus stared blankly, making his seat companion fidget and curse.

Bram ignored Kala's complaint, turning to face them from the front passenger seat. "Kala has done a good job of fooling the targets. They should follow her to the rendezvous point easily enough. Remember, be wary of the Sleeper. The other boy is still Unknown, so stay on your guard."

Kala *tsked* then nodded. Amadeus mimicked the second action. Since she had been befriending the two Psychic brothers for weeks, this wasn't new information for them.

"Ryan," Bram said.

He knew about Ryan's split consciousness but refused to call him by another name. Amadeus met Bram's eyes.

"You will disable the boys and help Kala herd them behind Greenway's."

"Yes, Father," Amadeus said.

"Good boy." When Bram reached across the space to ruffle Amadeus's hair, his hood fell back.

Bram wasn't and would never be their father. But he had a sick need for his underlings to refer to him as such. Ryan hated they were called his "children." He found it disturbing, and Amadeus happened to agree with Ryan on the matter.

Amadeus tossed his bangs out of his eyes and tugged his hood back in place. Kala scrunched herself as far away from him as possible, despite the fact there was plenty of space between them already.

Amadeus thought of nothing. It was easier to hide things from Ryan if he didn't think too much. So he saved his energy for the upcoming task.

Bram had wanted to get his hands on a Sleeper for a while. With one pinch, a Sleeper could render someone unconscious for an extended period of time. Technically, with a few well-placed Slices, Amadeus could do the same.

However, he could only put someone out for a few hours at best, while a Sleeper could for days—months even, if they were powerful enough.

A Sleeper was easy for Ryan to incapacitate, but it was the brother he was worried about, since his ability was still Unknown. Kala had tried to get the boy to share his secret, but no dice. He could be anything from a Berserker to an Empath. Amadeus could handle just about anything except a Fortress. Well, a Shield could be an issue too—if they got the jump on him.

The vehicle stopped a block away from Tollway Avenue. The pair exited the car, and Bram's driver sped off, making his way to Greenway's. Kala shivered while Amadeus clenched his hands, frigid fingers pressing into his palms. He wanted to cut off the sensory receptors that reacted to the cold, but they were there for a reason. His body needed to react to the low temperatures so the warm blood would stay constrained to his internal organs.

The streets here were filthy. Makeshift markets and shops were crammed between tall, abandoned buildings. People sat huddled in sleeping bags or under newspapers about every twenty feet.

Kala kept sending him hateful glances as they walked.

"You coward," she hissed. "Cutting off everything that makes you human. Doing everything they say without having to deal with the torment. You know what Bram will do to these kids. Heck, look at what he's done to you."

She shoved Amadeus angrily, causing him to stumble into the road.

"You make me sick, standing there like a Mindless—one of Bram's little puppets. Perfectly compliant in every way."

Amadeus stepped back onto the sidewalk, but she shoved him again, harder this time. He stumbled into the road, and a car swerved around him, honking.

"I wish I could kill you," she said.

Kala hated him, and rightly so. Amadeus was the one who captured her brother. He was the whole reason she was here, working under Bram's thumb.

Kala went to shove him a third time, but he caught her wrist.

"Don't push Ryan," Amadeus said, voice even. "He'll be harmed."

"There's nothing you can do to *me*." Kala was a Fortress, immune to all other Psychic abilities.

"You're really screwed up, you know that? All this"—she yanked her hand back and made a big sweeping gesture toward Ryan's body—"is gonna bite you in the butt one day. And you are gonna *wanna* die."

"Ryan wants to die," Amadeus replied.

Her eyes widened slightly. "Oh..."

Amadeus walked ahead.

Kala huffed, all signs of awkwardness or sympathy gone.

"Why are you doing this anyway?" she asked. "They got someone you care about too? You owe Bram money? 'Cause I can get you money if you help me get Amare back."

Amadeus stayed silent. Speaking created more work for him, and he was already going to have to lock some of this conversation away as it was. The more he needed to lock away, the more Ryan might get suspicious.

"You are the worst," she muttered, then grabbed his arm. "This is where we split. The boys are somewhere around this place. Greenway's is two blocks north. When you see them with me, trail us. If it looks like I'm having trouble, do your thing. Got it?"

Amadeus nodded. He already knew the plan, but Kala took every opportunity to act like she was in charge.

She paused a moment before letting him go. He couldn't read her expression as she turned and jogged off, disappearing around the corner.

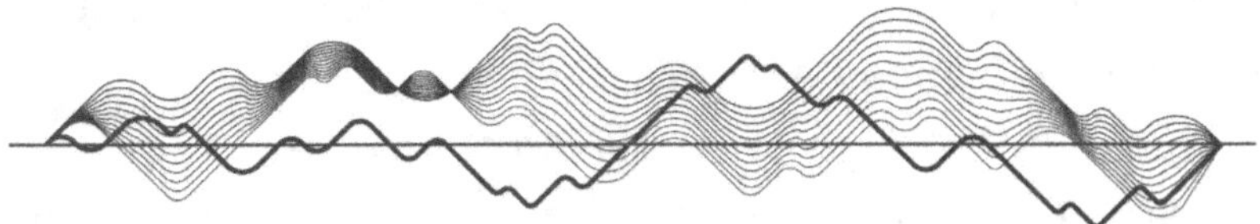

Chapter 3:
Amadeus

Amadeus followed Kala at a distance. She walked alongside their targets—two fourteen-year-old boys. They were twins, though they didn't look alike. David, the one with the shaggy blond hair, was the Sleeper. Maybe now Bram would stop threatening Ryan about snagging his roommate.

Amadeus kept his eyes on the second boy. Corwin had a mess of dark-brown hair sticking up in all directions, and they had no idea what he could do. Amadeus didn't want to get Ryan killed by being careless.

Kala and the boys laughed and talked animatedly the whole way. She was a good actress. In order to gain their trust, she'd revealed to them that she was Psychic. She'd told them that she knew a place where they could meet others of their kind.

Safe from the prying eyes of the Bureau.

It wasn't even a lie.

Kala stopped in front of an old brick building, purple neon light from the storefront sign lighting up her features. She chanced a glance back at Amadeus.

What is she doing? We're still a block away—

Corwin, the Unknown, went rigid. The boy's jaw clenched, and Amadeus ducked deeper into the shadows. The boy fisted his hands, forehead gleaming with sweat.

"What did you see?" His twin asked.

Corwin shook his head. He turned, stiffened, turned back, then froze again. It was like watching a deer get caught in the flash of headlights over and over. He did this a few more times before violently cursing and glaring—straight into the shadows where Amadeus hid. Kala reached out a hand, apprehension growing in her eyes. Corwin whispered something in David's ear and shoved his brother to the side. Then he made a beeline straight toward Amadeus.

Amadeus blinked his eyes, activating his ability. White, hair-like lines ran in a complex weave through Corwin's body.

He stretched out a hand and Sliced, severing the nerves in Corwin's spine.

The boy collapsed—a marionette without its strings. Corwin's face smashed against the concrete, knocking him out cold. People stopped and stared at the boy in confusion before scurrying on their way, clearing the street. Anything that looked like it had to do with Psychics sent normies running, because they were terrified of any event that might bring in the Bureau.

No one wanted to get questioned by the Bureau.

Kala fought to control the Sleeper. David kept pinching her and cursing—desperately trying to put her to sleep.

"Stop that," she said. "You know that doesn't work on me."

David ignored her, pinching her several more times and getting some good yelps out of Kala before she kneed him hard in the gut and he collapsed, coughing.

Amadeus moved to contact Bram, but Kala snatched the boy with one hand and touched the communication device in her ear with the other before he could speak.

"Came up on a bit of a hitch, Bram," she said.

"Kala," Bram chided.

"We've come up on a bit of a hitch, *Father*." Kala's face twisted in revulsion. "I think the other kid might be a type of Seer." She danced around a bit while the Sleeper tried to apply a good kick to her shins.

Amadeus had come to the same conclusion. The Seer had been trying to see all the possible outcomes of the future by making various split-second decisions. When none of them resulted in a positive outcome, he attacked in a last-ditch effort to save his brother.

The kid had to know he'd fail.

"Did they get away?" Bram asked.

"No, the *zombie* took care of the Seer, and I've got the Sleeper under control." Kala kicked David, making him gasp. She grimaced.

Amadeus could tell she was doing her best not to look the kid in the eye. He lifted a hand, ready to incapacitate David, but Kala shook her head.

"I've got it," she growled.

"What's the problem?" Bram asked.

Kala glanced between the building at their backs and Amadeus, then *tsked*. "Nothing. We'll cut through the Mystic Mart."

She's acting strange.

"I'll meet you at the back," Bram said.

Kala's eyes shifted to Amadeus. "Yes, Father," she replied.

Amadeus walked up to the unconscious Seer, still lying prostrate on the sidewalk, and lifted him with a grunt. He had cut off all the nerves that allowed the teen to feel from the neck down, leaving him in a form of temporary paralysis. Without his help, the effects would take a few hours to wear off.

Kala wrestled with the other brother. "OUCH! Quit that! I told you it won't work on me!"

Amadeus blinked, picking out the multicolored lines representing the Sleeper's emotional nerves. Then he numbed them all. Kala pulled the boy forward like a docile cow on a lead.

"I had it covered," she said.

Amadeus said nothing, instead opting to read the giant purple neon sign. *Mystic Mart*, it blazed in swirling letters, the light from the gas-filled tubes vibrating through the air. Brick walls and black-curtained windows kept the inside blocked from view.

Ironic. Shouldn't the Bureau be all over a place like this?

Why was a shop full of supposed magical or Psychically influenced items left alone when they made such a point of causing people to fear anything to do with Psychics? Then again, there was always a market for forbidden things. Maybe the Bureau secretly ran it, hoping to snatch up potential Psychics or glean information about them.

Kala didn't waste any time—she picked the lock with ease and walked ahead into the strange shop with the blacked-out curtains. Amadeus followed close behind, noting the gleam of sweat on the older girl's temple as her eyes darted to the side.

Hair lifted on his neck, but he didn't feel afraid. His body sensed something all the same, and he wasn't sure what to do with the warning.

"Kala—"

"Shut-up, Zombie." She tugged David toward the back of the shop.

Fine. If something bad happened, at least she was in front.

Amadeus appraised their surroundings. The Mystic Mart lived up to its name. Shelves upon crowded shelves were lined with unusual objects. The whole place was lit by mismatched shaded lamps and darkly colored lanterns placed haphazardly throughout the rows of mummified things and glowing jars of brightly colored liquids. Windchimes, crystal necklaces, ethnic masks, and dreamcatchers hung from the ceiling. Were those human teeth woven into the threads?

The muscles in Amadeus's neck pulled, so he looked forward, focusing on finding the exit and ignoring the boxes filled with bent silverware labeled *Psychic Talismans*.

What power did a bent spoon hold? People were so easily fooled. An eerie energy came from a few of the objects in the room. His mind was drawn to them, but he ignored the sensation. It was most likely a trap. If certain objects drew the attention of Psychics, it would be easy to sift them out and send them off to men like Bram or the Bureau.

Amadeus shifted the weight of the boy on his shoulders, and Kala mumbled quietly under her breath. She sounded anxious, her rambling adding to the bizarre ambiance.

They reached the backdoor, but before Kala unlocked it, she glanced at Amadeus and bit her lip. She looked...nervous? The hairs on his neck lifted further.

"Why don't I take him off your hands. He looks pretty heavy," Kala said, not looking him in the eye.

Perhaps offering him help bothered her in some way he couldn't reason out. Amadeus didn't care if she wanted the extra weight. He just wanted to get the job done quickly so he could get Ryan home.

Kala slung the unconscious boy over her shoulders, wincing slightly. She shifted his weight a bit then flicked her eyes down to his. There was pity there, or was that...regret? Kala shook her head and shooed David out the door ahead of her.

Amadeus let the door close behind them, touching his earpiece.

"Father?"

Silence.

"Bram?"

Nothing.

The earpiece didn't even fuzz with interference, meaning...

There was a Muffler somewhere nearby.

Had Kala affiliated herself with another group? Not the Bureau—she would never do that. But who else was there? A Mind Hunter gang? Or Bram's rival—Wesley's group. Had she found them?

He accessed his abilities, and everything changed to black and glowing white—mimicking a negative photograph. Dull, overlapping white lines outlined the door and every object around him.

He could see straight through the door and to the bodies pulsing bright white, like living tangled spiderwebs. Due to her abilities, Kala was invisible to him, but he recognized the Sleeper and the Seer, their nerves dimmed or cut short from his handiwork. A giant tangle of nerves he did not recognize made its way toward the backdoor of the shop.

The door Amadeus was about to walk out of.

Amadeus scrambled back. These weren't Bram's people. He was sure of that, and even though he was probably very close, Bram wouldn't get there in time. No wonder Kala had been in such a hurry.

She was planning this all along.

Amadeus blinked, deactivating his abilities. His eyes were getting tired, watering and itchy from overuse. He'd have to escape back out the front. It would be so much easier if he could sever the stranger's nerves, but he could only *see* nerves through walls, not sever them. The aisles rose over his crouched form as he wove his way back toward the front. Light from the streetlamps spilled into the room momentarily as the back door swung open then shut with a soft click. Amadeus froze.

Silence. Then footsteps, as if the man were walking on a decade's worth of dust.

Amadeus let out a slow breath and blinked, his eyes watering as his world switched to a black backdrop overlaid with bright, overlapping white lines. The moment he got a clear view of the man's tangle of nerves, Amadeus lashed out in his mind—simultaneously Slicing through vocal cords and leg nerves.

Nothing happened.

He cocked his head. *Another Fortress? No, his nerve network would be invisible.*

A strange pressure pushed against his efforts to cut off the guy's nerves. A Shield then, perhaps? Whatever this man was, they had been ready for Ryan's abilities. Amadeus dashed toward the front exit.

Shields could block other Psychic attacks weaker or on par with their own abilities. To be able to block Ryan's ability meant this man was a strong Psychic. Shields could also sense others' presence using a similar technique to Amadeus's own. They couldn't see nerves, but something else. Was it blood flow? Or heat signatures?

It bothered him that he couldn't remember. It bothered him that he was bothered.

The man dashed around the aisle, coming into view. He was huge, taller than Amadeus had originally thought.

Fear flared like lightning through his veins, releasing adrenaline in its wake.

Amadeus was turning back into Ryan again.

He gasped and dashed underneath grasping arms. He pushed the front door open, then bolted down the street hoping Bram might have left a few men at Greenway's. But still, that was an entire block away.

Ryan always put a timer on the severed nerves so he wouldn't get trapped for too long as the emotionless version of himself. The zombie.

I should've had more time.

He hadn't finished filtering and locking away the memories from tonight.

An edge of panic interrupted his thinking.

Don't be sloppy, don't be sloppy. Shut the doors, lock them away.

Amadeus was unraveling. Fear had broken through before other emotions. The sheer animalistic panic was making it hard for reason to surface. The emotion was...

Intoxicating.

He panted, shoving people aside in a mad dash. His powers were still activated, and many of them gasped in horror at his glowing eyes.

I need to hide.

A space. A hole. A crevasse.

But hiding wouldn't do him any good. He needed to get a solid gap between them, somewhere the Shield couldn't follow. He could *feel* the man gaining.

Numb up! Amadeus told himself, but...he didn't want to. He'd never lingered between the switch from Amadeus to Ryan. Never *felt*. He shoved the urge to linger aside.

He had to filter out parts of this night from Ryan.

Amadeus knew he was pushing past the limits of his body. He'd cut off his pain receptors. Being unable to feel made him initially faster, but the body could only take so much.

I've been running at full speed for too long.

He looked around frantically.

There!

He crammed himself between the narrow space of a nightclub and a taco joint. The buildings were so close together, even Amadeus found it hard to squeeze through.

The music of the nightclub pulsed through the wall against his cheek and chest. He shimmied into the close space, jerking in fear when his pursuer's arm snaked into the gap, snatching at air.

"Wait!" the man shouted, his face crammed between the buildings, making Amadeus giggle.

He clamped a hand over his mouth, swallowing the burst of hysteria. Other emotions were breaking through sooner than they should in the chaos of the moment.

"We're here to help you, Ryan!" the Shield said.

You're so full of it.

Amadeus found himself slipping away. Ryan's thoughts were blinking through.

"Leave us alone!" Ryan shouted back.

Wait. Us? I'm myself. I'm...who am I?

His mad scramble through the buildings made him feel trapped like a spider in its own web. Not because he was squished between two buildings. And not because an ape-ish man was straining his arm toward him like a cat pawing at a mouse. But because Ryan knew for the first time in years that the zombie had a will of his own.

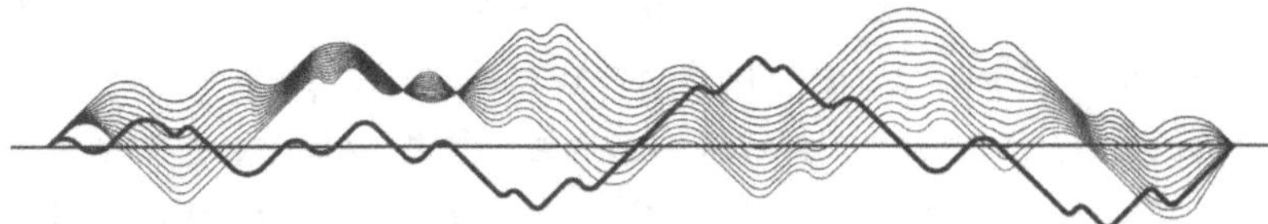

Chapter 4: Jory

Earlier That Evening

Jory huddled in the small concrete window seat. She'd drawn the filmy white curtains closed, creating a tiny sanctuary. While her forehead rested against the glass, fog clouded the clear surface, expanding with each exhalation of warm breath. She traced a small girl—circle head, triangle dress, little stick arms and legs. Then a boy. On a whim, she covered the boy's head with miniature curls. Finally, she connected the hands.

So simple, two people holding hands. She continued to draw, huffing over the glass when the image began to fade, until an army of people surrounded the little stick-girl. The image blurred as it dried—edges closing in—collapsing into itself until she was alone again. Even the boy with the curly hair vanished from view.

Jory swiped her hand over what remained of the image, pulling her legs up and burying her face in her knees.

Being an Empath sucks.

Jory flinched, the metallic click of the apartment door unlocking, echoing in the empty space. It slammed shut a moment later.

Sebastian's surge of emotions hit her like a wave. Grief, embarrassment, anger—they filled her to the brim. His date hadn't gone well, but what had he expected?

Jory felt everyone's emotions as if they were her own. It was downright crippling. Before her parents died, she had been able to control it. But after the accident it was like her brain had gone through a meat grinder, then mushed itself back together like a slab of ground beef.

Sebastian's emotions continued to steamroll her.

Just talk him through it, and it won't be so bad.

"What happened?" she called out from her hiding place.

Jory pulled the sheer curtain aside. Sebastian wore a crisp white dress shirt, bright against his black skin. A tan suit coat was slung over his shoulder, which he tossed over the back of the couch. Sebastian groaned and fell face-first onto the cushions, long sapling legs shooting out over the armrest.

Depression fell over her like a thick gray fog.

He mumbled unintelligibly into the navy cushions.

She glanced sideways at him.

"Am I supposed to understand that?" When he didn't answer, she sighed, "I told you not to go."

Jory crawled out of the window seat and plopped down next to her roommate. She pulled up her feet and settled into the far corner.

Sebastian rolled to his back and pulled a travel-sized bottle of hand sanitizer out of his pants pocket, squeezing out a generous blob. Even though he'd grabbed a fresh bottle before leaving just one hour earlier, it was already half empty. He rubbed it into his hands briskly.

"Careful there, don't wanna start snorting the stuff," Jory said.

He gave her a once-over. "Wouldn't hurt to sanitize more than once a month."

Jory rolled her eyes. "I bathe more than once a month."

"Sure you do."

She sighed, running a hand through her tangled hair and wincing when she hit a snarl. It wasn't *that* bad. He acted like he could be her father, when in reality he was only four years older than her eighteen years.

"What happened, Seb?" she prodded, turning the conversation away from her personal hygiene.

Sebastian buried his face in his hands. "We got through the appetizers before I told her I couldn't stay any longer. Sweat was pouring out of my armpits like Niagara Falls, and my palms could have watered a cornfield."

Sebastian had a deep fear of women, stemming from a traumatic relationship with his mother. Jory was the only older female who didn't elicit this reaction. Despite this, he made frequent attempts to push past his fear. The man was a hopeless romantic, and if it wasn't for his problematic past, Jory had no doubt he'd have a relationship with someone by now.

Sebastian lifted his head, noting a Chinese take-out box on the coffee table. His eyebrows narrowed at her aloof expression. "You ordered in."

"And that's surprising because?"

His stomach rumbled.

"You wouldn't want to touch my leftovers anyway."

"Of course not. I don't want your beef and spit. But I bet you left the dumplings on the counter." He leapt off the couch.

"Don't even think about it." Jory scrambled off the couch only to get her feet tangled in the throw blanket and fall face-first. She hissed in pain, rubbing her nose vigorously.

"I licked them! Every last one!" she shouted.

"You did not. The box still has the sticker-tab-thingy on it," he said, unperturbed.

Shoot, he's right.

"Would you two shut up already?" Jory's brother Ryan walked out of his room, rubbing his eyes.

He was wearing a black long sleeve shirt at least two sizes too big, the sleeves hanging over his hands like mantis claws. People always thought they were twins, with their warm beige skin, thick black hair, and pale eyes.

Except mine are a watery blue.

Anger seeped from her brother's body like pools of frothing red bubbles. *Why is he so angry?*

Ryan stared at her flatly.

Sebastian walked into the room, popping a dumpling into his mouth. "Mmmmm, still warm."

"Isn't it against the shrink code to steal?" She tried to act nonchalant, but Ryan's feelings were incredibly pungent. They oozed right under her skin, making her blood boil.

Sebastian shrugged.

"I think it makes sense," Ryan said, betraying no hints of rage. "Idiots don't have morals."

Sebastian glanced at them with a longsuffering look, then began ticking off his fingers. "First of all, I'm a child *therapist*, not a shrink. Second, I have excellent morals, as you well know. Third, I pick up half the rent while the two of you barely cover the second half."

Ryan's anger surged, crimson bubbles frothing around him.

Jory knew she was the only one who could see them. The only one who could see everyone's emotions leaking out in bright swathes of color—a living, breathing expressionist painting.

Her brows knitted. It was eerie that Ryan was able to feel so deeply while keeping his face completely void of emotion. Jory rubbed her temple. The roomful of emotions was getting to her.

The anger-bubbles retreated back into Ryan's body like someone sucking froth into a straw. She let out a sharp breath at the sudden absence of emotion. How did he just make them disappear like that? Boredom misted off her brother in a dull gray cloud.

"I'm going back to bed, and the two of you need to seriously shut up, before I make you," he said.

Jory and Sebastian immediately clamped their mouths shut.

While Ryan walked back into his room, Jory shook her head, fear dissipating. For a pleased moment she thought it might be her own fear untainted by anyone else. But then she realized Sebastian had it practically leaking out of his ears. She sighed.

Ryan rarely threatened them. The mere thought of what he could do when he was angry sent chills down Jory's back.

Their eyes met. "He wouldn't. Would he?" Sebastian asked.

Jory shrugged her shoulders. "Honestly, I don't know. Ryan's…Ryan, you know? And he's done it before."

"He shouldn't be allowed to have that kind of power over people, especially at his age." He sighed, despair shrouding him again in a deep-blue wave. Now that the distraction of the dumpling conquest was over, and with Ryan out of the room, Sebastian's gloom had returned. Jory's shoulders slumped with the weight of it.

"Come on, Seb," she choked out. "You know I can't be around you when you're like that."

He glanced at her and winced. "I'm sorry. I'll try to control it. It's just, I really felt good about this one. I thought, she's fun, quirky. I like quirky. Don't I like quirky?"

Jory nodded vigorously to get the conversation moving. The sooner he got this out, the sooner his emotions would stabilize, and her heart wouldn't feel like *it* was the one breaking. It sucked that she could lock her own emotions away in a little box but couldn't do it to anyone else's. It hadn't always been that way. But she had forgotten how to separate the two.

How did I do it? Something with…with… She wracked her brain and sighed.

"Come on," she said.

After Sebastian stuffed a few dumplings into his mouth, his emotions stilled into a lingering moroseness.

"Wouldn't it be better to wait? Try to meet someone organically, get used to them, like you did with me? Maybe even find someone like *us*?" she asked.

He sunk into the cushions. "You're different. And finding someone like us? It's not like there's a dating app just for people with Psychic abilities. And honestly, Jor, I was lucky enough to meet you and Ryan." He paused. "Well *you* at least. Ryan's a—"

"Troubled youth," Jory finished for him.

Sebastian lifted his eyebrows, but she ignored him.

"Anyway, I think you need to relax. It'll happen when it happens. Stop trying to force it. And if you never meet anybody, you'll always have me."

Golden love and appreciation shone off him. Not sexual love, but the kind you would share with a friend, or a sister, even. The same love pulsed in her heart, and she couldn't help being warmed by it.

Most people her age had finally started to get themselves sorted out. They knew who they were and what they wanted from life. Jory had absolutely no clue. She was everyone and no one, and she had no idea how she truly felt about anything.

Did she really love Sebastian, or were his own feelings for her just bouncing back? Maybe if she wasn't an Empath, she'd hate him. She loved Ryan, she knew that. He was only ever irritated with her or gave off a thick screen of guilt, which worried her. And despite that, she still loved him. This was the one part of herself she was one hundred percent sure of.

She couldn't leave the apartment. Having walls around her made a difference, and being in her own room away from everyone was the only way she could be alone with her emotions. But even then, she wasn't sure if she really felt a certain way because *she* felt that way or because she had been influenced by someone else's feelings on the subject at some point in her life.

So, she did experiments.

Earlier that evening she'd watched an episode of *Undead Walking* by herself. She'd wanted to see if, without Sebastian there, she might enjoy it. It was the same with all sorts of things. Sebastian didn't like pineapple on pizza, Ryan didn't like sushi (or any fish, really), so she didn't either. Ryan hated country music, but Sebastian loved it, so she felt conflicted on the matter. She would wake up in the middle of the night craving chocolate-covered pretzels only to find Ryan huddled inside the pantry stuffing his cheeks full of them, like a chipmunk preparing for winter.

All of this led to staying up all hours of the night, staring at the ceiling and questioning every aspect of her life, or shoved in the pantry with Ryan eating pretzels until she wanted to puke.

Consequently, she looked like a haggard middle-aged woman with baggy eyes and hair down to her butt (with perhaps a dreadlock or two). She should have been in college, making stupid choices that changed her into a smart, worldly adult.

But instead, each hour of her life was spent within the apartment walls on the highest floor, shoved into the farthest corner of the building with nothing but storage and empty apartments around and under her. No one wanted to live on the ninth floor, especially when the elevator was wonky as heck.

And what did she do all day? Entered data for personal training clients from Saber Fitness.

She looked at Sebastian, who was nibbling on the last dumpling. When irritation buzzed through her, she smiled. That emotion was hers.

"What are you smiling about?" Sebastian asked, one eye-brow raised.

"You're just a selfish pig is all," she said.

He looked offended but then glanced at the dumpling and shrugged his shoulders. "Only when I'm depressed."

Jory rolled her eyes. "Sure."

She grabbed her box of Chinese from the coffee table and picked up her blanket from where it had tripped her. After resting a hand on Sebastian's shoulder, she locked herself in her room.

Jory wandered through her dreams as if stepping between worlds. She was huddled in her apartment hunched over her computer, her hair rapidly graying. The next moment, the walls began inching in until she was encased in a cube made of cement that began to crush her. She knew she was dreaming.

She always knew she was dreaming.

It didn't make the fear any less tangible.

Just before she got mashed into a bloody mess of bones and sinew, she found herself staring up at an endless blue sky dappled with white clouds. She looked down at her body, finding it had changed drastically. She was young, not even six years of age.

"What would you like to see today, Anna Banana?"

No one had ever called her Anna...had they? It sounded hauntingly familiar. She looked to her left and saw a boy. He had large, long-lashed brown eyes. His curls caught the sunlight peeking through the sky. Bright rays splashed across his face, turning his eyes from brown to amber.

"See?" she asked, cocking her head to the side.

He nodded. "I can take you anywhere, Anna. Where do you want to go?"

"Somewhere without any people," she said, a soft sigh escaping her lips.

He placed his hand on her shoulder and smiled. A dimple appeared on his cheek.

"Silly," he said. "They're not real, remember? You just think they are."

She thought for a moment, closing her eyes.

"The circus," she said, a small, hopeful smile brightening her face. Ryan had gotten to go to the circus, and he was only three. It wasn't fair.

The boy's smile grew, and he threw his hands into the sky. "The circus it is! Be ready to be amazed, Miss Georgianna!" His voice sounded very grand. He closed his eyes, stretched his hands further out, paused, then brought them together in a great CLAP!

Color burst from his palms, moving around them, swirling and coalescing into a myriad of shapes—of shadow and light. She felt as if they were in a painting until slowly, everything took shape. A massive red-and-white striped tent popped up above them. A tightrope appeared here, a large hoop of fire there.

Everything was a wonder. But more wonderful than all of it were the people.

So many people. Vendors calling out about popcorn and pretzels. Children laughing and crying. Men and women gathered together, hundreds of them! So much noise, all crammed *into a tent. Elephants stomped about with little dogs wearing hats riding upon their backs. Dancers twirled, ribbons in hand. There were clowns and balloons and...and...*

And she felt nothing.

Nothing but her own emotions and, if she reached out, the excited feelings of the expectant boy in front of her.

She laughed. Felt her lungs expand with breath and restrict as bursts of giggles escaped her. When she spun, the world of color spun with her. Tears began to fall down her face. It was all so beautiful—the people, the color, the warmth of the bodies.

The boy smiled triumphantly at her laughter, but his face crumbled at her tears. She squatted down, her head buried in her arms.

"Is this what it's like for everyone else?" she whispered between quiet sobs.

It wasn't fair.

Quiet descended upon them. She looked up to see the boy crouched in front of her, the vision of wonder gone as suddenly as it had appeared.

"You'll get the hang of it," he said, patting her back. "Remember the threads, just like your mother said."

She nodded, wiping tears from her eyes. He lifted his thumb, brushing away the leftover wetness there.

Strangely, his face began to change. His eyes sunk in and became dull, his cheeks sallow. He was wasting away in front of her. Crumbling into dust.

"Wait... Wait!" she cried desperately. "What's happening?"

His arms began to disintegrate. "You have forgotten me."

She shook her head. "No, no I haven't. I would never. I—"

"My name," he whispered.

Just his face remained. "What is my name, Georgianna?"

The sky grew dark. His name? Of course she knew it. It was...

His eyes spoke endless sorrow as they faded.

Loss.

It burrowed deep into her soul as everything around her became black.

Panic. Cold, sweaty, shaky panic.

Jory woke with a start. Her breathing came in great gasps and her heart pounded, blood rushing through her ears and practically gushing in her veins.

Though the dream was fading, the panic did not. It raged like a great storm, pushing through the walls, hitting her in waves—persistent, demanding.

Wait... It's coming through the walls? If the panic isn't from me...

"RYAN!" Jory scrambled out of bed, yanking the door open. Multitudes of emotions began to pulse through her. She staggered to her brother's door, but pulling it open was a momentous feat. When she finally peeled it all the way open, she felt as though a semi crashed into her. Tears burst from her eyes one moment only to stop a second later as anger tore her apart. Fear, confusion, sorrow, nausea, anxiety, guilt. A cacophony of feeling. But over it all, the panic.

Ryan sat curled under an open window—the one leading to the fire escape. Bitter wind made the curtains swirl about his huddled form. He made no sound, simply rocked back and forth.

"Ryan?" Jory gasped.

He ignored her.

She crawled toward him, the sheer weight of his emotions pushing her down. She grasped his shoulders and shook him. "Ryan!"

His eyes snapped up, finding hers. They were wide—haunted. At the sight of her, his face crumbled in despair.

"What have I done?" he whispered. "I know now. I remember. I found the doors. I unlocked them...some of them. I can't see what's in the others. He's done horrible things, Jory."

He took a deep, shaky breath.

"*I've* done horrible things." His eyes unfocused as they stared past her.

"Ryan, who's he? Who's done these things?"

He began to chuckle—soft at first—then hysterically.

Jory stared at him in horror.

He's insane. Jory was barely keeping control of her own mind. So she did the only thing she could think of. She slapped him.

Ryan stopped, stared at her blankly, and then began to laugh again.

Sebastian walked in, rubbing the sleep out of his eyes.

"What the?"

"Put him to sleep," she said.

Sebastian's mouth dropped, and he waved his arms as he spoke. "Wait, what? Why? For how long?"

"I don't care, just do it," Jory growled at him.

Sebastian blinked several times in shock.

Jory was breaking. Ryan's hysteria was eating away at her. She could do something about that, though. Couldn't she? Separate herself somehow?

No, I'm losing myself.

Sebastian's sense of urgency finally kicked in. He ran over, pinching Ryan's muscle between the neck and shoulder. Ryan's peals of hysteria were cut off and his eyes shut, body slumping to the side.

The loss of his emotions made Jory gasp and shudder. She fell forward, hands slapping onto the wooden floor. They stung, but she didn't care. She could breathe—could think.

Sebastian shook his hands in worry.

"He's going to miss school, you know," he said, his voice panicked. "I got ahead of myself and put him out longer than I meant to."

"How long?" she whispered. Compared to Ryan's emotions, Sebastian's hit her like a pebble against a brick wall.

Sebastian rubbed his neck nervously. "Ummmm..."

"How long, Sebastian?"

"A week."

She groaned. "Idiot."

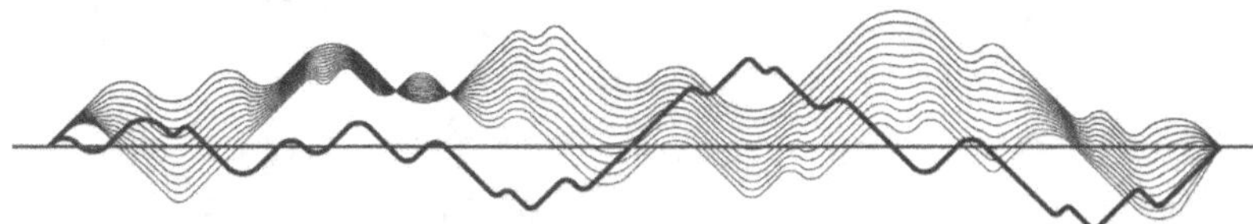

Chapter 5: Ryan

I'm in control.

I am.

Ryan took his time, going through the process of tinkering with his emotions—dimming the thin colorful strands clustered around the bright, white, physical nerves. He didn't numb them as much as he usually did. He couldn't depend on that anymore. *I have to wean myself. Like an addict.* Acclimate to his grief. To his guilt.

I've created a monster.

An unfeeling machine that wreaked pain and havoc on other Psychics just like him and his sister.

I can't do it anymore. There's no way I can justify all of that. Not even for Jory.

He wished he had left the doors in his mind closed.

What am I gonna do?

Amadeus terrified him. *Amadeus.* That other *thing* had named itself. After one of his favorite composers, no less.

What if he comes out on his own? What if he takes control? What if he erases me?

Ryan shuddered.

He pushed the thoughts away, opening his eyes. They were heavy and sticky, and his throat was coated with thick, gooey phlegm. It made him want to cough. He was in his room, an IV connected to his arm. Ryan's stomach made a sick, sloshy, growly-type sound.

Man, I could seriously go for some pretzels. Ryan blinked, running through the events leading up to now. Everything was so fuzzy after his initial discovery. *How did I get home?* He grazed a thumb over the IV on his wrist.

Familiar brick and cement walls surrounded him. The curtains were drawn, but a soft light from under the door trickled in. An old record player was nestled in the corner—vintage classical vinyl stacked neatly beside it. Ryan's violin leaned against a small leather sofa bed he had shoved against the opposite wall.

A man in his early thirties was curled up on the sofa. Damon had gray streaks at his temples—strange for a man his age. The rest of his hair was black, and all of it was pulled back into a sleek, straight ponytail.

Wait, what happened?

Damon was a doctor, well known to the underground Psychic community. He was a rare find among Psychics—a Silvertongue. He could convince a person's mind that it could do whatever he wanted, even persuade a body to heal faster. Mind over matter.

Psychic abilities could be tested for in the hospital, and if a Psychic was discovered, they were shipped off to the Bureau. Because of this, the Psychic community was protective of their resident doctor.

When Ryan tried to clear his throat, Damon jumped up in response, rushing over to him. He handed him a glass of water, which Ryan drank greedily. The water hit the empty pit of his stomach, which gurgled in response.

"How do you feel?" Damon asked.

Despite being ravenous, physically he felt better than he had in a long time. Ryan couldn't remember the last time he had gotten more than a few hours of sleep.

Emotionally, well...emotions were another matter completely. At least he could numb them up a bit. Be objective. Push them away.

I can deal with them later.

"Okay," he answered.

Damon nodded. "What do you remember before you fell asleep?"

Ryan did not want to go there. The chase, the discovery. Hadn't he gotten lost at one point? Yes, that was right. After he'd shaken off the Shield, he'd wandered in crazed circles. There had been a light. A flickering, candle-like glow and a calm breeze brightening and pushing him home.

Was that all in his head too? Just like Amadeus.

Amadeus...

Amadeus had tortured people.

He had hidden away parts of Ryan's memories—people, conversations, and events tucked away in the dark corners of his mind.

Soon Bram would be after him to complete another mission. If he refused, Jory and Sebastian were screwed.

But I can't do what Bram wants anymore.

Thinking about it made him want to puke up all the water he just drank.

"I don't remember," he finally answered, avoiding Damon's gaze.

Damon's eyes narrowed before he nodded. "Fine. You can hash out whatever happened with Jory later. But, Ryan?"

Ryan glanced up momentarily, only to flick his eyes away. It was difficult for him to make eye contact with anyone for longer than a moment or two, let alone meet Damon's earnest stare.

"You need to talk to someone about whatever is going on in here." Damon flicked Ryan's head, making him wince.

"And here." Damon placed a firm fist over Ryan's heart. "That's my medical advice to you." He stood up, arching his back to stretch. "Oh, along with eating and drinking lots of fluids, of course. I gave Jory some advice on what to give you to eat."

"How long was I asleep?" Ryan asked.

Damon disconnected the IV and took the lead out of Ryan's wrist. As he packed everything into a chestnut-brown leather case, he said, "It should have been a week, but I was able to convince your mind to wake up after four days instead. That Sebastian has quite a strong ability. It took more coercing than I thought it would."

Ryan went rigid. No one touched him. No one.

"Sebastian put me to sleep?" *Frickin' freak.* "SEBASTIAN I'M GOING TO KILL YOU!"

He heard a small yelp and scramble of feet from the other side of the door.

That's right, you wuss. Run.

"And that's my cue to leave," Damon said with a grin. "Call me if you need anything, Ryan." He shot him a meaningful look before stepping out the door.

"Jory, stop hovering. He's fine," Damon said as his door inched closed.

His sister entered a moment later, settling at the edge of his bed. Her face looked more haggard than normal, the bags under her eyes grayer, her hair descending in an even madder ebony tangle.

But her voice was the same as it had always been—low and soothing. "You scared me there for a bit. What happened?"

"I'm fine," he muttered under his breath.

She bounced her leg up and down and rubbed her wrist.

Wait for it...

When she opened her mouth to speak, he held back a sigh.

"Ryan, you have to tell me what's going on. Something is seriously off with you. When I came into your room, you were practically catatonic. Your emotions were, and are, erratic—disturbingly so."

He felt a strong urge to cut off a few emotions—to burrow into the emptiness.

To hide. Hide the ugliness inside him.

But he resisted it.

Why was it so hard?

He kept his practiced nonchalance in place.

"I'm fine. Nothing happened." He was irritated. Irritated with himself for being, well, himself. And irritated with Jory for prodding into his business.

Ryan was being unfair to her, he knew that. But that knowledge didn't change his awful attitude.

He couldn't bear to open himself up like that, even to his sister. He couldn't let her see what he had become.

A monster.

Even if he had done it to protect her. That fact alone would be the most horrific for her. That he had done all those things in order to keep her from Bram—from the Bureau. And just as important, keeping Bram from revealing Ryan's secret.

She can never know.

He waited for her to lash out at him—force an explanation or yell at him about the way he was acting. She didn't. Maybe she had sensed something in him. A fragility that hadn't been there before.

He couldn't remember her coming into his room that night.

Did I say anything? Do anything?

Why did Sebastian put me to sleep? He wouldn't have done that unless something really bad had happened...right? He's too much of a coward otherwise.

"You had some visitors while you were, um, resting."

It was then that Ryan noticed a red folder, fat with paper, along with a crisp white envelope.

Bram.

He resisted the urge to snatch the envelope.

Had Jory seen the contents?

Fear reached out, clenching his heart with its cold fist. He muted it without hesitation, receiving immediate relief.

Then shame.

He almost muted that too, but caught himself.

Had Jory noticed? Felt his fear...then lack thereof? He chanced a peek under his shaggy mane and saw that her fists were clenched and her leg was frozen mid-dance.

Yup. Definitely noticed.

"Who dropped off the letter?" he finally asked, voice even.

"Seb answered the door. He said it was a boy about your age," she answered. "Was he a friend of yours?"

Her question was innocent enough, but he knew the fear he had felt had warned her this was no ordinary letter.

Ryan kept his eyes down. "Maybe. Did he mention his name?"

Her leg bounced its nervous dance again. "I'm not sure, but Seb did say his eyes were an interesting shade."

"Orange," he said without hesitation.

"Yes," she answered.

Bram had sent his Oculus. Padraigin. The orange-haired teen had been there during Ryan's first official mission with Bram.

Bile rose in his throat, but Ryan gulped it down. It sank to his stomach like a golf ball. He'd forgotten about that night, until regaining the memory with all the rest. That first mission was when Amadeus had been born, when Ryan had torn in two, unable to handle what he'd done.

There had been a woman. Bram had wanted her for his team and he'd used Ryan to break her. She'd looked so much like his mother.

How far would Amadeus have gone? If Bram hadn't stopped him?

Would he have killed her?

Killed her like—

"Ryan?" Her voice was muffled, washing over him like a distant wave crashing against the sand.

Come on, Ryan, focus. Keep to the problem at hand.

Padraigin had the ability to share sight with another person.

And that person was Bram.

Was he watching now?

"Ryan?"

Be quiet. I need to think.

Perspiration sprung from his pores, wetting the back of his neck and forehead. It made him shiver. Could Bram know? Know that Ryan was going to go back on their deal?

"Ryan?"

Jory's hand reached for his.

"What?" His voice was barbed, fast and sharp as a scorpion sting.

She pulled her hand back—clutching it to her chest—tears brimming.

"What aren't you telling me? What's wrong? Are you in trouble? Please, just...just tell me. I can help you."

He began to laugh, which surprised him. But he couldn't stop it.

"You? Help me? You can't even leave this apartment! What could *you* do?"

His laughter bordered on hysteria.

He had to cut it off, but he couldn't concentrate.

Jory smacked him across the face, doing the job for him. The interaction gave him a strange sense of déjà vu.

"Good," she muttered. "It worked that time."

Wait. What?

She pursed her lips and shoved the folder and envelope into his hands.

"I think you should rest," she said, getting up to leave.

"Wait," he said.

She turned—hopeful, expectant.

He looked down, not wanting to see her disappointment. "You said visitors. Who else came?"

There was a pause, and for a moment he thought she might not answer.

"I'm not sure. Some redhead from your school brought your missed assignments. Apparently she's moved in across the hall."

"Weird. What psycho would *choose* to live on this floor?"

Jory sighed. "Don't ask me. *We* live here."

"Exactly."

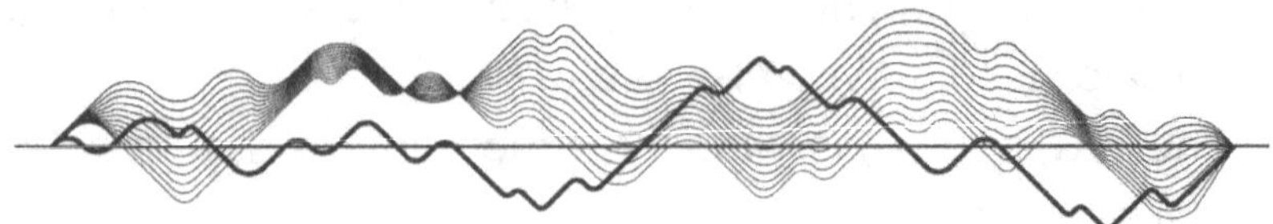

Chapter 6: Jory

Jory floated in an ocean of threads—a colossal weave of pure emotions. They pulsed in a variety of color and density. Tight, orderly weaves here, lawless jumbles there. Harmony and chaos intermingling in a vast array of colored strings.

Hesitantly, she reached out, lightly touching a soft green one she associated with peace. She paused. Her tan skin was strangely pale, or perhaps not so much pale as washed out—transparent. She was there and not there. Her fingertips seemed longer, thinner, as if someone had pulled them until they became like fresh taffy—malleable and soft. In fact, her whole body was this way. Wispy and ethereal, her hair wrapped around her.

The transparency turned her locks a dark, watery gray, like she herself was part of a watercolor painting. It weaved and stretched in a lazy way, mingling with the threads around her. She couldn't quite spot where her hair ended and the threads began.

The thread in her hand was cool against her fingertips and vibrated softly. A vision took form in her mind. The string belonged to an elderly man dreaming of a garden in which a young woman sat in a sea of roses, humming softly.

"I've missed you," she said, a sweet smile painting her face. The old man smiled and heaved a long, wistful sigh. His thread dimmed with the breath until both thread and dream were gone.

He was dead.

She felt him die.

Jory hugged herself with the loss. A thought scampered across her mind, dark and deadly. She shoved it aside, shivering, and willed herself forward, floating through the threads like she was a part of the weave herself. As she drifted, she touched various strings, each connected to a different person.

Many were sleeping and dreaming like the old man had been. She fought the urge to dive into their dreams.

It felt wrong to witness them.

The threads changed color and temperature as she drifted. Flaring and dimming in a wild dance of color and light. The effect was mesmerizing.

Many people consisted of multiple threads, and some were hopelessly tangled. Stopping at one such bunch, she reached out and began to untangle them. It was a delicate, tricky business, like picking out knots in a slim jewelry chain.

As she picked away, she discovered that the strings belonged to a young woman whose spouse had left her with five hungry children. Jory hummed as she worked, trying to Soothe her.

Some of the stronger negative emotions stung when she touched them, but the pain was bearable. As she worked, the strings hummed an angry dissonance until they were sorted out, after which they settled into a contented thrum.

Jory continued on, spotting an angry red thread slowly changing to a glowing white, like metal in the heart of a flame. She veered away, not wishing to graze against it.

Somehow, she knew she couldn't help that one.

She was surprised by how comfortable she felt here. These emotions were so clearly separate from her. Anger, joy, pain. She could touch them, but only if she wished to.

Jory untangled and Soothed as she went, feeling herself being pulled through the great weave toward a strange disturbance. It felt eerily familiar, like the touch of her father's hand as it ruffled her hair or the warm, rich taste of her mother's stew.

It called to her. She knew this set of threads. They pulsed out a painful keening that pierced through her heart. She was almost there, and a voice called to her with each soft pulse of light.

"Anna... Georgianna..."

But before she could reach it, another great mass of broken, swollen threads loomed before her.

Ryan.

The mad tangle sent fear running through her veins.

Ryan's threads had been knotted off systematically, all at various points and degrees of tightness. Some were tied off so tight the strands had distended—building pressure like a kinked hose or like boils close to bursting, pus-filled and inflamed.

She beheld it all with a mixture of horror and disgust.

Ryan, what have you done?

Jory rushed over, pushing the call of the other familiar threads away. She felt them sigh and retreat. Her heart responded with a sigh of its own that she couldn't explain.

But Ryan needed her now.

When she placed her hands in the mass that was her brother's emotions, she immediately snatched them back with a hiss.

So much pain. Pain mingled with a confused clash of feelings that left her lost.

Taking a deep breath, she clenched her teeth and gently eased her hands back in.

It hurt. It hurt so much. The threads would consume her.

Jory separated herself from them in a practiced motion that came to her as easily as breathing. How had she forgotten?

She didn't have time to try and remember. Ryan needed help now.

Jory closed her eyes and began to hum, latching onto the various threads. Calmly and carefully, she worked through them—releasing pressure slowly here, soothing soreness there.

She didn't get far before a dark presence loomed at the edges of her mind.

"Stop."

Jory froze. It was Ryan's voice, but not. Something about it was wrong...alien.

"Ryan?" she said, tentatively.

"Yes...and no," the presence replied.

What did that mean?

She stroked the threads as realization dawned. This thing was as much a part of Ryan as an arm or a leg. Jory kept her breathing slow even as her heart raced. "I want to help you, help Ryan."

The darkness swirled like ink falling in water until a ghostly form resembling her brother stood before her. Except the eyes.

They looked dead. She hugged her arms close to her body. When it spoke, it sounded speculative.

"You cannot mend it all, and the mending would be short-lived. Even if you could, he does not want you here. You shouldn't be here. You must not See. Not you." It paused before continuing. "Strange. I...I don't...like you. You're the reason for all of it." Its eyes sparked with venomous hatred. It made her recoil, causing her to float slightly away. Could this thing really be a part of Ryan?

"All of what?" she whispered.

The thing that looked like Ryan bared its teeth and hissed.

"The pain. You did this to us. I want to—" The hate in its eyes dimmed as suddenly as it had come. It shook its head. "No, I should not want things. Should not. I'm not functioning properly. You have to go."

She reached out. "But—"

"GO!" Rage and apprehension warred in its eyes, battling each other in a strange conflict of suppressed emotion. "Or I'll make you."

That sounded eerily like her brother.

She couldn't leave. She had to know what she had done, what she could do to make it right. "But, Ryan—"

"Ryan belongs to me." The inky Ryan raised its hand in a familiar gesture.

It couldn't use Ryan's abilities.

Could it?

Pain flared in the nerves coursing through her veins like fire through a trail of oil.

She tried to scream but no sound came. Writhing in agony, she found herself wishing for anything else.

Even death.

"Anna!"

The voice cut through the fire in her blood, and she gained enough lucidity to see the inky Ryan disperse in a swirl of black liquid as a powerful brightness pushed against it.

For a moment, she thought she saw a pair of soft brown eyes.

"Wake up, Anna."

Jory woke, clutching her blankets. She breathed heavily, her pajamas sticky with sweat. It took her a moment to take in her surroundings. It was too dark.

No wait, that's right. I went into my closet.

She had burrowed into a mountain of pillows, blankets, and clothes in order to muffle the emotions emanating from Sebastian and Ryan. She had fallen asleep whispering her mantra, trying to separate herself from anything outside her walls.

It's getting worse. I used to be fine staying behind a set of walls, but that's changing now.

The city was just outside. Only a wall of brick and concrete separated her from all of them.

All those people.

"The walls are good..." she whispered, starting her mantra, but the words froze in her throat.

She broke out into another sweat, memories from her dreams filtering into her thoughts.

I was having a nightmare. No...more than a nightmare.

It came rushing back, but the dream was riddled with holes.

She remembered the threads. She had tampered with the threads. Had that been real? Had she separated herself from them? How had she done it? The memory fuzzed and skipped like bad reception on a vintage TV. She screamed into her pillow in frustration.

Why can't I remember?

There was something else. Something more impor-tant.

Someone. She rubbed her wrist self-consciously, chafing the skin harder and harder as the itch in her mind grew larger.

He haunted her dreams, but who was he?

And then she remembered the thing. The Not-Ryan. She scrambled out into the living room to find Ryan shoving an apple into his mouth and swinging his backpack over his shoulder. He lifted his head, swinging his mussed hair to the side.

When his eyes met hers, she knew immediately.

He has no idea. No idea what that thing did to me.

All she managed to get out was a breathy, "What are you doing?"

He hitched the backpack strap on his shoulder and gave her an *isn't it obvious*-type stare.

Tentatively, she reached out with her mind to find that his emotions seemed perfectly in balance. Had her brief contact with his emotions really helped? Or had he simply tied them off to fake a semblance of stability?

She straightened, trying to look authoritative. "You should stay home. I don't think you're in any state to go to school."

He looked to the side, not meeting her eyes. He hardly ever did. Ignoring her, he walked across the room and out the door. When it slammed shut behind him, she winced.

The laughing, teasing brother she used to know had shriveled into this brooding, defensive boy she hardly recognized.

And it's all my fault.

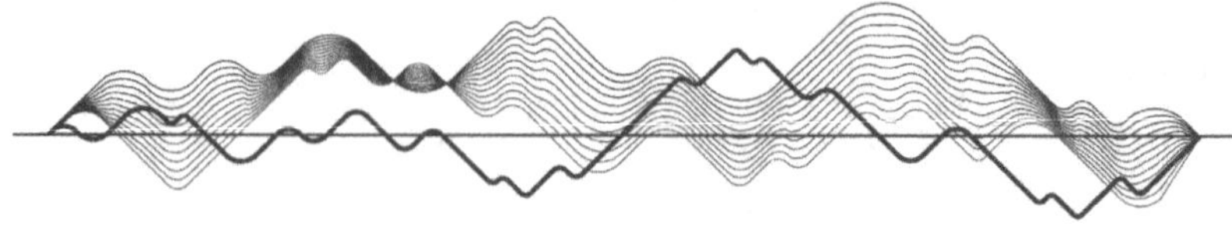

Chapter 7: Ryan
Three Years Ago

They're dead.

Dead.

The mint-blue Volkswagen slowed as the blonde woman made a sharp turn. Eileen Kilpatrick—the only contact mentioned in his parents will.

Their bodies bounced as they left the smooth, tarred road for a gravely dirt path. The tires crunched over the ground leading into the thick Northern California forest. Wintertime had laid its icy hands on the countryside so that the trees towered over the path like deathly sentinels—their leafless branches stretching out with long, knotted fingers.

"It's beautiful in the springtime," Eileen said, eying Ryan through the rearview mirror. "The trees and plants are bursting with green, and the sun is bright, and..." she trailed off, biting her lip.

Ryan clutched his violin case, hugging it close to his body as his breath puffed against the chilled glass window. He glanced at Eileen again. She flexed her fingers and placed her right hand in front of the heater, sighing in relief. Ryan had watched her knuckles go white clutching the wheel as they traveled up the mountains. There hadn't been any railing around the outer edge, and Ryan had pictured the little car shooting off the cliffside several times over the drive.

Maybe that would have been for the best.

Anna—No, that wasn't right. She wasn't Anna anymore. She was Jory now. The man with the orange eyes had said that would be better for her. New memories, new name. Her full name was Georgianna, so Jory was still a play off her real name.

His sister sat with her knees scrunched up to her chin. She had been screaming incoherently—arms wrapped tightly around her head for hours. She'd only calmed down when they left the packed winding streets of San Francisco for the wider freeways. Now they drove down an abandoned windy road, an eerie silence replacing the tortured cries from before.

The orange-eyed man was supposed to fix her, not make her worse. She's broken. What if she's like this forever?

Jory rubbed the blue armband on her wrist, eyes locked on Ryan. Her mouth moved in wordless speech, eyes wide in confusion and pain. Ryan ignored her, shoving himself more firmly into the side corner of the car. He knew she could feel his guilt.

Stop looking at me, stop looking at me, stop looking at me. Ryan's thoughts were a repetitive whirlwind as his sister's eyes continued to bore into him.

After about ten minutes of dirt road, they came to an aged stone wall. Moss and lichen curled up the mismatched stone. It circled about a large old house with pointed rooftops and dark, wooden shingles. Black, swirling gates loomed over them in the dusky twilight.

"In the summer, we get butterflies and ladybugs. It really is quite pretty," Eileen said, voice cheery.

She's so fake. Ryan pressed his face into his black violin case.

"Just through here," Eileen said.

He peeked up—thick blocky letters curved over the top of the gate, spelling out **Stark's Home for Troubled Youth**.

Days later, Ryan crept along the dark, narrow hallway of *Stark's Home*. He stopped, took a slow breath, and pushed a heavy wooden door open a crack. A slim stream of light spilled across his feet. He crouched low and peered inside the room, doing his best to stay hidden on the outside.

Inside, Jory sat huddled against the far wall. Standing in front of her, a young man clutched his left arm—nails digging into his dark, earthy skin. Eileen reached a hand up and placed it on the teen's shoulder. He flinched, jerking away from her.

Eileen pulled her hand back. "Oh right. Sorry."

She took a deep breath.

"Sebastian," Eileen said, tucking her pale-blonde hair behind her ear, "could you give the poor girl some rest? I can't get her to say a single solitary thing. She's just been rocking and mumbling for the past three days. She won't eat and hardly drinks. The only thing I can think to do is knock her out and plug in some fluids. Could you do that for me?"

Knock her out?

Ryan gripped the armband in his hands. *Remove anything that might trigger her memories,* Bram's dark voice echoed in his mind. He touched his cheek where she'd scratched him when he'd torn it off her wrist.

Sebastian glanced at Jory, sweat breaking out on the back of his neck.

"Ummm, y-you know, I'm n-n-not very good with women. I help with the kids, I'm good with kids, they're not...you know. And putting her to sleep m-might not even help her. She could come out worse, like my mom did..." He trailed off, shriveling under Miss Kilpatrick's stare. He coughed nervously. "So, yeah, I'll just do it then."

Sebastian scuttled over to the corner where Jory sat whispering and tracing swirls on the wall. His sister locked eyes with the teen. Sebastian froze. She rubbed her naked wrist and flicked her eyes from Eileen to the door where Ryan sat crouched on the other side.

She knows I'm here.

"M-my mom was an Empath," Sebastian stuttered. "Like you."

Jory continued to rock but tilted her head to the side.

Sebastian laughed nervously. "You feel my fear. I can see it." He took in a shivering breath, and blinked when Jory copied him.

"You're so small...like a kid. Like Riri or Calub, or..." He laughed again. "You have no idea who they are. Ummm m..."

Sebastian glanced back at Eileen, rubbing his neck nervously. "For how long?" he asked.

Eileen took a moment to answer, considering.

"A few days should do. I'm sure she'll regain her control after her mind gets some rest." An edge of worry colored her words, and Ryan gritted his teeth.

Please. He sent out a silent prayer. *I know I'm past saving, but she has to get better. She's all I have left.*

Sebastian crouched, approaching Jory slowly, his knobby knees thrust upward. Ryan thought he looked like a grasshopper, all knees and elbows.

"Hey," Sebastian said, his voice low and soothing. "Deep breaths, okay? Can you do that with me?"

Jory nodded, her long raven-black hair bobbing up and down. They took a few deep breaths, and once she stopped trembling, her crystal-blue eyes cleared up just a little.

It was working. This guy was getting through to her. Relief and a pang of jealousy stabbed at Ryan.

"Hey, um...can you, ummmm..." Sebastian reached his hands out then stopped, fishing out some latex gloves. After pulling them on, he paused only a moment before placing them on the sides of her face. They looked ginormous, swallowing his sister's cheeks.

"Georgianna?"

"Jory," she said softly, voice raspy from crying.

Hearing her speak—hearing *her* tell Sebastian that was her name—opened a pit in Ryan's stomach. Bram had done it. He'd really done it. Anna was gone. For the thousandth time, Ryan wondered if he had done the right thing. Was this girl even his sister anymore? Tears welled in his eyes, and he shoved the thought down.

"Jory. Okay, cool." Sabastian shuffled a bit, then said, "Close your eyes, Jory."

Jory closed her eyes.

Sebastian cleared his throat. "Okay, imagine the walls around you. The walls are good, um...they're strong. Everyone else is gone. It's only you, me, and Miss Kilpatrick. No one else. No feelings but yours and the people here in this room."

Jory peeked her eyes open and glanced at the door. Ryan flinched away.

"The walls are good," she said.

"That's it," Sebastian nodded vigorously. "The walls are strong. Everyone else is gone."

She repeated his words, then said the whole thing twice more before sighing gently.

Ryan watched closely as Sebastian pinched her shoulder. Understanding came then. *He's a Sleeper.*

His sister's head went limp. Sebastian tried to situate her against the wall, but her head lolled to the side anyway.

"Um...could you... She'll get a kink in her neck like that." Sebastian looked at Eileen.

"How did you do that?" Eileen asked.

He shrugged. "I don't know, I pinch and then—"

"No, no, how did you calm her down like that? I've been trying to help her for days." She shook her head slightly.

Sebastian gave Ryan's sister a tender look. As much as Ryan hated to admit it, he'd helped her.

His sister slept peacefully—the lines that had contorted her face smoothed away like he'd swiped his hand over drawings etched in sand.

She'll be okay now...right?

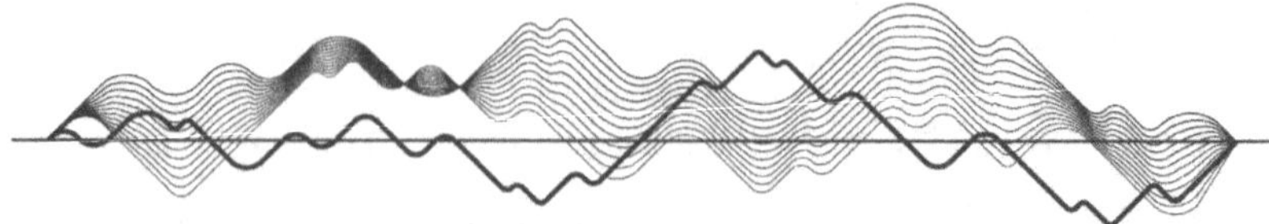

Chapter 8: Ryan

Present Day

The elevator door began to close, but before it shuddered shut, a short redhead ducked in. She had to be the one his sister had talked about.

Ryan did his best to give off the strongest "get lost" vibes he could. He hunched his shoulders, stuck his ginormous headphones over his head, and turned up Bach's *Cello Suite No. 1* on his phone as high as he could without blasting his eardrums. He shrugged his head to the side, taking in his warped reflection in the old metal walls of the elevator.

Despite his efforts, he could still feel the stare of those inquisitive dark eyes.

Why didn't I just walk down the stairs? The elevator was faulty and only went up to the seventh floor, so he'd already had to trek down two flights before braving the rickety metal box. He imagined the cords snapping—the rush as they thundered down before crashing at the bottom.

What would happen? Would they be suspended in the air for a moment as they fell? They wouldn't stick to the bottom of the elevator. It made more sense to him that they would slam against the ceiling of the elevator before smacking against the ground on impact.

The elevator moaned, metal grinding against metal. It had to have been pretty loud to reach past the music blaring in his ears. Ryan risked a quick glance to his left to see the girl look up nervously. The urge to reassure her rose in his chest.

He squashed it. *Stupid testosterone.* She didn't need anything from him, and he didn't need to strut around puffing out his scrawny chest to try to impress anyone. Besides, what *would* he do if the elevator malfunctioned and sent them to their deaths?

Probably just numb all her pain receptors, he thought. It would be the most he could do—a small mercy on the off chance that the impact didn't immediately kill her. She could wait peacefully as she bled out.

And I could die knowing I did one thing good in my stupid, pointless life.

The elevator shuddered before coming to a stop. The girl crouched slightly—a defensive stance. When the door opened, she stood straight, brushing her arms off self-consciously. She tossed her hair as she walked briskly out, as if to tell the world she hadn't been totally freaked out a moment before.

He walked a few paces behind her, feeling a bit stalker-ish.

What else am I supposed to do? We're going to the same place.

When Jory had mentioned a classmate coming by with his school papers, he certainly hadn't imagined this person strolling confidently in front of him.

Her unnaturally red hair brushed her shoulders as she walked. She had obviously bleached and then dyed it to the deep shade of red it was now, like pooled blood. He could clearly see at least an inch of black growing out at her roots. A large jacket that fell just above her knees was mere inches longer than the jean shorts she wore. Thin, black-gloved hands swung at her sides. Twin silver rings graced her middle fingers, their finishes dull.

The rings looked strange on the outside of her gloves. Girls made weird fashion statements.

Her pale legs sprouted beneath the jacket—lean and muscled. Probably a dancer. She had the build of one—small and thin with just enough curves for him to know she was older than her height suggested.

He watched her back, realizing for the first time that she might be shorter than him. Shuffling a little closer—trying to keep his feet quiet so she didn't see what he was doing—he looked down at her head. He had at least an entire inch on her, maybe more. His eyes widened, and he smiled.

I'm taller. I'm never taller.

A strange feeling rose in his chest. Like smugness, but not quite. It was mixed with a subtle curiosity that urged him to get just a little closer.

She halted, and it took him several stuttering steps backward to keep from bumping into her. Her loose, army-green jacket flared behind her as she spun around to face him. Planting her hands on hips, her mouth moved—mumbled sounds pushing through his headphones. She scowled, reached forward, and flicked the earpiece. He flinched before pulling them down to his shoulders.

"What?" he mumbled while staring at the ground.

"I said"—her voice came out clear and melodic—"when you're done sniffing my hair, you can stop the creepo act and just walk beside me."

His head snapped up." I wasn't sniffing your hair!"

She smiled, gaining pleasure from his discomfort. "It's apple blossom, if you were wondering. I could lend you some, so you can smell it whenever you like."

His mind reached for his emotional receptors out of habit—a defense mechanism to protect himself from the censure of others. It took more than a little effort to stop the impulse and school his features without the help of his abilities.

Shoving his hands into his pockets, he shouldered past her, completely ignoring her comment. He imagined her pouting behind him, and the thought caused his lip to shift slightly upward.

The urge to look behind him and see her reaction was tempting. Without meaning to, his eyes glanced to the side. He stifled a yelp and shuffled away, almost tripping over the sidewalk. She had come up beside him, close enough to brush arms.

How did I not notice her there?

She laughed, throwing her head back.

Ryan's heart stuttered slightly at the sound. It was almost like the area around her was brighter than everywhere else, and he wished her umbrella of light could extend to him.

The girl struggled to calm herself, sucking in long breaths. A few puffs of laughter still managed to escape as she swiped her gloved hand over teary eyes. The moment she stopped, his mind began devising ways to get her to laugh again.

What is wrong with you? She's laughing at you. People have probably told her a bunch of stupid stuff about you and she's following you around for a good laugh later with her friends.

The thought planted him back in reality and spoiled her genuine air.

Tilting her head slightly, she stared at him. His eyes shifted away under her scrutiny.

She poked his shoulder. "Why do you hunch your shoulders like that? You're short enough without going all Quasimodo."

Her directness surprised him.

"Don't touch me," he said before striding ahead once more.

She caught up to him easily, and they finished the walk to the bus stop in silence. A soft winter breeze brushed past them, causing Ryan to shrug deeper into his hoodie. Hunching again. He scowled, hating to validate her comment from before. He almost straightened but knew she might interpret that as some sort of win on her part—that her comment had made him feel self-conscious enough to change.

He thrust his neck out instead, exaggerating the bent-over look.

Two other teens, Presha and Reed, were already waiting at the stop, standing oddly far from each other.

The on and off couple were off today. Ryan fought the urge to roll his eyes. Presha's arms were folded across her generous chest. Her shirt plunged low.

Ridiculous. It's literally the middle of winter. The fact that she was so obviously exploiting herself made Ryan want to take off his hoodie and shove it over her head. He sighed, knowing that his hoodie probably wouldn't even get past her shoulders anyway.

His eyes flicked to the redhead next to him. He still didn't know her name.

My hoodie would definitely go over her shoulders...

The scream of the brakes as the bus pulled up left him flinching. He cursed under his breath as suddenly everything seemed too loud, too close, too much. He hated how sensitive he was to everything now that his nerves were less restrained. The need to numb them, to retreat into himself, was stronger than he thought possible.

Ryan stepped onto the bus. Why was it so cramped? Why did it feel like everyone was looking at him?

He slipped into an empty seat. Sweat broke out on his forehead and he tightened his fists, pressing them against his abdomen as a sudden surge of nausea made his stomach clench. He slipped his headphones on once more, hoping Bach might chase the panic away, but the notes— blaring in his ears at full volume—just added to the chaos of the moment. He tore them off and let out a shaky breath.

I'm not strong enough. Just a little break. A little break, and then he'd open up his nerves again. It was a process, right? He knew he wouldn't be able to do much at first. Baby steps. *One baby step back, just for a breather.*

"Hey, are you all right? Ryan?" The feather-soft touch of her hand on his arm and the strange sweetness of his name brought him out of his derailing thoughts.

He rested his forehead against the icy glass of the window and sighed.

Wait.

His body went rigid. He fingered the note from Bram in his pocket nervously. "How do you know my name?" he asked softly.

She laughed. "Idiot. I brought you your homework, remember? The teacher told me your name."

He felt like lifting his head and smacking it against the glass. *Of course.* His brain was in such a fog.

"I'm Kellry, by the way," she said with a smile. She tilted her head toward the classical notes blasting from his headphones.

He still hadn't turned down the volume. His muscles went rigid at her nearness.

She lifted her brows in genuine surprise. "Wouldn't have pinned you for a classical guy. I pictured something more moody—like screamo or 90's emo."

When he didn't respond, she huffed out a breath and leaned back against the seat. There was a good pause before her voice came out softly, "How are you feeling, Ryan, really?"

The question fell on his mind with a whisper of warmth, and without thinking he answered. "Empty."

"Ah," she said, dramatically. "Like you ate a tapeworm."

His right eye twitched. "What?"

She shrugged while picking out dirt from under her nails. "You know, a tapeworm? You swallow it and then it eats all your food. People do it so they can eat a buttload of junk without getting fat." She glanced at him and smirked. "You should fix that, by the way."

"I didn't eat a tapeworm!"

"I'm talking about your eye twitching. Not sleeping well?" She grinned at his scowl. "And you don't *eat* a tapeworm, you swallow it."

"I know you swallow it!"

Ryan rubbed beneath his eye where he could feel the rapid pulsing. He wasn't going to admit to her that his sleep was near nonexistent.

Her eyes brightened, and she bit her lip. A giggle escaped anyway.

A strange sensation tickled the back of his throat, but he swallowed it. The inane argument had diverted his attention from what he had just done.

He'd answered her.

Why had he answered her? He didn't tell people the truth about his feelings. He definitely wouldn't believe it was because she was a slightly attractive—fine—*immensely* attractive girl who happened to be giving him the time of day.

Was she Psychic? He'd heard of those able to detect others' intentions, or influence others into answering them.

Kellry pulled out her phone and began to browse through messages and various notifications.

He took the opportunity to pull his hood over his face and activate his abilities. He hoped she was distracted enough by her phone—and that his hood shadowed his face enough—to keep the soft green glow of his eyes hidden. He peeked over at her, examining the vast network of nerves in her body. He swallowed a gasp.

What the heck? How is that possible?

She had *extra* nerves. A whole slew of strange connections in her body that he had never seen before. They moved differently from the others as well, swirling and dancing around the traditional nerves everyone else had.

Typically, Psychics possessed certain mental nerves that shone brighter than others. But this was something different altogether. What in the world *was* she?

He examined her mind closer, pushing past the alien nerves he was so unfamiliar with.

But there was nothing, no patch of unnaturally bright neural connections, which would be a clear indicator of a Psychic.

So it *had* been because he'd merely been influenced by her. He wouldn't allow her to use her feminine wiles to trick him into answering her like that again.

But if she wasn't Psychic, what were all those other connections?

She glanced up from her phone. He closed his eyes, shutting off his ability in the same motion.

"Take a picture. It'll last longer," she said with a grin.

He shook his head and looked out the window. "You think too highly of yourself."

"Actually, I think I have a pretty accurate view of myself, and I'm basically awesome." She poked his shoulder. "How about you? How do you view yourself?"

He smirked and glanced her way, finally looking her in the eyes.

"That's not going to work anymore, Kelly," he said. "You're lucky I answered your first dumb question. Are you a Psychic or something?"

The question was meant to scare her, but she just shrugged.

"Something like that." She gave him a wicked grin that sent a whole slew of butterflies fluttering around manically in his stomach. She poked him again, harder this time. "And my name is Kellry."

"Okay, Kelly."

He gained a small sense of satisfaction when her brows knit together in irritation.

"And seriously, don't touch me," he added before turning away from her again.

Why would she suggest that she's something like a Psychic? That's insane. Most Psychics lived in fear of moments like these—of being accused of having any type of special ability that would separate them from good society. In fact, her moving in, going to his school—this whole conversation was strange.

He clenched his fist around the note in his pocket. It crumpled into his palm, creases biting against his skin.

Get well soon. Looking forward to seeing you at our next meeting.

The innocent words made the blood drain from his face. The next meeting had been preset, before Kala's betrayal to Bram and Ryan's failure to secure the brothers.

Before Amadeus had broken him. Before he knew he couldn't accept being Bram's pawn anymore.

Five days.

That was all the time he had to figure out what the heck he was going to do.

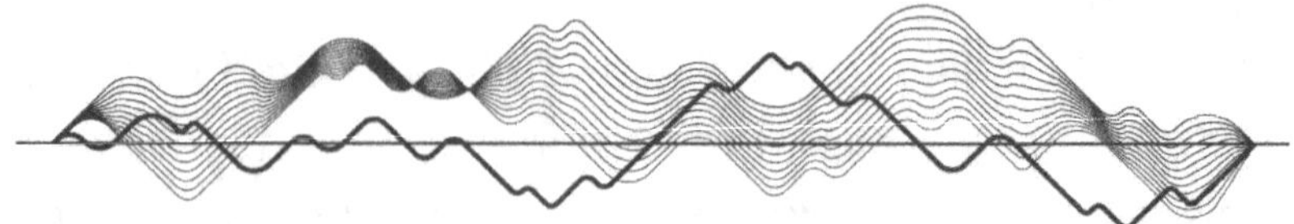

Chapter 9: Jory

What the heck am I going to do?

Jory sat at her small walnut desk, pounding the keys of her little laptop as she entered endless streams of data. Her eyes were tired and sore, causing the numbers to swim across the screen, and her stomach gurgled, reminding her that she hadn't eaten yet that morning. As she typed, her hands shook slightly—a result of her nerves flaring up in pain the night before.

An image of the Not-Ryan formed in her mind—eyes cold and calculating, inky swirls forming on the edges of his ghostly body. She shivered and lifted her feet onto the chair. A blanket was wrapped firmly around her body and over her head. She hugged her legs to her chest and rested her forehead on her knees, breathing deeply—feeling better in the enclosed space.

She wished she could have examined Ryan further this morning. She wished she could have kept him home. Ever since the night she'd found him half-crazed, she knew he was far from okay. His confession of guilt—of doing horrible things, along with the monster lurking inside him, did not bode well. What had he done? Who had sent the strange note that had shattered any semblance of calm he had been trying to muster?

She half expected to get a call from the school saying he'd snapped, or that his powers had gone out of control and the Bureau had been called. If that was the case, they would come for her next.

They always do.

Something tickled the back of her mind.

The Bureau. She had a strong feeling she had encountered them before. But if she had, wouldn't she have been taken?

Images of men and women in black suits flashed across her mind. She rubbed her temples. *Where did I see them?*

She took a long, deep breath through her nose and breathed out slowly through her mouth.

Ever since her parents had died, her mind had been left in a fogged shamble. Her childhood was a choppy mess. Remembering her parents and the life they had as a family before the accident was painful, so it made sense that her mind had blocked chunks of it out. It was like one of those fight or flight things that Sebastian talked about, or maybe that was a term for something else. Either way, she knew it was some sort of survival technique the brain used to help people cope with past trauma.

Maybe shying away from the memory for so long had been a mistake. Ryan needed her...had needed her for a long time. Back at the *Home for Troubled Youth*, it had taken a while for her to come back to herself. But with Sebastian's help, she had somehow regained a bit of the control keeping her sane.

It's my fault Ryan had to fend for himself during that time. Who was there for him when I was out of my mind? Who tucked him in and told him everything was going to be okay?

Even as a young teen, he had been afraid of the dark. Was he still afraid? He had spent those first few months alone—amongst strangers—coping with the loss of his parents and the possibility that his only remaining family member was a certified psycho.

Jory had tried to make up for it. Tried to get them out of there as soon as possible. She'd quit school, gotten a job and an apartment. Got him back in school. The people at the Home hadn't felt she was ready to leave since she wouldn't be able to live a normal life until she remembered how she had managed before. She'd left anyway.

We've never actually talked about what happened. Maybe if I could remember that day more clearly, I could connect with Ryan. Help him cope with his convoluted feelings. Taking deep, even breaths, she closed her eyes and searched her mind. Everything seemed so scattered, until a memory surfaced.

A birthday. She had been...fourteen? Maybe. Mom had gotten her a pair of leaf-green sneakers. Jory had beamed as she shoved them onto her feet and stood up immediately, jogging in place. *"They're perfect, Mom!"* Her mother's happy smile had been so sweet. Dad had gotten her a box full of headbands in all styles and colors. And Ryan had made her a card.

Why sneakers? She had loved them because...she had loved running.

Her eyes snapped open.

That's right. I was in track.

She had been on the team at her school. Her dad had always said it was a shame she didn't have longer legs. If she could win first place at their backwater high school with her short little corgi legs, with a tall stature she could have been an Olympian.

And she had loved green because peaceful emotions let off a green aura.

Tears pricked the corners of her eyes.

I love to run and I love green.

She did. Not because someone else near her did.

Or she *had* loved those things. She hadn't run in years and would probably faint from a short sprint. She was so out of shape.

If I've forgotten these things—these core parts of my personality—what else have I forgotten?

Another piece of the memory pushed to the surface of her mind—another gift. One of those fuzzy armbands. It was a pale-blue color.

"For your sweaty wrists." The words floated across her consciousness, the voice paired with a laugh and a dimpled smile.

Who?

She was so close, so close to remembering...

She pushed her palms against her temples.

Remember, remember, remember. He's important.

Tears pricked the corners of her eyes once more from the pressure of her palms and the pent-up frustration in her heart.

But the memory slipped from her grasp, fuzzing, escaping into the recesses of her mind again.

She threw her blanket off in frustration. She wanted to punch something, scream, cry. She wished she had something from her past, something tangible—an old stuffed toy, a photo, a piece of jewelry. Something to jog her memory. But she had nothing. All their belongings had been stolen or lost, and with her mind in tatters, she hadn't taken anything with her.

But Ryan might have.

She marched into his room. Unlike most teenage boys, he always left his room spotless. There was nothing on the walls. No video games, no books—just a bed, a small futon, a desk, a tall dresser, and piles of classical CDs and records. A large antique boombox and record player kept his violin case propped up. The boombox had been a gift from Jory for his sixteenth birthday.

Jory shook her head and hastily began searching through the desk and dresser drawers. She pushed back the thought that she shouldn't be going through his things—that he deserved his privacy. This thought was what had kept her from searching through his belongings on several other occasions when her worry for him had been almost unbearable.

She paused, hands deep in his drawer. Nothing.

She checked under his mattress, pillow, and inside the closet.

Nothing, nothing, nothing.

He had to have something! She started stomping around, trying to see if a floorboard was loose. The bed creaked as she shoved it aside and stomped some more.

She wasn't sure if she was actually expecting to find anything or if the rampage through her brother's room was just some sort of outlet for her helpless frustration. Either way, when her foot fell into the floor with a loud SNAP, popping the board up like a seesaw with a fat kid on one end, she was genuinely surprised.

Chips of wood and dust pattered to the floor as she pulled her foot back. She glanced around the room, feeling like someone should pop out any moment and say, "Stop, you!"

The room—of course—was empty, so she bent down and lifted the floorboard away. She'd cracked it. There was no way Ryan wouldn't notice.

Oh well.

She reached underneath the boards and almost immediately touched something. Grabbing it, she pulled out an old shoe box. She scooted away from the gaping hole in the floor, leaned against the bedpost, and set the box in her lap.

I actually found something.

She stared at the box for several minutes, then ran a finger through the thick gray skin of debris on the outside. Ryan obviously hadn't touched it for a long time. She took a deep breath and opened it.

A small, well-loved stuffed lion sat at the top. The fabric was faded and the black paint of the nose was almost completely worn off. The neck had a strangled look to it—all wrinkled with the stuffing shoved down deep into its little body. Ryan would always wrap his arms tight around its neck at night.

Jory rubbed the left ear, stained a dark shade of brown, between her fingers. She smiled at the ratty, clumped-up fur on the little ear from Ryan's constant sucking and chewing as a small child. What had he named it? Daniel? Dustin? Pumpkin? none of them sounded right.

She placed it to the side and gasped when her mother and father stared up at her. Her father was holding a young Jory in his lap. He had black hair and rich skin, a mirror image of hers and Ryan's. The only difference was the eyes. Framed by large, chunky black glasses, they were dark as the earth after a storm. Their mother sat leaning on his shoulder, her arm wrapped in his. She had always looked so delicate to Jory—almost frail. She had light-blonde hair and fair skin. Jory remembered tracing the thin blue-and-green veins, so clear on her mother's thin wrists. Her irises held almost no color at all, perhaps a bit of blue.

How long had it been since she'd seen their faces? Jory rubbed her face onto her sleeve, wiping away the dampness there. The picture had become wrinkled, and one corner was badly burned, but it was beautiful all the same.

She wondered why Ryan had kept *this* photo. There were plenty of pictures of their whole family. She felt anger rising up her stomach, rising until it clenched in her throat. Didn't Ryan think she might want to see this? The stuffed lion she could understand. Maybe he was embarrassed to still have the toy that had soothed him through the night as a child. But the photo?

She put aside a couple other knickknacks, including a pocketknife with her father's initials engraved on the handle, a bag of shells, and a spool of thick thread. She held the spool for a moment longer than the other items—a strong sense of déjà vu weighing heavy on her mind. Her fingers traced along the edges of the wood—worn smooth. The action soothed her in an eerie way. The back of her mind tingled, and she closed her eyes instinctively. She was so close to something.

After a moment, she let out a huff of breath and set the spool to the side as well. Glancing back into the box, she froze. A fat envelope sat at the bottom. JORY was spelled out in Ryan's handwriting—the black slanted letters stark against the white paper.

She lifted the envelope and broke through the seal. Her eyes widened when she pulled out a fuzzy, pale-blue arm-band. Goosebumps prickled across her skin. Was it a coincidence that she had remembered *this* gift mere minutes before?

Something poked out of the top of the band. It had been stuffed inside...a piece of paper? As she pulled it out, she realized it was another photo. She unfolded it and immediately broke out into a cold sweat.

It was him.

The boy from her dreams. He was real.

He was older in this photo, maybe fifteen or sixteen. Wild bronze curls fell across soft brown eyes. His head leaned against her own in the photo—his curls spilling across her hair and his arm wrapped snugly around her shoulders. His smile was large and bright. It tugged up a little higher on the right side, a dimple gracing his cheek.

His gaze was focused on the camera, but his eyes seemed to stare directly at her—through space, time, and reality. They held her, entranced and immobile for a long time. But what disturbed her the most wasn't the fact that this boy was in the photo.

No.

It was the look of complete and total adoration on her own face as she stared at the boy beside her.

She had known him. Loved him, if her large doe-eyed gaze was any indication.

But she had absolutely no memory of him, meaning something was *very* wrong.

Could someone have altered my memories?

The ability was rare—so rare, in fact, that some believed it didn't really exist. But if it did...and she *had* come across it...

What happened to me? This can't be normal, can it? Some sort of weird selective amnesia that applies to this boy alone?

How many of her memories were occupied by this person? And why did Ryan have all this tucked away—hidden from her? What did he know?

Her breathing became faster—her heart beating a riotous dance in her chest.

What has Ryan been up to these past three years?

A knock at the door made her heart stutter.

Despite the loneliness, Jory didn't mind the hours she spent alone in the apartment. It certainly was better than the alternative. But it was moments like these that she hated. She could always tell when Sebastian or Ryan was at the door. She knew the feel of their emotions better than her own.

The person at the door was a stranger.

They knocked again.

She stood, slipping the armband onto her wrist and tucking the picture deep into the pocket of her sweatpants. As an afterthought, she grabbed the spool of thread as well and dropped it in her pocket with the photo. Anyone who braved the ascent to the ninth floor only did so for a reason. Perhaps it was an especially persistent solicitor?

Jory stopped in front of the door and immediately saw a thin film of nervousness mixed with anticipation seeping into the apartment from whoever was waiting on the other side. Her hand hovered over the door-knob. That particular combination of emotions made her anxious. It could mean a whole slew of things—from how someone felt before a great performance to what people felt before committing any sort of crime.

If I wait, they'll just leave.

A young voice carried through the doorway.

"Um... Are you there? I'm here because...well, it's about Ryan?"

The boy sounded unsure and far too young to be anyone in Ryan's circle.

Does he even have a circle? I really know next to nothing about him.

Whether it was the hope that she might glean something from this person about her brother or the fact that he sounded like he wasn't older than an eight-year-old, she found herself opening the door. To her surprise, the boy was actually a young teen, perhaps as old as Ryan. Short blond hair sprouted from his head. What surprised her even more was the person behind him—a woman close to her own age with a mass of white braids and the darkest skin she had ever seen. The contrast was striking.

Jory's eyes widened. *I can't feel anything from her.* It was like she wasn't even there. A ghost. Goosebumps exploded across her skin.

Jory took a step back, but before she could shut the door, the blond boy reached his hand out—his anxiety practically spilling out his ears. She felt her own heart pound with the emotion and rubbed her wrist, needing to do something with the nervous energy overwhelming her. When she felt the armband, she was strangely soothed...like she could reach further into herself.

The boy's falsetto voice broke through her thought. "Hi, I'm David. I'm a f-friend of your brother's. I'm really worried about him." His other hand rubbed the back of his neck.

"You mind if I come in so we can talk?" His arm shook slightly, stretched across the space between them.

He didn't introduce the girl behind him. She just stood there, quiet and still. Could she actually be a ghost? Jory stared at his hand like it was a scorpion's tail—ready to sting her if she touched it. But if he *was* here about Ryan, it would make sense why he was so unnerved.

Hungry for any knowledge about her brother, she closed the space between them, taking his moist hand in hers.

"I'm Jory."

Guilt filled the boy's eyes and wormed into her body, making her jerk her hand back. The boy held fast, squeezing her hand tightly.

"Sorry," he whispered.

He pinched the skin between her thumb and pointer finger. Blackness descended immediately as she entered the world of dreams.

The boy from the photo sat cross-legged in the darkness. He was young again, eight or nine years of age.

His eyes crinkled at the corners when he smiled.

"Hello, Anna."

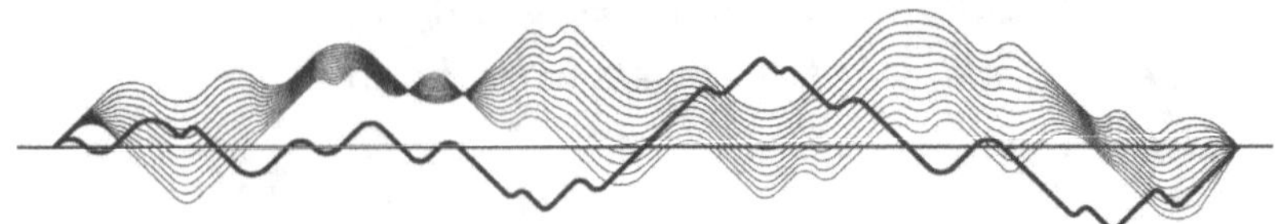

Chapter 10: Ryan

Ryan laid his face against the cool wood of his desk. He wrapped his arms around his head, nestling his skull like an egg. *If my head could hatch like an egg, what would come out of it?* It would be disgusting—something any smart person would shoot on site.

What a mercy that would be.

After his unsettling ride to school, Ryan had gone through the monotonous motions of his high school life—floating from one class to the next. Now that the dumb redhead had brought it up, he noticed he hunched his shoulders constantly. All the other active life swarmed around him like ants in an anthill—babbling to each other, insipid and small.

"Have you heard?" Laura whispered behind him. Her posse of friends sat in a horseshoe formation around Ryan's desk.

Assigned seating was the worst. He kept his head down, trying to ignore the baseless gossip these girls considered conversation.

"What?" one member of the group asked. The thirst for drama and intrigue dripped from her maw.

Shut up. He was so tempted to say it out loud, but the need to stay invisible outweighed that urge. *I could make them shut up. Snip a few nerves.* He put the thought aside, but not before imagining the ultimate satisfaction of hearing Laura cough and sputter like a beached whale.

Laura's smug voice carried from behind him once more. "It seems like more and more of those Freaks are being found. Found or..." She paused, trying to pull her listeners in closer.

"Or?" another girl asked.

Ryan could picture the smirk on Laura's face.

"Or...disappearing," she said, mysteriously.

Ryan tensed. A hollow laugh filled his head. *I'm one of those so-called "Freaks". I'm also one of the reasons for them disappearing.*

"That's not really news, Laura," a haughty girl whispered back. "The Bureau has been doing their job for years now. The tests being done on those things are going to improve technology and medicine. And they're probably disappearing because they realize their lives are pointless, so they do themselves—*and* the world—a favor by killing themselves or something."

"Just because your mother works for the Bureau doesn't mean anything, Trish," Laura said. "Besides, if the testing they've been doing is really so groundbreaking, why haven't the public seen any results? And if we need them so badly for improving our lives, that doesn't make *their* lives worthless."

Trish huffed.

"Is it really okay, though?" A timid girl to his right spoke up, voice unsure. "To experiment on people? I've heard some things. It's worse than what they do to animals."

"You're so naïve, Chrissa. They *are* animals. In fact, they're *worse* than animals. They're monsters, abominations, a genetic mistake. God's plague to mankind." Trish was practically hissing with disdain by the end of her rant.

Chrissa mumbled under her breath, "There's no need to bring God into it..."

Ryan felt anger and shame intermingle with each malicious word. He was the aphid. The aphid pretending to be an ant. And if the ants looked past his fake black coating, they would see him for what he really was—their next meal.

He sat amongst his carnivorous peers in History, his last class of the day. The most pointless class of all. Not because history itself was pointless, but because this particular class—with this particular teacher—was pointless.

Mrs. Tilldree allowed them to write whatever helpful hints they wanted onto a half sheet of paper. Whatever fit on this paper was fair game for the test. So people would sit diligently writing notes in the tiniest script possible in order to get as many free answers as they could. Ryan was one of the few who didn't even bother with it. You never knew what would be on the test, and honestly, it was ridiculous anyway.

Or maybe it wasn't—maybe it was smart. Kids cheated no matter what. This gave the teacher power over the situation. And it gave the lazy kids no excuse when their papers were returned with butt-low scores.

However, no matter how he thought about it, watching *Saving Private Ryan* to experience the "reality" of war was a bunch of bull. Which was what they were doing now. How had she even gotten permission to show this movie?

They had already watched *Black Hawk Down*, which Ryan had gratefully slept through a few weeks before. He peeked over his arm to see that Mrs.Tilldree was intently reading an untitled book. Untitled because she had a blank sheet of white paper folded around the cover. He didn't know who she was trying to fool. Everyone already knew she read all sorts of smutty literature full of long-haired, buffed-up Nancys that made adult women swoon.

Sometime later the bell rang, signaling the end of the day. Ryan flinched slightly, having fallen asleep at some point during the second half of class.

He shrugged his backpack on, blinking the sleep out of his eyes, and trudged out the door. Weaving around the people beside him, he avoided as much physical contact as possible. He was almost to the bus when Kellry's tiny figure popped out in front of him.

"Go away," he grumbled, walking around her. He wanted to get home. He had made it through the day without any backpedaling, and Kellry had the irritating ability to rile up his emotions in a way he couldn't quite get a handle on.

He hoped his dark vibe would shoo her away like the pesky dog she was. It worked on everyone else. But before he took a second step, she was in front of him again.

He glared at her but she just stared back, a mischievous smile on her face.

"Let's go somewhere," she said, conspiratorially.

"Find someone else, Kelly," he said, taking a step to the right.

She shuffled in front of him and frowned. "It's Kellry."

He smirked. "Okay, Kelly."

He stepped to the left but she hopped in front of him again. They did this sidestepping dance a few more times before Ryan's anger flared in a dangerous way. He needed to get away, so he turned around completely.

She giggled, stepping in his way again.

"ENOUGH!" his voice rumbled, loud and beast-like.

People going their various ways glanced at him questioningly. When he didn't react, they hurried on their way.

Kellry stood frozen, her eyes wide.

He averted his gaze, hating what he saw in her eyes.

Fear.

He deserved it.

His hands were fisted at his sides—his arms straight and rigid. The anger was unbearable. Ryan was angry with himself for being such a sorry mess of a person, and he was angry with Kellry for coaxing the mess out. It was too much. The anger, the shame, the frustration. He closed his eyes and focused on his ability. He'd take it all away.

A cool hand touched his wrist—a whisper of a breeze cooling the sweat he hadn't realized was sprouting on his forehead. Strange. It hadn't been windy at all that day.

"Let's go somewhere. I think you need it more than I do," she said, voice gentle.

His anger dissipated at the sound of her voice. How was it possible for one person to spike then sooth his emotions within the space of a few moments?

He opened his eyes to find her staring at him intently—worry causing a small crinkle between her brows. He wanted to smooth it out with his fingers—say he was all right, tell her not to worry.

What am I thinking? I'm worthless. And she's...beautiful and untouchable. Not for me.

He glanced away from her earnest stare.

"Why me?" he asked.

She tilted her head to the side. "What do you mean?"

He shrugged his shoulders and looked to the side. "Nothing. Where do you want to go?"

Her grin was downright sinister.

The hot bun in his hands released a thick swirl of steam into the cold late-afternoon air. Ramshackle shops and businesses huddled together down both sides of a long, narrow street. Most of the buildings boasted a second story where the owners lived. Bright-red lanterns hung, strung across the rooftops in a festive zigzag that made up South Bres' run-down version of Chinatown.

Clothing lines tangled themselves with the lanterns, along with strings of wires that served as phone lines. Street vendors displayed their wares of waving cats and delicate tea sets hand-painted with cherry-blossom branches.

Though the effect was haphazard and a bit chaotic, Ryan couldn't help but find a strange charm. This was honestly his first time in this part of the city, and Kellry had insisted they grab a bite at a hole-in-the-wall bakery here. So they had hopped on a city bus and rode in awkward silence until they reached Sakura Street.

So now Ryan found himself awkwardly staring at a...pork bun? He thought that's what she said it was. Kellry chatted away in perfect Mandarin with the couple that ran the bakery.

He'd thought she might have some Asian background in her blood. *Did she grow up here? Are they her parents?* Ryan shifted uncomfortably and darted his gaze to his shoes when the couple's eyes shifted over to him. What was she saying?

Finally, Kellry jogged her way over to him. She took a hearty bite out of her own bun and put her hand to her mouth as the steamy meat and bread made her eyes water.

"Ho-o-ot." She huffed out the word, waving her hand in front of her mouth.

The savory scent wafting up made his mouth water.

"If you don't eat that while it's hot, I'm gonna kick you," she said after swallowing.

Ryan glanced at his bun apprehensively. "Shouldn't I wait till it cools down a little? I think you might've burnt a piece of your tongue off just then."

She shook her head. "It's best like that."

When he hesitated, she smiled encouragingly. "Go on."

He raised an eyebrow and took a bite. Sweet, meaty flavor burst across his taste buds. The heat warmed him from his face down to his toes.

Kellry's smile grew. "Told you it was good."

He shrugged but eagerly took another bite. Laughing, she linked her arm through his, stopping him mid-chew. Before he could think about her being so close, she was off, tugging him down the street, showing him all her favorite shops.

Evening snuck in, burnt-orange rays of sunlight dimming then disappearing completely behind buildings as darkness weaved over them. Lanterns blinked to life and a soft orange-red glow filtered over the street, turning the run-down businesses into a market from a fairy tale. The place was much busier now. The people hustled about laughing, shouting, and whispering to each other.

Living.

Jory would have loved this place before...when she was whole.

They took a sharp turn into a darkened alleyway and stopped.

"Where are we?" he asked. Apprehension ate through his stomach, and the hair on his arms and the back of his neck lifted. He blinked and almost choked with panic when he realized he couldn't reach his abilities.

The Shield. He'd walked right into it, right into the wide bubble that cut off all Psychic ability. If Ryan had been outside the bubble, he would have at least been able to see the nerve connections of those around him, even if he wouldn't have been able to attack them directly. But he was inside the barrier, which cut him off completely.

Sweat broke out all over his body, making him shiver in the evening air. All that ran through his mind was a constant stream of curses.

I'm such an idiot.

Why did I ever believe for one second that this girl was genuine?

No. Deep down he had known. He'd known the moment he'd seen those strange nerve connections in her body, probably even before that.

That's right. I knew something was up the moment she moved into the apartment on the ninth floor.

Had he been that hungry for human interaction?

For a friend?

"Ryan, calm down." Kellry's voice broke through the din in his head.

He turned to her, heart filled with malice.

She flinched and opened her mouth to speak but stopped when three figures winked into view: the hulking Shield, a dark-haired guy toting a baseball helmet, and a large man with dark, hateful eyes Ryan recognized all too well.

Roman.

Profanities filled every corner of his brain.

Why the heck is Roman here?

Kellry stood in his way. He moved toward her, but she slapped her hands across each other and fire erupted—twisting and curling like mini flame-nados in her hands.

What the—how is she doing that? He had never heard of anyone with an ability that involved fire. Plus, if they were inside the Shield's influence, she shouldn't even be capable of using her abilities.

Before he could even think of a way to get around her flames, Roman was on him. The man was made entirely of muscle, and he didn't hesitate to spin Ryan's puny body around and land a solid, breath-stealing, bone-crunching punch into his gut.

Pain flooded through Ryan's abdomen, overtaking any thought or action that might help him out of this impossible situation.

He lay huddled on the ground, coughing and sputtering. He gasped and gripped his side—pain flaring with every breath. Feeling so helpless was strange. Ryan had never needed the help of physical strength. He could always manipulate those around him to do almost anything he wanted.

He cracked his eyes open to see Roman's fist crank back for another go.

I'm going to die.

There was no way he could survive another one of Roman's punches. The man was a Berserker and had obviously activated his ability before the Shield was in place. Even if his powers were shut off now, the residual release of muscle-enhancing chemicals had already been triggered. Roman could punch a chunk out of a cement wall when his ability was fully activated. Ryan had no chance.

A flash of red bled into his blurred vision.

Kellry?

She stood in front of him, arms splayed wide. Her army-green jacket flared out in an invisible breeze. Roman's fist was already swinging through the air, and even if he wanted to, he wouldn't be able to pull back from that momentum. Ryan reached out a hand, desperately trying to grab the crazy girl in front of him.

Roman halted a moment, struggling mid-swing as a gust of powerful wind pushed against him until the unseen power forcefully threw his fist to the side. He staggered and crashed to the ground. The man glared at Kellry, venom in his eyes.

"What did you do?" Roman asked.

"That's enough, Roman," she hissed at him, ignoring his question. "Drake wants him alive, you idiot. You could have killed him. Stop letting some grudge get in your way. Nothing works without him."

Who was Drake?

"He deserved it and a lot more for what he's done. Drake gave me permission to punch him." Roman stood and brushed himself off.

Kellry narrowed her eyes. "One! One punch to sooth your damaged ego. And certainly not aided by your abilities."

The Shield stepped forward.

There was no mistaking him—tall, wide, and grim. He was the same man who chased Ryan that night he'd discovered Amadeus and tried to squeeze through the walls. He stood between Kellry and Roman.

"That's enough," the man said, almost inaudibly.

Roman and Kellry immediately took a step back and turned away from each other like two siblings pouting after fighting over the same toy.

"Can we go? Kellry, you're so worried about your little buddy you haven't even noticed that he might be dying as we speak." The dark-haired guy was leaning against the alley wall, hugging his baseball helmet to his chest. He flung his hair to the side with a toss of his head.

Ryan coughed, and blood splashed onto the ground. It filled his mouth with the warm taste of salt and iron.

"See," baseball-boy said, nodding in Ryan's direction.

Kellry turned toward him, panic clearly written on her face.

The Shield walked over and picked up Ryan easily, cradling him like a baby. The movement made his stomach and side pinch and burn. He gasped and coughed again, blood spraying the front of the large man's shirt.

Gross. He wanted to curse at the man but couldn't seem to find his voice. Everything felt so surreal. Lights appeared, warping the edges of his vision. All he could think about was the throbbing in his abdomen and the sharp pain in his side.

"We have to get him to Lane. She'll know what to do. Ref, get your helmet back on. I need to make a call," Kellry said.

The guy with the baseball helmet shook his head. "Not safe yet. Let's head back to base, then call the Silver-tongue."

Kellry glared at Ref. "Fine," she said, her voice a growl. "Let's go then."

Ryan lost all ability to think clearly after that. With the Shield running—and his injuries being jostled to and fro—there was no way he could keep track of his own thoughts, let alone the maze of alleyways they were going through. At one point, they got in a car. He tried to find his bearings, but the pain consumed him and turned his world black.

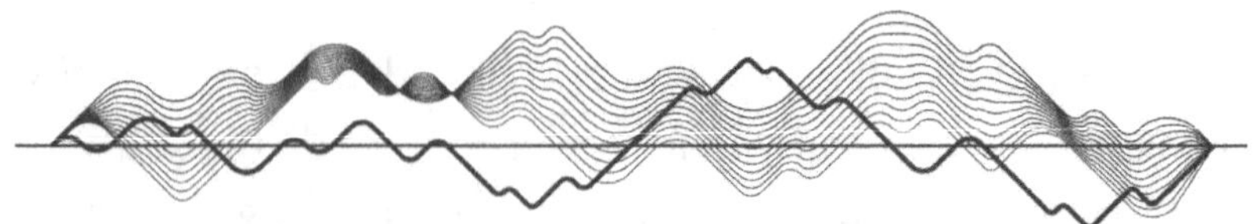

Chapter 11: Ryan

"Give him time. He had several cracked ribs and a good amount of internal bleeding." Damon's voice floated through the mess of Ryan's consciousness.

What happened? He tried to open his eyes. *Where am I? And why do I feel like a bulldozer ran over me?*

"We don't have any time. The meeting is three days from now."

Kellry?

"It doesn't really matter if we miss the meeting. Drake can get you idiots another opportunity." The voice was sharp and definitely female.

The snide woman continued. "And *you*—" She paused dramatically, disdain practically spilling off her words and reminding Ryan of the girls in his class. "You should go. I don't know why Kellry called you in the first place, Damon. I had everything under control."

"As much as you don't want to admit it, Damon has more medical experience than you, Lane. The only reason Ryan has healed this quickly is because *he* was here." Frustration coated Kellry's words. "You accepted the help. Get over yourself and thank the guy."

Ryan finally got a handle on where his eyelids were locat-ed and opened them slowly. The lighting in the room was dim, which he appreciated. His vision was blurred, but it cleared fairly quickly.

Kellry stood, hands fisted at her sides, glaring into the eyes of the girl in front of her. Ryan had originally thought she was much older—her grumpy, old, crone-like voice had made him sure of it. Now that he could see her, she looked very close in age, height, and coloring to Kellry. Her sleek black hair was speckled with thin white streaks. He assumed this must be Lane.

When Ryan attempted to swallow, his throat constricted and he broke out coughing.

Lane turned toward him, and when she did, he couldn't help but choke mid-cough. The shiny puckered skin of a burn victim crawled up half her face and into her hairline. She had shaved most of the hair on that side of her head. Part of her skin had melted over one eye where a foggy, scarred iris peered through, and the side of her mouth pulled up slightly in a permanent half-grin.

The effect was pretty grotesque.

If it wasn't for the burns, she would have looked almost identical to Kellry.

Lane frowned at his reaction.

He blushed, embarrassed.

Kellry followed Lane's scowl. Worry and guilt intermin-gled in her eyes when their gazes met. She took a step for-ward, but Lane shoved her aside and planted herself at his bedside. He looked up at her, silently expecting her to do the typical doctor-type things, like ask how he was feeling or wave a flashlight in front of his eyes. But instead, she stretched her arms out over his body. Her hands hovered over his abdomen, fingers splayed.

She closed one eye, since the deformed one didn't seem to have the ability to close, and began to hum softly. The notes were low and deep in her throat. He didn't recognize any sort of melody, just a strange mixture of tones. As she hummed, his body began to tingle while his blood rushed through his veins, changing speed and temperature with Lane's hypnotic song.

Curious, Ryan tried to hone in on his ability, but to his frustration, he found he still couldn't reach it. The Shield must be hanging around somewhere. These people obviously knew his powers were not to be taken lightly. Trying to lift his head to find the man, he cursed loudly when he realized he was unable to.

Lane peeked open her good eye at his outburst, and he clamped his mouth shut. She closed her eye again and continued. He was dying to know what type of ability she was using. How was she able to control the flow of his blood? As far as he knew, blood was like its own separate organ. It didn't have any nerves or connections to the brain that he was able to see.

The feel of it reminded him of Kellry's fire. Another ability able to function beneath a Shield.

Claustrophobia immobilized his body, causing his mind to switch into panic mode. He cursed again, glad he still had control of his vocal chords. The humming intensified, and his body grew more rigid in response.

His anger grew, breaking through the bindings he had so meticulously placed. Something in him snapped, along with anything resembling tact.

"You're a real piece of work, you know that?" he growled.

Lane's eye peeked open in response, glaring at him as she continued to hum.

"Ya, that's right," he continued, "your face looks like half of it fell in a meat grinder. You really oughta go back and have them finish the job."

The words were terrible. Things he would never say. But whatever she was doing burned like acid in his blood, and his reason had disappeared with the pain. He couldn't numb himself—the Shield still blocked his ability. All he could do was lash out at the source of his distress.

Lane's humming intensified and his blood got hotter—feverish. Sweat began to spill out of his pores like it was being sucked out, soaking his clothes

"STOP!" he yelled. He began to scream and curse as the pain escalated. He continued to rant about the healer woman—insulting her in ways that made absolutely no sense as the moisture rapidly drained from his body.

I'll be a mummy soon if it doesn't stop.

The thought made him giggle and then laugh. He was losing it—his mind was unraveling, and he had no way to stop it. Kellry's hands grasped the sides of his face, forcing him to look at her. His eyes locked onto her large dark ones, and he began to calm.

The pain stopped abruptly. His body was released from Lane's control. He could hear Damon yelling at her in the background but couldn't focus on what was being said. All he could see were Kellry's eyes, all he could feel were her gloved hands on his face, and all he could hear were her soft words.

"It's all right, Ryan. Shhhhh. It's okay. Look at me. I'm sorry, I really am. We're not here to hurt you, I promise." Unshed tears rimmed her eyes, but her voice remained steady and calm.

His hands reached up and pulled her down to him, gripping her in a fierce hug with his face buried into the curve of her neck and shoulder. His hands entwined within the softness of her hair. He stayed like that for a while, breathing in her scent and slowly sorting out his brain. Somehow, with her present, he was able to do it *without* the help of his abilities. He couldn't access the emotions themselves, but he was able to calm himself, sooth the rage that controlled his actions.

I can be in charge of my emotions. Can't I?

"Ryan...ummm." Kellry's voice came out muffled and strained.

Ryan let her go and they looked away from each other. He wanted to grab the pillow beneath his head and hug it over his face. If he ended up suffocating, that would be just fine. What in the world had possessed him to grab her like that? Wasn't he mad at her? She'd lied to him.

You lie to everyone, yourself included.

That was true. He didn't have the right to be angry with her. He also didn't have the right to pull her into a bone-crushing embrace, but it was too late for that.

A familiar pinch in his wrist heralded a lead snaking into his skin. It was attached to an IV pouch filled with fluids.

"I shouldn't have had to do this." Damon frowned.

"Hang in there, kiddo," he said, patting Ryan's shoulder.

Damon turned to leave but not before giving Lane a burning glare. She shrunk under his gaze.

"And *that* is why you are not ready to be out in the field," he said, his voice even and cool. "You let your anger and all the baggage in your life—that you *choose* to hang on to—conduct every action you take. You could have killed him, Lane. *That's* why Kellry called me. Your talent is completely and utterly wasted on you."

He left.

Lane stood there gritting her teeth. Ryan spotted a little vein on her head pulsing furiously. She turned to storm out the door as well but stopped abruptly when it swung open to reveal an attractive man in his mid-twenties. Ryan didn't swing that way, but there were no other words to describe this particular male specimen. He was rarely affected by such things, but with Kellry in the room, Ryan suddenly felt totally and utterly average in every way.

Lane froze in front of him, the haughty lift to her head—the whole "holier than thou" attitude—smothered in an instant. She stood, head tilted down slightly. She looked up through the lashes of her good eye at the man in front of her in such a sickly, adoring way that Ryan could have vomited right then and there if he really wanted to.

It seemed every moment he was exposed to this woman he disliked her more and more.

"Damon left in a hurry," the guy said. "I can't believe you managed to get under his skin again."

She tucked a strand of hair behind her ear and pouted.

"He didn't have to be here," Lane said, folding her arms across her chest. He patted her head and she blushed, a small smile breaking through the pout.

Ryan saw Kellry roll her eyes at the exchange. Lane noticed. She huffed dramatically and whipped her white-speckled hair behind her as she stomped out the door. She obviously was only able to switch to her humble, adoring mode momentarily.

Mr. Attractive shook his head at her grand departure and turned to Ryan.

"And here lies the Slicer—Bram's faithful little peon who strikes fear into any poor Psychic that crosses his path. You don't look so scary to me." He smiled, and a row of straight, bright-white teeth flashed into view.

Ryan wanted to punch that perfect smile right off his perfect face.

"If I'm so harmless, maybe you should have your Shield back off," Ryan said, trying to sound as bored as possible.

The man's smile grew wider, almost sinister. "Yes, but I'm afraid the real monster would come out to meet us then...wouldn't he?"

He knows about Amadeus. Ryan knew it, though he didn't understand how.

Ryan narrowed his eyes. "Who are you?"

"Drake Wesley," he said.

And with that, Ryan understood exactly what was going on.

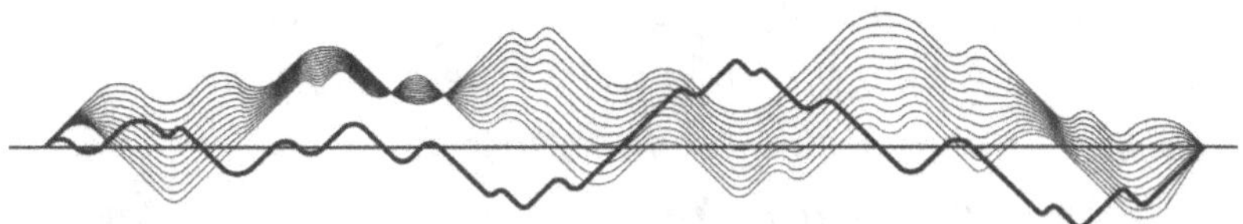

Chapter 12: Jory

Somehow, despite the black void around them, the boy in front of Jory appeared crisp and clear. It was like staring at a black canvas on which the boy had been painted floating in the center.

She stood in front of him on a surface she could not see or comprehend, feeling neither hot nor cold. It was almost like stepping into a tub of tepid water.

When the boy waved a hand, a short table appeared. A teapot followed, landing softly along with two large mugs. She stayed where she was, rubbing her arm up and down in a nervous pattern.

"Sit," the smiling boy said. "You still enjoy peach tea, right? Heavy on the cream?"

He dropped a couple tea bags into her mug and lifted the teapot, pouring steaming hot water inside. The steam coiled and spun delicately through the air, into the darkness.

"Ummmm..." She wasn't sure what to say...or feel.

The boy held a strange mixture of sadness and pain within. Deep, emotional pain for sure. Physical pain was present too, but muffled. Far away. He ignored it effortlessly, like it had become a part of his identity.

He was real. Which meant he existed in the real world somewhere. What was happening to him there?

When he glanced at her wrist, the smile grew. "You're wearing it again. I thought you'd lost it."

She held up her arm, the pale-blue band hugging her wrist. "So...this really was from you, then?"

He nodded. His eyes looked so sad.

She walked forward and sat across from him. He removed the tea bags from the mug and poured in a generous amount of cream along with some sugar. They sat quietly as he stirred the drink, the foggy coils of steam swirling and dissipating as the liquid cooled.

He lifted the mug and held it out to her. Tentatively, she reached out her hands and grasped it, her fingers a hair's breadth from his. The mug was warm against her fingertips. She cupped it fully between her hands, the temperature comforting in her palms.

She glanced around her. "So, what is this place? Am I dreaming? Are we in my head?"

He shook his head. "It's similar to your Tapestry. Some might call it a separate plane or dimension. Only the two of us exist here."

Tapestry... What Tapestry? Was that the place with all the threads?

"Why appear to me this way?" she asked as she brought the mug to her lips. "You aren't really a child."

"It's better this way, trust me. And how would you know I'm not a child?" There was a hopeful tinge to his words. He poured himself his own tea, drinking from his mug while hers still rested against her lips.

She tilted the mug and took a long drink—the sweet creamy liquid causing a slight tingling down her throat. She let her shoulders sag slightly at the comforting warmth and sighed. "I found your photo. Well, I found a photo of us hidden among Ryan's things along with this." She held up her wrist. "It was strange."

He leaned forward slightly. "What was strange?"

"I had a memory right before a birthday, the same birthday I got this. And then I found it right after."

"You remembered me?"

She shook her head.

"I...I remembered your voice...your smile. I couldn't get anything else until I saw the picture. It was then that I realized you were real." She clutched a hand over her heart as an incredibly raw, deep sorrow seeped into her. Glancing up, she saw it reflected in the boy's eyes. The sorrow streamed off him like a steady, constant rain.

"I'm so sorry," she said, tears welling in her eyes. "I can't imagine what you must be feeling. I mean, I can...but that's exactly why I'm sorry. I don't understand why. Why did I forget you? Why are all my memories a complete mess? We were close. I could tell. What were we? Friends? M-more...umm... more than—"

She was too self-conscious to finish that sentence. Her eyes had strayed into her lap, and she glanced up once more to see an amused smile on his face.

"More than what?" he asked, mischievously.

She felt her mouth gape slightly, like a fish.

"More than...you know..." She blinked a few times and then frowned. "I can't have this conversation with a ten-year-old."

He laughed.

"I miss this. You have no idea how much." He hugged his arms around his abdomen.

The sound of his laughter tickled a foggy corner of her mind. He stopped suddenly, wistfully staring at some far-off point behind her. She turned around, but there was nothing there. Turning back, their eyes met.

"Why am I here?" she asked.

"To remember," he said, tone cryptic.

She dropped her head in her hands. *"I've tried. Everything's a mess. It's like...like someone took one of those mummy forks, shoved it up my nose, and whisked my brain around. Maybe even pulled some chunks out."*

He propped his elbows on the table and rested his chin in his hands. *"That's an interesting thought."*

"I guess," she grumbled. *"It's a little morbid."*

He raised his eyebrows slightly. *"Maybe, but I think you might be onto something."*

Jory looked up. *"Really?"*

He tilted his head to the side and gave a slight nod.

"You mean someone got inside my head?" she whispered. The thought had come to her before. That seeming impossibility that someone could have altered her memories.

The boy's eyes hardened.

"Yes," he said.

Her leg tapped furiously against the ground. She hadn't noticed she was doing it till her knee slammed up against the underside of the table.

"Ouch!" She hugged her leg to her chest and bit her lip against the pain. *"How am I supposed to do anything about that?"*

What was she supposed to do? If someone altered her memories, then that was it, wasn't it? Was there a way to get the real ones back? Wait. Could there possibly be fake memories? Had someone pulled out a few...or locked them away? Or had they ripped out the real memories and sewn in fake ones?

How much of her life was real?

How much was a lie?

Her mind was swirling out of control.

"The walls are good," Jory whispered. "The w-walls are good."

"Anna. Anna, it's okay. Anna, please, we don't have much time. I'm starting to lose you."

"My name isn't Anna! It's Jory!" she shouted.

He was quiet a moment before asking. "Jory?"

Jory looked up to see confusion, and then disgust and horror play over his face.

"I can't believe they took your name too." For the first time, anger crept into his eyes. He aged suddenly—one moment a child, the other moment a young man. He was underfed, cheekbones slightly sallow, but the eyes and curls were the same.

"Who took my name?" she asked. She was so confused. What was happening?

He glanced at her and then down at himself.

"I can't...I...I'm losing the illusion—" He looked at her, eyes filled with desperation. "I don't know how many more times I'll be able to do this. Listen to me, Anna—and your name is Anna—you must look inside yourself. Find the inconsistencies—they're there. Trust me. You can do it, I know you can. Remember them, remember me. Please. It has to be you. I can't unlock them for you." He reached forward as if to rest his hand on her cheek, but the dark world began to crumble.

"I wish I could touch you. I—I—"
The dream disintegrated into dust.

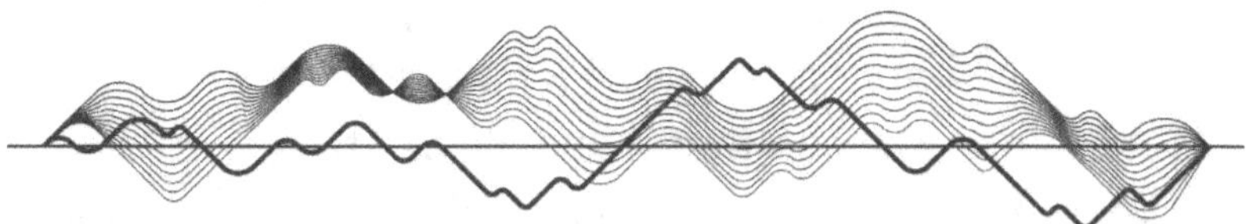

Chapter 13: Ryan
Two Years Ago

Ryan huffed out a nervous breath, tucking his hands deep into his armpits against the cold night air, trying not to look as conspicuous as he felt. Darkness coated the city, and the tall, dentist-mirror streetlamps began to wink on in quick succession.

They waited across the street from a ritzy, high-rise condo. It was so tall, and huge smudge-free windows gave the illusion that the structure was made almost entirely of glass. Manicured trees lined the street—miniature iron fences protecting the trunks. Perfectly mowed, vibrant green grass and square bushes rimmed the outer wall of the building.

Everything about the place drove home that North Bres was everything the South wasn't. Clean, opulent, lush. Not one cigarette butt littered the asphalt, not one piece of gum sat on the sidewalk. There weren't even any leaves collecting along the edges of the street or piling beneath trees. It was so perfect, almost alien.

I want to go home. But then, he didn't really have a home now. Starks certainly wasn't. More importantly, Bram would take his sister if Ryan didn't do this. Bram would tell her everything Ryan had done and then make her work for him. *I made a deal. She lives a carefree life. No memories of what happened, of what I did. And I—*

"Take a breath. The first one's always the hardest."

The teen next to him stood tall and confident. Padraigin O' Riley looked just as his name suggested—ridiculously Irish. Bright-orange hair sprouted from his head, and freckles upon freckles covered every inch of his fair skin. His name and stature made him the poster boy for a young Irish warlord.

Ryan wiped the sweat gathering on his palms onto his jeans. *The first one's always the hardest?* Could he really do this? Abduct someone?

A taxi pulled up in front of the condos, and a thin woman with long, wavy, pale-blonde hair stepped out. Ryan's heart leapt into his throat.

Mom?

A cool night breeze ruffled her hair, and she tossed it to the side while tucking the unruly strands behind her ear.

It wasn't her. Of course it wasn't her. His mother was dead.

"That's our target," Padraigin said quietly.

Ryan's blood went cold. "Wait, what? Her? She's the spa lady?"

Padraigin gave him a hard stare, then blinked, eyes turning bright orange. He'd activated his ability, connecting his mind—his sight—with Bram.

"Let's go."

Ryan cursed under his breath. Padraigin was on the move, and Ryan had to jog to catch up to his long strides.

Ryan knew this woman was a Pacifist, a branch off an Empath. She could calm those around her but didn't feel others' emotions like his sister could. She owned her own spa, and from the looks of her residence, was doing quite well for herself. Of course no one knew she was a Psychic. Until now.

Idiot. You should have stayed under the radar. It was only a matter of time before the Bureau or some Mind Hunter gang would have come along to claim her.

As they caught up to her, trailing behind her perky staccato steps, Ryan couldn't help but feel like a stalker fresh off the stalking boat. Not that there was such a thing as a stalking boat, but that was beside the point.

She slid her security card into the front lock, and Ryan watched as it clicked from red to green. The door swung open, and he was surprised by how fast it began to shut again. They wouldn't make it in time to snatch it.

"Hey!" Padraigin called out. "We have a friend in the building, but the useless idiot isn't answering his phone. Mind holding the door for us?"

Ryan held his breath but didn't need to worry. Padraigin had cut off his ability for the moment, so the true color of his eyes—a bright, leafy green—had surfaced. They were striking but not unusual. Not like Bram's orange irises.

The woman eyed Padraigin, an appreciative smile glittering across her face. She pushed the door open with one hand. When the fiery-haired teen caught the door, hand just above hers, he grinned. She seemed to melt under his gaze as his bright eyes entranced her like the glowing lure of an angler fish.

"Well, come on then," he said.

She blushed and ducked inside. Padraigin eyed Ryan, gaze flicking toward the doorframe. Ryan ducked inside, quickly palming the device that Mike—Bram's guy for all things tech—had worked up. He called the tiny black piece of invention his "Naughty Kitten".

"She'll make a right mess of things, won't ya, love?" Mike had said tenderly to the device before handing it over to Ryan. "Now you treat her right. Don't be slapping her around. Nice and gentle-like."

Ryan shivered at the memory. All of Bram's toadies were a bunch of weirdos, and he wasn't an exception. But Mike? Mike was nasty.

Ryan gripped the inside of the doorway as he crossed into the complex, placing the paper-thin device. It stuck, just as Mike said it would, and the door slammed shut. He shoved his hand back into his jacket pocket and pressed the button that would link it over to Mike.

They crossed the plush, carpeted walkway. His feet sunk into it with every step while Ryan wondered how in the world they kept it so bone-glaring white. When they paused before an elevator with mirror doors, the woman glanced up at Padraigin through her lashes.

"Where do you need to go?" Padraigin asked, voice smoother than whipped butter.

She bit her lip. "Level six. How 'bout you, handsome?"

"Level eight," Padraigin answered. "But I can walk you to your room if you'd like.

"I'd like that very much," she said, voice practically purring.

Geez, lady, you don't even know if he's legal. This was too easy—she was more than willing to dish out where she lived. As the doors whooshed shut and Padraigin pushed the number six, Ryan felt bile crawl up his esophagus. This was it. No going back now.

While the numbers lit up, the bile rose with the elevator. *Two, three, four, five...* He was going to puke. Taking a deep breath, he cut off the multicolored threads associated with panic, anxiety, and fear. Calm rushed over him, like that flame retardant stuff firefighters threw over a budding forest fire. The stomach acid retreated, leaving a burning sensation behind and a bitter taste in his mouth. He'd never numbed his emotions this much before. After everything, he felt he *deserved* to feel pain and any gut-wrenching guilt that ate away at him.

The relief was heady. He felt relaxed, confident. He was in control—over himself and the situation.

He could do this.

The door pinged and slid open soundlessly. The trio walked out, Ryan lagging slightly behind.

"So who are you visiting?" the woman asked, her eyes lingering on the bulge of Padraigin's biceps beneath his black T-shirt. From the back, Padraigin seemed as stoic as ever, except for his fingers tapping a rapid, fidgety beat against his thigh.

"He's not the one who actually lives here," Ryan said in a bored tone. "I think he just crashes here a lot. His name's Brian. Have you met him?"

Padraigin gave him a sideways glance, eyes appraising. Ryan couldn't tell if he'd done well or just screwed everything up.

The woman paused, looking at Ryan with blinking eyes as if she was surprised he could even speak. She tapped a finger over her pouty lips and shook her head. "Can't say I have."

She stopped in front of a door with thin, curling black numbers reading *604*.

"Well, this is me." Though she'd pulled her keys out of her purse, she didn't open the door. They jingled softly as her fingers fiddled with the key ring. "Why don't you send the kid up to your friend and you stay for a drink?"

Ryan rolled his eyes. He and Padraigin were only two years apart. But the older teen towered over him, making him feel smaller than he was.

Padraigin turned his roguish grin up ten notches, pheromones spilling off him in buckets.

"Now that's an idea," he said, voice pitched lower than before. The lady giggled and turned the key in the lock. Padraigin followed her inside with Ryan right behind him. He heard the soft ding of the elevator door opening again down the hall and gritted his teeth. Naughty Kitten had done her job.

Ryan glanced around the room. Her taste was modern—eccentrically so—with strangely angled furniture and steel fixtures, everything ranging from white to black to gray. Huge canvases decorated the walls, covered in thick, nonsensical brushstrokes in the same color scheme as the rest of the condo.

He had entered the world of a modern day black-and-white film. Ironically, everyone in the room was dressed in similar shades as well. The only thing that hadn't gotten the memo was Padraigin's bright-orange hair. It stood out in all its glory, defying this world devoid of color.

The woman turned, eyes darkening when she noted that Ryan had entered along with the hot Irish boy.

"Go on, kid. Can't you take a hint?" she asked.

Padraigin rested a hand on her shoulder and leaned in close to speak into her ear. "Sorry, Tasha, but he's not going anywhere."

She blinked, blood draining from her face.

"You know my name?" Her eyes widened then flicked to Ryan and practically bulged. But she wasn't looking at him. Her eyes were focused higher, on something *behind* him.

A large, beefy hand landed on Ryan's head. The hand weaved into his hair, jerking his head back so he was forced to view the man's face. Ryan's jaw clenched, Roman's dark eyes sparkling above him.

"Loser," Roman said.

Ryan smirked and activated his ability, Slicing all the physical nerves connected to Roman's left arm. It slid off Ryan's head like a lump of meat and smacked against the muscle-head's side.

Roman growled, but a soft *tsk* whispered behind him and he backed off like an injured animal, arm swinging listlessly at his side.

Bram entered then, shadowed by Mateo—dark, lithe, and deadly. Ryan had always assumed Mateo was near his age, but it was hard to tell.

Tasha shifted a foot backward. "Who—"

Mateo darted forward, swinging behind her and delivering sharp, precise blows to the insides of her knees. She collapsed, sinking into the dark boy's grasp. A knife flicked out into Mateo's hand, its tip barely glancing against Tasha's neck. She gulped, and the motion caused her skin to graze against the knife. A thin trickle of blood leaked down the hollow of her throat.

"Let's get comfortable," Bram said. He sunk into one of the black-leather couches and crossed one leg over the other. "You've become careless, Tasha."

Tasha lifted her chin as the knife pressed harder against her pale skin. She closed her eyes, taking a slow breath before laying a steely glare on Bram. Ryan couldn't tell if the confidence flashing behind her hardened gaze was false or real.

"Whatever you want me for, you'll have to pay. Same as everyone else." Her words were haughty, full of bravado. Bram smiled, linking his hands in his lap.

"As much as I admire your fearlessness, I'm afraid you have a *very* wrong idea of what's going to happen."

Her confidence faltered for only a moment. "What do you want?"

Ryan admired her boldness, her fiery eyes. It was sad, really. Such a fire would have to be quenched, because Bram always got his way.

And Ryan would have to do the quenching.

"Here's the deal. I've been feeling a little under the weather lately. I need someone with your specific skills to ease my mind."

"Fine," she answered. "I'll Soothe you. Then leave."

Bram's laugh was soft.

"No, you'll be coming with us—happily. Trailing behind me like a good girl." Bram tilted his head, a predatory smile blooming across his face. "I need constant care, you see. My mind is home to countless lifetimes of memory. It gets loud—messy. Sometimes I act out. Like now. I'm feeling a bit overwhelmed and don't have the patience for you to come to your senses slowly. So let's get going, shall we?"

For a moment, all was still as the two faced each other, then Tasha spat and saliva smacked onto Bram's cheek. It drizzled down his face as his strange orange eyes hardened and his smile widened. He wiped it off nonchalantly with the back of his hand.

"Ryan?" Bram's voice floated across the empty space, dark and heavy. Ryan flinched and hugged his arms to himself, stepping forward.

"Why don't we give Tasha a little taste of what happens when one is...uncooperative." Bram gave him a meaningful glance.

"How about I give you a little taste of what it means when I say go—" Tasha gurgled, her jaw slackening as all the nerves in her tongue, throat, and the lower half of her face were cut off. Mateo released her, backing off as she threw her hands up to her neck. Now numb, her tongue flopped around, sliding out of her mouth one moment and choking her the next.

Tasha coughed and sputtered, eyes bulging in fear. Ryan's stomach turned. She looked so much like his mom. He looked at Bram.

Tell me to stop, tell me to stop. As he sent the silent plea, Bram looked from the writhing woman to Ryan. He kept looking—no order, no inclination that he was going to allow Ryan to lose his hold anytime soon.

Nausea claimed him. Not from fear, because he'd rid himself of fear. But from grief and anguish that this woman was suffering at his hands. Ryan began to shake.

A few lingering moments later, Bram nodded and Ryan hurriedly connected the nerves once more. As Tasha gasped for breath, Ryan fisted his hands, nails biting into palms.

He pictured his sister, her unruly black hair and crystal-blue eyes. Pictured the way they got all squinty when she smiled and ruffled his hair. The way she used to laugh. She'd laugh again, but not if he gave up now. Not if he stepped aside so Bram or the Bureau could snatch her away forever.

There was nothing he could do. Even if it made him hate himself, even if it made the whole world hate him.

Tasha had regained her breath, unleashing a torrent of profanities in Bram's direction. Bram smiled sadly and shook his head. He looked at Ryan and fisted his hand, placing it over his chest.

Ryan shook his head. *I don't want to.*

A tick pulsed in Bram's jaw, and his eyes darkened to liquid amber. Ryan's pulse quickened, sensing the thin wall holding off the man's wrath rapidly dissolving.

Swallowing hard, Ryan held up his hands, feeling for the right points to trigger. *There and...there.* He'd practiced this. Under Bram's tutelage, they'd worked through the ins and outs of what Ryan was capable of. They'd used other members of his group as guinea pigs to train Ryan until Bram deemed him ready.

The training was grueling, chipping away at him, shriveling him up inside. When he'd done this with the others, he'd felt as though he was watching himself from beyond his own body. After a point, he would look on numbly, like he was someone else. Someone else had flared Roman's stomach nerves until he vomited uncontrollably, someone else had increased the pressure on the nerves in Rashida's brain until her ears and eyes bled.

Ryan took a deep, ragged breath and fisted his hands. Every nerve in Tasha's body ignited in an explosion of pain. Each and every connection. Ryan turned it up, increasing the pain an increment at a time.

Tasha began to scream. Roman placed his good hand over the woman's mouth to muffle her as she writhed. The large, muscled man looked at Ryan with disgust. Roman hated that Ryan existed.

Ryan hated that he existed too.

Tasha's eyes found Ryan's, pleading and desperate. They tore at his heart. Bile rose in his throat as the woman, so like his mother, choked on her own puke. Roman cursed as Tasha's bodily fluids escaped between his fingers. Heart twisting, Ryan looked at Bram.

Tell me to stop. Tell me to stop. Tell me to stop.

Bram gave an almost imperceptible nod. Ryan unclenched his hands, and Tasha's body shuddered on the floor with the sudden release of pain. Her eyes stared into Ryan's with a mixture of pity and sorrow.

Pity? Sorrow? A tenderness he couldn't fathom filled her gaze, twisting his heart further and further. Wrenching and tearing. *Don't look at me like that. Hate me. Fear me.* Tears rimmed his eyes, threatening to spill over with each shuddering breath. He couldn't do it. Tasha was looking back at Bram now, murder in her eyes.

Just give up. Please give up.

Despite cutting off his fear and panic, the riotous, ugly scream from every other emotion was breaking him apart, tearing down the walls he'd built. If he didn't get a hold of himself, he was going to freak out. Dissolve into a manic mess.

Or maybe... Maybe he could cut them off all the way. He'd done it before with terrible results. But that was because he only cut off one, or a few. What if he cut off all of them?

What would happen then?

It was never permanent—what he did. In an hour or so, Roman's arm would regain feeling. How much pressure he put on the cut determined roughly how long it would last. He thought it was like how a Sleeper's ability worked. He could put a similar timer on it, just in case, so he wouldn't be void of emotion for too long.

It would be okay... It had to be okay.

Bram nodded once more.

Ryan looked at Tasha, whose defiant eyes widened with panic. She shook her head.

"No, no, no, no, no please, you can't. Just stop, you don't want to, I can tell you don't want to. So don't, please." Tasha's pleas fell against Ryan like fists to his gut. Her hair was wet with her tears, strands tangled over her face, her mascara running down in smudged streaks.

"Please," she whispered.

Bram held up his hand, telling Ryan to wait.

"Do you know why we came to your place Tasha?" Bram stood and stepped over to her. He crouched in front of the woman.

"It would have been all too easy to get you whilst you were wandering about on the streets. But I like my children to know that I can easily apprehend them anywhere.

Especially the place they feel most safe. Take my boy Ryan here." He lifted his eyes to Ryan.

"He was at a place filled to the brim with Psychics. But I came to his bedside and whispered in his ear and he knew, didn't you, Ryan? You knew you couldn't get away from your father."

Ryan nodded numbly.

"Come now, Ryan, what have I told you? How do you answer when we're having our friendly chats?"

"Yes, Father," Ryan answered, trying not to choke on the word.

"You're sick." Tasha's face contorted in disgust.

Bram sighed and nodded to Ryan once more. And in that moment, Ryan felt something in him fracture, hairline cracks racing up his body and through his heart like he was made of fine china. He couldn't hurt her anymore. Not as he was now.

So he Sliced. He cut off every emotion he had. All the guilt, pain, and sorrow. Any traces of happiness or empathy. He had to think, so he left his ability to reason and felt himself fade away into blissful nothingness. Almost as if he was dead.

Dead? He wasn't dead, but he was...something. Not Ryan.

He stared at the woman in front of him. Why did Tasha persist in needing further persuasion? It was obvious she wasn't going to leave this place without joining Bram.

He could persuade her. He could do it quickly, efficiently. That way he could get the real Ryan home. Ryan was suffering. He could fix that too. He could fix Ryan.. .with time.

Without any hesitation, he cut off the nerves to Tasha's lungs, and as they collapsed, he flared the pain in her organs. Without air to breath and the acute pain, the woman began to spasm.

Bram's eyes narrowed, and he looked at Ryan with a calculating stare.

It was interesting to watch the woman dying. Because she was, in fact, dying. Wouldn't it be better if she died? Then Ryan wouldn't be asked to torture her anymore. Perhaps, if he killed everyone in this room, Ryan wouldn't have to deal with Bram's orders ever again.

No.

That wouldn't work. Based on past experience, killing people did more damage to Ryan than good.

"STOP, RYAN!"

He released his hold, realizing Bram had given his nod to halt and he hadn't noticed.

Padraigin, Roman, and Mateo stared at him with fear and apprehension.

Tasha sucked in a gasping breath and began to sob, her suffering the only noise in the room. Bram nodded to Roman.

"Get her. It's time to leave." Bram gave the new Ryan, the *not* Ryan, a meaningful look. He recognized the need and reconnected Roman's arm nerves so he could lift Tasha. She shuddered, fingers twitching, then they all filed out silently.

Bram grabbed his shoulder and looked into his eyes.

"And who might you be?"

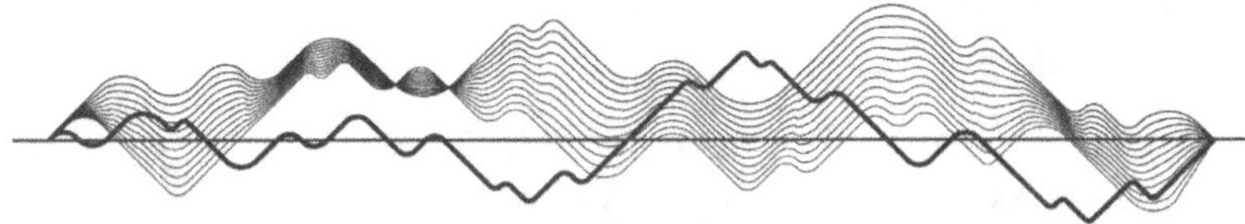

Chapter 14: Ryan

Present Day

The day Ryan's mind broke was a memory he'd failed to suppress—Tasha's tortured gaze haunting his dreams most nights.

At the time, he thought there was no other way to keep his sister safe. But every now and then, he'd played with the idea of finding another Psychic group, one that rivaled Bram's and could help keep him and his sister safe. However, that idea had dissolved as soon as it was born. If he tried that route, Jory would most likely be brought into his dark world and all too close to the secrets he so desperately worked to keep hidden. Not to mention, the reputation Bram had built around Ryan ruined any chances he had to get other Psychics on his side.

Now Ryan sat face-to-face with Drake Wesley. Bram's oldest friend and biggest rival. Someone who would want Ryan dead.

So why am I still breathing? What does he want from me? And when did Roman switch sides?

Roman had disappeared several weeks ago, and Bram had been tight-lipped about the Berserker's whereabouts.

It had probably driven Bram mad to lose a member of his team to Drake Wesley.

Fear bubbled up in his chest.

If Bram found out that he had been taken by his arch-frenemy, he would retaliate. He might even claim Jory in his absence.

"Did Bram tell you about me, Slicer?" Drake Wesley grabbed a folding chair and whipped it out, turning it backward. He set it next to Ryan's bedside, straddling the seat. After resting his arms on the back, he nestled his chin on his wrists.

Ryan shifted beneath the bedsheets, hesitant to speak. Now that he knew who Drake was, he didn't want to screw everything up with a sarcastic remark. He needed him. And he hoped he had been taken for the reasons he was thinking...and not because Drake wanted him eliminated.

But he wasn't dead yet, which was surprising. If Drake knew about Amadeus, he had to know Ryan was a wild card.

That was a mild way of putting it, because even Ryan didn't know what Amadeus was capable of...or if he was still there. Now that he had figured out that Amadeus was working separately from him, maybe he wouldn't come back. He only surfaced when Ryan completely cut himself off from emotion. If he didn't do that, Amadeus couldn't come back. *Right?*

He shifted his attention back to the present issue. Ryan had known instantly from the look on Drake's face that the guy knew about Ryan's other self.

How does he know? I only just discovered him. I need to figure out what he knows...and how he knows it.

Ryan tried to shift his position a bit more, to sit up, but he couldn't find the strength. In a moment, the Shield was there. The world blurred around him as the man flopped Ryan onto his wide shoulder. Ryan tensed, panic prickling his insides due to his helplessness. But all the large man did was prop up Ryan's pillows and fluff them before gently laying him back in a sitting position. Ryan hugged his abdomen in anticipation of pain, but there was none. Just a lingering soreness.

My ribs were broken. I know they were.

Ryan stared back at the Shield's kind brown eyes. The man gave Ryan a questioning look, eyebrows knit in concern.

"Uh... I'm comfortable now, thanks," Ryan said.

The Shield backed into a dark corner of the room and melted into a large bean bag chair that had been hidden from Ryan's previously limited view. An awkward crunching ensued as the giant settled into the chair, the beans inside trickling over each other like one of those large rain sticks.

He turned his focus back to Drake, who watched him expectantly.

"He mentioned you. Once or twice," Ryan said, finally answering Drake's question about Bram.

Drake burst out laughing. "Did he? Once or twice? Come on, kid, let's be honest with each other."

Ryan smiled despite his efforts to dislike the guy. *Why do I want to dislike him? Is it simply because he's good looking? Stupid.*

Ryan gave himself a mental shake. He wouldn't let himself slip into such a shallow ditch. *So the guy has a perfect face. That has nothing to do with me. I have no reason to be threatened by him.*

Despite acknowledging this, he couldn't help sneaking a glance in Kellry's direction. What did *she* think of Drake? She happened to be looking at Ryan at that moment. The two locked eyes and then swiftly glanced away from each other. Drake didn't miss the exchange.

The man frowned in a brooding way, staring at Kellry longer than Ryan thought necessary. Drake might be in his early twenties, but Kellry was still a teenager. The dislike he had pushed away came creeping back like a heavy cloak, weighing down his thoughts.

"Why am I here?" Ryan asked. Preemptively, his hands fisted in defense, clutching the thin white sheets blanketing his legs.

Drake gave him a calculating look. "To recruit you...or eliminate you. Your choice."

Ryan blinked in surprise and then smiled. He liked that Drake was so direct. It was refreshing.

"As long as you can guarantee the safety of my sister, I'm all yours. I'd like to keep her as far away from all this as possible."

Drake shifted in his chair. "Kellry was right, then. That's quite the bond you share. To do so much, go so far for someone. Many here, me included, felt you did it all because you enjoyed it. That you were Bram's loyal little dog. And while that's good news to us that you're not—to hurt so many people, just to keep *one* safe?"

Ryan shrugged. "It's human nature."

Nevertheless, Drake was right. Even if there was more at play than Jory's life. Hidden truths were at stake—truths that he would never admit to Jory, or anyone else.

"Can you do it?" Ryan asked, ignoring Drake's jab at his reasoning.

"What if I told you it was done?" Drake asked.

Ryan's eyes widened. Done? What did that mean?

"I'd say that sounds a bit too simple," Ryan answered.

"There is one hitch. You might want her far away from this, but there is no plausible way we can protect her if she is."

Goosebumps flared across Ryan's skin. All this time, he'd fought desperately to keep his sister in the dark. She couldn't know. About anything. Drake couldn't have brought her here.

"What did you do?" Ryan asked darkly.

Drake narrowed his eyes. "Trust me. This is for the best. Do you really think Bram would have kept his hands off her forever? If you understood anything about his plans, you would have known this to be false. It was only a matter of time before she and her boyfriend got roped into all this."

Ryan's panic and anger raged in his chest. This man was destroying everything he had worked for. Even if, deep down, Ryan knew he was right. *Wait a second... Boyfriend? He couldn't mean...*

"What boyfriend?"

"The tall, skinny guy. He was living with you. Right?" Drake asked.

Ryan sighed, sinking back into his pillows.

"He's not her boyfriend. He's just Sebastian." He shrugged. "Anyway, he doesn't matter. What do you mean it's taken care of?"

"We brought her here. She's asleep, for now."

Ryan closed his eyes, breathing deeply. His heart was beating too fast. It filled his mind with its senseless thumping. He wished it would stop. It would be so easy to just cut the muscle nerves around the arteries. But he couldn't think that way. Ryan had to find new ways to cope. New ways to keep the need to numb himself at bay.

It was just so difficult. He was so angry. Angry...and afraid.

The breathing helped a little. But not enough. He needed to be able to calm down. To think objectively.

So he numbed himself a little bit. Just enough to think clearly. The effect was immediate and staggering in the relief it brought him. Tears pricked the corners of his eyes. How could the absence of feeling...*feel* so good?

He took another steadying breath. The temptation to retreat further into nothingness gnawed at his insides, but he ignored it. Only a little bit, no more. His heart calmed to a normal, steady rhythm.

I have to think.

Wait. He glanced over at the Shield. The large man watched him like a hawk. But the absence of his gift was clear. The shield was gone. Ryan could use his abilities. How long ago had he lifted it? When Ryan said he would help them? Or maybe he could only hold it for so long.

"She can't know," Ryan said.

"Know what?" Drake had sat quietly during Ryan's silence. He arched a brow at the demand.

"What I've done," Ryan whispered. "I'm sure Roman's told you, and he doesn't know half of it. I don't want her to know *any* of it."

Drake sighed. "I can't promise that, Ryan. There are a lot of people here and they *all* know, to an extent, about you. You've garnered quite a reputation in the Mind Hunting world. I can't control what they can and cannot say."

"They say nothing, or I kill everyone here. Or you kill me. Whichever comes first." Ryan wouldn't kill them, but they didn't know that. They thought he was a cold, heartless beast. He needed to tap into that belief now, because if everything unraveled, then what had it all been for?

The Shield stood, and Ryan didn't have to reach out to know that the protective bubble had enveloped him once more. Good thing the numbing effects were already in place, but he wouldn't be able to calm himself further or do anything to the people around him.

He felt a whisper of heat and turned his head to see Kellry holding a flaming dagger in her hand. The fire licked up and down the edges of the blade, which was mere centimeters from his throat. Kellry's eyes were sad, but the blade in her hand was steady. Her jaw set. She wouldn't hesitate.

His heart pinched, but he ignored it.

"That's a neat trick," he said sarcastically.

She brought it closer. The heat breathed against his neck.

"Shut up, Ryan. This is serious."

When Drake held up a hand, both Kellry and the Shield backed off.

"If you really wanted to kill us, you would have. You had a chance. A chance to get at least one of us," he said.

Ryan shrugged. "Maybe, but I'll die before my sister finds out the truth about me. I can promise you that."

Drake studied him, their eyes locking in silence.

"Fine." Drake's voice was calm and even, as if he was talking to a caged animal. "If I get them to stay quiet about your past, you'll help us?"

Ryan nodded. "I'll help you."

"Good." Drake stood. "We'll talk more after you've had some rest."

"Wait!"

Drake folded his arms across his broad chest. "Ya?"

"My sister, she…" How did he explain this? "She has a hard time being around people. She's an Empath, a strong one. Honestly, if she had a handle on her abilities, I'd have a run for my money."

Drake hitched an eyebrow.

Ryan held his hands up. "I'm serious. She's *that* strong. But the fact is, she's completely overwhelmed by them. She can only handle one, maybe two people in the same room as her."

Drake nodded slowly. "I'll make sure her situation is dealt with care. Now rest. I'll be back to brief you on our plans."

After the door closed, the Shield rose from his seat. Walking over to Ryan, he held out his hand.

"Jack Graydon." His hand enveloped Ryan's in a firm handshake. "It's good to officially meet you. You've been met with harshness and anger from the others. I'm sorry for that. Know that not all of us feel that way. And I truly meant what I said that first time. We want to help you, Ryan. I see your struggle, your pain."

Jack's eyes held sorrow and understanding. Ryan stared at his sheets, unable to meet the earnest stare. Jack brought his other hand up, enclosing Ryan's completely with his own. "People don't understand that being Psychic not only gives us gifts, but terrible burdens as well. Keep in mind I'm here whenever you need me."

Ryan stayed silent, unsure of how to accept this stranger's kind words. They were a trap, they had to be.

Jack patted him on the shoulder, meaty hands heavy, then left.

Now it was just him and Kellry. Thankful that his emotions were manageable for the time being, he sat calmly despite Kellry's eyes boring into the side of his face. He ignored her until she finally let out a loud harumph-ing sound and plopped herself next to him on the cot.

A bright, flowery scent wafted over to him.

What did she say her shampoo was called? Flower Berry? Cherry Blossom?

He shifted over and looked to the side, shoving the thought away. Her closeness made him stiff and awkward. There had been girls who liked him in the past. Dark, moody girls who thought he was mysterious and interesting.

Well, he certainly had more going on beneath the surface than your typical high schooler. A bit deeper and darker than they would ever know.

Ryan had ignored them all. Easily. They weren't anywhere near his type. But...his type was never anywhere near him. This meant no girlfriends or anything close to one. Which was a good thing, since he was too messed up to have one in the first place.

But before his parents died, he had been different. Happy.

He was the kid everyone gravitated toward. Even being the shortest in his class, he still drew in a large group of followers. He was honest, confident, and laughed off any small trial he'd faced in his young life.

If nothing had happened that day...if no one had come for them, if he'd had control of his abilities... What would he be like now?

Would Kellry like that person? Would he?

Kellry was different from any girl he'd ever met. When he was little, he'd gravitated toward the sweet, shy type. After he'd changed, that type took one look in his eyes and ran off like a doe.

Why is she here? Did Drake put her up to it? Tell her to get close to the crazy kid and find out his secrets?

But she had seemed genuinely concerned for him.

She was bright and determined. Why spend any of her valuable time with him?

"Momma J doesn't talk much, but when he does, it typically hits home," she said.

He stayed silent. It was easier that way.

"Hey, come on, Mr. Death Wish." She shifted right up to his side. "Where ya gonna go now? Try to scoot away and you'll fall off."

He hugged himself. If he stayed quiet long enough, she'd leave. It was childish, but it was still effective.

Except when it came to Kellry.

When he glanced over at her, she was staring at her gloved hands.

"Sorry about the knife, but if you were gonna switch to psycho-mode, I needed to protect Drake." She glanced up, caught him looking, and gave a small smile.

He looked away. Her scent, her nearness, her comment about "protecting Drake" all irritated him. He felt his shoulders stiffening. He needed space, to be alone. Her apology was empty. She was basically saying that if his crazy broke out, she wouldn't hesitate to kill him to save her...what? Mentor, friend...boyfriend?

She nudged his shoulder with her own. "Wanna talk about it?"

He glared at her. "What *don't* you already know?"

"You're so touchy," she said, rolling her eyes. She leaned back into the pillows. "How about this. I'll tell you a secret and then you tell me how you're feeling."

"You're so weird. Why do you want to know my feelings? Why not something important like information about Bram?" he asked.

She waved a gloved hand. "Roman told us a good amount, and any holes will be filled later when Drake talks to you. I want to know your feelings because...because I think it's important."

He studied his hands, absently tracing the creases in his palms. What was her angle?

"What secret?" he asked.

She sat up and bounced, jostling him. He grunted in discomfort. Her hair was up in two buns today, and short tendrils had slipped from their pins to fall in loose curls around her face.

"So he does get curious," she said.

"If you're going to gloat, I'll Slice your leg nerves and shove you off the bed."

"Ooooooo scary. But then I would be stuck there on the floor, and trust me, my annoyability is a gift in itself."

"You could army crawl out."

She tilted her head. "Yaaaaaa, but I wouldn't."

He gave her a pointed stare.

She laughed. "Okay, okay. The secret. Ummm..." She clasped her gloved hands together. "So, the secret is I've been following you around for the past four months or so." She glanced over at him, baring her teeth in a nervous smile.

Wait... She couldn't have. Where had she followed him? What had she seen? Even if he hadn't noticed her, Mateo certainly would have.

"That's impossible. You would have been seen. Mateo—"

She rolled her eyes. "Mateo is too full of himself for his own good."

Ryan's eyes flew open in genuine surprise. How could she dismiss his abilities so easily? "You *know* him?"

Kellry shrugged and leaned into Ryan's shoulder like it was the most natural thing in the world.

"The modern-day ninja? Ya, I know him. You could say we're childhood acquaintances. I know how he works...f or the most part." She picked at her gloves, pulling them up slightly and then tugging them back down again.

Ryan's brain was running a mile a minute. What connection did she have to Mateo? The teen was around Ryan's age, give or take a year or two. Though it was hard to tell since his features had an ageless quality to them.

He was severely loyal to Bram and had been with him way before Ryan had been pulled into the group.

Looking at the girl beside him, he had to wonder: Who the heck was she? He remembered those strange swirling lines he'd seen, and the fire she manipulated. But there was more there, like how she'd completely blocked Roman's Berserker-strength punch.

"Your turn," she said brightly.

He blinked. *My turn? Oh, the feelings question.*

"I don't think so," he said, shifting his shoulder up and jabbing her temple in the process. "I don't think we quite covered the fact that you've been following me."

"Ouch!" She rubbed the side of her head with a scowl. "I was comfy. Do you know how hard it was to get comfortable on those pikes you call shoulders?"

"You shouldn't have been there in the first place," he mumbled.

Kellry ignored his comment, probing the rigid bones.

"Seriously, do you even eat? I feel like I could make some impressive veggie skewers with these." She pinched the bones in question and he flinched.

He swatted her hands away, a slow half-smile creeping up the side of his face.

"Stop deflecting the question. Why were you following me?"

Kellry grinned mischievously. "I told you I'd tell you a secret, and I did."

He glared at her.

She giggled. "You're cute when you're mad. Your nose twitches a little."

Ryan fought the urge to grab his nose. He wanted to be mad, he *was* mad...but not really. Something about Kellry was completely disarming. He enjoyed her laughter and loved how she allowed herself to relish every emotion. She committed herself to each one, and he envied her effortless control over herself.

This was the most stable he'd been in a long time. And it was only because he had given in and subdued his emotions to a manageable state.

She took his silence for irritation and sighed. "Be grateful I *was* following you around. Anyway, now you have to tell me how you're feeling. So spill."

He stared at the wall, unable to meet her eyes. Talking about how he was feeling felt...impossible.

"If you had asked me that a while back, I wouldn't have been able to tell you. But I guess if I *have* to put it into words, it's like I feel everything at once, or a few things too much. I jump from emotion to emotion like a drunk downing liquor. Every glass pulls me deeper, and I begin to lose myself. And I can't do anything to stop it...or I can, but the solution is more scar—I mean, dangerous, than just pushing through the emotions myself."

She placed a hand on his. The gloves were thick like leather, and he wondered what holding her actual hand would feel like.

"You're doing better than you think, Ryan. I wanted you to know that I've been watching you because I know you have problems. I suspect—" She shook her head. "You're headed in the right direction, so don't ever go back to what you were."

He couldn't meet her eyes. She knew something, had seen Amadeus at work—seen him emotionless and evil. After seeing that, how could she be willing to sit with him now? What did she want from him?

His hand sat limply within hers, but she grasped his tighter. "What can I do to help?" she asked.

Ryan's breath caught, his heart stopping and starting again in a strange rhythm. He felt the tears building pressure at the back of his eyes but fought against them.

This is bad.

He cared for her too much. He was too dysfunctional to care for people. When was the last time someone had offered to help him?

Jory.

She was the only other person in this world who cared for him, but he could never accept her help, because if she was really going to help him...she'd have to know.

But Kellry had seen him. Seen who he was. Seen the darkness. And she had stayed, for reasons he couldn't begin to fathom. Honestly, he didn't care. So what if she was using him? He deserved it. Maybe it was okay for him to lean on her until she decided she'd had enough and left.

Or maybe she really did care for him. Maybe one day he could tell her his secret and she wouldn't hate him. Wouldn't run. *Maybe I'm an idiot. I'm definitely an idiot.*

But the thought of talking to someone about it, someone who wouldn't see him as a monster, was too good to be true.

That could never happen.

And yet he still found himself curling his fingers around hers and whispering one word. "Stay."

"What?" she asked.

"Just stay."

"Okay," she said softly, leaning against his shoulder once more.

When Ryan woke, Kellry was gone. He couldn't remember the last time he had slept so deeply. The rest, the knowledge that his sister was safe, and the cool spot on his shoulder where Kellry's warmth had been left him feeling peaceful for once.

But then the guilt came.

Evil.

Worthless.

...Murderer.

It was like lying on the bottom of an ocean, the salty liquid making him feel weightless, and the dark, black-blue of the depths distorting any light trying to filter down.

In this abyss, he couldn't smell anything, taste anything, feel anything. Only a bone-deep chill seeping into his flesh. He'd gaze up while spending a weary eternity drowning beneath a surface impossible to reach. And honestly, thinking of the effort it would take to get there was too overwhelming, anyway. He was lost, adrift among the bottom feeders of a dark, vast world. Here, any glowing lights were a trap drawing him into a monstrous maw.

"Finally awake, are we?"

A man wearing jeans and a white tank top leaned against the wall to Ryan's right. Lean, corded muscle shaped the arms crossed against his narrow chest. He was of medium height with a slim build. Ordinary enough if it wasn't for the large black baseball helmet on his head. The orange SF logo of the San Francisco Giants was emblazoned on the side, looking incredibly out of place.

Ryan recognized him as the dark-haired guy in the alleyway. He wondered what his ability was and if it had anything to do with the headgear.

Fisting his hands, Ryan lifted his arms above his head and stretched, surprised when all he felt was a lingering stiffness in his abdominal muscles. He sat up and lifted his shirt.

No bruising.

He ran his hand over the unblemished skin. "How?"

The man shrugged. "That's Lane for you. With the Silvertongue's help, of course. I'm Camden, by the way. Feel free to call me Ref—everyone else does."

Ryan nodded. "Ryan... Just Ryan." His mouth felt thick and sticky from sleep. His breath was probably terrible. He wondered what he'd have to do to get a toothbrush and paste in this place.

Ref pushed off the wall with his shoulder and walked toward the door. "Clothes are on the chair. I'll be right outside."

He was out the door before Ryan could say another word. He swung his feet over the side of the bed and noticed a pitcher of water, an empty glass, and an apple. His throat flared with thirst so, ignoring the glass, he drank straight from the pitcher. He downed the liquid with furious gulps that spilled onto his chin and chest. Water entered his stomach, sloshing around in the emptiness.

His mouth felt better. Cleaner. But it still had a strong odor. He noted the clothes on the indicated chair and chucked off the large white nightgown-thing. His briefs and jeans were freshly washed, the blood he'd spat all over himself absent.

What happened to my hoodie? He made another sweep of the room. *And my shoes?*

After shrugging into his shirt, he ran his fingers through his hair, combing through the tangles as best he could. It was long, possibly long enough to tie back. When was the last time he'd cut it?

Wait... Where are my headphones, and my phone? Ryan checked the pockets of the jeans and glanced around the room, but the items weren't there. He missed his music. He was so used to tuning everything out with the help of his favorite composers. With a sigh, he snagged the apple and walked out the door, tapping against his leg as if pressing violin strings.

Ref was waiting for him in the hallway, leaning against the opposite wall. The guy straightened and walked off down a narrow hallway without a word. Ryan followed, biting into the crisp skin of the apple, the dramatic chords of Bach's *Violin Partita No. 2* playing out on his pant leg. The chords in his mind kept his breath steady.

He wondered where he could possibly be. The walls were empty but clean. Their upper half was painted a dark forest green, while the bottom portion was covered in dark, almost black wooden paneling. The effect made the hallway look even narrower than it already was. There were no windows, just plenty of doors, which made him think of an apartment building or hotel.

They made their way down an even narrower set of stairs, walking straight down into a large basement. Ryan blinked. Bright fluorescent lights covered the tall ceiling, reminding him of school. The room was huge, gymnasium sized. A little over half was covered in spongy, mat-like stuff. The rest was plain cement.

The room was empty, save for Drake.

Ryan glanced to his side but Ref had already gone back upstairs.

"Let's chat," Drake called to him.

Ryan bit into the apple with a loud crunch.

Here we go.

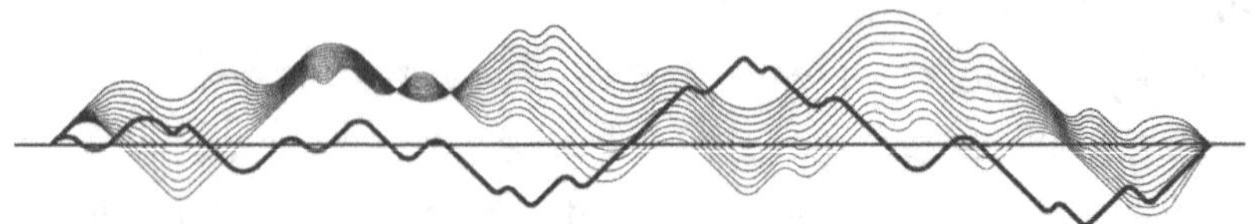

Chapter 15: Jory

"The walls are good, the walls are strong, everyone else is gone. The walls are good, the walls are strong..."

Jory hugged her legs to her chest, breathing slowly and muttering her mantra under her breath. She could feel them. The others, just beyond the walls. There were so many people here. So many emotions.

So close.

She rubbed the armband absently, trying to recall the details of her last dream, to distract herself from all the people right outside her door.

Who was the boy from the Tapestry?

Who was *she*?

According to him, her name was Anna. Well, it wasn't too far-fetched. Her name was technically Georgianna. But no one had ever called her that. They'd called her Jory.

Jory... She reached deep into her mind, trying to recall childhood memories. But whenever she tried to pinpoint a specific moment, it fuzzed like static.

Find the inconsistencies. She scrubbed her face with her palms. *But it's all inconsistent!*

She grabbed the lone, flat pillow on the cot, buried her face in it, and screamed, trying to release the tension that had built inside her.

She couldn't find either name in her distant memories—Anna or Jory. But one thing she did know was that the boy in her dreams was real and possibly in trouble.

He looked so frail.

His eyes, the way he looked at her, and the feelings that radiated from him toward her... A wild blush flushed her cheeks, and she buried her face in the pillow once more.

Why can't I remember him? What else do I need to do to unlock my past?

To unlock the truth.

If I could just remember his name, I know it would unlock so much more.

What is it?

She pressed her palms against her forehead, willing the pressure to pull his name from her hacked-up memories.

She glanced at the armband. The armband Ryan had hidden away.

Her brother was keeping secrets. If he had kept them this long, there was no way accusing him, even with proof, was going to get him to fess up about their past. Reluctantly, she slipped the armband off and stuffed it in her pocket along with the spool of thread. It made her pocket bulge conspicuously. She would have to find a better place for it.

But for the present, she had more pressing matters to attend to.

Like, where on earth was she?

Jory had woken up alone in a dark room locked from the outside. Dim light filtered from under the door, and she could make out the silhouette of a small dresser with a lamp. The cot she'd slept in creaked slightly as she rocked. She ran her hands over the dresser and lamp until she found the switch and turned the light on.

Where was she? Had she been taken by the Bureau?

Images of the woman and boy who had come for her flashed across her mind. The boy was obviously a Sleeper, like Sebastian. But the woman...

Ever since they had left *Stark's Home for Troubled Youth* and started living in the apartment, Jory had done everything she could to keep away from anything Psychic related. She knew the teens had nicknames for all the known abilities, but she hadn't had the mind to keep track of them. Even when she had been living in the home amongst almost thirty rescued Psychic children, she hadn't paid attention. Mainly because it had taken everything she had to stay sane at the time.

She'd latched herself onto Sebastian, and Ryan had been left to fend for himself.

Was that why Ryan had hidden those things from her?

Had he been mad at her all this time? Bitter?

Did he hate her? Or did it have to do with that *thing* inside him? The inky Ryan.

The curly-haired boy in her dreams had mentioned a place—said that it was similar to where they had been. Was that the place with all the threads? Where that monster sat waiting?

It had to be.

"My Tapestry," she whispered. If he had known about it, it must have been a part of her past. She knew she had been able to control her ability before her parents had died. But because of the trauma, she'd forgotten how.

Did the Tapestry have something to do with that control? She rubbed her thumb along the wooden spool of thread and blinked.

When had she taken it out of her pocket? She rubbed her fingers along the worn edges and fingered the thick green thread.

Green for peace. Her mother's voice floated across her mind. A random, errant thing, like feathers falling from the wings of a startled bird.

Her mother had been an Empath, like her. Though not nearly as strong. Had the thread been from her? It had to be.

And then, unbidden, a new thought came.

It made her fingers tremble and halt their exploration of the spool of thread. Could she go there at will?

The thought terrified her. The thing inside Ryan was there. And she could access people's minds there, tamper with their emotions.

She could do other things there as well. The old man... When he'd died, she'd seen his thread disappear. When it vanished, she'd realized something about herself.

Jory shivered, ready to shove the spool back into her pocket.

But what if I can find the boy there? Find him or find other answers? Perhaps even a way to control my abilities. Be around people again.

She grasped the spool, rubbing her fingers against the wood and closing her eyes.

How do I find it? Do I meditate or something? How do *people meditate? Should I fold my legs? Hum?*

She did both.

And it was then, while she was sitting cross-legged on the cot, mumbling "Oooooooooohhhhhhhhhhhhhmmmmm-mm," that the door opened.

Not the metaphorical door to her mind. The actual door.

"Am I interrupting something?"

Yellow darts of curiosity and a bright fog of excitement engulfed Jory. Her eyes snapped open immediately. She stuffed the thread in her pocket, taking in the tiny figure in front of her.

A jaw-cracking smile broke out onto Jory's face.

"Riri!" Jory leapt off the bed. She stumbled and sat with a wince, since her legs had fallen asleep. Sharp pricks ran up and down her lower limbs as the blood began to flow freely through them once more.

Riri giggled and tackled her in a warm embrace. The prickles in her legs erupted with the movement, but she ignored the sensation, hugging the girl with all her might.

"You're ginormous. Here, let me look at you." Jory pushed her back slightly.

It had been over two years since she'd last seen her. Chestnut waves were pulled back in a messy ponytail. Hazel eyes hovered over a prominent nose and wide mouth. Once Riri grew into her features, she was going to be strik-ing, but for now, her awkward phase was beginning.

Jory smiled affectionately, only to frown a moment later. "Where are we, Riri? Is Calub here?"

Riri shook her head. "I wanted him to stay at *Stark's*. He's still too little."

Jory laughed. "Too little? Too little for what? Ri, you're not even ten yet."

She tossed her ponytail to the side. "The Boss needed me. Besides, it's not like I can't go back whenever I want. I visit Calub often. Kid hardly knows his sis is gone." Riri glanced around. "We have got to get you another room. This one sucks butt."

"Riri!"

"What? It does!"

Jory laughed, Riri's excitement overtaking her mood. It was relieving and frustrating at the same time. She wanted to have control of her ability so badly, to be completely ruled by her *own* emotions. As she slipped the spool of thread back into her pocket, the thought pounded against her head that she had to figure out how to enter the Tapestry.

"Riri, where are we?" Jory asked. "You said you can come and go, so they didn't kidnap you too?"

A loud huff escaped the girl's lips and she shook her head. "I told them to explain things to you more before Eunuch put you to sleep. But looks like he got a bit trigger happy, it being his first mission and all."

"Did you just say Eunuch?"

Riri laughed. "Ya, Roman came up with the nickname. He said it's 'cause his voice is really high. But I don't get it."

She looked up at Jory innocently. "What is a eunuch anyway? No one will tell me."

Jory almost choked on her own spit. *Cough.* "Uhhh..." *Cough.*

Riri rolled her eyes and pouted. "Whatever. There's the internet, ya know. I'll just look it up myself."

Jory laughed nervously. "You do that."

The girl nodded and they rose from the floor to sit on the cot together.

"Anyway, we're at Drake Wesley's base. He's uh... Well, he's...Drake." She looked at Jory as if her explanation made complete sense.

Jory shook her head. "I don't follow."

Riri groaned.

"Whatever. I hardly know anything, anyway." She frowned and smoothed out some wrinkles in the sheet. "Being a kid sucks butt."

Jory pinched her nose. "Would you stop saying that? It's gross."

"Ow!" Riri rubbed her nose and grimaced. "Corwin says it all the time!"

Jory pinched her again, on the side this time. "I don't care if *Corwin* says it. It's vulgar, so quit it."

"I don't even know what vulgar means! So stop pinching me, butt sucker!" Riri stuck her tongue out and jumped off the bed before Jory could attack her again.

"I'm going back to Sebastian, so you can stay here and pinch yourself!"

Sebastian. He's here?

Jory reached out. "Wait, Ri!"

Riri went to shut the door, but before she could, some-one grabbed it and peeked inside.

"Mind if I pop in?"

Riri glanced back at Jory and stuck her tongue out again, then turned to the other girl. "Watch out—she pinches."

After Riri left, Jory took a deep breath. Kids were tough to deal with sometimes. Their emotions were often all over the place, and each one felt incredibly deep, almost wild. The new girl shut the door behind her. Uncertainty hovered around her before she spoke.

"I was told it should be all right as long as only one person visits you at a time. But if you want me to go, I can come back later. I just thought you'd like to talk to someone who can actually explain what's going on." The girl tucked a strand of pin-straight, brown hair behind her ear. Long, rough-cut bangs swept across her forehead, framing a pair of hazel eyes. She looked young, not quite twenty.

"No, please stay." Jory tried to smile but the girl's uncertainty made it difficult. Jory's lips quivered slightly. At her reply, however, the uncertainty blew away, Remy's shoulders relaxing as the soft green of peace filled the room. She settled on the edge of the cot, hands clasped in her lap.

They sat quietly for a moment, and the girl shifted and began to grow anxious once again.

"This is awkward," she finally said, blowing out a frustrated sigh. "What do I even say?"

"Why not start with telling me where I am and why you all decided it was a good idea to sic a Sleeper on me." Jory frowned, forehead wrinkling as frustration and anger grew within her. "A name would also be nice."

Redness bloomed beneath the girl's skin, flushing across the bridge of her nose. Embarrassment worked its shaming hands, clutching Jory's chest and causing the blush to creep onto her own features.

It was exhausting having this girl's emotions mingle with her own. It was getting worse. Compared to Sebastian's waves from sorrow to excitement and Ryan's random psychotic bursts of emotion, this should be nothing. Instead, she found herself being swallowed by it all, almost as if she was more affected than the people who the emotions belonged to.

"I'm so sorry, I should have started with that. I'm Remy. You're at a base of sorts. I can't tell you our exact location. Um..." Remy held her hands tightly together. She stared at them a moment before continuing.

"David put you to sleep because we heard you struggle going outside. That being around other people burdens your mind," she said.

Jory narrowed her eyes. "David. Is that who Ri said was called Eunuch?"

Remy rolled her eyes. "That's Roman's doing. David is certainly not a fan of the name, and I'm not as good with familiar names as everyone else here." She stared into her hands and rubbed her thumbs over each other as a wistful sadness trailed from her body.

"David acted too soon. He's still green and got a bit spooked and put you to sleep before Kala could explain further. Basically, we are an organization that rescues Psychics from Mind Hunter gangs and the Bureau. If we're successful, we either relocate them or recruit them."

Remy paused and peeked over at Jory. "Do you remember Ms. Kilpatrick?"

Jory felt her heart skip as she turned to her. "How do you know Eileen?"

"That Home she took you to is one of several around the country that we partner with," Remy said, smiling. "Ms. Kilpatrick is a Huntsman, and as such, she has the ability to pinpoint other Psychics. It's very rare."

Jory sat quietly for a moment, processing this information. She had been an absolute mess when Eileen showed up at their door after her parents had died. Those memories were more blurred than most. Why had her mind completely crumbled? She had always told herself it was because of the trauma—she simply had a weak mind.

Now, she had to challenge this way of thinking. According to the boy from her dreams, her mind had been tampered with.

When did it happen?

She closed her eyes and focused, her hand sneaking into her pocket once more, rubbing the spool of thread.

"Jory?" Remy spoke, interrupting her thoughts.

Jory shushed her, concentrating.

The memory was hazy at best. A neighbor... No, a policeman came and told them there had been an accident. Wait. Or she had been there when they got in the accident, she had been in the car and then a bright light and...and a white room? The hospital? That's where she saw the policeman...or nurse?

Strange.

The memory seemed to shift and morph—ambient, like an old lava lamp. Faces changed from male to female, young to old. Policeman, to nurse, to a man in a black suit. Syringes pierced her skin. They were cutting into her skull. These weren't her memories. That hadn't happened... That wasn't her. Was it?

Had she been in the accident? Had Ryan? Isn't that something she would know?

She had always avoided the memory, and Ryan had flat out refused to ever talk about it.

Her parents had died in a car accident. A fluke incident that had crashed into their family like a great space rock, leaving an empty crater.

She'd been running from memory, running from everything. Unwilling to delve deeper and discover what a patchwork doll she had become. Pieces torn out here, patched up there. Sewn up with mesh and holes that absorbed all the emotions around her until she was unrecognizable. Swollen and beat up, dirty and useless.

But...it was more than just being overwhelmed by those around her. More than her own incapabilities.

What had happened?

Remy's feelings of concern pelted her from the side, making it impossible to concentrate on her memories.

There was no way she was going to get a handle on her memories without solving how to separate her emotions from those around her.

She needed to get her powers under control.

She needed the Tapestry.

At least...that was the only thing she could think of doing.

She relinquished the tattered memory with a sigh. Opening her eyes, she saw Remy staring at her intently. The girl quickly glanced away, awkwardly rubbing her thumbs over each other.

She must think I'm such a weirdo.

"All right," Jory finally said. "So I'm at some sort of base for hero Psychics. You still haven't told me why you took me, and apparently Sebastian as well."

Remy switched from rubbing her thumbs to playing with the tips of her long brown hair.

"I don't know much. I'm kind of a um...glorified secretary here. I handle any paperwork or odd jobs."

Was dealing with me an odd job? Jory thought with a slight frown.

Remy let out a breath, slightly deflated. "But I'm pretty sure you were being targeted by Bram."

Bram? Who's that? Wait. If he was after her, then what about—

"Where's Ryan?" Panic crept up into her chest.

Remy froze. Fear oozed out of her, dark and sticky like molasses from a freshly tapped tree. The look in Remy's eyes spoke of horror and disgust. The feeling rolling off her made Jory want to vomit. Her stomach churned and clenched. Through all this, Remy remained silent, ignoring her question altogether.

Why? Jory had felt this before, when she'd encountered the inky Ryan from the Tapestry.

Remy stood, her finger pressed to what Jory assumed was some sort of earpiece. Maybe Bluetooth?

She glanced over at Jory nervously. "Okay, yes... Yes, I understand. No, I-I... Yes, I mean, she's awake. I'm not sure, do you want me to ask? No, I didn't."

Remy's eyes darted over to Jory again. "I thought you wanted me to... Yes, yes, sorry." The way Remy was getting cut off, plus her increasing anxiety and overall shifty behavior, put Jory on guard.

When Remy finished talking to whoever it was, she looked over at Jory once more.

"I..." She paused, her fingers tangling themselves in the ends of her hair. "Your brother is here. We intercepted him on his way home from school, so you have nothing to worry about. He's...doing well. I'm sure he'll come to see you soon. Anyway, I'm supposed to take you to the main area. The girls' side, anyway. There are showers and a lounge, and I can grab you something to eat. Everyone's cleared out of there, for now."

Jory understood. Everyone had left the area so she could clean up and have a meal without having a mental/emotional breakdown. It was a kind gesture but for some reason left her feeling irritated.

Jory nodded and stood, her legs slightly wobbly.

Remy held out a hand. "Need some help?"

Jory felt the urge to slap her hand away, to bark a sharp remark and scowl. She swallowed it. Remy was being genuinely kind. Jory was just so tired of feeling like a burden.

She settled with a firm "No, thank you" and waited for Remy to get several paces ahead of her before following. She knew she should probably stick close enough to have a conversation. To glean more information from the "glorified secretary." People like that always knew more than they let on. However, she just couldn't muster up the energy to do it.

A few hours later, Jory sat, belly full and skin soft from bathing. She gritted her teeth, wondering for the hundredth time how she had conceded to having her hair brushed by a nine-year-old.

"Uuugh, how did you let it get like this? Gross." Riri jerked the brush through her hair, causing a ripping sensation akin to being scalped.

"Oww! Ri, I'm pretty sure you're supposed to start at the ends," she said through gritted teeth.

"I am."

"Oh."

Riri grunted slightly as she pushed the brush through her hair. Tears pricked the corners of Jory's eyes.

"There are like these clumpy bits. They look kinda like long, hairy turds. Can I just cut them off?" Riri asked.

"No!" Jory slapped her hands over her head. The brush yanked out of Riri's hand, having lodged itself in the wet, bushy mess.

A fog of amusement entered the room. Remy had left to take care of "things" a while back but had returned in time to overhear Riri's comment.

"Here, let me." Remy walked over to a nearby cabinet and pulled out a spray bottle and comb. "You really shouldn't use a brush when it's this tangled. Riri, could you go grab the conditioner from the shower?"

Jory flinched when Remy began but quickly relaxed under the sure hands that worked through her matted hair.

"You're really good at this," Jory said appreciatively.

Remy pieced out another section of hair, speaking softly as she ran the comb through. "My sister and I both have thick hair. She was like you and neglected it the majority of the time. I did this for her a lot."

Sorrow and loss dripped from her words like a misty rain.

Jory didn't pry further. She knew what that feeling meant.

Two hours later, Jory stared into the mirror at a stranger. Gone were the bags under her eyes thanks to the beauty rest granted by Eunuch (she had forgotten his real name). Remy had patiently worked through her hair until every mat and tangle had been worked out. About a pound of hair had been pulled out in the process, but Jory had plenty to spare.

With a few confident snips, Remy cut off four inches of ratty, uneven ends. Even with that much gone, it still fell to the middle of her back. Remy then proceeded to french braid Jory's hair into one thick plait starting on the right side of her head around to the left so that the braid fell over her left shoulder.

"I brought you a sweater and some jeans, courtesy of Kellry, since she's the only one here even close to your size." Remy handed her the proffered clothing.

Who's Kellry? She was surprised there *was* someone close to her size. She was even smaller than Ryan, which was saying something.

Jory slid the dark-green sweater over her head and stepped into the black skinny jeans. They fit like a glove, which felt super weird since all the clothing she owned was always several sizes too big, for comfort reasons. She never left the apartment, so she hadn't really cared about what she wore.

Looking in the mirror, she appeared thinner than she felt she should be. She held the spool of thread and wristband awkwardly in her hand. The pockets of the jeans were sewn shut, which Jory felt was pointless.

She glanced around the bathroom. The room was split into two sides by a waist-high wall. Bathroom stalls and sinks made up one side while eight open showers with floor-to-ceiling four-foot partitions covered the back wall of the other. Marbled tiles lined the floor and crawled up the walls, stopping about two feet from the ceiling.

"What is this place? What kind of building is it?" Jory asked, pulling absently at the unfamiliar braid.

Remy glanced around the large room. "It was a small apartment complex or dorm, I guess. There used to be a college. I mean, the building is still there, but the college itself lost funding and students. When the school went under, this building lost its tenants and Drake picked it up dirt cheap."

"It's nice. Clean," Jory said.

Remy smiled. "We all work hard to keep it that way."

Riri burst into the room, eyes gleaming with excitement. She had left shortly after Remy took over, because apparently watching someone else's hair get brushed proved "super boring."

"Ryan started a fight—you gotta come see!" She giggled with excitement as she turned and scampered back out.

Remy took a step forward, and Jory moved to follow, but the girl lifted a hand. "You should stay here. I'll tell Sebastian he can come see you now. I'm sure it's a harmless scuffle."

By the apprehension swirling off the girl in waves, Jory knew Remy was lying.

She clenched her teeth. With that *thing* resting just beneath the surface, she hoped Ryan wouldn't do anything he'd regret

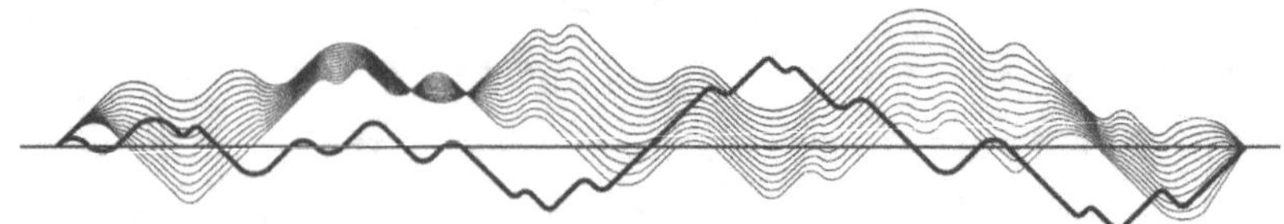

Chapter 16: Ryan

"So that's it. That's your plan?" Ryan rubbed a hand over the back of his neck as he stretched it from side to side. Drake and Ryan sat, leaning over blueprints and notes. They'd spent at least an hour exchanging information. Ryan's muscles pulled tight then eased slightly after the stretch. He sighed with the release of tension.

"That's it. Simple, straightforward. When you've got so many people and variables involved, that tends to work out the best," Drake said.

Ryan scanned over the papers. "Ya, but a lot of this is based on complete conjecture. You act as if you know who Bram is going to place where. How he'll react in certain situations. I know you guys have a past, but the Bram I know isn't this predictable."

Several people entered the room, and Ryan folded into himself. His shoulders hunched, and he let his hair fall into his face. Where was a good hoodie when he needed one?

Drake noted the shift in Ryan's posture and glanced up.

"Ah, good. You're all here." Drake stood and slapped a hand on Ryan's shoulder. He flinched in response, but if Drake noticed his discomfort, he ignored it, keeping him close to his side.

Ryan recognized several people in the room. Kellry watched a short distance away, her eyebrows creased. Ref rested in his typical position against the wall, helmet shoved under his armpit. The Sleeper kid and his brother were also there, hovering in the background next to the hulking form that was Momma J.

Lane was slowly inching her way over to Drake's side. He'd known her for mere minutes and couldn't overlook her sick adoration if he tried. A few others he hadn't met hovered about, hostile glares pointing in his direction.

A lanky shadow crouched at the bottom of the stairs, elbows propped on tall, knobby knees. Sebastian, watching him with a hooded stare. A small form bounced behind him, but he couldn't quite make it out.

"As you already know, this is Ryan Zamora. He is a Slicer and a great asset to our team. Many of you have voiced your concerns to me, repeatedly." Drake gave a meaningful glance to a few of them before continuing. "Rest assured that I take all your worries seriously, and I can promise you they will be addressed, but for now, there are more pressing matters at hand."

"More pressing than the fact that Bram's hound is sitting in the middle of our base of operations?" The girl who spoke had tilted, leaf-green eyes and russet-brown hair that fell in loose waves to her shoulders. Her eyes were filled with an intense hatred toward him, which Ryan felt was a bit too personal for a first meeting.

Could she be from a memory hidden deep within his psyche? He thought he had unearthed everything Amadeus had hidden from him. Perhaps the flood of recalled misdeeds wasn't over.

"Ya, Treasa's right. He might look like a wuss, but he's a torturer, a sicko. We go on the mission with him there and I'll be killed before you can say 'hobs knobs.' I'll be too concentrated on watchin' my back to pay attention to my front." The man had a thick, full beard, and the sides of his head were shaved short while the rest was pulled into a thick topknot.

Drake didn't answer their protests. "Ryan and I have an agreement," he said firmly. "Part of this agreement includes all of you. Any of you who have interactions with Georgianna Zamora will refrain from mentioning Ryan and his past dealings."

The bearded man snorted out a laugh, but when he realized he was the only one, he swallowed it awkwardly.

"Wait, you're serious? You're telling us she doesn't know what he is?" He pointed an accusatory finger at Ryan. "What right does he have making demands of us? Girl has a right to know she's related to poison."

Ryan had been ducking his head down through the entire exchange, shifting in his chair and gnawing on the inside of his cheek until he tasted blood. But with those words, his head shot up, jade eyes glowing. Everyone in the room froze or shifted into defensive positions.

His eyes locked onto bearded-man, and his voice came out dark and icy. "My sister is left out of this, or I'll stop your heart before you can say 'shove off.'"

The man stepped right in front of Ryan, a confident smile splitting his face. "I am more than willing to beat your skinny little—"

"Boys, boys, boys." Kellry stepped between the two, placing a hand on the man's chest and patting Ryan on the head. "Take a chill pill, Krueger. Drake knows what he's doing."

He shouldn't like having her hand resting on his head. It made him feel as if he was an overexcited dog, but the moment it lifted away and settled on her hip, he felt a momentary sense of loss. His ability deactivated, the intricate weave of nerves dimming in the bodies around him.

Momma J hovered behind Krueger like a dark shadow. Krueger sighed, holding his hands up in surrender. "I can feel your sulk through the back of my shirt, Momma. I'll retreat. My mind hasn't changed, though. If that piece of trash is on my team, I'm walking."

"Has the bickering stopped, ladies?"

Ryan blinked in surprise when Kala stepped forward. It felt like ages since everything had gone down at the Mystic Mart. The red string in her white braids had been exchanged for mint-green beads that made a soft *clack-clack* sound when she shook her head.

"You are all well aware that I worked with Ryan on multiple occasions. And I've explained to you the uniqueness of his case. I can promise you he is not loyal to Bram," she said.

She's standing up for me. Why?

Krueger's eyes widened, his head tilting to the side. "Uniqueness? According to you, this kid's got split-personality stuff going on. The Ryan sitting in front of us might be all bark and no bite. But as soon as the other one comes out, we're all limp noodles. A pretty little pasta salad."

Kala rolled her eyes. "Ryan has control over it. That side only comes out if he wants it to, right, Ryan?" She looked to Ryan for confirmation.

Ryan felt sweat form in between his shoulder blades. The answer forming in his brain went something like *Um... Uh... No... Maybe? I don't know. I used to, but then he gained sentience and I'm actually terrified he might surface and take over my body any minute. Therefore, Operation Pasta Salad might not be as far-fetched as you all think.*

"Psh, of course I do," he said, grasping at all the confidence he could muster. It wasn't much.

"Liar," Krueger said. "It's obvious."

Drake waved a tired hand. "Let's put an end to this so we can move on. We all trust Kellry's word, and she says he's good."

There was a series of reluctant nods around the room until Lane grumbled something unintelligible.

Drake jumped slightly when he saw that she was almost shoulder to shoulder with him. Ryan bit back a grin, eyes locking with Kellry, who shared his mirth. When she smiled, Ryan glanced down quickly, unable to maintain eye contact.

Lane scowled. "Kellry isn't perfect. He could have tricked her."

Drake's eyes turned steely and Lane glanced away. He ignored her comment.

We're not getting anywhere like this.

Ryan took a step forward. "I'm not going to hurt anyone. And I certainly have no loyalty to Bram, especially since my sister is here. If you find any reason to doubt me, kill me." He looked at Lane directly, which was harder than he liked to admit.

She narrowed her eye, causing the skin on the burned side of her face to pull taut. "Fine," she said, albeit grudgingly. She held up a finger. "One wrong move, and I'll sing your blood to boiling."

Krueger spat to the side. "I wouldn't trust her abilities. I'd sooner call her pretty."

Harsh... Although, I think I might've said worse.

Lane's scarred face flushed.

"I would be careful, Krueger. I'll make you bleed out through your sweat glands. With your gaping pores, you'd have blood practically spewing from your pits." Lane lifted her chin and looked down her nose at him. "It wouldn't take long."

What are they? He glanced at Kellry. *They're sisters. Kellry's fire ability must be the same. Their abilities must be linked to those strange nerves I saw.*

Ryan glanced down, activating his ability, and snuck a peek at Lane.

There! The same lines. Strange, swirling, twisting lines. Except Lane's seemed to glow a faint blue where Kellry's were a wispy white.

He glanced over at Kellry and blinked in surprise when their eyes met. She was staring at him intently, the only one in the room who noticed he'd activated his ability. She didn't look suspicious, just questioning. He blinked again and his eyes went dull. She folded her arms and gave him a meaningful stare.

We need to talk, they said.

Ryan glanced down into his lap, wincing. Drake had yet to remove his hand from his shoulder. His viselike grip tightened further as Lane and Krueger bickered.

The grip irritated him, and the noise did too. His taste of peace from when he had numbed his nerves earlier was long gone. Ryan closed his eyes, trying to picture something quiet, something to calm his explosive anger. He needed these people to trust him. He didn't want to go back to Bram.

Somehow he knew if he did, Amadeus would come back.

And that terrified him.

"Would you guys shut up! You all promised me. You promised you'd get Amare back. We need *him* on our side to do it." Kala shoved a finger in Ryan's direction.

Ah, of course. She stood up for me because she needs me out of the way to get her brother back. If I was still with Bram, they'd have little or no chance. Ryan didn't know why that disappointed him.

Drake's hand tightened further. What was his deal? He didn't seem to be a very talented leader. Maybe it was because Ryan was used to the absolute obedience that Bram commanded. Even taking that into account, with everything Ryan had seen so far, he wasn't very optimistic. These guys didn't even seem to like each other very much. How had they been able to get in Bram's way all this time?

The bickering had expanded, and people were joining in, mostly siding with Krueger. The anger festered, growing unbearable. Ryan clenched and unclenched his hands so hard that his nails pierced through the skin.

Underneath the din, Ryan muttered just loud enough for Drake to hear, "That hurts. Let go of me."

When Drake looked into his eyes, they widened in alarm. He let go of Ryan's shoulder immediately and took a step back.

Ryan stood, his presence now long forgotten as the fighting grew. He took in the scene in front of him, trying his best to process his rage.

Roman and Kala were shouting, their bodies mere centimeters away from each other, faces flushed. Momma J held David's and Corwin's collars as they shouted, barking like chihuahuas. Treasa shoved a finger into Lane's chest as Lane gritted her teeth and hissed back angry words. Ref leaned against the walls and picked the dirt out of his nails, and Sebastien watched from the stairway, the only one with his eyes glued on Ryan. Kellry held Krueger's shirt in her fists and shouted something in his face. Krueger's eyes changed, the dark irises growing until his eyeballs were black marbles.

He was activating his ability.

And Kellry was in the line of fire.

Ryan's rage consumed him, his ability snapping to existence in a heartbeat. It bloomed to life with a ferociousness he had never felt before. Time seemed to slow. Kellry's eyes widened in disbelief. Drake's hand stretched out, entering Ryan's peripheral vision. He must have seen Krueger's activation as well. But he was too slow.

Everything needed to stop.

The nerves were bright and clear, clearer than they had ever been. Ryan reached his hand out and, with incredibly quick, precise movements, began to Slice.

He started with Krueger by Slicing the optic nerves and severing the connection to his ability. He then severed the nerves in his spine. Krueger collapsed like a poorly made block tower. Kellry grunted as Krueger's shirt jerked out of her hands. She stumbled forward, almost tripping over him. Ryan's lip twitched in satisfaction as Krueger lay in a heap, shouting out in fear against his combined paralysis and blindness.

Ryan's next moves were just as quick if not quite as drastic as he Sliced an arm here, a leg there. Some vocal chords. The others cursed as their arms flopped to their sides or their legs went numb, their bodies falling to the ground. Lane gripped her throat, her voice stolen. Her voice grated on him the most.

The movements came so naturally, so easily. It felt good to shut them up. A darkness hovered at the back of his mind.

The only ones untouched were those uninvolved in the bickering. Those... and Kala, since she was immune, and Kellry, since, well, since she was Kellry.

It was over in moments. Drake's hand dropped to his side listlessly as he took in the scene in front of him and turned to Ryan, eyes wary. Kellry glanced from Krueger to Ryan and then back again, mouth agape.

"If I wanted to escape—" Ryan's voice cut through the shock and stupor. "If I wanted to hurt you, I would have done so a long time ago. You all are so pathetic. You think you can accomplish anything like this? Bram doesn't need my help to tear you apart. He'll easily enslave you all."

It was so ridiculous, the looks on their faces. So comical. He began to laugh quietly, hysteria biting at his insides.

He felt a pinch on his shoulder. "Time to sleep, mate. Can't go Slicing everybody up like that. It isn't nice."

Ryan felt his vision fog. *Aw heck. When did Sebastian sneak up on me? The lanky id—*

Darkness consumed him.

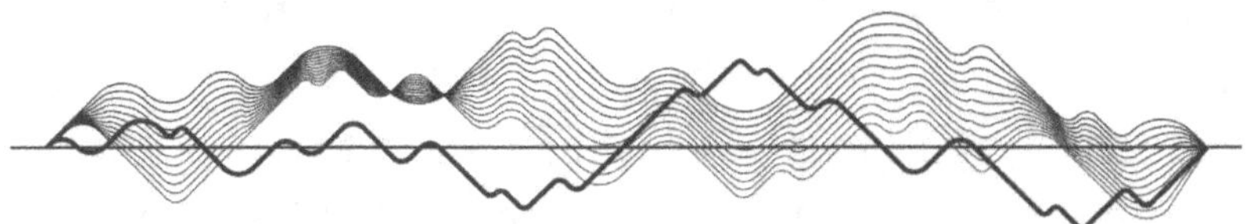

Chapter 17: Ryan

Ryan woke, his body sitting up reflexively. It made him dizzy. Someone smacked him on the head and he fell back with a curse and a groan.

"What the heck, Roman! He just woke up. Geez!" Kellry's voice made Ryan want to smile. He'd never had someone stick up for him so often.

"He sat up like a mummy from a coffin. Besides, he deserved it." Roman grabbed Ryan's lower jaw. Ryan squinted his eyes open, still not used to the light. "If you numb my arm up one more time, so help me, I'll... I'll..."

Ryan tried to jerk his head away but was unsuccessful. Two seconds after waking up, he already felt angry. He hated it. He liked feeling emotionless. It put him above all the petty stuff people pulled. Above people in general. Trying to force his emotions down and act controlled without using his ability was stupid hard.

He gritted his teeth and measured his breathing, then forced his heart to slow while trying to dull the fire in his eyes. He tried to give off the feeling that he simply didn't care.

"You'll what?" Ryan asked, his voice even. "Break my ribs? Try to kill me? Been there, muscle-brains. Go ahead, pound me."

He spread his arms out, inviting him to try.

Roman scowled and shoved him back as he let him go. Ryan's head smacked against the floor. He propped himself up on his elbow and spit to the side as he rubbed his chin, his head pounding. Even without his abilities, Roman was strong. He hoped his jaw wasn't bruised. However, the way his blood pulsed, along with the soreness blooming beneath his skin, told him otherwise.

"Hey! What did we say? Come on, you guys, let's introduce ourselves properly and get this over with." Kellry huffed as groans and mumbles of consent filtered throughout the room. She leaned down, one gloved hand on her knee while the other reached out to Ryan.

"Come on, ya big idiot, get up." Kellry smiled encouragingly, and Ryan ducked his head to hide his own smile as he reached out and took her hand.

You're really something, you know that? he thought as he peeked at her from underneath his lashes. Her hair was pulled into two messy braids. Loose tendrils escaped, brushing against the moon-white paleness of her neck. She was wearing her signature army-green jacket with the sleeves rolled and pushed up above her elbows.

Drake elbowed him in the side. Ryan realized he'd been staring and glanced up at the man whose eyes looked more than a little irritated. Ryan had a feeling it wasn't just because he'd incapacitated his team. What was the history between those two?

Got something to say, old man? Ryan thought with a smirk.

Ryan glanced around and realized that he couldn't have been out for very long since the effects of his Slicing were still in place.

"Fine. Tell shorty I'll say hi as soon as he fixes my eyes!" Krueger lay sprawled out on what looked like a pink yoga mat. Ryan bit back laughter but quickly sobered when the gravity of what he had done sunk in.

What had possessed him to do that? Sure, they were all being unbelievably annoying, but... He glanced at Kellry again. When he'd seen Krueger's ability kick in...when he thought she might be in danger, any control he was building up had been tossed to the side.

"You can wait. It'll wear off soon enough," Ryan said.

"Are you kidding me? I'll just have to wait? Listen here, kid—"

"Save it. I saw you activate your ability, so I neutralized you. Get over it."

The man quieted for a moment, then started laughing.

Is he nuts? Although, I was laughing like that a second ago. Is that what I looked like?

Ryan watched with interest as most of the people around him simply rolled their eyes or shook their heads.

"Ha! Fine, you got me... Hmmm. Everyone here calls me Krueger. I don't think the streets have a name for my ability yet. It's not very common. Basically, I can force you into a dream state and play with you a bit." He grinned.

"Any harm Krueger does in the dream state affects you in the real world," Drake said.

Ryan couldn't help his eyes widening. He'd never heard of an ability like that.

Momma J stepped forward. "I'm Jack Graydon, Shield. I know I introduced myself before, but you've been in and out of things. Sorry for the rude welcome."

"This here is David and Corwin." Jack gestured to the two young teens Ryan had gone after with Kala that night.

Corwin huffed, "I'm a Seer."

The boy rubbed his nose, which was slightly crooked. Ryan bit the inside of his cheek, wondering if the kid had broken his nose when his face smashed into the ground after Ryan Sliced his nerves back when he'd worked for Bram.

"I can see exactly five minutes into the future at will, no more, no less," Corwin continued. "Sometimes it'll activate on its own, but only if I'm in danger. And even then, only sometimes."

Interesting.

Corwin placed a hand on his brother's shoulder. Since Ryan had cut through their leg nerves, they were both sitting propped up against the wall.

"And this is Eunuch." Corwin grinned mercilessly. "He's a Sleeper, except he kinda sucks at it."

"I *never* agreed to that name!" David gritted his teeth, his voice shrill as a five-year-old girl. "And I don't suck. At least my ability isn't lame like yours—you're practically useless." He turned to Roman. "Why can't I be, like, the Terminator or Faint King? Eunuch doesn't even have to do with my ability!"

"Did you just say Faint King?" Krueger laughed hysterically. His hand twitched and he lifted it to his face, eyes blinking. "Ah ha! Finally!"

He proceeded to flex his fingers and blink his eyes. Everyone else who had been affected by Ryan's abilities was doing the same.

"Shut up, Krueger!" David yelled, hands fisting at his sides as he struggled to stand.

Kellry gestured to Treasa, who frowned.

"He heard my name," she said dismissively.

Krueger appeared at his side, rolling his shoulders and wincing before elbowing him in the ribs. "She's prickly, that one."

"What's her ability?" Ryan asked. He glanced up at Krueger, who, despite being average height, still towered over Ryan. He felt weird standing next to the guy he'd recently incapacitated. He wasn't quite sure what to make of Krueger but for some reason couldn't bring himself to dislike the guy.

He leaned down and whispered into Ryan's ear. "Girl's an Oculus, or is as close to one as it gets. I'm pretty sure it's something different, though. Similar, but she's keeping things to herself, that's for sure."

The girl in question shot a dark glare in their direction. Krueger straightened and saluted her with a wink. She tsked and walked toward the stairs. Several others filed out behind her, including Jack and the boys. Both were still bickering about nicknames.

Krueger leaned over again. "Can't deny she doesn't look half bad walking away." The man grinned mischievously, and Ryan coughed up a small laugh. The man narrowed his eyes and glanced at Ryan again, looking him up and down.

"You're certainly not what I expected, kid."

Ryan ducked his head and shrugged.

"You're kinda unhinged, you know that?"

"Yeah..."

"Well, I'm kinda a hothead myself so...yeah."

"Yeah." Ryan shifted his gaze awkwardly.

"All right, then." Krueger gave him one more searching look and then trailed after the others.

"You get along with the weirdest people." Kellry folded her arms across her chest and smirked.

"*You're* weird," he muttered.

"Which proves my point," she said, lifting her chin with a grin.

"Who says we get along?" he grumbled, shoving his hands deep into his pockets.

She raised an eyebrow and shook her head.

Ryan glanced away and realized that Drake was still in the room.

The man sat with a thud and sighed, resting his face in his hands. It was now just the three of them. Well four, but Ryan didn't want to count Lane. She still couldn't talk. Ryan had put a bit more emphasis on her Slicing than the others, and he had been ignoring her constant glare for the past several minutes.

Kellry walked over to Drake, placing a hand on his shoulder. "Well, that was a disaster."

Drake reached up, grasping her hand in his. Ryan felt pulses of irritation ticking in his forehead and hoped a vein wasn't visible.

"I know. This whole thing is a huge mess. I can say I'm the leader all I want, but it doesn't mean anything."

"Stop it, Drake. Thinking like that is what's making you fail. You have the ability to lead, so stop feeling sorry for yourself and take charge. You've brought these people to-gether for a reason." She knelt in front of Drake and he lifted his head, meeting her eyes. Ryan fisted his hands inside his pockets. He shouldn't be here. He felt like a complete outsider at this moment.

Kellry's gaze was firm as she looked into Drake's inane, gorgeous face. "I'm not going to lie to you. You've made mistakes. Honestly, you're lucky the team pulls together and works well under pressure, but...that's only going to get us so far."

Drake nodded and smiled. "What would I do without you, Kell?"

She smiled back. Ryan felt a gag coming on. *Stupid pretty boy with his stupid pretty lines.*

He looked away from the two and found a mirrored expression of his feelings in Lane's face. It was twisted in anger and longing.

Jealousy was an ugly thing. Is that what he looked like? Ryan forced himself to school his own feelings. He took a deep breath. More than ever, he wished he could numb his emotions. The desire was overwhelming. It was too easy, too close to his fingertips. It had been so intoxicating when he'd done it before.

Why can't I? I can control it. He'd done it before, and everything had been fine. Right?

He shook his head. That was a path he could not...no, *would* not follow. Amadeus was too real and too close for Ryan to let his guard down now.

"Get some food in you."

It took a moment for Ryan to realize that Drake was talking to him.

"Come on, ya weirdo, let's eat together." Kellry skipped over and slung a casual arm through his, tugging him forward.

"Okay, Kelly," he said.

She slapped his shoulder. "It's Kellry!"

"Yup...Kelly."

She grumbled and pulled him harder. He grinned, enjoying her frustration, then glanced down at her.

If I kissed her, I'd have to lean down. He'd always wondered what that was like.

He took a deep breath and looked behind them as they reached the stairs. Drake stood, a small frown on his face as he watched the two of them go.

Too bad jealousy didn't look bad on *his* face. He just looked like an injured prince. Lane stood behind Drake like a shadow. She tapped his shoulder, causing the man to jump.

"Geez, Lane, don't scare me like that. How long have you been there, anyway?"

Ryan couldn't help but feel a little sorry for her.

Only a little bit. He wasn't a saint.

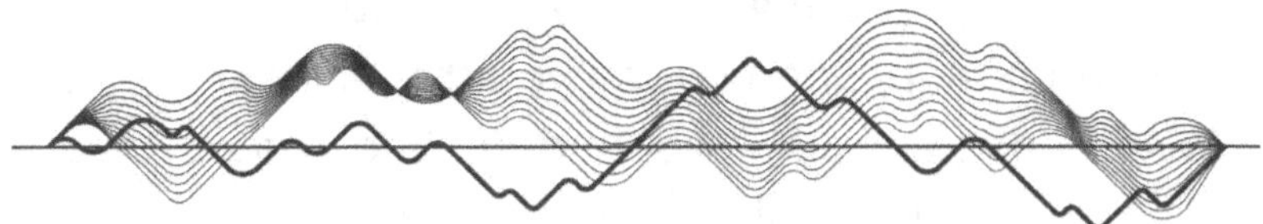

Chapter 18: Jory

"Jory, are you sure? I thought we agreed you weren't going to do this anymore."

They were back in her small, windowless room. Jory lay on the cot while Sebastian sat, legs wide, to compensate for the small chair. The lamp was dim, creating muted, overlapping shadows spilling across the floor and ceiling.

Sebastian held her hand while his forehead creased into multiple folds. He wasn't wrong to worry. Before—at the Home and even after they'd moved in together—Sebastian would use his abilities to help her sleep. Soon, she couldn't sleep without his help. Sometimes she would even convince him to let her sleep for an entire day. It was just too overwhelming to be around so many people, so being *forced* to sleep gave her a brief respite.

They both knew it was unhealthy. And it certainly wasn't helping her get a handle on her abilities, or life. So Sebastian had slowly cut her off. She still struggled with insomnia.

"Stop worrying, Seb. It makes you look old." She reached up, smoothing his lines away with her fingers. "I need to do this. Every time I've entered deep sleep, I've gotten clues about myself. With the Tapestry, or with..."

"The boy, or boy-man, I guess?"

"Yes." She'd told him everything—from the Tapestry to the boy, and that thing she'd seen in Ryan.

"So Anna, then. Should I call you that from now on?"

Jory shook her head. "No, I-I don't know what to believe...or what's real. I only remember being Jory. Honestly, even if I do get my memories back, if somehow I'm able to fix it all, I feel like this Anna person will be a stranger to me."

Sebastian tilted his head thoughtfully. "Okay."

He furrowed his brow again. "So, if you enter the...Tapestry?" She nodded and he continued, "When you enter that place, there's a good chance you could come across that thing again."

She took a deep breath. "I'll stay away from Ryan's threads."

Sebastian fidgeted and rubbed the back of his neck. "Can't you just wait till I get back? I don't like that you'll be here alone."

"I'll be fine. Remy's around." She took his hand. "So they really didn't tell you anything? About what they're doing or where they're going?

He shook his head. "Just that they'll tell me when and *if* they need me. Other than that, I'm as in the dark as you are."

Jory frowned. "That's a bit concerning."

He shrugged.

"Well thanks again for keeping an eye on Ryan for me. I know it must be hard for you," she said.

He looked away and sighed. "Why, because I'm a coward?"

Jory squeezed his hand.

"You're not a coward, Seb. After everything in your past, you're brave." She paused. She was asking so much of him. "You don't have to do this. There are going to be women there, and staying on top of Ryan won't be easy. You could get hurt. I don't know what's going on with him. What secrets he's keeping. You said that Drake told everyone that he'd made a deal with Ryan not to mention his past. Why? Why would he do that? What has he done to make everyone hate him so much?"

Sebastian's eyes darkened, and Jory felt his fear creep through her toes and into her bones.

"I don't know," he whispered. "But it wasn't merely hate—they were terrified of him, Jor. And the way he took them out? It was effortless for him, like breathing. Then he just laughed. He's unstable. If I don't go, I'm worried he could really hurt someone."

He looked at her and smiled, forcefully trying to lift the mood. "Don't worry, I'll look out for him and I'll see what I can find out from the others. They promised not to talk to you, not me."

"Well, well, Sebastian Davos. You gonna be my spy?"

"Looks like it."

Their false smiles faltered and melted away.

"Be careful, Seb. This Bram guy sounds dangerous, and Ryan—"

He gripped her hand tighter. "Let me be the one to worry about your brother for once. And as for this Bram fellow, I'll stay under the radar."

"Sebastian."

"I'll be fine, Jory. Let's do this. You ready?"

"I am." She paused, remembering something. "Wait, just a sec."

She reached over to the nightstand and grabbed the spool of thread. She'd already slipped the armband back on. She took some of the thread and twisted it around her finger.

"Wait a few minutes first. I'm going to try to um, like. ..visualize it. I'm hoping it helps."

Sebastian nodded as she closed her eyes. She breathed deeply, in through her nose and out through her mouth.

In and out. In and out. In...and out. Picture the Tapestry. The bright lines, the weaves and tangles. The raw emotions pulsing, just within reach but separate from her.

She felt a soft pinch on her shoulder and a kiss against her forehead.

"Hang in there, Jor," he whispered.

"Put the yarn away, dearest. It's time to go."

She was in her childhood home. Jory looked down at her hands, finding they were small and browned by the sun. She ignored her mother for a moment, weaving the circle of yarn through her fingers to form the various patterns of Cat's Cradle. She enjoyed the game because it helped her focus her mind. The patterns were constant and reliable. If she slipped her fingers through here, wove through there, she would successfully move her way through each pattern in an endless cycle that kept her mind from the buzz of emotions in the outside world.

When a pale hand grabbed hers, the diamond weave for Jacob's Ladder went limp. "Anna. I said put it away. I know you're nervous, but I'll be right there with you. I promise."

Her mother knelt in front of her, eyes kind, pinky outstretched. "Pinky swear." Her mother's pale hair wisped around her face.

Jory stared at the outstretched finger and nodded. Pinkies entwined, her mother leaned forward and kissed her forehead. Jory rubbed the spot, a strange sense of déjà vu holding her still for a moment.

"Good girl. Let's go."

The memory pulled Jory forward through the front door and outside.

"Anna, concentrate. Look at me."

Jory shook her head, confused. It was like she had been sucked from one place to the next. The two now sat on a red park bench. Children laughed and played, cried and screamed. Parents chattered, scolded, and sighed. It was early afternoon and the park was packed to the brim with people.

And with people came emotions.

She could handle it. She knew how to make the wall.

Jory breathed deep, concentrating on a wall of defense against those around her. She built it brick by brick until she sighed with relief. All done.

Was this what she had forgotten how to do? How to properly make the wall? That didn't feel quite right.

Her mother took Jory's hands in hers, her pale, translucent skin a stark contrast to Jory's own.

"Close your eyes. Picture the Tapestry. We've been there many times now, so I know you can do it."

Sweat beaded on Jory's forehead. What was her mother saying? They'd been there before? Together? She couldn't remember it. But she had gone there herself. She pictured what she knew. Her mother's thumbs rubbed against the tops of her hands.

"Good, you see it. Now comes the tricky part. Up till now you've shielded yourself from those around you. You've built strong walls to keep others' feelings away from you, but cracks always form, don't they?"

"Yes," she whispered.

"That's because that was always a temporary fix. Until you were old enough to understand and see the Tapestry. Until you understood the responsibilities that came with that access. I know it was a bit scary at first. I never realized you'd be able to manipulate so much there. You are a strong Empath, Anna. Much stronger than me. You must learn complete control."

Hearing her mother's voice waver, Jory opened her eyes to see worry and fear.

Was she afraid of her?

Jory shut her eyes tight. The fear in her mother scared her, because her mother was never afraid.

"Now, let go of the wall, Anna. Break it down. You must let it all in. Only then will you be able to take your place in the Tapestry. Only then will you be able to see how to separate yourself from the emotions of those around you."

Jory felt panic rise like bread in an oven, inflating her chest and making her hands sweat.

"Mom," she whispered. "I can't. It...it hurts. There are too many people." Tears squeezed out of the corners of her eyes. "I'm scared."

"I'm here. I've got you. Trust me. You must let go and bring the Tapestry here."

Jory opened her eyes. "Bring it here? But we go there. It's a different place. I can't bring it—"

"Sweetheart, I've already told you this many times. The Tapestry is here. Here, all around us. It's like layering lenses. Bring one in front of the other. Come now, close your eyes and let go."

The fear didn't go away but neither did her mother's hands—they held hers, giving her strength. Jory began to close her eyes, but before she could, she noticed a dark figure hovering in the background. The man stood, all in black. He lingered behind the swings, his figure stark and strange amongst the playing children. His eyes glowed a bright orange.

He shouldn't have been there. He didn't belong.

He smiled, his mouth wide and predatory.

"Anna, close your eyes," her mother urged.

"There's a man. He's looking at me." She gripped her mother's hands tighter.

Her mother turned and frowned. "I don't see a man."

The dark form held her eyes then surged forward with inhuman speed until his face was side by side with her mother's. He pressed his cheek against her mother's face, his grin widening. Her mother didn't blink, unaware of the being beside her.

Jory opened her mouth to scream but her throat seized.

"Anna, what's wrong? You must picture the Tapestry."

Orange eyes pierced through her own. The man shook his head slowly.

Jory felt all her muscles tense. Did he not want her to access the Tapestry? What would he do if she did? Was he even there? Her mother couldn't see him.

She had to reach the Tapestry. He wasn't real. He couldn't be real. She shut her eyes again and focused, slowing her breathing.

Let it all in.

The thought was beyond terrifying. Despite that, she had to try. She knew she had to try. She opened her mind and let the wall collapse. Immediately, emotions battered against her—tearing into her. Joy, anger, jealousy, love—they poured through her like a broken tap, flooding her senses in a ceaseless deluge.

"Access the Tapestry. Separate the threads."

Her mother's voice floated toward her. She focused and began to see the threads, hundreds of threads weaving and connecting the people around her. Her own threads mingled among them. She grasped them, twisting them around her fingers like a game of Cat's Cradle. Before she could pull them from the weave—before she could separate herself from the storm of feeling—pain seared through her chest, ripping a hole through her. She opened her eyes and gasped.

The Tapestry's lines lingered over her vision, flickering in and out as she fought for air. The man with the orange eyes had stabbed a homeless man curled up under a tree. The man's agony ripped through her. Blood spilled onto the grass.

That isn't right! That wasn't what happened!

The man sped to a young mother and kicked her knee in, crushing the bone. The woman screamed, dropping to the ground. Jory jerked her hands away from her mother and grasped her own knee, screaming in pain.

This wasn't real, but the fire of pain lancing through her body spoke otherwise.

"You're not real! You're not here! This isn't what happened!" Jory screamed at the man, and he smiled. He rushed to her once more, faster than her eyes could follow. He grasped her face in his hands, jerked her head upward, and leaned in, his breath cool against her ear.

"I am here," he whispered. Goosebumps erupted over her flesh. She couldn't push him away.

"No, no, no, no, no, no, no." Tears streamed down her face. She was losing herself. She'd already lost the Tapestry, and now her mind was open to a barrage of emotions and searing pain.

"Focus, Anna." Her mother's words filtered through the storm inside her like a ray of light breaking through the clouds.

Anna... She was Anna, and she was also Jory. She'd done this before and she could do it now. Focus. Focus. Focus!

She pulled the Tapestry back, thrust her hands into the threads, and separated herself from them. As simple as a child's game. Clarity ensued, followed by peace. Jory opened her eyes and found herself floating within the Tapestry. The memory had dissipated, the man with the orange eyes gone with it.

The threads pulsed in a symphony of light and color. She gazed down at her watercolor hands and smiled in triumph.

She had done it! At least she'd repeated what she'd done long ago. Jory hoped she'd be able to recreate her success once she regained consciousness.

Now that she had some control over her abilities, she stretched forth her hands. It was time to find the boy.

Jory had realized the last time she was here that she was drawn to the threads of those she was close to. She closed her eyes and concentrated. Ryan's and Sebastian's threads called to her almost immediately. Hoping to keep her presence unknown, she quickly drifted away from the direction of Ryan's threads.

How could she find the boy's threads? She didn't know his name. All her clear memories of him were recent. She breathed out, picturing his face and the feelings she had when she was with him. Curly hair, a dimpled smile, warm eyes. A familiar sensation tugged her. She followed it, weaving through the Tapestry, avoiding the touch of the threads around her so she didn't become distracted by them.

Until finally, she found him. It had to be him—she knew it in her heart.

His threads pulsed in pain, fear, and despair. Bright crimson and deepest ebony. What could she do?

Her heart sank.

She was afraid to touch the threads, because then she'd feel the pain too. Stronger than her fear was the fact that she couldn't leave him like that. Sucking in a deep breath, she thrust her hands into the threads. She gasped as her mind linked directly to his. He was awake, which was unfortunate. If he had been asleep, maybe she could have talked to him.

Tiny pinpricks of pain in her head and all over her body made her wince, and her muscles jerked and shuddered. A throbbing headache made her stomach roil. The nausea caused her lips to dry and brought bile up her throat. Despair and heartache weighed heavy in her chest. Strange. Someh ow...somewhere underneath it all was an unwavering white thread of hope. Hope and determination braided together in a tight weave that kept her somewhat sane.

But this wasn't her. It was him. His pain, his threads. His hope. She took another deep breath, trying to separate herself from him. Just enough to regain her own sanity. She was so close to him, so deeply connected she could feel the beat of his heart in her chest as if it was her own.

His mind felt so familiar, which was both comforting and eerie.

"Anna... Anna..." he whispered under his breath.

She could hear him! Hear his spoken words. How was that possible? Could she do that with others, or just him?

"I'm here," she said. "Where are you? I need to find you."

Jory felt his head snap up. She hadn't realized it had been hanging before. Was he hanging from something? Strapped to a wall, maybe? She couldn't tell.

"Anna!" he gasped. Tears gathered and wet his eyelashes. She could feel the shuddering relief within him.

Anna! *His thoughts bloomed within her mind.* Anna, I cannot speak aloud. There are cameras, and they record every move and noise I make. *He paused, his mind searching hers.* You still do not remember me fully. *Disappointment filled his heart, but he pushed it away, his thread of determination strengthening.* You must remember me, remember everyt hing... I... *His voice trailed off. He was hiding things from her.*

Once you remember, come find me within the Tapestry once more. I'll be waiting for you.

His mind pulled away from hers, the threads slipping from her fingers.

"No! No wait, please! Why! Why do I have to remember! Why can't you just tell me?"

You always were so impatient.

He pushed her away.

"No!" She reached forward once more but the Tapestry was fading. She was falling.

Falling into a black abyss.

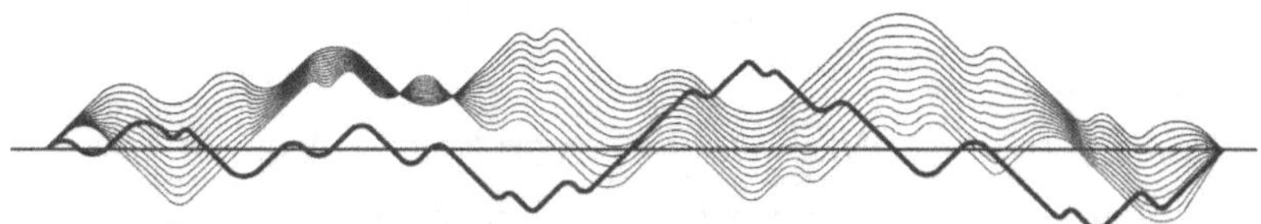

Chapter 19: Ryan

Ryan had never felt the need to murder someone.

Until now.

Drake was so beyond dead. Ryan would start with his face of course. For some reason, though, no matter how he pictured mutilating him, Drake still managed to look good in his imagination. Even his own dark thoughts couldn't break through the perfect absurdity that was Drake's face.

Ryan, Lane, Sebastian, Krueger, and Treasa sat huddled in a small pocket of sewer pipe surrounded by a dense wall of excrement-filled water. Ryan couldn't help but be awed by Lane. The sewage pipes arched and curved around them. Using her strange abilities, Lane had pushed the putrid water away. The water flowed around their bodies like an invisible sphere. Their small bubble-pocket thing moved with them as they slowly inched forward toward the grate.

"Whatcha thinkin about, Slicey?" Krueger asked from behind. His breath smelled of old beef and cabbage.

"None of your business." Ryan hitched his shoulder up, hitting the bearded man in the chin. "Get your scruff off my back."

Krueger grunted in pain. "Quit it, newbie. You know I can't move any more than you can. Oi! Sleeper, give a man some space, would ya?"

Ryan scowled. "Why are you even here, Sebastian?"

"Reasons," Sebastian grumbled from behind Krueger.

A wet, squirty sound ensued as Sebastian squeezed out yet another glob of sanitizer. He had been periodically rubbing it over any exposed areas the entire time. Sebastian continued to mumble angrily under his breath. Krueger cursed as he pushed further into Ryan's back. Ryan bumped against Lane, who glared darkly at him with her good eye until he inched back.

"I'm concentrating, you earwig," she hissed. "Keep your distance unless you want about twenty pounds of sewer water smashing on top of your idiot head!"

"And I told you to move away, not snuggle up closer," Krueger grumbled to Sebastian.

"Something touched my elbow. Are there mutant fish in this sewer?" Sebastian whispered. He spurted out another glob of sanitizer. When he tried to squeeze out some more, the bottle made a pathetic breathy sound.

"I'm doomed," Sebastian said quietly.

"Why are you whispering?" Krueger asked, too loudly.

Sebastian winced. "Well, we're on a mission. Don't you whisper on missions?"

Ryan couldn't help but roll his eyes. What a loser.

"You're all pathetic." It was the first thing Treasa had said since they'd branched off into teams.

He couldn't help but agree with her.

"Might not want to tick off the lady. She could literally fill your mouth with a load of crap." Krueger's breath still reeked, but it was sweet compared to the raunchy pit they now found themselves in.

Ryan held his shirt over his mouth, but it didn't help. He gagged for the hundredth time and once again pictured stabbing Drake in the face.

"The smell's right juicy, isn't it?" Krueger asked innocently.

The words made Ryan gag again. He could hear Sebastian making similar noises behind him, which didn't help.

"Shut up." Both he and Lane managed to speak simultaneously. They glared at each other.

What are you looking at, hag-face? he wanted to say, but Krueger had a point. She *was* keeping the poop wall at bay.

Krueger's voice butted in again. He really should listen to his own advice. "Couldn't you push the liquid poo a little farther away from us?"

Sebastian moaned softly at Krueger's words.

"Yes, please, please, please," Sebastian mumbled under his breath.

Ryan had wondered the same thing.

Sweat trickled down the side of Lane's face. "Do you understand how hard it is to push it away as far as I am? It's heavy! Besides, Kellry was *supposed* to be here too."

"How would she have helped?" Ryan asked, curious. Could she burn it away? Evaporate the liquid somehow?

Lane winced, and the sewage sloshed threateningly around them. "None of your business! Just shut up already!"

Ryan clamped his mouth closed. The reason they were making such an effort wasn't just because they didn't want to trudge through the filthy water. It was because the water itself was a dump site for hazardous chemicals as well as refuse. He wondered if it might have been wise to invest in some proper masks. He imagined the five of them emerging from the sewage with extra arms and toes sprouting from their bodies.

Kellry.

It bothered Ryan that Drake had changed the teams last minute.

He gritted his teeth, thinking back on that moment.

"Kellry, you're with me," Drake said. Ryan didn't miss the shifty glance Drake threw his way.

What a prick. Scared I'll steal your girl? *Ryan lifted an eyebrow at the man, and his glance darted away.* That's right, I'm not stupid. *Ryan wondered if Kellry knew what an emotionally compromised lamewad Drake really was.*

Kellry frowned. "Wait, what? Drake, I can't go with you. I'm on Lane's team." Kellry gave Drake a meaningful look, but he ignored it.

That's right, she doesn't wanna go with you. *Ryan knew his thoughts were petty. But Drake was an idiot if he thought Ryan didn't see through him.*

"Aw, but boss, now we're short a lady," Krueger said.

"Treasa's going with you."

Treasa instantly stepped forward, green eyes sharp. "I'm supposed to go with Kala. I—" She gritted her teeth. "I think it unwise if I change teams now."

Back then, he'd wondered what had gotten Treasa so riled up. He stared at her now as she glared at the murky water around them.

"Almost there," Lane muttered, face taut with concentration. Ryan wondered how her ability worked. When Lane had been healing him, she'd hummed. Strange, deep melodies that had vibrated through him. Where had she learned the melodies? Did the sequence of sound even matter? Why wasn't she humming now?

After several more steps, and after Ryan dubbed his shoes completely ruined and unwearable, they made it to the grate.

Water flowed from the huge pipe through the grate, where it spewed forth like a waterfall into the tunnel below. It was a short waterfall, dropping down about five feet or so. The tunnel was ten feet wide with a tall, curved brick ceiling. Slim, ledged walkways hugged the walls and guided the river-like flow of sewage. Before the water made it through an even larger grate, a narrow tunnel branched off to the left.

"Okay, Krueger, do it quickly. Once I block the water off, it will build up fast. I won't be able to hold the pressure for long. You'll have about a minute." Lane's breath came out in short bursts, and the back of her shirt was drenched in sweat.

"Say please," he said with an evil grin.

Lane gritted her teeth and let out a low, growly sound.

Krueger threw up his hands in defense. "Kidding, kidding. Down, kitty. Daddy will get to work, okay, punkin?"

Lane ignored him as they all slowly began to file around her until she ended up in the back. She turned around and thrust her hands out.

Ryan wondered if the use of her hands was necessary or reflexive. Oftentimes Psychics used their hands to complete actions, like Sleepers with pinching, or how Ryan swept or clenched his hands when fulfilling different aspects of his ability.

As Lane thrust her hands out, the water responded, whooshing backward. The gush escaping the pipe turned quickly to a stream and then a trickle.

Krueger leapt toward the grate, quickly pulling a battery-powered saw out of his pack. He angled it against the bars and flipped the switch.

Nothing.

"Ummmm... Is it just me, or shouldn't it be buzzing...or cutting?" Sebastian's voice trailed off at Kruegers glare.

"Shut your butt, pencil-boy. I'm on it." Krueger mumbled a colorful string of curses as he shoved his hand into the pack. Ryan was impressed with his creative uses of curse words and tucked a few phrases into his arsenal to use for later.

"Is there a reason you aren't sawing, you useless pack-horse?" Lane screeched through clenched teeth. She gasped and the murky mass lunged toward them, gurgling and sloshing. Sebastian crouched down, shying away from the wall of water while Lane managed to barely get it under control.

"I'm gonna die, I'm gonna die. I'm gonna drown in a sea of germs. Oh Lord, save me from this death made by Lucifer himself!" Sebastian rubbed the bottle of Purell between his hands like a string of prayer beads.

Ryan felt sweat break out on his own forehead. As irritating as Sebastian was, he wholeheartedly agreed that death by sewer water was not the way he wanted to go. And he had plenty of much cooler ways tucked away in his mind. But that was the point—in his mind, he had always *chosen* the way he died. To have his life taken in such a pathetic way would just be stupid.

Krueger gave a short whoop and pulled out some spare batteries. "Gotcha!"

"Are you kidding me?" Ryan couldn't help his jaw from dropping. "You didn't change the batteries? If we die because of this, I'm gonna—"

A loud whirring drowned out his voice as the saw came alive.

"Yeah baby!" Krueger yelled as he sawed through each bar as if slicing through soft cheese.

"I'm at my limit!" Lane's knees slowly began to buckle. The invisible force was crushing her. Her elbows bent back—hands strained and shaking.

"KRUEGER!" She screamed as the water began to steadily push toward them. They backed up slowly with tiny, inching steps.

Ryan glanced at Treasa. She had been quiet the entire time. Her face was white as a sheet, her eyes huge as the water came near. Frozen.

"GOT IT!" Krueger kicked the last bar out of the way and jumped down. "GO, GO, GO!"

They didn't hesitate, although Ryan did give Treasa a bit of a nudge as he leapt past her. She blinked at the touch and followed him down. Everyone except Krueger climbed up on the left ledge.

He stood at the bottom as Lane scooted backward, her heels hanging over the edge.

"Jump, Twoface. I got you!"

"I...hate...you...so...much," she managed to say between panting breaths. She let herself fall backward and Krueger caught her, slinging her over his back and scrambling onto the ledge just as a great gushing wall of refuse plunged down.

They all pressed themselves tightly against the brick as Lane lifted one shaking hand. The wall of water curved away from them, coursing down its path and down to the main grate. After a minute or so, it slowed, changing from a torrent to a stream before lowering to its normal depth. Lane dropped her hand and crumpled against Krueger's side.

He looked down at her and sighed, lifting her into his arms.

"Put me down, you idiot. You almost killed us all! You couldn't have checked if the batteries were good before we left?"

Krueger's eyes flared, and he tightened his grip on her. "At least I brought extra!"

"You're useless!"

"And you've got several screws loose, Twoface, but do you see me complaining?" He jerked his head to the side and they all began to walk down toward the branching tunnel.

"She shut up fast," Ryan said.

"She passed out," Krueger responded.

For a minute, Ryan thought he was irritated, but when he looked closer he could see worry and perhaps a bit of guilt clearly written on Krueger's features.

"I thought I was going to die," Sebastian said.

"Speaking of dead, did you guys hear about the morgue?" Krueger asked.

Was he setting up some kind of joke? Any possible guilt that Ryan had seen on the man's face had disappeared.

Krueger walked confidently forward, leading the group toward the tunnel.

Ryan wasn't so sure of his footing. He couldn't take his eyes off the water rushing mere inches from him. The ledge was maybe two feet wide. And that was being generous. One false step and he'd slip into the water. A rat weaved around their feet, jumping into the murk, and Sebastian yelped, grabbing Ryan's shoulder. Ryan smacked his hand away, causing Sebastian to yelp again.

It was getting a little easier to control his emotions. And he'd been able to keep himself from giving into temptation by numbing his nerves.

Sebastian was trying his patience—testing the modicum of control he was so desperately trying to hold onto.

No one had answered Krueger, but he kept on talking as if they had. His voice was calm and conversational like they were sitting around a family dinner and not walking along a sewer ledge.

"Ya, so I heard yesterday that bodies have been disappearing from the place. Loads of them, all in one go."

Ryan froze. Sebastian smacked into his back but he ignored it.

"Krueger, wait. What did you say?"

The man grinned. "Interested now, ain't cha, Slice-man? I'm not making it up. It was on the news and everything."

"How many?" Ryan asked, trying not to panic.

Krueger shifted Lane, shrugging her over his shoulder like a sack of flour. "Um...I don't know. Ten...or was it twenty?"

That's a huge difference, idiot!

Ryan pressed his earpiece. "Drake! Drake, come in!"

Drake responded, voice hushed and strained. "What is it, kid? You're not supposed to be contacting us yet. This isn't the best time."

"It's Hans. He's here. He's got bodies."

"What! How do you know? Can you see them?"

"No, but Krueger said the morgue was emptied about a day ago. He said ten, maybe twenty bodies."

Drake cursed. "How did Bram know we were coming?"

The comm went silent for a moment until Drake's voice cut through. "The mission's a bust—get out of there. Now."

Ryan sighed. "Lane's passed out, Drake. We can't go back."

"What's going on?" Sebastian whispered behind him.

Ryan glanced up at Krueger, who had gone pale as a sheet.

"The...the Puppeteer... He emptied the morgue? How can you be so sure?" Krueger shifted his eyes over to the tunnel entrance. It was pitch black.

Ryan threw up his hands. "It's obvious! It can't be a co-incidence that a morgue loses all its dead people the day before we're planning on jumping Bram. We need to get out of here. Now."

Ryan pressed his finger to the comm. "Drake, can you get Riri to jump us out?"

"We'd be stranded, Ryan. I told you Riri only has three good jumps in her. She's used up one and is waiting for us to all meet up. If she jumps in to get your team, she'll have to do another jump to get mine and then there's the jump home. That's one too many jumps. She can't do it."

"I'm coming to you, Drake!" Riri shouted into the comm, making them all wince. "It'll take me some time to get to the vents on foot, but if Ryan's group stays put until I get to you, then I'll only have to do two jumps."

"When did this become Ryan's group?" Krueger mumbled.

"Can someone please tell me what's going on?" Sebastian shouted, breaking his whisper streak.

"You don't want to know," Ryan said, dismissing him. "Riri, that seems like our best bet. What do you think, Drake?"

"Ummm..." Drake paused.

Kellry cut in. "Riri, you need to get over here fast."

"Already on my way—there's no way I'm gonna let you be zombie-chow."

"Wait. What did she say?" Sebastian grabbed Ryan's shoulder again. "What did she mean by that?"

"Shut up, Sebastian." Ryan shrugged his hand off with a jerk.

"Get here as fast as you can, Riri. I need to get in touch with Kala. She's on the long receiver, so I'll get back to you in a bit," Kellry said.

What the heck is Drake doing? Painting his nails?

"I think I'm gonna faint. Can we get off this ledge, please?" Sebastian shifted forward, making Ryan stumble.

"Sebastian, find some balls, or I will. I swear I'll kick them clean off."

"If I don't have any, how would you kick them?" Sebastian grumbled.

"I didn't—I told you to find—whatever! Krueger, let's rest in the tunnel until Riri gets here."

"Who put you in charge? Maybe I don't wanna wait in the tunnel. Maybe I—"

"Krueger, I swear, get in the tunnel or I'm shoving you and Lane into the churning river of sh—"

"FINE! Fine, *leader,* let's all go in the tunnel!"

Ryan rubbed a hand over his face and took a couple long breaths. *Why do people have to be so stupid? Why am I the only one thinking clearly?*

They filed into the narrow tunnel and sat. Krueger dropped Lane on the ground and winced when her head smacked the concrete floor.

"You trying to kill her?" Ryan asked.

Krueger shot him a glare before glancing down into the darkness. A soft green light emitted from the high intensity glow sticks hanging from their necks. The light didn't reach far, making it impossible to tell how long the tunnel was. At a glance, it could be twenty feet or a mile.

From the blueprints, it had looked to be about five hundred feet give or take.

Ryan rested his head against the wall, telling himself that a good shower would eliminate anything that rubbed off and into his hair. He missed his jacket and wished he had his phone and headphones. The music would have helped. He tried to play the notes of Chopin's *Mazurka in A Minor* in his mind. Pictured pressing his fingers against the vibrating strings—the arc of the bow as he coaxed the clean, lilting notes. His thoughts pushed through, causing dissonance, the notes screeching instead of soothing. Abandoning the mental practice, he focused instead on a long, steadying breath.

How had this happened? How had Bram found out they were coming? The plan had been simple. Kala, Eunuch, Treasa, and Momma J were going to retrieve Amare back at

Bram's base where security would be thin. Padraigin, Mike, maybe one or two others would be there. Piece of cake.

Then Drake switched Treasa and Kellry around.

Now Drake, Kellry, Roman, and Ref waited, huddled in the large venting system above the warehouse where Bram was meeting.

Ryan's team had come through the vast sewer system underneath the building. The tunnel led to a narrow set of stairs that entered the warehouse's basement. The small warehouse was used only periodically to maintain this section of the sewer. People were supposed to come in and check the water here, but who were they kidding? This was South Bres, and no one cared less whether the water was turning into a dump site for harsh chemicals and who knew what else. It was supposed to be impossible to get into this section of the sewer except through the warehouse. But they had Lane.

The rest of Bram's crew would be at the meeting. This was supposed to include Ryan. Bram would have noticed Ryan's absence but shouldn't suspect treachery. As far as Bram knew, Jory was still at Ryan's apartment, leaving Ryan very much under his thumb. However, wasn't there a possibility he'd seen Drake take her?

Drake had suggested Ryan go to the meeting like planned, but Ryan had refused. If Bram had any suspicion Ryan was a traitor, Mateo would be on him in a second.

Ryan shuddered. Mateo was the deadliest person he knew. Being a Fortress made him immune to Ryan's abilities, and he was skilled in ninjutsu or jujitsu...or something.

Treasa crouched away from them, head in her hands.

"I'm not supposed to be here," she mumbled.

"Could someone please tell me why we stopped the mission? You were joking about the zombies, right?" Sebastian was whispering again. Which honestly might not be a bad idea now. His voice mingled with the soft dripping from the walls and small scattering of tiny rodent feet. Sebastian stood, knees bent to keep his head from scraping the ceiling.

A faint scuffling, scraping sound echoed down the tunnel. The small hairs on Ryan's neck rose in response.

"Do you guys hear that?" Ryan asked quietly. Everyone froze. The sounds continued.

"Maybe it's just some really big rats?" Sebastian asked.

No, it was them. The Mindless. They were here.

Ryan looked over at Krueger.

"What do we do, leader?" Krueger asked, almost inaudibly.

"So *now* I'm the leader? How'd they even know we were down here?" Ryan hissed back.

"I wasn't supposed to be here!" Treasa shouted. Her hands were tangled in her hair and she was breathing heavily.

"Quiet, you idiot. They can hear." Ryan grabbed her wrist and shook her, but it was too late. The shuffling had stopped and everyone stayed rigidly in place. Sebastian held both hands over his mouth, shaking his head slightly. Krueger glanced toward Lane's still form and gritted his teeth.

A thunderous moaning echoed toward them, followed by the sound of many feet sprinting down the tunnel.

"RUN!" Ryan yelled, grabbing Treasa's wrist and yanking her forward. Krueger snatched Lane and tossed her into Sebastian's arms.

"Take her!"

"What? But she's—"

Ryan barreled toward Sebastian and shoved him back onto the ledge they'd just come from.

"Go. They're here."

"There's nowhere to go!" Sebastian yelled back.

"Just do it!" Ryan screamed at him. Sweat had erupted from his pores, and his hands were slick against the wall as he ran down the narrow ledge. They had to get back. Ryan had seen what the Mindless could do, and he had sworn he would never be on the receiving end of their master's ire. Yet here he was. An echo of Krueger's earlier string of curses ran through his mind, crowding out any coherent thoughts.

Sebastian hobbled back the way they had come, clutching Lane's body against his chest. She looked ridiculously small in his spider arms.

Ryan heard a loud whirring and glanced back. Krueger had taken out the saw as he shuffled backward on the ledge. His foot slid slightly, and Ryan reached out to snatch his collar and yank him back before he fell into the rushing water.

"Thanks, kid!"

Ryan nodded and pressed a finger to the comm. "Drake, they're here. They're down here in the tunnels."

"How'd they know about the sewers?" Drake shouted back.

"How the heck should I know?" Ryan spat back.

Drake cursed. "Riri's not here yet."

"I'm coming!" Her voice came out strained. "I'm trying to find my way through the vents."

"Well find it quick, because the Mindless are—" Ryan coughed as his throat seized. Shadows morphed and took shape as creatures emerged from the darkness.

They rounded the corner in a rush, arms whipping around their bodies. In their haste, one of the Mindless was shoved into the dark water. It thrashed uselessly as it got carried to the grate.

Well that's one down. Maybe if we can get them into the water—

It slammed into the bars. Arms shot up at the impact, latching onto the grate. It climbed up the metal, its arms and legs wrapping and crawling across the bars like some strange insect.

Well there goes that idea...although it could still buy us some time.

"Ryan, what's happening?" Kellry asked over the comm.

The other Mindless, distracted by their fallen brother, turned their heads back toward him in unison. Dead eyes flicked and rolled under pale lids. Ryan was panicking hard, heart racing. He needed to calm down to think. But it was so hard when he was so scared.

"They're not dead, they're not dead. They are just... just... Sweet heaven, they *are* dead! Ryan, do they eat people? Do they eat brains? Are they going to suck the marrow out of me? I want my marrow!" Sebastian was hysterical, which did not help Ryan's state of mind.

Ignore him. What could they do?

"If we get them into the water, it might give us some time. Go for the legs," Ryan said to Krueger.

"Can't you Slice their nerves? Maybe even their connection to Hans?"

Ryan winced. *I can't.*

The first one reached them. With a great battle cry, Krueger whipped the saw in a wide arc. He cut away an arm and got the tool halfway into its torso before the saw lodged in place with a buzzing, stuttering gurgle. Arms groped around the sides of the mutilated Mindless. Luckily, because of the narrowness of the ledge, only one could charge them at a time.

They pushed forward with brute force. Krueger's knees buckled, and he yelled out.

"I said go for the legs!" Ryan shouted.

Krueger roared and kicked his leg forward, connecting solidly with the dead guy's chest. He managed to dislodge the saw a little, but not all the way.

"Ryan, do something!" Krueger yelled. "These meatbags are gonna kill us!"

Ryan's breathing was too fast. He was getting light-headed. "I can't! Their nerves aren't normal. They're dull and hard to grasp onto. I've never been able to do it!"

"Well this is a great time to try, don't you think? Come on, Slicey, you can do it!"

How could the idiot sound so cheery?

Krueger yanked at the saw while trying to get it started up at the same time.

"Some meat must've lodged in one of the gears," Krueger hollered back.

Sebastian began to vomit. The hurling noise made sweat break out on Ryan's forehead and turned his stomach. Any thoughts Ryan tried to form were drowned out by the incessant groaning.

The Mindless with the saw in his gut thrust out his remaining arm, snagging Krueger's neck in a crushing grip.

A gurgled "Ryan..." escaped Krueger's lips before a sickening crunch sounded. The Mindless released Krueger, who let go of the saw and tumbled back into Ryan, blood spurting from his lips. The blood spattered onto his face, hot and wet.

There was no time to think. No time to wonder if Krueger was dead or dying. No time to cry, no time to breathe. The Mindless was lunging forward, clawlike fingers reaching for his throat. Numbing came as easily as air. Instinctively, he muted everything within himself—every emotion. It was reflexive and immediate. Time seemed to slow.

Just as he remembered, the nerves in the Mindless were muted and dull. Ryan reached for them to cut through, but it was like waving a knife around underwater. He narrowed his eyes, straining. He had to find something. There had to be something.

A muted, glowing nerve, barely brighter than the rest, pulsed at the back of the Mindless' head right at the nape of the neck. Could that be it? The connection?

As he reached out to Slice it, a dark shadow appeared in his mind. Long, black, sticky tendrils latched onto his brain. It crawled over his mind and sunk in its feelers like a living thing.

Amadeus.

Ryan shut off his ability, reactivating all his emotions in one painful lurch.

The gutted Mindless who had just crushed Krueger's windpipe snagged Ryan's wrist, tugging him to the side toward the water. Somehow Ryan knew he wouldn't be able to crawl out like the Mindless. Hardly able to concentrate on what was happening, he wrapped his other arm around Krueger's body, hanging onto it as they were both shoved over the edge. He had to save him.

What do I do? What can I do?

Sebastian grabbed Ryan's arm with one hand, the same arm that clutched Krueger's spasming body. Simultaneously, he threw out his other hand, pepper spray bursting out of a pocket-sized can and into the Mindless' eyes. It let go of Ryan, flailing back into the others.

"Take that, you rotting piece of garbage!" Sebastian yelled, tugging both Ryan and Krueger back up onto the ledge.

He's stronger than he looks.

Ryan glanced back to see a wide-eyed Treasa struggling to hold onto Lane.

The spray caused the thing to stagger back, but only for a moment. It let out a gurgling screech and lunged forward again.

Ryan activated his ability and Sliced the faint, pulsing nerve. The Mindless immediately went limp, toppling into the rushing water. That only took care of the one. The Mindless that had been swarming behind the first surged forward. Ryan panicked when he realized he'd have to find the pulsing nerve again. What if it was in a different place?

And even if it wasn't, it was so difficult to spot sitting clustered within several other nerves.

Not to mention he wasn't anywhere close to getting his crap together enough to concentrate.

"Treasa! Treasa, you need to connect to Riri. She needs to See so she can make the jump!" Kellry's voice pleaded through the comm, but Ryan doubted the girl would get it together enough to do anything. As Kellry continued talk to Treasa, Ryan stopped listening. It was too late.

The Mindless lunged, and Ryan found himself giving up. Why was he fighting so hard anyway? How many times had he wished for death so he wouldn't have to go through the trouble of orchestrating it himself? Now, death quite literally bared its slimy white teeth at him.

Krueger's lifeblood was spewing all over him. *I want to live. I have to save him.* Just before the bloodless fingers closed over his face, Ryan shut his eyes and a warped *tzzzzzzit!* sound filled his ears.

Riri.

Hands tangled into his hair and with another *tzzzzzzzit!*, they were out.

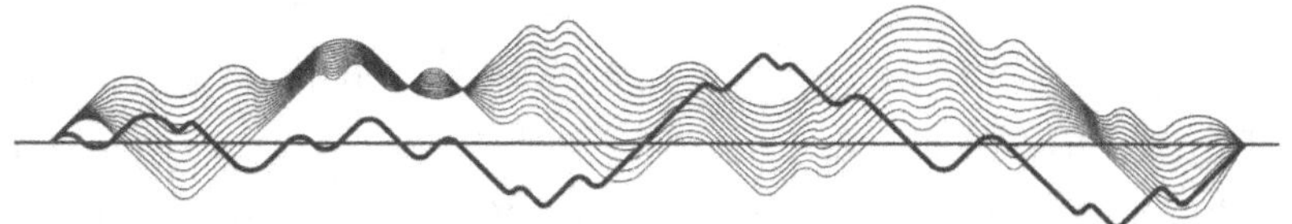

Chapter 20: Jory

If she stayed in this room forever, with no phone, no clock, no windows, would time stand still? With no possible way of knowing, how would she count the days, weeks, mont hs...years?

Jory had lived that way for so long. Up on the highest floor, tucked away in a forgotten corner of a deteriorating building. She'd kept her curtains drawn, only distinguishing morning from night by the soft glow sifting through the blinds and splashing onto the ceiling floor through gaps in the drapes. With the comings and goings of Ryan and Sebastian, the time had passed in a strange, monotonous blur, days melting into each other. She had drifted through them, pulled by the current of time. She had aged on the outside, but had anything changed on the inside? Was she still stuck in time, forever grieving over her parents' deaths while cowering deep within her shattered mind?

She pictured herself there—a little orphaned girl tied up in a tangled mess of thick thread, huddled in a dark room, eyes to the floor.

She'd stayed that way. Stagnant, never challenging her past, never pushing toward the future. Forever young and helpless...and selfish.

Not anymore.

Jory glared at the pillow on the floor. It was limp and battered, and the feathers had exploded from it in her fit of rage when she had woken up. She had screamed and cursed and cried until finally flopping back onto the bed, arms splayed in defeat—one leg hanging listlessly over the edge. A few feathers still wafted down, swaying and swirling slowly until it came to rest on the floor. One landed on her nose. She stared cross-eyed at it before blowing it off and sighing.

"Why can't I remember you?" she whispered. A few more tears escaped, trailing down the sides of her face and into her ears. She rubbed them with the palms of her hands.

Everything about him was so familiar. His voice, his smile, even his heartbeat. She had never felt the need or longing to be with anyone. Her and Seb's relationship was one hundred percent platonic.

But him? Ever since that first dream, a huge, gaping hole had opened in her chest, like an old wound had been ripped apart, and now she thought about him constantly. She rolled to the side and slipped her finger under the blue armband. It had been easy to make a small slit and fold up the photo to stuff it inside. Pulling it out now, she opened it and traced his features.

Bronze curls, brown eyes, dimpled cheek, medium height and medium build.

Knock. Knock. Knock.

Jory folded and stuffed the photo back into the band as Remy opened the door an inch.

"They're back! Ryan and Krueger—" She bit her lip. "There's a lot of blood, and Lane isn't waking up. I know you can't handle it, but you're an Empath, so you might be able to wake her up." Worry and fear swirled around Remy, but hope glowed through her eyes as she stared into Jory's.

Krueger? Lane? Who were they?

Jory nodded and they rushed through the halls and down some stairs into a huge room. Emotions assaulted her like a fleet of arrows to the chest. She stumbled and fell, her hands slapping onto the ground. Her eyes opened wide and bulged as her hand shot to her throat. Reflexively, she tried to throw up a wall, Sebastian's chant beginning in her mind. The wall failed.

Anger, panic, guilt, fear, worry, and so much more battered against her, keeping her glued to the floor. Then the pain came. Stabbing, throbbing pain, so bad she couldn't breathe!

Not me. Not me. Not me. The Tapestry, get a hold of the Tapestry. Someone is dying!

Shoving her hand into her pocket, she yanked out the spool. She pulled the green thread off, sending the spool rolling and spinning across the floor. She tied the ends and wrapped the string around her wrists, then pulled it through with her middle fingers, creating the first pattern in Cat's Cradle. Closing her eyes, she saw it. In the darkness behind her lids, the Tapestry floated, waiting for her. She took a deep breath and stopped fighting, letting the emotions and the pain envelop her. She gritted her teeth and threaded her fingers into the next pattern. As the motions calmed her, she opened her eyes, willing the Tapestry to stay.

It flickered over her vision, but she continued through the steps of the child's game and it held in place. Dropping the string, she thrust her hands into the glowing threads around her. It was so strange how something no one else could see was so tangible to her. They all pulsed furiously, each emotion filled with passion. With precise movements, she detangled herself from them, removing her threads from the great weave.

There was no time for relief. Standing, she reached out, finding the collapsed woman's thread, green with the peace of sleep. *Lane.* She pinched it and willed her awake. Lane shot up, hand clutching her chest. Jory blinked rapidly at the sight of her mutilated features.

"What! Where?" Lane glanced around and spotted Ryan.

Ryan hollered at a bearded man, clutching his body as tears streamed down his own face. Blood was everywhere. Mainly leaking out of the sides of the man's lips.

Remy's words lingered in her mind. *Ryan and Krueger. That must be Krueger. When was the last time I saw Ryan cry?* Jory didn't know. She couldn't pull up one memory of her brother in tears. Not even after their parents died.

Lane staggered over to the two and placed her hands over Krueger's body. He was still and pale. His thread looked dull, close to fading from the Tapestry.

Jory held onto Lane's thread, willing the calm to continue. The woman responded, calming visibly and beginning a strange, low chant. Jory grabbed onto the man's thread as well and, taking in another deep breath, she delved into his consciousness. The pain dulled now as Krueger's thoughts and regrets faded away.

Jory watched as a vein pulsed in Lane's head.

She's losing him. With Lane's threads in one hand and Krueger's in the other, she felt deeply connected to them. Her breath caught as Krueger's heart sputtered and stopped.

No you don't! Come back! Live! Jory felt a tug on her own life force. She watched in awe as bright-white tendrils swirled down her arm and fingertips and around the fading thread.

Ba-Bump. His heart stuttered back to life, and she sighed in relief.

She tried to sever the connection, to stop the flow, but nothing happened. She was being drained—her thread fading, her heart slowing.

She was dying.

Stop! Stop! Wait! Jory watched her own thread grow fainter and fainter as Krueger's grew brighter and brighter. As if sensing the danger, Ryan's head swung up, and he met her eyes for the first time. His eyes widened in alarm at the sight of her.

She reached out her hand, releasing Lane's threads. "Ryan..."

His eyes flared to life, glowing a bright green as he looked directly at the threads.

Can he see them?

After a moment, he whipped out an arm and made a swift cutting motion. Her connection to Krueger dissolved. She gasped as her thread brightened and her heart beat a little stronger.

Jory clutched her chest. *I almost died... If Ryan hadn't stepped in, my life force would have been completely drained away.* Hands shaking, she worked to slow her breathing and stay grounded enough to follow the conversation that seemed to float over her head—muted and fuzzy.

"I-I don't understand..." Lane had stopped humming, staring down at Krueger's rosy cheeks—at the deep rise and fall of his chest.

"He healed so quickly. He was so close to death. How?"

Jory's eyes widened at the man who rested a hand on Lane's shoulder. He looked like a combination of every perfectly sculpted Greek statue.

"Rest now, Lane. You've done enough. Maybe your ability has grown?" he asked.

Lane shook her head, her good eye fixed in disbelief. "Drake, it wasn't me. It felt like something or some*one* was—"

She looked up, glancing around the room until her eyes stopped on Jory. They shared a quiet understanding. Lane nodded her head in Jory's direction then proceeded to sag against the wall, completely spent.

Jory looked back to Ryan and the bearded man. A tiny redheaded teen, sharing a strong resemblance to Lane, hovered behind Ryan. Black roots contrasted with her bright-red locks.

Wait, I've seen her before. Didn't she move in across the hall at our apartments? She said her name was...Kellry?

"Where's Amare? Are they back yet? Did they get him out?" Riri asked.

Riri lay in a limp heap on the floor. Her face was practically green with nausea. This always happened when she reached the limit of her Teleportation abilities. Jory reached for Riri's thread, swallowing the bile in her own throat at the touch, and Soothed her. Almost immediately, Riri's face returned to its normal healthy hue.

It was so easy. Everything had happened so fast, but now that there was a semblance of peace, Jory took a moment for herself. She looked at all the people around her, at the mesmerizing weave of threads. They tangled and pulsed and reached toward each other in a mad dance that only Jory could see. A riot of emotions.

And she only felt her own.

It was so easy.

Anger bloomed in her chest.

Her past had held the answer, and she knew there were more answers still hidden there. Whoever had locked those memories away and taken this peace from her was going to pay.

Jory's fingertips tingled as her eyes were drawn to a thread changing very quickly from relief to white-hot anger.

Ryan.

He stood, resting Krueger's head on the ground with care.

"Are you going to answer her, or should I?" Ryan's voice was eerily calm. A darkness hovered there—she could see it building in his eyes. His question was directed toward the man Lane had called Drake.

Drake gritted his teeth and looked away, shoving his hands into his pockets.

Ryan's eyes burned and he turned to Riri. "No, Ri. They're not back. We haven't been able to contact them since the sewers. For all we know, they're all dead."

"Ryan. Why would you say that?" Kellry frowned and then sighed as Riri started to cry. "Great, see?"

"Yes, I do see. I seem to be the *only* one that does." Ryan turned his glare back toward Drake, pointing an accusatory finger at him. "If you hadn't followed your own stupid agenda, we would never have been in this mess in the first place."

Drake's eyebrows rose, then his eyes grew angry. "Watch yourself, Ryan."

Ryan laughed and walked right up to Drake. "Or what? What are you going to do? You know *exactly* what I'm talking about. Get it through your pretty-boy head. *You* caused this. *You* changed the teams because of *your petty jealousy.*" Ryan shoved his finger into Drake's chest, punctuating the last three words.

With A scowl twisting his face, Drake's eyes shifted to Kellry and back to Ryan. He opened his mouth to speak, but Ryan wasn't done.

"If Kellry had stayed with us like she was supposed to, she could have burned all the Mindless to a crisp in seconds. Krueger would never have had to fight, and he *never* would have gotten hurt. And if Treasa had stayed with Kala, we wouldn't have lost our only way of communicating with the other team when their signal was lost. What was the point of having an Oculus on our team when we were within a few hundred feet of each other? Not to mention that Treasa completely lost her head. If Riri hadn't come when she did, everyone on *my* team would have died."

Drake opened his mouth and closed it. Everyone stayed completely still. Silence clung to the room, dark and heavy, and no one could speak due to the weight of it.

Jory stared at her brother in amazement. Who was this? He was so passionate—so full of life. What had happened to the dull, emotionless Ryan? The one who didn't care about anyone? She looked at the man named Krueger. How long had Ryan known him?

Kellry broke the silence, walking up to Drake and Ryan. "What does he mean, Drake? What petty jealousy?"

Drake wouldn't meet Kellry's eyes. He glared at the floor, fisting his hands until they shook.

"What does he mean?" Kellry pressed.

Drake clenched his jaw. "Don't make me say it, Kell."

Kellry's eyes widened, and everyone jolted when hysterical laughter burst from the corner where Lane rested against the wall.

"FINALLY!" Lane shouted, throwing up her arms and then dropping them limply on the floor. She laughed some more, but as it faded, she sighed. "That was brilliant. Don't get me wrong—I still hate you, Ryan, but..." She grinned. "Finally, I don't have to look at her idiot clueless face ever again."

Kellry's face was horrified. She looked between Drake and Ryan and then Drake again. Then anger began to bubble up in her as well. Jory sighed, watching as it flared to life. *Here we go.*

"You took me off Lane's team because..." She shook her head. "Because you were jealous of *him*?"

She pointed a finger at Ryan.

Her other hand rested on her chest. "Because you have feelings for *me*?"

Drake stayed silent.

Kellry's words choked out, tears brimming in her eyes. "They almost died. My *sister* almost died, Drake. Jack, David, Kala, Amare...we have no idea what happened to them." She bowed her head and hugged her arms around her slight frame. Ryan reached out a hand and rested it on her shoulder, eyes tender. It was a look Jory had never seen expressed in her brother's face.

Kellry rested her hand on Ryan's while Drake's face darkened. Ryan turned to him.

"What is this group even for?" Ryan asked. "Saving Psychics? Or Pretty Boy Drake's personal vendetta against Bram? Because trust me when I say you have been lucky so far. Bram is smart, and whatever losses you think you've dealt him, he'll give right back. He might not own an empathetic bone in his body, but he knows what he wants, and he knows what he has to do to get it. His team works like clockwork. Despite being a psycho creep, at least I know when I do a job for him it will go right, and every Psychic's life will be prioritized. Every order will be given and taken without question." Ryan looked at the man in disgust. "Get a grip and lead this team right, or—"

Drake's head shot up. "Or what? *You* will?" he snarled.

"Ha. Heck no. Do I look like I wanna be in charge of these idiots? No, if you don't step up...she will." He shoved his thumb at Kellry.

Drake stared at Ryan in disbelief.

"I think he's got a point." Roman stepped forward, clapping a hand on Kellry's other shoulder. "Whenever things go down, she's the one who steps up and calls the shots. She's the one who told Riri to be on standby in the first place. She's the one who talked sense into Treasa so she could concentrate and connect with Riri and get us to teleport over."

"Not to mention..." Roman glanced at Ryan. "She was the only one who voted not to kill Ryan. She was sure she could get him on our side. She tracked, made contact, and brought him in without so much as a scratch."

Kill Ryan? Why would they need to kill him?

Jory looked at her brother. Pure adoration emanated from him toward the girl named Kellry, but no surprise whatsoever. He wasn't at all phased by the fact that they all had, at one point, wanted him dead.

What in the world is going on?

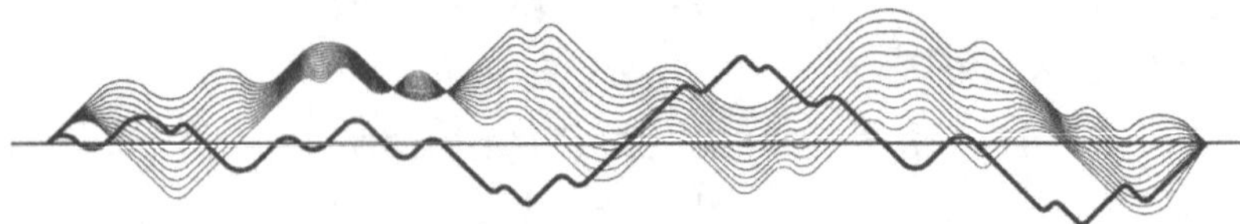

Chapter 21: Padraigin

Everything had gone according to plan.

Padraigin looked up into the charcoal sky. He lay on the roof of Bram's base of operations with the cold cement pressing against his back. Only a few of the grand celestial bodies that dappled the night were able to peek through the dense fog and battle against the city lights below. If South Bres was swill and fodder, North Bres was filled with the pigs and cattle that fed off it. Padraigin was sick of it. He missed being able to see the stars. He wanted to go back home.

Back to the Bureau.

But orders were orders.

He reached a hand up to the night sky, the black silhouette covering one of the only stars peeking through the heavens. Slowly he brought his hand back down to cover his eyes. He'd always loved the stars. He wasn't sure what it was about them, but time and time again his eyes were drawn to the night sky. He let out a slow breath. How much longer would this assignment go? He'd been with Bram for over two years now.

Just make your move so I can go home.

Kala's face came into view, her ebony eyes framed by a mass of white braids—her expression twisted and hateful. He gritted his teeth.

A hardness had formed in the pit of his stomach. It hardly weighed him down—but it was there all the same, a pebble-sized seed that twinged randomly. However, it was small and easy to ignore.

Even after a night like tonight.

Eight Hours Earlier

Paddy, Paddy!

His sister's voice spoke to his mind—anxious and angry.

What's wrong? he asked.

Bad news, Paddy. That useless piece of horse dung changed me to a different team.

Why had Drake changed things? Padraigin could feel their connection buzz. Treasa was upset. She'd never learned to school her emotions like he had, and he was definitely the better actor of the two. Her anger, her irritation at anyone she deemed inferior or incompetent—which was practically everyone—made her vulnerable. She needed to calm down.

Did you hear me, Paddy? I'm not coming to you—I'm stuck with these idiots. We're already in the sewers.

He sat up, hands fisted, blood freezing in his veins.

Why didn't you tell me before?

He could picture her shrugging. *It wouldn't have changed anything,* she said. *Besides, your mind was clouded, or you were connecting to Bram. This is the first time I've been able to reach you properly.*

Padraigin clenched his hands. *Treasa, get out of there.*

Idiot didn't even bring a working saw. If we're crushed by sh— wait what? What's wrong?

The Mindless, Treasa. Bram had Hans send them to the sewers.

The connection to his sister's mind staggered.

They were going to go to the vents!

Padraigin swallowed the lump that formed in his throat. *Bram changed his mind, didn't want to take the chance of killing off Drake. Besides, they'll have more room to move in the sewer. Get out of there. Now.*

I can't! There's no way back, I—

The connection severed, which could mean a slew of things. The most likely one being her concentration had been broken by an outside source.

He pressed his fingers against his temples. *Treasa! TREASA!* It was no use. She was gone. He cursed and slammed a fist against the cement.

"Easy there, tiger." Rashida walked over, impossibly long legs lending to her strides as she slinked over to him. Lean, muscled arms propped against her hips, and she leaned toward Padraigin with a seductive smile.

Rashida always looked seductive—she couldn't help it. Every move she made was smooth and graceful. Today she wore a black tank top tucked into a pair of form-fitting tan pants and a chunky black belt housing two handguns hung at the sides of her generous hips. Black army boots laced up to mid-calf, completing the ensemble. The outfit accentuated her curvaceous figure and left Padraigin feeling all sorts of uncomfortable.

"Kala is at the gate with a few little friends." She grinned, showing straight rows of bright-white teeth beneath a prominent nose. "It's showtime."

She reached out a hand and ruffled his curls, then straightened and walked off. Her thick black braid whipped around her as she turned, smacking him on the wrist.

Padraigin frowned at her back. There was nothing he could do for his sister from here. *Don't die.* He knew his silent plea wouldn't reach her.

Standing, he followed Rashida into the building and down a flight of stairs before slipping into the foxhole where Mike lived.

The man sat, fingers typing away while glancing feverishly up at the circle of monitors around him.

"How much does Kala know about the base?" Rashida asked.

"Why would I know?"

Rashida lifted a brow and Padraigin scowled. It wasn't what she thought. Kala was just another one of Bram's tools. He could care less—the fact that Padraigin *did* know the answer to Rashida's question was only because Padraigin was trained to be observant.

"Not much," Padraigin said finally. He rubbed the back of his neck, thinking. "Certainly not about Mike's setup."

Rashida smirked and leaned forward.

It was a lie. Kala knew everything. Treasa had told him when Roman joined up with them, and again when Ryan had done the same. Both had spilled their guts to Drake's team. Padraigin hadn't told Bram. He answered to the Bureau. Besides, Bram would have wanted to know how he knew Roman and Ryan defected, and that would have blown his cover.

He watched the monitor to his left as a young teenage boy approached the guards outside. The boy crept up behind them and thrust a hand out, pinching one on the neck. The guard immediately dropped, forced into deep slumber.

It was the Sleeper Bram had been after. *Looks like he'll get the kid after all.* The second guard's hand snagged the boy by the throat. The Sleeper rose in the air, feet kicking. Both of the Sleeper's hands held tight to the meaty wrists at his neck. When the Sleeper let go with one hand and snaked it up to pinch the arm of the guard, both collapsed.

Padraigin shifted his attention to Kala, whose white braids were pulled back in a thick ponytail that practically glowed on the screen. He knew she'd be back, because she would never leave her little brother behind.

She should have stayed away.

Kala rushed to the fallen boy and helped him up. A large man joined them, checking the bodies of the two guards. He pocketed two knives and a handgun before they carefully made their way into the building.

"Aren't they cute?" Rashida asked with a wide grin. "They *can't* believe it would be that easy."

"Is the big guy going to be a problem? He looks like one big protein shake." Padraigin glanced at Rashida.

She shook her head. "Nah, I've seen him before. He's a Shield in every way. He might try to throw his weight around, but he wouldn't stand up in a real fight. All defense."

"If he's a Shield, won't you be at a disadvantage? You won't be able to access your ability."

She ruffled his hair again. "Aww, you worried, cutie?"

"Maybe," he said with a toothy grin and winked.

"Flirt," she said.

Padraigin shrugged. "You started it."

"I'm too old for you," she said, "And I know I'm not *quite* dark enough for your tastes."

Padraigin scowled and Rashida laughed. What was wrong with him? Why did it bother him so much when she alluded to Kala in this way? Returning to the professional he was, he schooled his features.

"So, should I be worried?" he prodded.

Rashida shook her head. "Just because my abilities are gone doesn't mean I can't fight. It's like missing an arm. It's annoying, but I still got another arm and two legs to do the job."

Padraigin nodded and sighed as they watched the group move farther and farther through the building.

"Little mousies following the cheese," Mike mumbled as he typed away.

The entire building was rigged to Mike's specifications. He locked and unlocked doors, turned lights on and off, and sent orders to the men patrolling with a few swift touches of the keys. He lured the group through the building, giggling to himself as they reached for locked door handles or ducked down a hallway to escape the men being sent their way.

"Stop playing with them, Mike. I'm bored." Rashida pulled a gun out of its holster and nudged Mike in the head with it.

Mike stopped typing, turning his head back and around like an owl. Padraigin knew Mike couldn't really turn his head that far. It just looked that way with how his back was hunched up. It didn't help that the man's brown hair tufted out the sides of his head or that his round yellow eyes peered beneath thick, dark, slanted brows. Even his tiny nose hooked down like the beak of an owl.

"You know I don't like those things, love," Mike said with a glare.

Rashida sighed, shoving the gun back into the holster.

Mike ignored her and turned his head back to his work. "They'll be stumbling into the boy very soon."

A greasy grin crept across Mike's face. "Oh I do love working for Bram. He always makes things so interesting."

Padraigin gritted his teeth, that pebble of anxiety twisting in his stomach. His father's face flashed into his mind. *You're my lens and key.* The words settled his thoughts and calmed his stomach.

"Oh lookie, they found him." Mike giggled as he turned up the audio in the room.

Padraigin watched the black-and-white screen as Kala lunged forward to embrace the ten-year-old boy, tears streaming down her face.

The boy screamed and pushed her away.

"Amare...what?" Kala's voice filtered through the speakers. Her head whipped around until she found the cameras.

"What did you do to him!" she shouted.

"I thought you said she didn't know about Mike's set-up." Rashida cocked her head to the side, eyeing Padraigin.

"She doesn't. She doesn't even know Mike," he lied.

It felt like Kala was staring directly at him. Her glare was icy, and he clenched his fist to keep from flinching away.

"Mike, you slimy weasel, what's wrong with him?" Kala glanced back at her brother and reached a hand toward him. The boy flinched away. As she choked against her tears, Padraigin began to dig his nails into his palms. He'd seen worse.

Rashida raised a skeptical brow. "Uh-huh. Ya, she doesn't know him at all."

"How interesting." Mike leaned forward into a small microphone and pressed a button. "Well, hello there, love. The boy's perfectly healthy, just had a few heart-to-hearts with Bram is all."

Mike's voice echoed from the audio as he spoke through the speaker system.

Kala cursed and motioned to the Sleeper. Amare shook his head as the older boy approached.

"That's my cue." Rashida's grin spread from ear to ear as she broke through a trapdoor in the middle of the floor. Padraigin watched on the screen as she dropped from the ceiling and approached the stunned faces.

Sighing, Padraigin walked over to the gaping hole in the floor and dropped down into the room below just in time to see Rashida darting straight toward the hulking Shield. A strange, invisible bubble passed through the air, making him stagger. The man had activated the Shield. Padraigin wouldn't be able to access his abilities.

The Shield threw up his arms in defense as Rashida's leg swung up in a high arc. He caught the kick with his wrists, his solid form absorbing the blow. Then he reached out and snagged her ankle. She immediately twisted out of the grip, her body spinning in midair, bringing up her other leg. She twisted, using the large man's weight against him as her foot connected with the side of his face.

He grunted, and Padraigin winced at the crunching sound that ensued. Blood flowed from the man's nose, and he dropped to the ground like a great stone rolling off a mountain.

Rashida landed on her feet and bounced on her toes a moment before turning to Kala and the Sleeper. The Sleeper gritted his teeth as Rashida walked calmly toward him. The boy stood frozen like a frightened deer as she inched forward, her smile still glued in place.

"Wait," the boy said. He reached a hand out, but Rashida stepped over to him and tapped his shoulder in an unforgiving way. The boy dropped to the ground as if Rashida had been the Sleeper. Kala glared at her, hate strong in her eyes as Amare huddled in the background.

"What did you do to him?" she asked with a growl.

"You know how Bram works," Rashida said simply. "Have anything else to say?"

Kala looked at her brother. Fear, grief, and hate swam in her dark eyes.

"Amare, it's me." Kala placed her hands on her chest. "Kala."

Amare stared at her like she was poison while Kala's eyes brimmed with tears of anguish and fury. Padraigin's gaze fell to the floor.

Rashida frowned. "What did I tell you? You can't just leave, princess. Can't just walk out on someone like Bram and leave poor little brother behind. You have to accept the consequences."

"Screw you!" Kala shouted, tears streaming down her face.

Rashida sighed, eyes tight. "Come on, Amare."

She jerked her head toward the door. Amare burrowed into Rashida's side and took her hand, following her. A strangled sound escaped Kala's throat when Amare glanced back at her, his brow furrowed with fear.

"You can take care of one simple girl, can't you, Padraigin?" Rashida asked, almost condescendingly.

He ignored her.

"Tie up the others," she added without looking back. "We'll figure out what Bram wants to do when he gets back."

The door slammed shut behind her. The metallic thud sounded so loud, so final—like a lid on a coffin.

Padraigin walked over to Kala, but she shifted her feet into a solid stance.

"Don't, Padraigin," she hissed. "I'll smack the ginger right out of you."

The threat made his lip twitch. Padraigin shook his head. "You know I have no choice."

"I thought you of all people would understand," she said, eyes pleading.

He almost took a step back. Why would she think that? They'd only shared a few conversations, nothing noteworthy.

"Kala—"

"Padraigin, please. Tell me what Bram did. How did he screw with Amare's brain? Did he take me out completely?"

It was the way she'd said his name. Or maybe just hearing his name on her lips. "No, you're still in his memories." He pursed his lips. "You're still his sister, but you abused him. In Amare's new reality, Bram saved him from you. That's why he believes he's here."

Kala shook her head in disbelief. "Amare can fight it. I know he can."

Padraigin grimaced. "Why'd you leave, Kala? You knew this would happen."

"I couldn't let him take those boys. I couldn't be part of that."

"Was it worth it?" Padraigin asked, scornful. "You saved two strangers but lost your brother in the process."

He nudged his head toward the Sleeper. "And one of the boys got caught anyway. So what you did really didn't mean a thing."

Kala shook her head violently. "No, you're wrong. It meant everything. I could never have forgiven myself for turning those boys over to a monster like Bram. I *will* save Amare. I will make Bram change him back, or I will spend the rest of my life proving to him that what's been done to him is a lie. There's no way he could have taken everything from us. Not everything."

Her words cut him, unexpectedly opening up a vulnerable space inside he hadn't known was there.

Kala had made a *choice*.

Everything was a choice, but acknowledging that made him uncomfortable. He had followed orders for so long, telling himself he didn't have one. The Bureau, his father, and Bram. He'd accepted his mother's treatment, accepted that he was a tool, accepted that his identity merely consisted of his next order. A lens and a key.

He subdued Kala, ignoring her curses as he tied her up. Ignoring the hateful, beautiful dark eyes that seared and tore into him.

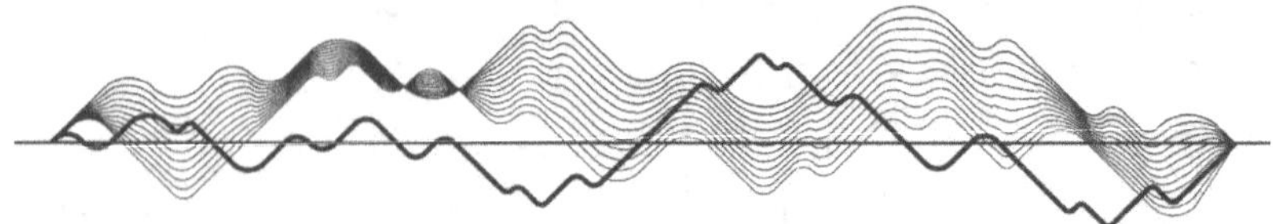

Chapter 22: Ryan

Ryan looked at the ground around him.

Crimson splattered up the walls, flecked on furniture, painted windows.

Why was there so much blood? It didn't make any sense. His ability didn't work this way—it didn't make people bleed. Did it? He was so caught up in the redness, the wetness, the surprising warmth of the liquid across his face that the sobs coming from the corner of the room didn't register at first.

He glanced over at his sister. She stared wide-eyed at him, an ongoing scream of pure terror escaping her mouth in agony.

She looked at him like he was a monster risen from the nightmarish stories they read to each other when their parents weren't watching.

What had he done? He looked at the bodies. He hadn't done that. This wasn't real. That wasn't them.

"I'm sorry," he whispered. "I didn't mean to, I—"

Anna's screams echoed in his mind until Ryan's eyes shot open.

He was at Stark's, and the other children were sleeping soundly in their beds. Their snores, coupled with other unfamiliar creaks and groans of the night, made it hard to sleep at all.

"Good dreams there, boy?"

Ryan glanced to his right to see a darkened silhouette crouched next to his bed. Glowing moonlight framed the monster's form as it leaned toward him. Ryan opened his mouth to shout, to scream, but nothing came. His voice was stolen by fear.

Orange eyes glowing, the monster smiled. "I see no recognition in your eye," it said, "which is to be expected. Don't worry, boy. Soon you will know me very well. You need a father, don't you? Everyone needs a father."

Ryan felt wetness and warmth gather in his sheets as he peed himself.

He recognized it then. Not a monster, but a man. He hovered in his dreams, sometimes like a phantom or a reaper watching Ryan silently from the background.

Sometimes, Ryan felt as if the man egged him on. That he convinced him to lose control. He was real? The man leaned close, lips almost touching Ryan's ear.

"I know your secret, Ryan. I know what you did. Let's make a deal."

For the second time, Ryan woke up.

A dream within a dream.

Ryan hated those. He pinched his arm hard and bit his tongue till it bled, welcoming the pain of reality.

He was awake, and Bram was far away. Not at the Home, not at his bedside.

After accepting that Kala and the others had been compromised, they relocated to an old brick house miles south of their original hideout. Apparently it belonged to Krueger. Or some late relative of his. It had multiple rooms, but they were all small and covered in stained wallpaper.

He shared his space with Ref, who didn't argue about the arrangement. Ref wasn't much of a talker. The guy was a closed book, and Ryan couldn't tell if he didn't give a crap and a half about him, or if he was actively stoking the flames of a smoldering, eternal hatred.

Either option was just as likely.

Their room had to have been a nursery at some point in time. Clowns in various poses danced across the white wallpaper speckled with rainbow polka dots.

When in time was that ever a good idea? Eighties? Nineties?

A giant, yellowed stain covered his side of the wall, and he wondered if it was just age or if some kid had peed on it in the past.

Maybe Krueger did it, he thought, and smirked. Ryan couldn't picture Krueger as a child. He kept imagining a tiny body with Krueger's adult head, man bun and all. Chainsaw in hand.

It wasn't yet dawn, but with only two bathrooms and one shower between them, Ryan took his chance to clean up.

After rinsing off, he shook his head like a wet dog, flinging droplets of water in all directions. Soft gray light sifted through the skinny, horizontal glass window above the shower. The glass was that weird wavy kind meant to lend privacy. It was cloudy, and in the corners an orangey-brown goo grew in seldom-cleaned, damp places.

Clinging to the sink, he leaned toward his reflection, taking in the shaggy hair and haunted green eyes. The wet strands hung across his vision. Jerking his head to the side, he flung them out of the way. A strange temptation to buzz it all off made his hands itch.

Where would I hide, then?

What a lame thought. He shuffled through some drawers until he found what he was looking for.

Holding the scissors awkwardly, he hacked at his hair without direction. The scissors were old—surprise, surprise—and slightly dull, but as each chunk fell, a strange feeling of liberation washed over him.

He needed to change.

In those few charged minutes in the sewers, Ryan had realized something.

He didn't want to die.

As much as he fantasized over it, glamorized it, he didn't actually *want* it.

And feeling Krueger's lifeblood pump between his fingers had made him realize how precious it was. It made him realize how badly he wanted to be useful. How badly he wanted to be a true member of a team. How badly he wanted to be reliable, to prove himself.

Then there was Jory.

She'd regained some control of her abilities.

Did she remember what had happened? Everything he'd fought for, everything he'd done to keep her in the dark was unraveling.

Ryan had seen the danger at once when he'd watched Jory's nerves weaving themselves into Krueger's body—feeding into his life force. He hadn't stopped to think when he'd Sliced through the connection, releasing Jory from giving it all away.

Now both of them lay on cots while Damon, the Silver-tongue, tended to them.

Ryan cut the last chunk of hair and looked in the mirror once more.

He looked stupid. His eyes were too big and it was weird seeing his eyebrows when he hadn't seen them in so long. They were like furry black caterpillars above his eyes.

But his jawline was strong, and he felt new...ish.

"It's okay to hate what you've done," he said to himself. "To hate what you are. You know what you are, Ryan. You're selfish and you're an idiot. You've been an idiot for a long time. You suck. But that's okay, because it stops now."

He shoved a finger at his reflection. "You're done being an idiot. You're done sucking."

"That was quite the pep talk."

Ryan turned abruptly, gripping the towel that hung loosely around his waist.

Kellry leaned against the wall, grinning.

"You're in the boy's bathroom," he said. What was he, five?

"Um, I don't think so. There's practically one real bathroom in this place. Especially since Roman clogged up the other toilet." Kellry glanced at the floor. "You made a mess. It looks like Sasquatch shaved his legs in here."

Ryan shrugged, running a hand through the cropped mess on his head.

She appraised him, her eyes not only raking over his face and hair, but the rest of him as well. Her scrutiny was unnerving, and he gripped the towel a little tighter.

"It looks good," she said, finally.

"What?" he asked in disbelief.

She laughed. "No, really. Here, it just needs a little more work."

Kellry grabbed a stool from beneath the sink and made him sit.

"Pull the towel up a bit," she said. "I can see your buttcrack."

Ryan flushed and pulled the towel up, grumbling.

"Just kidding," she whispered in his ear.

Her warm breath made him shiver. He felt the sudden need to dunk his head in a bucket of ice water.

"Come on," she said, nudging his back, "lighten up."

How am I supposed to lighten up if you keep doing stuff like that?

Soft snips filled the air as small bits of hair dusted his ears and shoulders. His skin began to itch, but he sat still as Kellry worked quietly, periodically running her fingers through his hair to find the uneven patches. She hummed a strange song he'd never heard before. The soft trills and deep intonations reminded him of the otherworldly chant Lane had performed on him.

"I've never heard that song before," he said.

"I wouldn't think so," she said. "It's from my home."

She sifted through the drawer and picked up a buzzer, proceeding to trim and shape the hair at the nape of his neck and around his ears. When she clicked it off, she walked around to his front and began snipping some more.

She was so close, having to lean in to work on his bangs. He wanted to grab her waist and pull her to him, to nestle his face in the curve of her neck. The feeling was so overwhelming he almost numbed it.

He wondered if these emotions felt so new because he'd perpetually numbed his feelings for so long. Would he feel this way about any girl hovering this close to him?

No.

Kellry was different. Kellry was—

"What are you thinking about?" she asked.

You.

What he said was, "Any update on my sister, or that idiot?"

She paused her snipping and grinned. "It's almost like you care about that idiot."

Ryan frowned, itching to break eye contact, but Kellry held his gaze.

"Maybe," he said after a moment. "Maybe I just don't want all that effort wasted, since my sister almost killed herself saving his hide."

Kellry laughed, and her breath tickled his face with hints of mint and lemon.

Does her mouth taste like it smells?

An overwhelming need to test the thought had him leaning forward. Her laughter was cut short with a short inhale that sent his heart racing. He continued his advance, and her lids fluttered closed, lips parting slightly.

It was terrifying how natural it felt to bury his hands in her silken hair and trace his fingers down her neck. To feel the prickle of goose bumps on her skin in reaction to his touch. The need to feel close to someone—to feel close to *her*—raged within him like a caged beast.

A loud echoing stream had them both frozen, lips just about to brush against each other. Kellry snapped her eyes open, but Ryan buried her face in his chest.

"If you two wanna go tongue-tangling, you have to pick a better place." Krueger grinned unabashed as he continued to relieve himself.

He'd walked right in without either of them noticing.

If Ryan wasn't so happy to see the man up and about, he would have Sliced right through his pisser.

"Krueger, you couldn't wait a few minutes?"

The man shrugged, zipping up his pants. "Not when you've been blacked out for next to forever. Bladder fills up like the udders of an un-milked cow. I would've been mooing something fierce if I waited a moment longer."

Ryan hung his head, hiding a smile. Not only from Krueger's comment but from the faint snickering against his bare chest.

"Anyway, don't hang out here too long. I'm not the only guy who's gotta go. That tall germaphobe is dancing just outside. Doesn't want to disturb the young folk in heat."

Kellry snorted a laugh then whispered in his ear. "This isn't over." She stood, sending Ryan a wink before confidently walking out of the bathroom.

It was Ryan's turn to have goose bumps explode over his skin.

She's something else.

Sebastian dashed in a moment later, cheeks beet red. Ryan groaned, burying his face in his hands.

So close!

"You're so lucky you almost died, or I would kill you," he grumbled, eyeing Krueger through his fingers.

"Aw, shush your tush. I heard your sobs of woe all the way from the pearly gates. Called me back from my place amongst the bare-bottomed angels," Krueger said before slapping Ryan on the back.

Ryan threw a punch to Krueger's side, but the man easily dodged it. "I didn't sob over you, stupid. Besides, no way you're going to heaven."

Krueger shrugged. "Good thing it's not up to you." He grinned, looking Ryan up and down. "New do suits you, kid. You look like you could join the marching band or knock on my door selling some Thin Mints and Taga-longs."

"Shut up."

He chuckled, ruffling Ryan's hair before walking out. But before leaving, he turned, cocking his head back.

"Get some clothes on and go see your sister. She's not doing so hot. Besides, she seems to have a lot of questions needing answers." He gave Ryan a stern look. "Can't keep running from her, kid."

He's right. But there's no way I can tell her. Not everything. Ryan leaned his head back and closed his eyes, breathing deeply. The thought of telling his sister anything was sending him into a spiral.

"You know he's right." Sebastian's low timbre echoed off the tiled walls.

"Why are you still here?"

"Hey, you don't like me much, I get that. That doesn't change the fact that you know I care a heck of a lot for your sister. She doesn't deserve the way you've treated her, how you've shut her out."

I don't need this from you. Freaking gangly piece of crap.

"Shut up, Sebastian."

"Or what?"

Ryan opened his eyes, meeting Sebastian's stare with surprise.

"Or you'll make me?" Sebastian quoted the line Ryan had used on him multiple occasions. The line that had always gotten the coward to back off.

"I don't think you will, not now." Sebastian approached Ryan, squatting down with his ridiculous grasshopper legs. He rested his forearms on his thighs and took a deep breath. They were eye level now, with Ryan still sitting on the stool Kellry had taken out. Sebastian's gaze was soft, kind.

It roused the anger brewing so close to the surface. Ryan jerked his head away, glaring into the amorphous design of the gray tile.

"And that's not a bad thing," Sebastian said, voice as soft as his eyes. "You're different, Ryan. Something changed within you. Something important, and it's okay to let go of the old you. To let go of the hate. I can see it. I've always seen it. And no matter what you tell yourself, it's not me or this guy Bram you're angry with. It's you. Whatever happened, whatever you've done, you need to forgive yourself."

Freaking shrink.

Ryan wanted to laugh. He'd always been acutely aware of the hate he harbored for himself. It had shaped everything he'd done, everything he thought about. Fantasizing about suicide, keeping secrets, allowing himself to disappear behind a dark version of himself.

Ryan finally lifted his gaze, feeling years of self-loathing building up along with an emptiness that gnawed at the pit of his stomach and rose to his heart.

"And what if," he said, voice void of emotion, "I've done the unforgivable?"

Sebastian pursed his lips, wariness blooming in his gaze.

That's right, be afraid of me. It's only fair.

Sebastian didn't back down, didn't blink. "Then you need to spend every moment of the rest of your life making it right, Ryan. Even if it never will be. You owe that to yourself."

Sebastian stood, nodding. "And who knows, you might come to realize you're not so unredeemable as you believe."

The man left, and Ryan stared into his hands once more. He felt...bewildered. Sebastian's words held some truth. Not the redeemable part—that was a big pile of fairy vomit. The other part, the part where he spent the rest of his life making up for all of it. That felt right. Not for himself, though. For Jory.

He just wasn't sure if that meant telling her the truth.

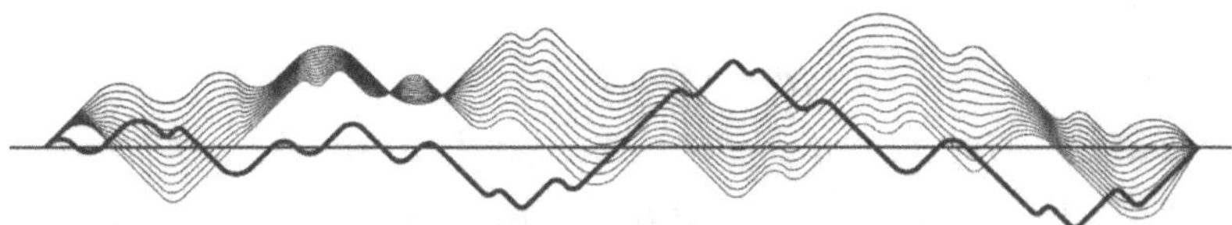

Chapter 23: Jory

She was lost.

Threads surrounded her in an undulating mass, as changing as the sea. They glowed and dimmed in a rainbow of phosphorescent color, and though she had separated herself from the threads, the pull of emotions urged her to Soothe and detangle. To weave.

Jory ignored the pull, trying to find her way. She felt trapped. Before, she could leave the Tapestry or bring it to her, but this time she'd been thrust within its depths. Consciousness and the real world were beyond her reach.

She wasn't dead, though. She knew that much. If she was going to be stuck here, maybe she could find some answers.

She'd had a growing suspicion ever since she'd experienced that memory with her mother.

Find the inconsistencies. That's what the boy from her past had said. There had been too many fissures and webs within her mind for anything to stand out. Then she'd seen the man with the orange eyes.

He had not belonged in that memory, and Jory felt a growing fear that this man might be the key.

Closing her eyes, she lifted her watercolor hands over the weave. So far, she'd been able to pick out the threads of those she knew. However, trying to find someone she wasn't even sure existed?

"I have to try," she whispered.

Taking a deep breath, she pictured the man—his predatory gait, his dark, silken voice, and the orange eyes beneath heavy lids. She sank her hands into the threads and pushed out with her mind, feeling more than seeing the ripple, like a stone dropping into a still pond.

Her mind raced outward with the ripple until she felt it. Felt him.

He was real.

Reflexively, she tugged. Her amorphous body shot toward the threads, hair cascading behind her—a long, waving stroke of a painter's brush. Within moments, she was there. The threads were strange, to say the least. They looked battered, with wisps of frayed string dangling all over. Some threads were snapped, waving listlessly like the tail of a dying horse in a winter breeze.

It made her flinch back, unsure what a mind left in such a state held in store for her.

She had to do this, though. She needed to know who he was.

One thread made her flinch away. Angry and pulsing from red to white hot, it was the one she'd steered away from all that time ago. Had it only been days since then?

She wanted to turn away, go back. I have to do this, *she reminded herself.*

So, with a steadying breath, she delved her hands into the weave.

White walls, white coats, blue gloves. And pain, so much pain. She had dived too deep. This man had run through the minds of hundreds—had cut, sewn, and re-sewn memories.

It was him. It had to be. This was the man who had taken her life from her.

Her hands shook slightly, and she had the sudden urge to find that green string, the one connected to his life force, and...

And what?

Kill him?

What am I thinking? I can't just kill someone. *Besides, she'd have to confirm her suspicions before she acted on anything.*

Concentrate on why you're here. Focus on the memories.

His actions had taken their toll.

Wait...

She was in his memories.

She could do that?

Jory had walked through dreams, seen thoughts—each time she used her ability, she found out more that she could do.

The man's name was Bram, and as she sank deeper, she witnessed flashes of memories. Memories of tortured children, time spent with younger versions of Damon the Silvertongue and Drake. But most of all, a hook-nosed man.

Brinsley. His name was Doctor...no, not Doctor. Director Brinsley. The white-hot thread was connected to this man, strung tight around every memory or thought of him. There was something disturbingly familiar about this man.

Kill.

The word whispered around the strand like a snake hissing and biting.

Bram had been a prisoner of the Bureau. However, as much as she wanted to find out more about his time there, more about this man, she needed to look closer to the present. She needed to find other information.

Bram.

Was this the same Bram Ryan was working for?

It had to be. The pieces were falling into place, and she didn't want to think about what that meant for Ryan.

Forcing herself from Bram's broken past, she searched among tangled memories and faces until she found the ones she wanted. The ones she was afraid to find.

Her mother, her father, and the boy with bronze curls.

She saw what happened—what really happened—and she saw Bram grasp her head and erase it all.

While her lungs gasped for air and her eyes streamed with tears, she didn't notice that her host had discovered her presence.

"Found you."

A giant orange eye opened in front of her. She released the threads with a jerk as her body was flung out into the Tapestry.

Jory sat up, sucking in air as if she'd been drowning. When the world spun, she fell back and shut her eyes. Her hands reached out, searching for something, someone.

Hands grasped hers.

"Woah, hey, hey, you're all right." The voice was male, soft and soothing.

"He saw me. He's here. He—"

"No one's here. You're safe. Just...take a second to calm down," he said.

Jory nodded, letting her head sink further into the pillow and taking a few long, deep breaths. Once she steadied herself, she reached out with her mind, the Tapestry easily falling into place around her. The threads next to her pulsed with anxiety, concern, and an irritated awkwardness.

Slowly lifting her lids, she met the steel-gray eyes of the man beside her. He couldn't have been more than twenty, with mussed dark hair and a light shadow of a beard over his jawline.

Releasing her hands, he stuffed his into his pockets and straightened.

"Um, you thirsty?"

Her throat was incredibly dry, so she nodded and he went to pour her some water from a blue pitcher sitting on a side table.

When she went to sit up, her arms shook. He reached out a hesitant hand, and she nodded her approval. Helping her into a sitting position, he tucked the glass into her hands.

"Thanks," she said, handing it back after a long swig. "Um, who are you?"

She looked around at the peeling, flowered wallpaper and lace curtains.

"Oh, ya, um. I'm Ref. I mean, I'm Camden, but everybody here calls me Ref, so..." He shrugged and leaned against a back wall.

"And I'm Krueger, in case you were wondering." An old sheet with more tiny yellow flowers partitioning the room was flung aside to reveal the bearded man she'd saved.

"And this is my late Nan's place. Adorable little broad."

Krueger grinned, threw off his covers, and walked over to her. As he sat on a stool next to her bed, his face grew serious.

She hadn't noted Krueger's presence. She'd removed herself from the weave and could no longer sense the emotions of those around her unless she actively reached out to the threads.

"Thank you. For what you did. Not exactly sure what it is you did, but I'm grateful and I won't forget it. Looks like I owe both you *and* your kid brother," Krueger said.

Ryan.

She had to talk to him. The question was—could she trust him? After everything he had kept from her? About himself, about their parents?

"Where is he? I need to talk to him," she finally said.

Krueger shrugged. "Somewhere around the place."

He stood. "Now if you'll excuse me, I need to take a mighty piss. If I see your brother, I'll send him over."

Jory nodded her thanks, and he strolled from the room.

He's so healthy.

Krueger had been so close to death, and now he was walking around like nothing had happened, while she could barely lift a glass. Would she be like this forever? Having given up her life force without a second thought and stuck in this weakened state?

And then there was Bram. What did he mean when he said he'd "found her"? And what was she going to do with the truth she had seen? It was so bizarre. Her mind still fought with the knowledge, still remembered the car crash. She needed time alone. She'd seen how Bram had done it now—how he'd stitched other memories over her own. Her memories weren't exactly erased, just buried beneath a swath of false images she needed to remove.

And once she did, she'd find *him*. Find the boy hidden within her memory. He'd been there that night. She'd seen him in Bram's memories, but his name was still lost to her.

She glanced at Ref, who still leaned against the wall, his gaze fixating on anything but her.

"Can I ask you something?" she said.

His eyes shifted to hers and he nodded warily.

"Why are you all so afraid of my brother?"

He scrubbed a hand through his hair and walked over before slumping into the stool beside her.

"We're not really supposed to tell you," he said finally.

She narrowed her eyes and folded her arms across her chest. "And?"

Ref sighed. "And, well..." He shrugged, something Jory realized he did a lot.

She stared at him intently until he heaved out a long breath. "Fine. Not like any of us really agreed with it any-way."

He rubbed the nape of his neck, forming his thoughts before speaking.

"Your brother's been Bram's right-hand man for a few years now. The work he did for him was pretty horrific stuff. Any Psychic in South Bres has heard of him by now. His reasons are his...and I think you should talk to him about whatever excuses he has for doing what he's done."

Venom had slowly crept into Ref's voice during his short explanation.

"He's won over a few people here. Kellry, Krueger, Momma J, but the rest of us..." He shrugged. "He's useful, and I'd rather have him working *for* us than against us, but that doesn't mean I could ever trust him."

Jory nodded. She couldn't blame him, because she wasn't sure she could trust Ryan either. Ref glanced at the empty doorway and grinned darkly.

"Speak of the devil," he whispered, before standing and walking over to pick up a large baseball helmet.

Ref glanced at her once more, eyes tight. She tilted her head in confusion before he walked out the door.

Ryan came in, staring at Ref's back as he walked away.

"When did he become so talkative?" he grumbled.

Jory blinked, noticing her brother's hair was short. It reminded her of the old Ryan. The Ryan who laughed and played soccer. The Ryan who won spelling bees and scratched his head over difficult equations. The haircut also brought out all the stark differences from his younger self. His jaw was sharp and masculine now, and baby fat from his youth no longer coated his cheeks. She could clearly see the creases in his brow as he turned his eyes toward her.

"Hey Jor," he said softly.

"Sure you shouldn't call me Anna?" she asked.

Ryan flinched and paled.

"You...you remember," he said. His fingers wrapped into tight fists and his jaw clenched. For a moment, Jory was sure he would scream out curses or punch the wall. But after a moment, he slumped against the doorway, fingers unfurling. Ryan looked into his empty hands, then let them fall to his sides. When his eyes found hers, they almost looked...hollow.

"I didn't remember everything. Just bits and pieces," she said after a long moment of silence. She wouldn't tell him everything she knew. It was his turn, his chance to prove himself, and for that, he needed to start talking.

"Why, Ryan? Why work for Bram?"

He hunched his shoulders and ducked his head, not meeting her eyes.

Jory rolled hers. "Get over here and sit."

He didn't move.

"SIT!"

Ryan flinched again then sighed. Shuffling over, he sank into the stool and rested his forearms on his thighs. He stared into his hands again, and when they began to shake, he laced his fingers together to still them.

"When Mom and Dad... When it happened, you broke. Bram offered me a deal. Told me he'd erase the trauma and rewire your mind so that you wouldn't go after the Bureau, wouldn't go after *him*. Get you to a point where you could function. He said that it would be easier on you if you started fresher. That if small details, like your name, were changed, you'd be less likely to derail again. All I had to do was work for him, and he'd leave you alone. Wouldn't try to recruit you."

Ryan looked up at her, lines of sorrow and guilt etched in his face and in the empty pits of his eyes.

"I did what he asked me. I told myself I was doing it for you, but now I...I don't know anymore."

His hands began to shake again, and Jory noticed that no matter how tightly he clenched them, they didn't stop.

"When I couldn't stomach what Bram required of me, I cut off my emotions. Sliced them away until no humanity was left within me. I did...oh gosh, Jor, I did horrible things."

When his voice caught, he clutched his head—digging his fingers into his skull.

"And something happened," he continued. "That night when you found me in my room, I realized I had unintentionally created something. Someone."

He's talking about that thing I saw in the Tapestry. That black, inky version of himself. "He's still there, Jor. He sits at the back of my head waiting. Waiting for me to slip up, to give him a chance to sink his hands into my consciousness. And I'm scared that if he does, I'll be lost forever."

She wanted to hate him. To yell at him for being such an idiot. If he'd only talked to her, they could have gotten through all of this together. Instead, she grabbed his collar and pulled him into a hug.

"Come here, you idiot," she said. And with those words, a dam broke. Tears soaked into her shirt as her brother cried, and for a moment, it was just like those times when they were small. When he'd fall off his bike or when a storm brought booming thunder and bright flashes of light.

She'd hold him then and stroke his hair, humming softly till the sobs ebbed away.

Jory held him now, clutching him to her chest. However, she couldn't deny that as much as she loved him, what he'd done—what he'd allowed himself to do in her name—left a sick, sinking feeling in her belly.

I can't trust him.

Not just because of that thing that hid in the shadows of his mind. But because his story didn't match the truth.

He'd said that he didn't want her going after *him*. One person.

When he should have said *them*.

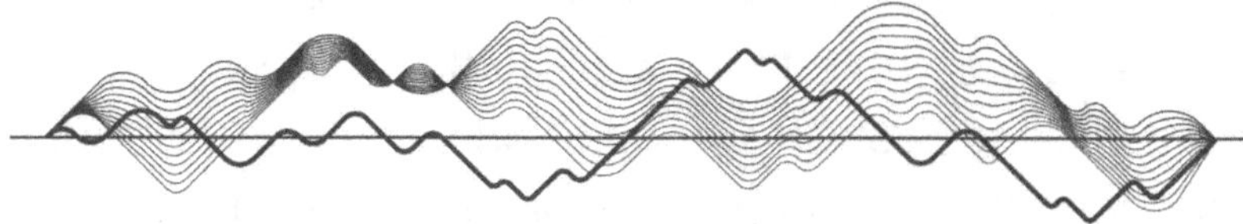

Chapter 24: Padraigin

Stark's Home for Troubled Youth.

The letters were hidden amongst a play of moonlight and shadow cast through the branches of a skeletal tree. Padraigin didn't have to see them clearly to know what they said. He hopped with practiced ease over the mossy stone wall and crept to the window on the east side of the building. He wished he had more time to appreciate the myriad of light thrown across the night like glittering dust particles. The refuge for Psychic children was high in the mountains, gardens lush with winter vegetables. Most importantly, the city glare was far behind him and the stars guided him as he approached.

All right, Paddy my boy, get yourself inside.

His father's voice streamed into his head, clearer than any radio or earpiece. Cormac wouldn't settle for less than perfection. So perfection would be what Padraigin delivered.

I'll have to block you out for a bit to switch abilities, Padraigin said.

I know that, boy. Do your job. You're my lens and key. And neither of those things need a voice or a brain.

It was one of his father's favorite things to say, and the words had long since stopped bothering him. He found comfort in them, a sort of freedom even. Padraigon didn't need a voice, didn't need to bother with a conscience. A conscience led to indecision, and he didn't have the luxury to be indecisive. He nodded. A lens and a key—that's all he ever needed to be. Padraigin shut off his Oculus abilities and closed his eyes, making the shift.

When he opened them again, he knew they were as orange as Bram's. Except where Bram's were a prolonged stain of an experiment gone horribly wrong, Padraigin was the success. The success among many, many failures.

His father was proud of that.

Padraigin tapped into his other ability. The soft click of the latch on the window flicking open rang loud and harsh in his ears.

He didn't hesitate to vault inside. The air was heavy with silence. Children and caretakers slept behind scores of locked doors, but this would be no obstacle for Padraigin.

He tightened the gas mask on his face.

Speed was the key.

He delved into his Infiltrator abilities, and immediately the house changed to a 3D blueprint. He could see through and into every wall, every door, and every lock. Everything layered over each other in an orderly map of lines, gears, and interlocking parts.

He traced steady fingers over the vials in the crisscrossing leather straps on his chest. Focusing, he ran down the hallway, unlocking doors with his mind as he passed and chucked vials into the rooms. The crash of glass chased him, and plumes of smoke hissed out of the open doorways.

A woman darted out of the bedroom at the end of the hall, gun in hand.

Eileen Kilpatrick. The Huntsman and the ultimate prize of this endeavor. He jerked to the side as her finger pulled the trigger. A bullet sang past his left ear with a deafening bang. He had to give her credit for the complete lack of hesitation as she aimed to kill.

He tossed another vial and grunted as her second and third shots grazed his head and lodged in his shoulder. The fourth hit his chest, lodging into his bulletproof vest. A great whoosh of air escaped his lungs, and he was flung backward. He landed on his back, head smacking the wood flooring. The bullet may not have pierced his flesh, but the impact of the blow left him feeling as though he had been beaten with a baseball bat.

He coughed, waiting for the killing blow, but Eileen never shot a fifth bullet. Groaning, Padraigin staggered to his feet. The gas had done its job. Eileen sat crumpled on the floor, blonde head sagging into her chest.

Without missing a beat, Padraigin switched to Oculus mode.

Took you long enough, his father said. *Ah, very nice. I'll send Brinsley's men in to retrieve her and the others. Get out here. We have other safehouses to hit before the night is through.*

His father's presence eased back out of his mind.

Minutes later, Padraigin sat in the helicopter, headgear squeezing his skull as thick gauze was wrapped over his wounded shoulder.

"You're better than this, Padraigin," his father said, dis-approval thick in his voice.

"I can still do the job," Padraigin said dully into the mic of his helmet as the blades of the helicopter whumped and cut through the night sky.

"Go easy on him, Cormac. He did well." Director Brinsley smiled, watery blue eyes bright behind coke-bottle glasses. His hooknose arched over his grin. Padraigin kept his gaze from traveling to the shiny, ridged skin that crawled up the old man's neck, lower jowls, and bare head. Scar tissue from burns an Elementalist child dealt him years ago. Back when Bram escaped.

Padraigin's father sniffed and looked out into the passing landscape. His orange curls, so similar to Padraigin's own, whipped about his head.

"Everything is working out splendidly," Brinsley contin-ued. "How's your head, boy?"

"No pain, no dizziness," Padraigin answered.

Brinsley gestured toward Padraigin, grin widening. "See? No negative side effects from using his ability. Finally some success, and now that the facility is repaired and the reno-vations and expansions are complete, we are finally ready."

"Bram is still out there, Director," Cormac said.

Brinsley arched a brow thoughtfully. "Yes, yes, well." He looked at Padraigin. "You're sure he didn't look further into your mind. See us?"

Brinsley's cold eyes probed Padraigin's features, search-ing.

"He sees what I want him to see. You trained me well."

Brinsley snorted. "It wouldn't surprise me if he knows more than you think, boy."

"Then why keep me around? Bram could have killed me, silenced me countless times."

Brinsley gave a slight nod. "Yes, but he could also feed us whatever information he wanted." He tapped his temple and grinned. "It's the game, boy, always the game."

Padraigin was unsure exactly what "game" the director was referring to, but he nodded.

Brinsley's smile slipped away, leaving a thin, grim line. "Despite that. It still baffles me that you couldn't stick a knife in him."

"He's a careful man," Padraigin replied.

Brinsley heaved a sigh and waved a dismissive hand. "Yes, yes. Our little science experiment is a sneaky rat. Even with you watching him these past two years."

The director leaned back into his seat and grinned. "However, the thing with lab rats is they never truly escape. Bram has yet to realize that his taste of freedom was really just a door into a larger, much more complicated maze. Bram's days at playing hunter are over."

Brinsley chuckled softly and rubbed the bridge of his nose. "It's time to snap the trap."

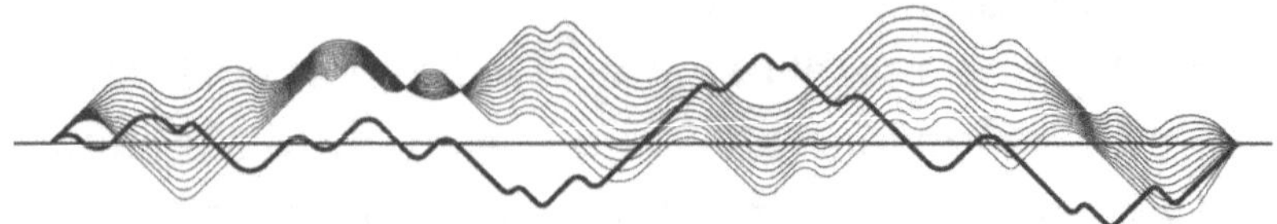

Chapter 25: Ryan

A tasseled lamp boasting forty watts at best cast a sick yellow light within the small living room. Ryan leaned against the wall, watching as Drake paced. Emerald-green, paisley wallpaper made the cramped space feel even smaller. Kellry and Lane stood while Treasa and Ref sat on opposite ends of a tan suede couch.

Krueger sat in a high-backed velvet armchair flaunting a maroon robe while Sebastian hovered awkwardly behind him. Roman stood in the archway leading to the dining room, arms crossed over his shirtless frame.

At the center of them all stood Riri.

"What do you mean they're all gone?" Drake ran a hand through his mussed hair.

"She means they've been taken." Kellry's words came out as a sigh, and she bit her lip deep in thought.

It was past midnight when Riri had woken the entire house with her panicked sobs. Her brother, along with every other Psychic at Stark's Home, had vanished.

Roman strode forward, grabbing the little girl's shoulders and shaking her slightly. "What about Eileen! Did you see Eileen?"

Riri shook her head, tears streaming down her face, and Kellry rested a hand on the large man's shoulder. "Let her go, Roman."

Roman gripped the small girl a moment longer then complied, growling under his breath as he straightened.

"It's Bram. He got her. He finally got her, that crazed piece of—"

Drake cut Roman off, waving a hand. "I'm not so sure. Eileen's resourceful, trained. If he could have pulled it off before now, he would have. You know that. That was supposed to be *your* job, remember? Besides, he wouldn't have taken all those kids."

"How were they taken, then?" Lane said, tapping a finger against her chin. "There were other adults. Not to mention several of those kids, especially the older ones, had notable abilities."

"It could have been retaliation for trying to ambush him," Roman said.

Kellry shook her head. "I don't think it's him. The Bureau could've done it. They certainly have the manpower." Lane flinched when Kellry spoke of the Bureau but nodded in agreement.

"I thought they didn't know where Stark's Home was. And what about the other Homes?" Sebastian added his voice to the conversation. "And if they *did* know where they were, why act now?"

Kellry turned to Riri. "Riri, I need you to think. Can you calm down?"

The small girl sniffed, scrubbing her fists across red-rimmed eyes.

"Start from the beginning," Sebastian added, words soft.

After two more shuddering breaths, she spoke. "Calub's been having nightmares lately. So sometimes at night I'll teleport to go check on him. I—I felt extra worried tonight, but I just thought he'd had another nightmare. When I got there..." She took a deep breath. "It was so quiet. I mean...it's always quiet, but it was a different quiet. Ghost quiet."

She shivered, and Kellry softly urged her to go on.

"The first thing I noticed was that all the doors were wide open, and it smelled...funny. I ran into Calub's room but he was gone, everyone was gone."

Tears welled up in her eyes once more.

Something's not right. But Ryan couldn't put his finger on it.

He kneeled next to Kellry in front of the young girl. "Hey, Ri." He was hesitant to speak because it felt weird voicing his thoughts, interfering in the conversation instead of just watching.

"Try to remember anything else, like sounds...anything unusual. Was there any broken stuff lying around like people had been fighting or—"

"I stepped on glass, lots of it, when I was running around looking in the rooms, but it didn't look like anything had been broken. The windows were fine, but there *was* a big dark splotch on the wood in the hallway." She looked down. "I didn't wanna look at it."

Kellry and Ryan exchanged a dark look.

Roman groaned, resting his head against the wall. As Ryan watched the man's hands clench and unclench, he was sure he was aching to punch someone.

Eileen was the whole reason Roman had left Bram's group in the first place. She'd been his target, and he'd fallen head over heels for her the second he saw her. Bram had even erased his memory and sent Roman after her again, only to achieve the same result.

"Why don't we have the chit jump us over, take a look ourselves?" Krueger asked, rubbing his beard.

Kellry shook her head. "She only has one jump left in her until she recovers, and besides, there might be others watching."

"Ow!" Riri winced as Lane grabbed her leg, yanking it up to sniff the bottom of her shoe.

"You sniffin' feet now, Twoface?" said Krueger.

"Shut up, you imbecile."

Lane pulled out a pair of tweezers and a short vial from a pack at her waist. "There's still some glass here, and she said she'd smelled something. I can smell it too—her shoes are coated in it." She pulled some tiny shards of glass from the girl's shoe and dropped them in the vial. Then she tugged off the whole shoe and stuffed it in a Ziplock baggie also procured from the pack.

"Hey!" Riri reached for her shoe, but Lane smacked her hand away. Ri clutched her hands to her chest and sniffed, her lower lip pouting.

Insensitive brat. Ryan wanted to punch the scars right off Lane's face but settled for a burning stare.

Sebastian hugged Riri and shot his own dagger eyes Lane's way. She ignored the glares.

"Drake, contact that idiot Damon to come and take a look at this with me. He's..." Lane trailed off.

"Smarter, better, more talented?" Krueger asked.

Ryan grinned at her scowl.

"More *experienced*," she corrected with a sniff before tossing her head and leaving the room.

Roman paced back and forth, grumbling to himself. "Well, what do we do?" he shouted, glaring in Drake's direction. "We need to get Eileen back. Now."

Everyone looked to Drake. When he didn't answer, eyes shifted toward Kellry.

"Well go on, then. Answer them, Kell." Drake folded his arms across his chest and jutted his chin out.

What a frickin' baby, Ryan thought with a tired shake of his head.

"Stop crying, Drake," Krueger said. "Honestly, any win you've got is because of that girl."

A snarl broke out on Drake's face, twisting his looks into something wholly unattractive for once. "I put this group together, and it's not up to any of *you* who gets to be in charge." Jutting a thumb to his chest, he continued, "I know Bram better than anyone here. I was there. I was with him when—"

Roman grabbed Drake's collar and thrust his back against the wall.

"I don't give a crap in the devil's pisspot what you know or don't know," Roman hissed. "I want results. I joined you with the clear understanding that if and when Eileen's safety was compromised, you would either do something or I was out. Well, here we are. If you want to lead, then lead. What are you going to do?"

"Honestly, no one cares about your frat days at the Bureau with Bram," Krueger added.

Kellry placed a hand on Roman's wrist. "We'll get Eileen, but throwing Drake around isn't going to make any of this go any faster."

Like a bear, Roman released a sharp puff of air from his nose and dropped Drake. Drake stood, brushing off his pants and straightening his collar.

"You like to forget, Drake—Lane and I were there too," Kellry said, folding her arms.

Ryan blinked. Kellry had been a captive of the Bureau? That would mean she not only knew Bram but several others on his team personally. It made sense since she'd mentioned in passing she knew Mateo, but she'd changed the subject when Ryan tried to pry further.

"You were just a kid," Drake said dismissively.

"That's enough, man," Ryan finally said. "If you're going to sulk, do it somewhere someone cares."

Drake's eyes darkened as he walked over to Ryan. His collar was still askew and his hair stood in odd angles at the back of his head. Beneath his disheveled state, every muscle tensed in anger.

"You," he said, voice cool, collected. "You think a torturing, psychotic brat like you could ever get any real respect? Everyone here hates you. The only kind words or support you receive are out of fear and an ultimate goal to catch you off guard and shove a knife into your puny back."

"Oi! Don't go speaking for everyone just because your perverted crush was put in the spotlight," Krueger said.

Drake let out a dry laugh. "Of course a complete idiot like you would defend him."

Finally showing your true colors, Ryan thought. He almost smirked, but the anger he felt only allowed a grimace.

Krueger shook his head. "It's sad how delusional you are."

"Me?" Drake laughed again.

Kellry took a step forward, but Ryan shook his head at her. She pursed her lips but stayed back, eyes sparking.

Ryan could feel the denial and hate roiling within him. He could also feel the truth behind every one of Drake's words. It was beyond infuriating that every single thing he'd said Ryan had already thought about. Multiple times.

The urge to numb the shame, the anger, and every conflicting feeling rose within him like a gathering storm. A black abyss waited there. And he *wanted* it to swallow him whole. That's what was so terrifying. He *wasn't* afraid of Amadeus. He wasn't afraid of the inky tendrils that reached toward him from the recesses of his conscience. He was afraid because he *wanted* to disappear, and Amadeus could offer him that. It was bone chilling how badly he wanted it. Especially when he allowed himself to think about his past.

No. Not anymore. Not now. I made a choice. Make up for it. It'll never be enough, but make up for it.

It started here. Getting past this debilitating hatred for himself. He couldn't let it cripple him anymore. There was truth in Drake's words, and that hurt, but there were more important things. Things beyond himself. Beyond his need to hide.

"I may be psychotic, but at least I can accept that." He looked up at Drake, who towered over him. A vein twitched in Ryan's skull at the way Drake eyed him from above. Ryan closed the distance between them and tilted his head back.

"You need to accept the possibility that someone might be better at this job than you. Get over yourself, man."

Drake blinked, and Ryan took the opportunity to shove past him and plant himself solidly by Kellry's side.

Ryan didn't miss the grin and thumbs up Krueger sent his way. The action left a satisfied warmth inside him that he hadn't felt since he was a kid.

Pride.

Eyes shifted around. Everyone seemed uncertain of who to look to. The only ones who didn't seem to care at all were Treasa and Ref, as both of them remained silent during the entire exchange.

After a few long moments, Kellry let out a long breath.

"We need to weigh our options," she said. "We know Bram has taken Kala, Jack, and David. Thanks to Krueger, we've got a place for now. We should be under the radar. We need to find out if this latest move was his too. Although, if he was to retaliate, he'd typically take a more direct approach."

She tilted her head in thought. "With us spread so thin, we need to regroup. See how big this really is. Which means we need to find out if the other Homes were compromised."

The others nodded, but Roman shook his head. "We have to go after Eileen."

"Okay," Kellry said, tilting her head to the side. "Let's go then, Roman. Where to?"

He clenched his teeth. "If you don't have any real—"

"We don't know who took her, Roman. If you want to leave, be my guest. But I never said she, and every kid that was taken, isn't a priority. We have to *think* and plan. We've lost people, and honestly, if the Bureau *has* taken her, there are some options we need to consider."

"Like what?" Roman folded his arms over his large chest. "A truce."

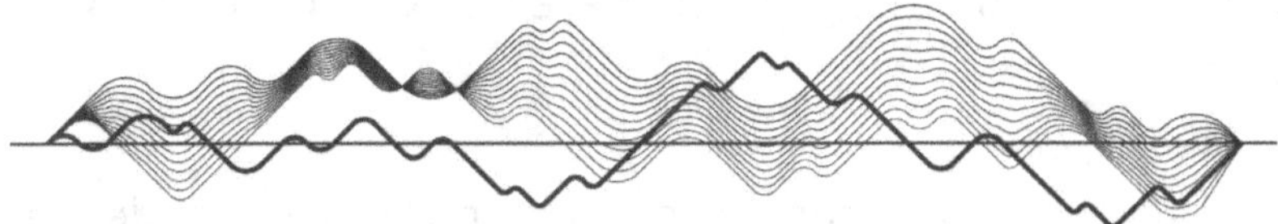

Chapter 26: Jory

When Riri's shouts and sobs broke through the night like a blaring siren, everyone had gone to her side.

Everyone except Jory and Remy, who had been told to stay and make sure Jory remained in bed.

Neither of them liked being left behind, but Remy seemed used to the treatment and simply sighed, retreating to Jory's bedside. Sinking onto the stool, she pulled out a small pocketbook and began reading.

"Get comfortable," Remy said without looking up from her book. "They'll remember us eventually."

Jory glared at the small yellow flowers on the walls. It had taken more effort than she liked to admit to sit upright. Her muscles and her mind were sluggish and brick-heavy.

Streaming off her life force had taken more of a physical toll than she'd thought possible. She looked down at her open palms and flexed her fingers, remembering the feel of her hands weaving into the complex weave of emotions. It was frightening realizing the scope of what she could do.

Some things were just within her grasp. Things that lay dormant but full of dark promises. She needed to stay away from that darkness, from anything that would lead her to use her abilities to such a degree.

Her thoughts shifted to her journey through the Tapestry. The way that large orange eye had opened up in front of her.

Found you.

Could he have meant something more than just detecting her within his consciousness?

They'd relocated while she was unconscious in case Kala and the others had been jeopardized. Then she'd woken the moment Bram "found" her...

Did he see where we are now?

She hated to be the reason they might have to leave a safe shelter so soon after arriving, but she didn't want to underestimate Bram's abilities.

If he did find me, we're all in danger.

"Remy."

The other girl looked up from her book, bangs swishing over warm eyes.

"I think Bram might know where we are. I need to talk to someone. Could you get Drake or Ref or someone and tell them to come see me?"

Remy's eyes widened, lips parting slightly. "What do you mean? Ref keeps us safe. We're pretty much a fuzzy blip to Bram."

Jory wondered exactly what Ref's ability was. It was comforting to know there were extra precautions besides locked doors, but could Ref block a telepathic connection?

"Just please...humor me."

Remy nodded warily, slipping her book back into her pocket. The moment she left, Jory felt a little better until gooseflesh rose on her arms. The hairs on her neck bristled, and she slowly looked around the empty room.

Am I being watched?

The feeling was so palpable. But when she locked onto the Tapestry, she couldn't feel anyone nearby. No other emotions but her own.

Eerie silence coated the air. With each breath, a strange tension built in her breast.

There's no one there.

Shadows shifted in the corner of her eye, and she jerked her head to the side trying to catch whoever might be there.

Nothing. No one.

It's nothing, Jory. Just relax, she told herself.

She let out a deep sigh, ready to sink back down into the bed, when a hand clamped over her mouth and a sharp point pricked her neck.

"Don't move."

The voice was male, casual. Like a friendly neighbor asking for a cup of sugar.

Ice crept down her spine as her throat bobbed against the blade. The fact that his voice was so calm caused the ice within her to compact and fracture. She knew he wouldn't hesitate to cross the thin barrier of flesh between his blade and the pulsing artery beneath.

"Get up," he said, lifting his hand from her mouth.

Jory gritted her teeth.

"Um...that's a bit"—she winced as the knife drew a bead of blood—"contradictory," she finished, trying to stay as still as possible.

He ignored her statement, pressing the blade deeper. A thin, warm trickle slid down her throat.

"Do you want me to move or not?"

"Get up," he repeated.

"I can't." She gulped as the cool metal traced an inch-long line across her skin.

"Then I will slit your throat," he said. Jory felt him shift behind her as if shrugging.

What should I do?

"I literally can't," she insisted, trying to entreat the stranger. "I'm sick."

"Get up." The shrug in his voice was so strong.

Jory closed her eyes, trying not to blink as the blade began to drive deeper. He was going to kill her. She tried to shift her legs, but they moved painstakingly slow.

"Hurry up," he said with a nudge into her back.

"I am!"

"Quiet now." His lips grazed her ear, making her shiver. He sighed, the sound heavy with irritation.

When the pressure of the knife abated, she sagged with relief, relishing the influx of air into her lungs.

A knee slammed into her back as he took her arm and yanked her off the bed. Unable to support her weight, her legs immediately buckled. Her hands failed to break her fall, and she heard the crunch of her nose breaking before feeling sharp, needle-like pain shooting up into her skull.

He crouched next to her and grabbed her braid, lifting her head until they were eye to eye.

She squinted, her face an explosion of pain. He was young. Sixteen at most. His irises were dark, almost black in the dim lighting of the room. He had a sharp, straight nose and angled eyes that assessed her silently. He cocked his head to the side.

"You were telling the truth." His eyes crinkled at the sides as he laughed almost soundlessly.

Jory winced and grimaced. The nape of her neck burned as he tightened his grip on her hair.

When his laugh trailed off, he studied her once more.

"You look very much like your brother," he said. "And yet...not at all."

Ryan, what kind of people have you been involved with?

The boy's head flicked up, and he closed his eyes, listening. He reminded her of a cat—she could almost see his ears twitch at sounds imperceptible to her. A smile crept across his face, and without hesitation, he scooped her up and leapt onto the windowsill, waiting and watching the bedroom door.

Ryan strode into the room and went rigid, jade eyes growing large and round with fear while color drained from his face.

Do something! Jory thought, frantic. Why was he just standing there?

"Move, Ryan, you—" Drake's words halted when he saw them.

Lacy curtains fluttered, catching the wind and shielding them from view for a brief moment. Jory's captor took the chance to leap from the sill and dart off into the shadows.

He wanted Ryan to see us.

A smug grin stretched across the sharp angles of her captor's face. Her head bumped against his chest, and she realized he was laughing again.

When she tapped into the Tapestry, she saw nothing. His presence was a void in the weave. She was helpless against him, unable to use her abilities in any way.

He's like that girl who came to the apartment. She'd learned since then that the girl, Kala, was a Fortress, unaffected by Psychic abilities.

He must be one too.

Ryan was afraid of this boy. She knew by the terror, the utter panic within him when he'd seen them.

She should also be afraid, but she was too tired and her head throbbed too much to think properly.

It's so weird being this close to someone and feeling nothing. Even though I can see him, he still seems invisible.

After a mad sprint, she was stuffed into an old black Corolla and they were off.

Blood ran freely down her face, and it felt like a chisel rammed into her temple with any bump or uneven surface they drove over. Krueger's Nan's was located in an old, established neighborhood surrounded by Northern California forest. The roads were steep and winding and hadn't been tarred in years.

The boy's casual demeanor never faltered as he sped down streets and screeched around corners. Jory closed her eyes, gritting her teeth at the intense pace.

Her abductor hadn't bothered to tie her up, blindfold her, or restrain her in any way. She'd even had to buckle her own seatbelt. Turning her head to the side, she watched him, noting that the smug grin hadn't left his face since he'd locked eyes with her brother.

"You're with Bram," she said, finally tilting her head back to try and slow the flow of blood from her nose. Warm and slick, it began to run down the back of her throat.

"Lean forward."

"What?"

"Lean forward. You don't want the blood draining down your throat."

"But then it's just pouring out of me."

"It's going to bleed either way. It should taper off soon enough."

"Don't you care about it getting all over your car?"

He shrugged. "Won't be the first time...or the last."

Creepy much?

Jory grimaced and leaned forward, the throbbing in her skull becoming more pronounced.

"You didn't answer my question."

"Was it a question?" he asked.

She sighed. "Fine, then who are you?"

"Mateo."

She squinted. "That doesn't answer my question."

"It does."

She glanced at him again. "What does Bram want with me?"

"He doesn't want you."

"Then why am I here?"

"You're dumber than I thought."

It was pointless to speak with him.

The bleeding tapered off, and she leaned back into her seat, breathing heavily from her mouth. Tender flesh indicated bruising around her nose and underneath her eyes. She was a proper mess—blood everywhere, from her hands to her shirtfront and pants.

After several minutes of watching the tree line speed past, she heard that quiet laughter again.

"What's so funny?" She kept her eyes on the green blur while she said it, because turning her head proved too much effort.

"Your brother's face."

She wasn't sure what answer she had been expecting, but that wasn't it. "Why?"

"He's fun to tease," he said.

She let out a harsh laugh and immediately regretted it when the chisel in her skull turned into a jackhammer.

"*This* is teasing?" she asked, wincing.

"*This* is a job. But I *waited* to tease him."

She took the effort to turn toward him, frowning. "Torment him, you mean."

"I'm sure that's how he sees it." He glanced at her, eyes appraising.

"You're not afraid," he stated.

"I don't have the energy to be afraid."

"You should be."

Jory wasn't sure how much time had passed. Somewhere on the freeway, exhaustion had beaten out the pain and she'd passed out.

How many times had she woken up like this?

"Don't try and sit up." The dark drawl crept through the space between them, seeping into her ears like worms.

"Bram," she whispered. A deep crimson hate glowed within her.

"After all this time, how did you figure it out? I left you close to catatonic."

"Screw you," she said. There was no way she'd tell him about the boy that had visited her in her mind. Not after what she'd remembered.

Bram sat in a dark leather chair in a shadowed corner of the room. Jory could make out his silhouette. His legs were the only visible part of his body, made clear by the moonlight spilling across his knees. His hands and forearms came into view as he leaned forward, resting them on his thighs, and his sleeves were rolled up to his elbows. Corded veins beneath the skin of his forearms rippled over lean muscle.

Face still concealed by shadow, his orange eyes glinted in the darkness like a predatory cat.

"Come now, Georgianna." His tone was berating, like a father speaking to an ornery child.

Don't call me that.

"Maybe you're not as good as you think you are," she said.

"Perhaps."

"What's keeping you from digging around my brain right now?"

Bram stayed silent, observing her from the shadows.

He didn't seem closed off to her questions, just selective about what and how he answered them. She tried a different approach. "What do you want?"

"To prove a point," he said.

"What point?"

"That you're all running a hopeless race. A loop that will forever bring you back to me. Drake's convinced himself his version of our cause is so much more noble, when really, we both want the same thing. Our paths will align eventually. His games are merely setbacks to the big picture, and thanks to you, I can pluck each of them up one by one."

Jory fisted her hands. *It was my fault, then. Bram found them because I went rummaging around in his mind.*

She narrowed her eyes. "And what exactly is your end goal, this path that you're all aiming for?"

He spread his hands out in a sweeping gesture. "To free the Psychics. Eliminate the Bureau."

Kill.

The word from his conscience lingered with her. His objective had been so clear. He was lying. Bram wanted revenge on the hook-nosed man, Director Brinsley. Freeing the Psychics was a front. A pretty promise to justify his methods to those who followed him.

"So why take me? I'm not a part of whatever plans you all have. I didn't come after you with the rest of them. I honestly don't know anything of any use to you."

"I chose you because Ryan betrayed our agreement."

"Because he stopped working for you?"

Bram grinned and shook his head.

The hairs on her neck prickled.

He stood, coming into the light fully. He looked just as he had in her dreams. Yet somehow more frightening. Each step he took closer to her bed made her want to flinch away, to tuck herself beneath the covers like a child.

She forced herself to meet his cold gaze, to take measured breaths.

He crouched down next to her, his face close enough for her to see creases in his forehead and flecks of silver in his hair.

"The agreement to work for me in exchange for scrambling up your brains a bit."

"What?"

"That's right," he said softly. "Ryan begged me to get inside your head. Erase strong, confident Anna, and leave Jory. A mewling, dependent nothing. Lost in torment from the death of her parents and the sea of emotions crushing her sanity."

No. Ryan said I was broken...that Bram had offered the deal to help fix me, not break me.

Her mind ran through their conversation, through the fogged memories of that night. But then...Ryan *had* lied. There had been another survivor that night, and he'd still acted like their parents were *both* dead.

She shook her head. "You're lying. He'd never do something like that."

"You know that's not true."

"I—" She gritted her teeth. She didn't know what was true anymore. "I-I won't let your words get inside my head."

"You don't have to. Not when it's the truth." A wolfish grin spread across his face.

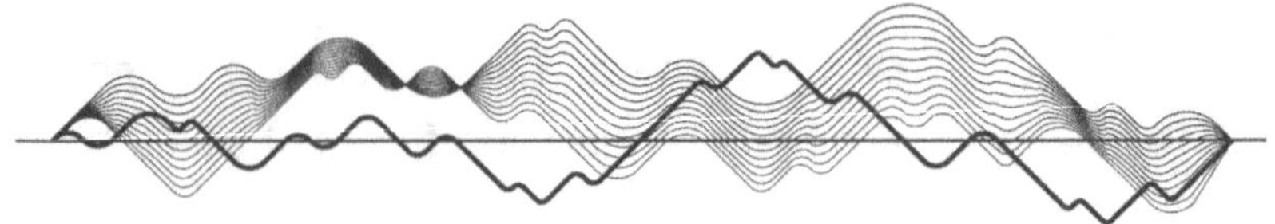

Chapter 27: Ryan

When Ryan punched the wall, his hand easily broke through. He pulled it out and punched again and again and again, crushing the sickly yellow flowers painted against the curling, plastered paper. A discordant symphony raged in his head—high, screeching notes fighting against each other.

Mateo had taken her. It was all over now. Bram would tell her. He'd tell her what Ryan had done as punishment for betraying him. These past years were for nothing. Everything he'd done had been pointless. All the lying, the sneaking, Amadeus taking up residence in the recesses of his consciousness.

All of it.

His selfish desire that they could go on being brother and sister, that she'd continue loving him, worrying over him. He'd just needed that one person.

I'm such an idiot. A self-absorbed piece of trash.

It was too much. He was so frustrated and furious with himself. Jory was in danger, and the first thing he'd thought about was her learning the truth.

It would be so easy to take the pain away—the shame. *Cut off your emotions,* the dark, inky shadow at the base of his skull whispered. *Remember?* Tendrils of slinky black fingers stretched out, pooling over his fracturing resolve. The voice seeped into his thoughts like oil into cotton. *Remember what nothing feels like?*

Ryan shuddered. He wanted to, *needed* to escape. *Just for a minute. One minute can't hurt.*

No! the other part of him shouted, sending Amadeus skittering away like a horde of diseased rats.

A raw snarl ripped from Ryan's gut to his throat as he went to punch the wall again, but a hand stopped his fist.

"Quit punchin' my Nan's daisies."

Ryan looked up at Krueger, his eyes blurred from angry tears. He clenched his teeth and hung his head, hand still fisted against Krueger's palm.

Krueger rested his other hand on Ryan's shoulder. "We'll get her back, kid."

Ryan's shoulders slumped further.

No, he would never get her back. Not now. Even if they were able to rescue her, she was lost to him.

Why didn't I just tell her? Confess when I had the chance, instead of twisting the truth?

At least then he would have come clean himself. If he'd been honest, maybe she would have forgiven him eventually. It was a slim chance, but it was a *chance*.

"Ugh, stop crying," Roman said. "And stop babying him, Krueger."

"All right, and why don't you stop moaning over Eileen." Krueger grinned at Roman's scowl then gave Ryan's shoulder a squeeze.

"He's not wrong. Get yourself together, kid," he whispered before backing away.

Kellry, Ref, Roman and Krueger had filed into Jory's room shortly after Mateo had run off with her.

Kellry leaned out the window, staring into the empty street and letting out a huff of air. Outside, the trees danced as if her breath had swept through them like a miniature gale of wind. The scent of damp earth drifted into the room, coupled with the moist air. Ryan wondered if it would rain soon.

"How did he find us, Ref?" she asked, propping herself up on the windowsill.

Ref stood in a darkened corner of the room, clenching his helmet in both hands. Ryan hadn't paid him any attention since he'd entered the room, since he was an easy person to look over.

"I don't know." The white-knuckled grip on his helmet tensed further and Ryan swore he heard bones grinding in protest.

"Jory said she thought Bram might know where we were. How did she know?" Kellry looked to Remy, who sat on the stool next to Jory's bed.

Remy shook her head. "She just knew. She was adamant I get someone."

A memory clicked in Ryan's mind and he cursed.

Kellry's dark eyes narrowed. "Spit it out, Ryan."

Scrubbing his hands through his short locks, he sucked in a long, slow breath.

"She dreamwalked."

"Wait, what?" Krueger lifted his brows. "I've never heard of another ability able to enter dreams besides mine."

Ryan nodded. "Ya, it's certainly not common, but some Empaths—strong ones—can. My mom was one of those.

But she didn't master it until she was an adult. Jory was wandering into dreams when she was a kid."

Krueger let out a whistle. "That girl might be even scarier than *you*."

"You're not wrong." Ryan's hands were shaking. If his suspicions were correct...

Like a dust devil, panic rose within him, picking up dirt and debris. It swirled and rushed, stealing his breath.

Breathe. Accept that you might never see love in her eyes again. That's fine. All that doesn't matter anymore. What matters is making it up. Changing. You can save her. That's what matters. Stop thinking about yourself.

Stop sucking.

The gathering storm settled. He had an objective, a purpose, so he zeroed in on that purpose like sunlight through a magnifying glass.

"What does that mean? So what if she dreamwalked?" Drake spoke from his darkened corner of the room. He stood, arms folded, chin tilted up. His perfectly sculpted brows arched, and Ryan almost smiled when he thought of shaving them straight off his smug face.

"It wouldn't mean anything if she dreamwalked into any of *our* minds. Well, maybe Krueger would be different. Anyway, what I'm saying is that if Jory went exploring into a mind that also had the ability to dive into another's consciousness, they might have been able to reciprocate the action."

Kellry's eyes widened. "You think she wandered into Bram's head."

"Yes."

She bit her lip, and Ryan watched as the wheels turned in her mind. "But why Bram, of all people? Do you think it was an accident?"

Ryan opened his mouth but someone else spoke over him.

"It wasn't an accident. She wanted answers," Ref said in a measured tone. He locked eyes with Ryan. "Answers she didn't get here."

Ryan looked down. He'd told Drake to keep everyone quiet. To keep Jory out of the loop, out of their plans. Out of Bram's sight.

There's nothing you can do about that now. Keep moving forward.

Ryan squared his shoulders, meeting Ref's penetrating stare.

"That's what I think too. Bram must have felt her presence and read into her own mind. That's how he found us."

Ref pursed his lips. His eyes spoke volumes. *This is your fault,* they said.

I know.

"So what do we do now? Bram's obviously making moves. He took Eileen and all those kids, and now he's coming for us," Roman said.

Kellry shook her head. "He's retaliating because we moved in on his turf, not to mention we've coaxed some of his people to our side. He found an opening and took advantage of it. Besides, he doesn't want to kidnap a bunch of kids. He wants adults, teenagers, competent people with strong abilities he can rally together to take down the Bureau."

"Kellry's right," Ryan said. "If he wanted to go against the Home, he could have done that a long time ago."

"And how do you know that?" Drake asked.

"Because he visited me there. He came in the middle of the night to my bedside just to show he could." Ryan's dreams were still haunted by those memories. Of the whispered plans for him and his sister if he didn't hold up his end of the bargain.

Krueger grimaced. "What a freaking creep."

Ryan turned to Drake. "Why are you questioning this, anyway? You said you didn't think he did it."

Drake shrugged. "You're obviously a liar. You've lied to your sister all this time, so why wouldn't you lie to us?"

The growing desire to scream at the man's obvious, idiotic grudge was beginning to reach a high point. Patience wasn't easy to master. Ryan tried his best to release the tension in his jaw before speaking.

"I have no reason to lie to you."

Drake arched his brow once more, and Ryan rolled his eyes.

This is impossible.

"But you had reason to lie to *her*?" Ref asked.

"Yes, Ref, I did! At the time, I really thought I did. Since when have you cared, anyway?"

Ref blinked before ducking his head down and staring at his helmet once more.

"We're getting off track," Kellry said. She hopped off the windowsill and strolled to the center of the room. "We need to work together to get those kids back. To get Eileen back. Bram has too many of our people for us to try to force things to go our way."

"We can't, Kell. We left Bram back then for a reason. He's not right in the head." Drake's voice took on a pleading tone.

Kellry swung out her hands in a sweeping gesture. "We have nothing, Drake! Nothing to barter with, and too few bodies to fight with. There's no way we can get everyone back now. We're sitting ducks."

"This is what he wants," Drake said.

"You think I don't know that? We've tried it your way, Drake. We've tried it on our own. We *failed*. Bram can get us in there. Sane or not, he has twice the brains of any one of us."

Drake clenched his fists, and for a moment Ryan thought he might add to the holes Ryan had created in the wall. Instead, his shoulders sagged and he nodded.

"He always said it was only a matter of time 'til we came back," Drake said. He shut his eyes and grimaced.

Soft gray light pushed through dark, low-hanging clouds, brightening the room slightly with the promise of dawn. Everyone looked to the window as a light drizzle misted from the sky.

"Pack up. We leave in one hour." Kellry marched out of the room, and Ryan couldn't help but smile.

She'd fallen into the role so easily. No one questioned her, they simply followed. Drake remained behind, staring listlessly into the dreary morning.

"It rained that day too," he said.

Ryan tilted his head. "What day?"

"The day Bram got us out."

"Of the Bureau?"

Drake nodded. "He was never the same. I never knew exactly what happened to him that day, but...he wasn't the Bram I knew after that." He shivered, turning to Ryan. Drake looked him up and down, lip twitching as if he were staring at a maggot feasting on the dead.

"What does she see in you?"

Ryan shrugged. "Beats me."

He let his own smug grin curl across his face before leaving the room, and a fuming Drake, behind.

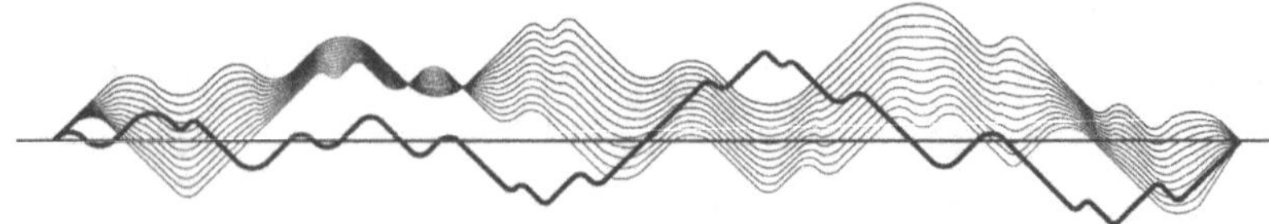

Chapter 28: Ryan

"What is *that*?"

Ryan couldn't help but agree with Lane as a proud Krueger hefted a staff-long branch. It wasn't the branch that had them blinking in confusion. It was the pair of red polka-dotted boxers tied at the top. They hung damp and limp like their hopes of getting through this day without leaving disaster in its wake.

Krueger gestured animatedly toward the boxers. "What are you talking about? It's obvious it's our flag."

"Flag," Lane said flatly.

"Ya, you know, a 'we know you kicked our butts, so please don't sic the ninja brat on us' flag."

"Aren't those supposed to be white?" Ryan asked, tilting his head back to take in the underpants as they fluttered weakly. The wind grew in strength and the drops of rain became fatter as the morning wore on.

"It *is* white," Krueger said.

"With a million red dots," Ryan said.

"What if they think we're declaring war or something?" Lane hissed.

Krueger shrugged. "Naw."

He glanced at the flag and grinned. "It's perfect."

Ryan ducked his head, hiding his grin.

"Krueger, what is that?" Kellry approached with the rest of the gang, shrugging a backpack onto her shoulder.

Ryan and Lane had followed Krueger when he ran from the car in search of a "pole." The others had taken their time walking from the supermarket parking lot where they'd left the cars.

"I told you to find some white cloth, not... Are those boxers?" Kellry asked.

Krueger inclined his head. "A pair of my silkiest."

Roman tipped his head up, examining the "flag." "You're an idiot."

Kellry waved a dismissive hand and began trekking through a stretch of maple trees. "Whatever, just bring it."

Ryan jogged after her, shrugging deeper into his black hoodie. He'd grabbed it before relocating to Krueger's Nan's and was relishing the familiar warmth. His headphones and phone still hadn't been returned to him. He'd have to remedy that soon, because the absence of his music was a crater-like hole he couldn't fill.

The damp began to seep through the polyester of his hoodie. Tilting his head back, he embraced the frigid beads of liquid as they splattered and streamed across his forehead and cheekbones. When was the last time he'd allowed himself to enjoy the rain? He took a deep, cleansing breath. Above him, a canopy of dead, orange-yellow leaves clung to spindly branches.

This particular strip of mountain maples separated a length of businesses and a large park. Bram's lair of operations lay just beyond South Bres' City Park.

The park consisted of stretches of yellowed grass, a large pond, thick-trunked trees, curving sidewalks, and one ancient jungle gym crawling with children. It was simple but well kept. Really the only clean, decent place in South Bres. There was a silent pact to keep the place up, and everyone respected it.

Drops coalesced on Kellry's clear-plastic poncho. Before they entered the park, she turned her head back, and the drops hovered around her face like dew suspended on a spider's web.

Her brows were pinched in thought, but when she caught him staring, her dark eyes brightened with a mischievous gleam.

"See something you like?" she asked with a sideways grin.

"Yes," he answered.

His straightforward reply caught her off guard and she blinked, pausing mid-stride, a soft pink glow beneath her pale skin.

Watching her reaction made him want to tease her. To grab her and kiss her slightly parted lips. He grinned, and her blush deepened.

Ever since he'd made his decision to move forward, to be better, he felt a freedom he hadn't felt since before Bram. A freedom he hadn't felt since before his parents died. And with this freedom came a sort of...permission to be the Ryan of his childhood. Bold, good-humored, even.

"Too slow." Roman pushed past them, shoving Ryan to the side. Ryan's hand twitched, itching to Slice through Roman's leg nerves and send him toppling into the thickening mud. He pictured the man squirming and cursing in the muck for a moment before sighing and letting go of the urge.

He glanced at Kellry's gloved hand and snagged it before proceeding forward. Her grip tightened in his, and the metal ring on her third finger pressed into his palm. He wondered again exactly how her abilities worked. How the friction between the rings was enough to produce such controlled flames. He remembered the strange flow of power that curled around her nerves. Once everything calmed down, he *had* to ask her about it.

Bram's base was a three-story office building crammed between an abandoned warehouse and an empty lot full of overgrown weeds. A rusted bathtub leaned against the side of the building facing the empty lot. It was filled with dirt. Parsnips, leeks, and kale sprouted in a makeshift garden from the recycled tub.

In an alley across the street, Ryan huddled with the others in the shadow of an apartment complex.

A fire escape climbed the wall beside them. Ryan eyed loose bolts in the metal and wondered if the escape would be the best route or if the residents would fall to their deaths instead of burning in a fire.

"So...do I just go out and wave it around a bit?" Krueger eyed the building, and Ryan raised a brow at the growing apprehension in the man's eyes. It was unusual to see Krueger unsettled; even when they'd almost been engulfed by a sewage wall, he'd managed to keep his cool.

"No one else is going to wave that stupid thing around," Lane muttered.

A loud screech had them all turning toward Ref, who had opted for his typical wall lean. The bottom ladder had come free of the fire escape, squealing down its track.

"I didn't do it." Ref's helmet was on, keeping him from interfering with any technology close by and tipping Bram off to their presence.

"Then what—" Ryan's eyes went wide, and he glanced up as a dark figure dropped from the steel platform above.

He landed in the midst of them, and for half a second everyone was still. Then Mateo burst into motion, sprinting toward Roman first. The large man cursed, but before he could even lift his arms in defense, the lithe boy leapt. His leg swung up and slammed back down into the crevasse between neck and shoulder.

Roman dropped like a rock.

Krueger began to wave the branch. Mateo stopped it with a wrist, ducking away to avoid being slapped by soggy boxers. Pulling the "flag" from Krueger's grip, he tossed it aside. He threw a swift jab toward Krueger's abdomen, but the man blocked it. A wild grin spread across Mateo's face.

Ryan knew how much the boy loved a challenge. Ryan had never expected that "challenge" to be Krueger.

Mateo swung his leg up again, but Krueger's forearm caught the kick. The man grunted at the impact while lifting his fist in an uppercut to Mateo's chin. Mateo flipped backward, pushing fingertips off the asphalt and landing on his feet.

"Come at me, you freaking grasshopper!" Krueger shouted.

Mateo's grin stretched wider.

Krueger lunged forward, but a swirling wall of fire halted his path. Ryan barely registered the *shing* as metal scraped against metal and Kellry stepped into the fray. Heat filled the alley and rain hissed and steamed away as it tried to drown the flame.

"That's enough," Kellry said.

It irked Ryan that he couldn't do more. If he tried anything, he'd only get in the way. But then, he wasn't the only one useless against the Fortress. Everyone else stood frozen.

"Long time no see, Kellry," Mateo said. The smile was gone, his eyes somber.

"We're coming back, Mateo. We're coming home," Kellry said.

Ryan glanced at Kellry, brows knitting downward. Exactly how much history was there between Kellry and Bram's crew? He hadn't really thought about it too deeply until now.

Mateo blinked, eyes wide. It was the first time Ryan had ever seen such an expression on his face.

Kellry's fire was fighting a losing battle as the rain turned into a downpour. She let it extinguish and walked across the space, hand extended.

Mateo snagged it and pulled her into a hug. Ryan stiffened and his jaw locked, teeth grinding together.

"Took you long enough," Mateo said.

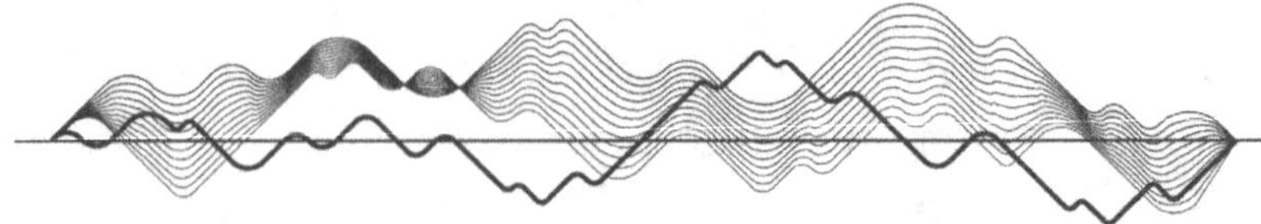

Chapter 29: Ryan

"What is that?" Mateo stared pointedly at the silken boxers lying miserably in a growing puddle.

"Don't ask," Kellry said.

"Aren't you going to come say hi, Lane?" Mateo tilted his head to the side.

Lane ignored him.

"Still upset about the crickets? C'mon, Laney, that was years ago."

She stiffened. "I could still make your blood boil."

"But you didn't."

"I knew Kellry would take care of it. She loves the spotlight, after all." Lane flicked her streaked hair off her shoulder and sniffed.

Ryan ducked his head, deep in thought. He'd noticed the first time he'd seen Kellry's flame that it worked outside the realm of Psychic ability. Lane's abilities were also in this category, so he assumed it was genetic. If they still had Momma J, he could have nullified a wide range of Psychic power. Then with Lane and Kellry on the front lines, maybe they would have stood a chance.

But then Bram had Hans, the Puppeteer. A man who could control dead bodies from a mile away. Furthermore,

Mateo wasn't the only skilled fighter on the opposing team. Rashida was behind those doors, along with a dozen thugs. Ryan had always thought of them as meatbags—that's how useful he deemed them. But then, why take the brunt of an attack when you could chuck out a few steaks to distract the dogs at your door?

"Hey friend." Mateo waggled his fingers at Ryan. "Nice to have you back."

Ryan scowled. "I'm not. Not really."

Mateo shrugged. "We'll see. I doubt that dark side of yours will stay quiet."

When Ryan didn't answer, the other boy winked at him before turning his attention to the rest of the group.

"I wondered where you got to, Roman. So you were the one who told white-braids about old Mike and the base."

Roman ignored the boy, rubbing his neck and shoulder.

Mateo winked at the large man and turned on his heel. "Come on, then, and Kell—"

Kellry met Mateo's eyes. "Yes?"

"This better not be a joke. If you Trojan Horse this thing, I won't hold back."

"You know I wouldn't lie to you."

He nodded. "What are you doing moping back there, Drake?"

"Shut up," Drake grumbled. "Let's get this over with."

Ryan couldn't help but agree.

He hung back as the others made their way across the street. Mateo was talking animatedly with Kellry. And as badly as he wanted to step in between the two, Ryan couldn't stand being next to the other boy.

When Ryan had fallen short on a job or made any kind of mistake, Mateo had been his punisher. But now, after everything, Ryan knew that the real reason he feared Mateo, the real reason he hated him so much, was because Mateo was a reflection of himself.

The way he felt about Mateo was the same way everyone else felt about Ryan. Hate, fear, and resentment.

Sure, Krueger had gotten over his initial disgust, and Momma J had been kind, but they'd never *seen* Amadeus in action. They'd only heard about him. But Kellry? Kellry had watched him for months. What was her excuse?

How can she even stomach being around me? The thought sent him spiraling deep within the pits of his mind. Guilt, self-loathing...just when he thought he could move past it.

Shut it off. Shut it all off. You can be above all this. You're better when you feel nothing.

I doubt that dark side of yours will stay quiet. Mateo couldn't have been more right.

A shoulder bumped him.

"Sorry," Sebastain mumbled.

Ryan had forgotten he was there. Sebastian, Corwin, Remy, and even Treasa had kept so quiet, hanging back at the edges of the group.

"Sebastian?"

Sebastian glanced down at him, reminding him of a baby panda staring down from the top of a stalk of bamboo. "Ya?"

Ryan shoved his hands deep in his pockets. "Are you afraid of me?"

Sebastian didn't answer right away. His lips pursed and his eyebrows pulled down in thought. "I'm afraid of parts of you."

Ryan frowned and nodded. "Fair enough."

"Not so much now, though," the tall man added quickly. "You've changed. But I'm wary. I know, I mean... Well, Jory knows too. She knows that there are things you aren't being completely truthful about."

Of course she knew. She was getting her memory back. Her abilities back. Soon Ryan wouldn't be able to hide anything from her. He winced, rubbing sweaty hands on his jeans. She was just beyond those doors.

Along with Bram.

Sebastian followed the others, but Ryan couldn't bring himself to take those last few steps.

His breath came short, and he stopped at the large, black metal door.

Shut them off, Ryan.

"Look at us. Couple of pansies."

Krueger had hung back as well. His hands were deep in his pockets, and he kicked a stray pebble off the cement entryway.

He glanced sideways when Ryan forced out a dry laugh.

"What are you afraid of?" Ryan asked. "You're a lot more capable than I thought you were."

A rueful grin lit Krueger's features. "That should probably hurt my feelings, but I get too much enjoyment out of people underestimating me."

The smile quickly faded, and he shrugged. "Let's just say people with any sort of mind powers make me want to wee my pants a little."

Ryan frowned. "Wait, but...aren't *you* in that category?"

"Yup."

"Then—"

"C'mon." Krueger bounced on his toes, shook out his hands, and puffed out two quick bursts of air before pushing the door open. Ryan took a step back, but Krueger's hand shot out the door and yanked him inside.

Vinegar and lime assaulted his nose. A special cleaning solution concocted by Hans. The scent permeated the air and clung to the dark, moody gray walls. Ryan found it ironic that a man who controlled dead bodies found so much joy in creating and implementing homemade cleaning products.

Ryan and Krueger trailed behind the group as Mateo led them down a narrow hallway and up a flight of stairs.

Ryan knew exactly where they were going. Mateo was reporting back, which meant they were headed toward Bram's office. Ryan blinked in surprise when they passed by the black double doors and stopped in front of another door.

Ryan had never been in Bram's bedroom and didn't hold the slightest desire or curiosity to change that fact. Two slabs of muscle stood outside the door. Nick and Brody...or Dick and Cody? He wracked his brain, but he'd never cared enough to remember their names properly. Never cared about anyone or anything besides Jory. He had always viewed himself as above all the meatbags filling the spaces in Bram's lair.

They're people too.

No, they're fodder, slop to spread in the troughs when the pigs come squealing to the lion's den.

Amadeus's voice was getting louder and more sentient by the day. Ryan shivered at the malice seeping out like black slime from the base of his skull. He rubbed the nape of his neck in an effort to muzzle the monster.

When Mateo jerked a nod, the two men moved aside, albeit shooting furtive glances as the group filed into the small space. Ryan trailed in at their heels but halted in the doorway, seeing Jory sitting up in bed.

"What's all this?" Bram asked with raised brows.

"They're throwing in the towel, Bram," Mateo said, waving a hand toward the group.

Ryan hovered in the doorway as Bram placed his palm on Drake's forehead and closed his eyes. Bram was sifting through Drake's mind. Drake winced, but then Bram grabbed Drake's forearms with a fierce grin on his face.

"I knew you'd come back. Now all this foolishness can stop."

Drake jerked away.

"All this foolishness? How many times have you almost killed us, Bram? How many times have you driven innocent Psychics within an inch of their sanity? Used pawns like him"—he jerked a thumb toward Ryan—"to torture and coerce others to your side?"

Bram rolled his eyes. "If you've come back only to whine, then go. You left, then did everything you could to get in my way. Besides, I never got close to killing *you*."

Drake gritted his teeth. "Why?"

"That should be obvious. You and Damon. You're all I ever had. We're brothers, the three of us. With bonds deeper than any bound simply by blood.

"You're not the man I knew within the walls of that place," Drake replied. "You lost something that day, Bram."

Bram nodded. "I did." He cocked his head to the side and grinned slowly. "Empathy isn't as important as you seem to think."

Drake's eyes widened, and he took a step back. Ryan could see the fear in each rigid muscle on the man's face.

Ryan didn't blame him. Bram was pretty much a borderline psychopath.

So many things clicked into place. The nonchalant expression he wore while watching others in pain, the cold, calculated decisions, and the complete lack of remorse.

Ryan knew all too well what it was like not to have empathy. Bram was wrong. Empathy was everything. He knew the staggering emotions that came when he switched between feeling it and not. How drastically his decisions changed when he could connect emotionally with the people around him.

Jory's stare bore into his head like a termite on steroids. He scratched his forehead and fidgeted slightly, shifting from foot to foot.

Look at her, you idiot. Isn't this what you've been waiting for? A chance to come clean? Tell her about the real deal with Bram. Tell her!

Not with all these people. They don't need to know. They have nothing to do with it. Besides, does it even matter now? Bram must have told her everything anyway, and if he didn't, wouldn't knowing just hurt her?

For a moment, Ryan didn't realize the last strain of thought had been the whisperings of Amadeus.

"Shut up," he mumbled, digging his nails into the base of his skull.

"Is it true?" Jory's voice rang out in the small space.

Ryan flinched.

There's no going back now.

He nodded, head low.

The air in the room grew tight, and Ryan felt a tangible shift in the energy around him.

It's Jory.

The realization triggered memories from his childhood. When she was young and hadn't gotten a grip on her abilities yet, he could feel the waves rippling and heightening the emotions of those around her to match her own.

Everyone turned to Ryan, hackles raised.

"You're admitting it, then? Admitting that you purposefully had Bram go into my mind to ruin me and my ability."

"Yes," he whispered.

"Why?" The desperate plea tugged Ryan's gaze to meet hers. He wished he hadn't when he saw the betrayal there. "What possessed you into thinking that was okay?"

The air was oxygen-less. His vision blurred and his breaths came out in rapid huffs. She had to understand. The way she was looking at him now, it was almost identical to that day.

"You have to understand." Ryan blinked as sweat stung his eyes. "If you had remembered what happened, you would have abandoned me that day. I couldn't lose you. Not after losing them."

"What do you mean, *them*?"

Jory's eyes grew wary and she jerked her head toward Bram.

"What did you do?" Her fingers clutched the blankets, and a new wave of malice rippled through the room.

Bram grinned and held up his hands.

"What I needed to do. To get what I wanted."

Ryan glanced between the two.

What are they talking about? What the heck do they mean?

He was missing some core detail.

"What—" he began.

Jory turned to him once more. "Tell me what happened that night, Ryan. Everything you remember."

Ryan's gaze shifted to the sea of eyes around him. His foot twitched, aching to double back and run.

"I can't." The two words choked him as they left his throat, tasting of bile. Jory's ice-blue eyes pierced his, and he cracked.

You don't have to face their judgment. Her judgment. When you're alone, you can face it alone. Like you always have.

"Ryan!" Jory's voice cut through Amadeus's purr.

Ryan dug his nails deeper into the back of his head.

Shut up! Shut up, shut up, shut up!

"I killed them. I killed Mom and Dad." The words fell from his lips like wilted leaves.

No one spoke. Jory's mouth parted slightly, and she was silent for a moment as his words registered.

"That's what you've thought all this time?" Her eyes shifted to Bram momentarily, poison leaking from her gaze. She shook her head. "No, Ryan. You didn't. You didn't kill them."

It was as if Jory had a string tied to her tongue as her words pulled the hysteria up from his gut. He clenched his teeth, holding back the mounting emotion.

"You saw me kill them," he spoke through his teeth, his jaw tightening further.

She shook her head again. "The beginning, Ryan."

His eyes pleaded with hers, but the ice in her gaze only hardened. The sea of eyes drowned him in their judgment. He examined the black laces woven through the silver brackets of his sneakers.

You don't have to feel the pain, the guilt.

His heart was pounding so hard as brick after crushing brick was piled onto his chest.

It's okay, Ryan, let go.

The bright-white web of nerves lit up behind his mind's eye. They branched out, a great tree within, slim roots reaching and stretching over every muscle, every vein. His heightened emotional nerves pulsed bright, and his hands began to shake. He didn't remember accessing his ability, but...it was so close now.

It's okay.

Just a little...

The relief was staggering. A long sigh pulled from his lips, the breath seeming to coil and disperse at his feet.

A little more.

He dimmed the nerves further.

His muscles relaxed and his fingers finally retracted from their claw-like grip on the base of his head.

"We were eating dinner." His voice was cool and even. He was going to sound so callous. But that didn't matter now. What mattered was that he was floating in the void, floating outside the sea of eyes.

"A hook-nosed man walked in. Then people filled the room like ants and grabbed us. They grabbed Mom by her hair and started dragging her. I wanted them to leave, to get their hands off of her. I lashed out with more power than I'd ever used before. Blood went everywhere. Dad had moved to help Mom at the same moment. I killed them, and several others that were...in the way..."

Ryan flexed his hands. His blood turned lukewarm, a feeling he always got when he was this close to completely turning off his emotions.

"Bram came, then. He knew the hook-nosed man. They made some sort of deal. He walked off with Aiden. And Bram got me and you. You looked at me like I was, like I was rotten—"

"Wait."

Even in his current state, Jory's quavering voice caught his attention.

"Say that name again."

"What name?"

"Who did Brinsley take?" Jory's voice had grown even more frantic.

"Brinsley?"

"The hooked-nosed man! Who did he take?"

"Aiden."

She didn't remember him. I thought she had already. I thought he'd be the first thing she'd remember.

Jory sat still for a long moment, mouthing the name as if she were tasting something she'd forgotten the flavor of. A lone tear ran down her cheek, then another, and another, until they were flowing in earnest down her tanned skin. Sebastian was at her side in a moment, taking her hand in his.

This is wrong. Me standing here like this...feeling next to nothing. It's wrong.

It was so hard to care.

"Keep going," her voice broke.

"Jory—"

"KEEP GOING!"

At her outburst, the waves of her sorrow, of her anger, broke some of the others down. Tears flowed down Sebastian's, Roman's, and Kellry's faces, laden by the strength of her emotions that pulsed through the air, filling them all.

Ah, there it was. The look he'd been waiting for.

That's right, Kellry. This is what I am. Get a good taste.

Finally, the others began shuffling out of the room, unable to withstand the tangible emotions strangling them.

Sebastian didn't move from her side, despite openly sobbing. Bram stood unaffected, one eyebrow raised.

"Tell me why it was so important to steal him away from me!"

"You would have gone after him," Ryan answered.

"Dang straight I would have!" Jory took a few deep breaths. "Finish. What do *you* think happened next?"

"Bram told me he'd be willing to just take me if I did everything he asked. He said he could change your memories, create a new reality for you. You wouldn't remember what I'd done. I didn't know that changing your memories would cripple your abilities so much. But it was done, and there was nothing I could do."

"You idiot."

Ryan blinked.

"Turn them back on."

Ryan's finger twitched. She knew, of course she knew he'd numbed himself.

"No."

"Do it, Ryan, or so help me—" She clenched her fists and took in another deep breath.

"Why?"

"Because you need to feel it, Ryan. When I tell you this, you need to feel every last bit of it."

He shook his head and she growled, thrusting her hands out in front of her. Her fingers weaved through a strange series of patterns that were hauntingly familiar.

Cat's Cradle. Their mother had used the child's game to help Jory hone her abilities.

He felt it then.

No, wait.

She was accessing the Tapestry. She was going to bring them back. Every last horrible, sickening emotion.

She didn't coddle him. They flared to life with a lurch that sent Ryan to his knees.

"Why would you listen to him? You should have told me, Ryan. You should have told me from the start." She took a deep breath. "You didn't kill them, Ryan."

Ryan's world spun. It couldn't be true. She was wrong. He remembered it so vividly. He relived it almost every night. How could she say that wasn't his reality? That night defined Ryan, down to his fingertips, to the blood that pumped through every vein.

"You're wrong!" He pulled at his hair and curled into himself.

"No, I'm not. I've pulled apart every piece that ego-trip sewed in there. I know the truth."

A soft chuckle came from Bram. "Do you. You sure about that, Anna?"

"Don't you call me that." Then suddenly, she grinned. A sinister smile Ryan had never seen on his sister's face before.

"Yes, I *am* sure, Bram. And I think that scares you a little. I threw you off your game that night. You didn't mean to leave me that bad off. But I fought back. I fought back, and you screwed it up, jumping out of my mind before you could make the seams seamless."

Bram frowned, and Ryan froze.

Could she be right? If she was right, then that meant Bram had gotten into his head first.

Everything was crumbling, falling like an avalanche of stone and debris. He tried to numb himself, but Jory was still in control.

"Ryan, listen to me. Dad isn't dead."

Her words didn't register. He shook his head.

"Dad isn't dead," she repeated.

Yes he is.

"Brinsley, the hook-nosed man. He shot Mom, then he took Dad. He would have taken us too, but Bram came and forced Brinsley to leave us behind."

"No... No, I killed them. I killed them and then I had Bram kill you. He killed Anna and I was left alone anyway." Ryan hugged himself then felt another set of arms wrap around him.

Kellry.

He jerked away.

"What are you doing!"

She still had tears coursing down her face.

"Ryan—" The tenderness in her voice undid him. She reached toward his face, but he slapped her wrist away.

"What's wrong with you! I'm disgusting, Kellry. Complete waste."

He had to get out of there. She was insane to look at him like that. His brain couldn't process what was happening in the room. So he did the only thing he could think to do.

He ran.

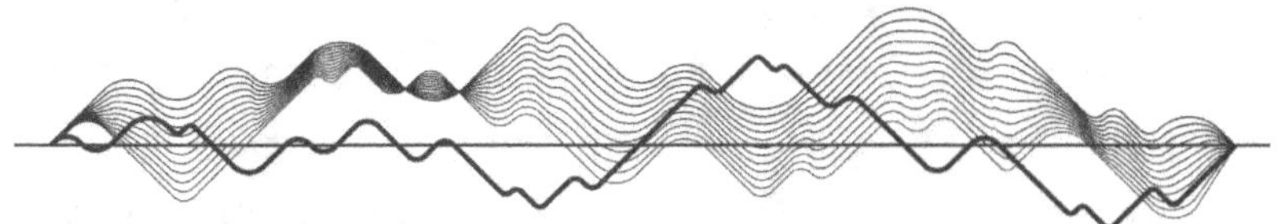

Chapter 30: Jory

Aiden. His name was Aiden. The moment the name left Ryan's lips, Jory's heart lurched.

But...she had lied. She hadn't completely sorted out her mind yet. Even after hearing his name, it was difficult to grasp onto the memories. Anything that included Aiden remained fuzzy, and any words they may have shared blended together in a muffled undertone.

Sebastian's sniffles filled the room.

"Is this h-how it's always b-been to you?" he asked. "It's so overwhelming."

"What are you talking about?"

"Your emotions, Jor. They're digging into me like rabid cats." Sebastian's face fell into his hands as he sobbed.

Shoot. He was right, but she had the opposite problem. Now that she could block out others' emotions, hers were spilling out all over the place.

She used to be so good at this. Having to master something she'd already mastered years ago was beyond frustrating. It should have been like riding a bike: Jump back on, start pedaling, and she'd find her balance. Maybe a slight wobble here and there, but that was expected.

Jory felt like she was jumping on the bike and pedaling, but instead of a slight wobble, every time she started gaining momentum she would crash into a pebble that would hurl her off the bike, down a hill, and into next week.

Bram turned to leave. Kellry was already gone, chasing after Jory's poor idiot of a brother.

"Why can't I remember him?" Jory asked Bram before he left. "Even now. What did you do?"

Bram shot a smug look over his shoulder. "Aiden was the key to all your memories, Jory. He'd been there from the beginning. The boy next door. Amazing how such rare, powerful Psychic families ended up being neighbors."

He grinned at her blank stare. "You're right about one thing. You did fight back. Harder than anyone before you. Your ability is really something special. If Brinsley had known, there's no way he would have let you go."

Turning on his heel, Bram faced her once more, his hands slipping into his pockets. He leaned casually to one side.

"I couldn't have you running off after your father and that boy. You would have fallen straight into Brinsley's lap. So I yanked out the person that would unravel everything inside you."

"And Ryan? You couldn't think of something even minutely less horrible than having him kill his own parents?"

"Not anything that would have made him so perfectly malleable to my needs."

"You're sick."

Bram shrugged. "Perhaps."

"You know what I think?"

Bram cocked his head. "No." He smiled. "But it wouldn't be too difficult for me to find out."

Jory returned the smile. "But that's just it, isn't it? It *would* be difficult. I'm more than you can handle."

We both are. Or else why would he go through such lengths to emotionally cripple Ryan the way he has?

"Your point?"

"My point is that I thoroughly hate you, Bram. More than I ever thought I could hate someone. And it seems like it would be all too easy for me to rid you from this planet."

His features remained completely impassive, but when Jory reached out to the Tapestry, she could see the threads of fear and anger flare.

"So you're going to kill me, then?"

"Jory!" Sebastian pleaded. "You can't do that. Even justified, you can't—"

Jory held up a hand, silencing her friend.

"No, I'm not. At least not yet."

"How kind of you to postpone my execution."

"I'm holding off because, believe it or not, we have the same goal."

"And that is?"

"Brinsley."

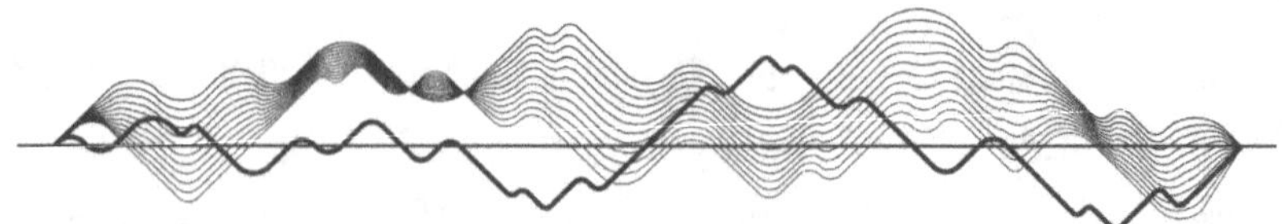

Chapter 31: Ryan

"Oof!" Ryan doubled over, grabbing his midsection.

"Your swings are too wide, kid."

Ryan hardly heard Krueger's advice over a mad coughing fit.

"Did you have to hit me that hard?" he asked, sucking in mouthfuls of air.

"Don't whine, or do you wanna sound like that douchebag baby?" Krueger danced from foot to foot and rolled his shoulders.

Ryan knew he meant Drake and shook his head while preparing his footing again.

"Good choice." A devilish grin split Krueger's face as he went in for the attack. Ryan threw up his arms, wincing as fists met his forearms.

A week had passed since they'd settled into Bram's lair. Ryan had completely avoided Jory and everyone else by locking himself away in an abandoned office space. It had taken three days to drag himself back out of the blissful nothing that beckoned him twenty-four seven.

Amadeus had become uncharacteristically silent since Ryan had given in. He wasn't sure if he should feel happy or wary about that.

Plus, facing the truth was practically impossible since he wasn't one hundred percent sure what the truth was.

His memories hadn't changed when Jory had told him what really happened that night all those years ago. Every awful, guilt-ridden feeling still clung to his psyche. Until Krueger came pounding on his door. He was the only one Ryan would respond to. There was just something about the big idiot that Ryan connected with. So on the fourth day, he was dragged from a pile of empty water bottles and half-eaten meals with an invitation to box.

Hitting the leather bag proved strangely cathartic. Ryan beat the thing until every bit of his energy was spent and he was left leaning against it, panting and sweating. After getting down decent form, Krueger started fighting him straight on. The man was ruthless, and Ryan went to bed with muscles screaming and bruises blossoming over every inch of his tiny frame.

"You need to talk to her, Ryan."

"Who?"

Krueger rolled his eyes. "Well technically, both the ladies in your life need some solid attention."

Ryan gritted his teeth, dodging a swing before it clipped his side. He went in with an uppercut, but Krueger batted the punch away like a cat swatting a ball of yarn.

"I can't."

"Why not?"

"Jory's in the thick of planning something with Bram." Ryan scowled. "How she can breathe the same air as that guy is beyond me. If I go near him, I swear I'll kill him."

"And Kellry?"

Ryan's defense faltered, and Krueger's fist kissed his jaw, sending him sprawling. Ryan cursed and spat red when his mouth filled with blood. His tooth had cut into the inside of his cheek.

"Kellry deserves better," Ryan said.

"Pretty sure that's up to her, mate." Though Krueger offered a hand and pulled Ryan up, he only landed in the exact same spot seconds later. Ryan threw an arm over his face and groaned.

"This is hopeless. I'm too small. I'd be pulverized by a twelve-year-old with any skill."

"He's right, you know. You can't teach him the same way you were taught."

Rashida leaned against the doorframe. She wore a white T-shirt tucked into form-fitting, high-waisted black pants. Her thick black hair was pulled up into a high ponytail.

Krueger's grin changed into something almost predatory. The man had it bad for the dark-skinned beauty and didn't care who knew it.

"Why don't you show me how, gorgeous?" He beckoned her forward. "How would a smaller opponent get the best of me?"

Ryan groaned again. She was hardly smaller than Krueger. Long-muscled legs strode straight past his mentor and over to Ryan. She crouched down.

Ryan eyed her warily. She'd avoided him before now. Well, that wasn't completely true. When Bram had first recruited him, she'd taken him under her wing. But over time, she'd pulled away until she began to ignore him completely.

"Stop trying to get a headshot. Aim for where you can reach." She smacked Krueger's midsection, and he wheezed. When she aimed for his crotch next, he quickly shielded the area.

"I think he gets the idea," Krueger said.

She cocked a hip and lifted her eyebrow slightly. "I think he'd like a demonstration."

"I'll let you demonstrate all you like *later*," he answered.

Rashida stared him down, queen of nonchalance. Unfazed, Krueger met her gaze with a coy, sideways grin.

"Can I go now? I feel like I'm ruining the mood," Ryan said from the floor.

"No, you stay, Ryan." She crouched next to him again. "It's good to see that you're not running away anymore. I can't stand people who refuse to face the consequences of their actions."

She shot a glance at Krueger and whispered, "Try to get in a good kick to the nuts for me."

She ruffled his hair before leaving.

"That woman is my woman," Krueger said after watching her leave.

"Sure, Krueger." Ryan stared at the drop ceiling—monotonous tiles interspersed with foggy lights that made him feel groggy if he looked too long.

Krueger sat next to Ryan and grinned. "She might not know it yet, but it's only a matter of time."

"Sure, Krueger."

Krueger smacked him on the head. "Shut up."

Ryan rubbed his head and laughed. "I don't know what you're thinking, man, but Rashida likes to fly solo."

"Not for long."

"Last time I checked, she didn't have a tag on her butt with your name on it," Ryan said.

Krueger grinned. "That's an idea! Hey, what do you think she would do if I slapped a sticker with my name on her butt?"

"She'd murder you."

They laughed and Krueger clapped a hand on Ryan's shoulder.

"All right kid, I'm out." He pursed his lips. "She's not wrong—you'll have more power if you aim for what you can reach. At least until you're skilled enough to try other things."

Ryan nodded and Krueger saluted him.

"Think about what I said before," he said over his shoulder while striding out. Ryan wondered if he was going to try another pass at Rashida.

He shook his head. *Dude has a death wish.*

Silence clogged the stagnant air like a damp rag in a urinal. Being alone sucked. His mind spiraled and his chest tightened.

Think about what I said before.

"I don't want to think about it," he muttered, throwing an arm over his eyes.

Bram and the others were going to take a shot at the Bureau.

She's going to go after him. Aiden and...Dad.

His dad was alive. He still couldn't believe it. Every time he started to feel a bloom of relief, of joy, the false memories would claim his mind.

An image formed behind closed lids. A body sprawled over his mother's still form, blood leaking from countless slashes. His father had died. He was dead. Ryan had killed him. He'd lived with that guilt for years. The nightmare refused to let him go.

What do I do now?

Everything in his life had revolved around keeping Jory safe and keeping her from learning the truth.

That had gone south. And if the Anna side had anything to say about it, there was no way Ryan would be able to keep her from running off into the most dangerous place in New Bres.

What do I even call her now? She's not Anna, but she's certainly not Jory either. She got angry at Bram for calling her Anna, but was that because she didn't want to be called that? Or because she hates Bram's guts?

Ryan scrubbed his hands through his hair. He was still getting used to how short it was. Kellry had done a pretty decent job on it.

He cursed. He couldn't decide if she was sincere or insane. What he *did* know was that she deserved better than what he had to offer. Where had he gotten off thinking any different?

What do I do?

Didn't you already decide that? Make up the difference, be better. Live the rest of your life paying an impossible debt because that's all you can do.

That's right. Just because the truth was out didn't mean his goal had to change. If anything, it had more meaning. Everything was out in the open now, and despite feeling like a garbage human, he felt an odd sense of freedom. Suddenly, his life was open to do whatever the heck he wanted.

I could run away, live the rest of my life feeding homeless people or adopting orphans or something.

He shook his head.

No. I actually care about these idiots.

If they were going into the house of psycho-bird-nose-man, then that meant he was going too.

Jory probably doesn't have her head on straight. I know mine is barely staying hinged. He took a moment to tentatively poke around in the back of his mind. He'd thought if he let himself start going numb again, Amadeus would battle for control, but the alter was nowhere to be found.

It was too convenient. There was no way Amadeus would have given up so easily. The brief illusion of freedom crumbled away like a stale saltine cracker in tomato soup, and the soggy, pathetic thought bobbed around in his mind until he tossed it away.

Idiot, he told himself. *I'll never be free.*

Of course.

Ryan huffed a sigh into his large bowl of tomato soup.

The lounge area consisted of several round tables paired with mismatched chairs and stools. Ryan sat alone in the farthest corner of the room. His chair was more like a small sofa. He leaned back against the faded gray upholstery, knees up to his chin with the lukewarm soup cradled against his chest.

Momma J and Riri sat at a table on the other side of the room. The Shield waved him over, but Ryan shook his head. Momma J shrugged and turned back to Riri, laughing at something she said.

It was good to see that Momma J and the others were okay. The moment the truce was made, Bram had reversed his work on Amare. Kala took him and left the next day, claiming she was leaving New Bres for good.

Lucky.

A dish clattered onto the table in front of him. He fumbled with his bowl, soup sloshing precariously.

"What the—"

Ryan clamped his mouth shut as Kellry sat directly across from him.

"I made you grilled cheese. Eat it."

"I have soup," he muttered.

She lifted a brow. "If you get any skinnier, Hans might mistake you for a corpse and try to add you to his undead army."

Ryan glanced at his bony wrists.

She's not wrong.

It was the most massive grilled cheese he'd ever seen. Thick slices of crusty golden bread attempted to house generous slabs of cheese. It spilled out of the edges in golden, gooey puddles. Ryan set his bowl of soup down and took a bite of the sandwich. It was delicious, but eating under Kellry's scrutinous gaze made him chew fast and swallow too soon. He coughed and thumped his chest several times before speaking.

"Kellry, I don't think—"

She shook her head and leaned back comfortably in her chair. "I'm not going anywhere. You finally crawled out of your rat's den, and I'm going to say my piece."

"Say your piece?" Ryan couldn't help the twitch in his lip. It wasn't even funny, but her earnest seriousness had him itching to smile. He took another bite to mask the urge. The crunch of the toasted bread was beyond satisfying.

She's insane, remember? She likes me, the garbage human. But then, maybe we could make it work? Buy a cute little house with padded white walls on the inside. I could help her into her straightjacket in the mornings, and she could watch me as I smack my head endlessly against the wall. It could totally work.

"Ryan, I've known a lot of awful people. Legit, off the wall, nasty sacks of humanity." Kellry pointed to Ryan. "You're not one of those people."

Ryan took a swig of milk. "Heh. What makes you so sure?"

"When I first saw you, you were in the middle of interrogating someone for Bram." She paused, biting her lip and looking away. After taking a deep breath, she met his eyes. "I had orders to kill you, Ryan."

Ryan's lips parted, and he took in a sharp breath.

She leaned forward, resting her chin on her arms. "Ya, I've killed people. Suddenly you aren't so bad, huh?"

"But, I *have*..." he trailed off. No, he hadn't, if Jory was right. He'd never killed anyone.

She grinned sadly. "You were helping Bram poach and torture people left and right with absolutely no remorse in your eyes. Our people were so afraid of you that any action against Bram came to a standstill. But you were also the only one who didn't live here with Bram. You walked home alone every night, the perfect target."

Ryan leaned toward her, closing some of the distance between them. "What changed your mind?"

"I followed you. But while you were walking home, you stopped suddenly. It was so weird. Everything about you changed in a moment. Your shoulders sagged, and your hands began to shake. And then you made this noise like a moose being stabbed in the gut."

Ryan snorted. "That's attractive."

"More like pathetic."

Ryan flicked a crumb off his plate. "I'm totally seeing how you fell for me now."

She shook her head, stretching her arms back. "Naw, that didn't happen until after we met in person."

Ryan perked up. "Really? When exactly—"

She waved her hand, her silver ring catching the gleam of the dull, luminescent lights. "That's not the point. That moment showed me there was more to you than some dead-eyed psycho."

Ryan rolled his eyes. "Thanks."

She grinned. "You're welcome. Anyway, I kept my eye on you after that, and I found out pretty soon that you were just being an idiot. I knew if I could get you and Jory away from Bram, you'd help us."

"Psh. Just being an idiot?"

She nodded.

"That's putting it lightly," he said.

"It's true."

Ryan held her gaze a moment longer, then slumped back into his chair with a sigh.

"So…" Kellry gave him a pointed look.

"So what?"

She folded her arms across her chest. "So are you done ignoring me now?"

She's going to hate me.

"I'm no good for you."

Her hands fisted and she leaned forward. "Ryan—"

"Listen, please. I like you, Kellry, more than you know, but I'm not right. Like, I'm not a whole person, you know? What I'm trying to say is… I need time to fix all"—he gestured to himself—"this. So to answer your question—no. I'm not going to ignore you anymore, but I can't be what you want me to be…with you. Am I making any sense?"

"You are. Which is annoying because I actually have to respect that." She groaned, then stood. "Finish that sandwich. It was made with frustration. Also, don't expect me to back off that easily. If you can't figure out how to 'fix yourself,' or whatever, then you're just going to have to deal with the fact that I don't care if you're broken."

Ryan couldn't help the wry smile as he watched Kellry's slim form glide away. Frustration tasted dang good, so he didn't have any issues finishing the sandwich.

When the last bite was gone, he sighed.

I can't put it off any longer.

No guards stood outside Bram's bedroom door, just Treasa.

Why is she here?

Her leaf-green eyes narrowed. "Get lost."

"*You* get lost." Ryan reached for the door handle.

"Hey!" She snatched his arm as the door pushed open, and they stumbled through.

Immediately, he was grabbed by his shirt front and shoved against the wall. His breath left him in one mighty swoosh. Ryan accessed his abilities, and a bright, glowing nerve tree bloomed in his opponent's body. He Sliced through shoulders and knees. The other boy crumpled with a loud thump, and Ryan's feet touched the ground once more. He bent over, coughing, hands gripping his knees.

"Ryan, I wasn't expecting you."

Padraigin's orange curls spilled around his head.

"Padraigin? What the heck were you thinking?"

Padraigin grunted, trying to sit up without the use of his arms or feet. Ryan's eyes widened when the other boy managed it with relative ease.

Guy's got some solid core.

"Thought you were someone else."

Ryan fidgeted. Padraigin had been his mentor—had looked out for him before he ditched Bram.

"Padraigin, what—"

The door creaked and Padraigin froze, eyeing the door. Ryan lifted a brow and glanced back as well. Treasa stood awkwardly, gaze glued to the floor. When no one appeared, Padraigin gave a sheepish grin.

"Do you mind?" Padraigin eyed his arms and legs.

"Oh, sorry. Just a sec." Ryan reversed his handiwork, reviving the nerves once more.

Padraigin shook out his arms as he stood and clapped a hand on Ryan's shoulder. "You've changed."

"Not enough," Ryan said, looking away.

Padraigin squeezed his shoulder. "Hey, don't be too hard on yourself. I know what it's like to be tied to another's will. To follow orders."

"It doesn't excuse what I've done," Ryan said.

Padraigin's grip tightened further, almost painfully.

"Ya, I guess not," he replied after a long moment.

"See you around." Releasing Ryan's shoulder, he strolled out. The older boy didn't spare a glance for Treasa, but Ryan swore he could feel energy between the two. It was in that moment that he noted how their irises shared the same shade of leafy green.

Treasa ducked her head and scurried off, heading the opposite direction from Padraigin.

Weird. Why was he in here?

Nothing was out of place, at least as far as Ryan could see. He glanced from the simple desk to the bed, but Jory wasn't here.

I wonder if she ever knew this was Bram's room? They must have set her up properly somewhere else.

"Need something?"

Ryan spun. Bram's orange eyes glinted, a large, lopsided grin displayed on his angled face.

"If you're looking for your sister, she's been moved to the third floor."

Ryan brushed past him.

"It's good to have you back with us." Bram's words echoed after him.

Once he was well away, Ryan muttered, "I'm not *with* you."

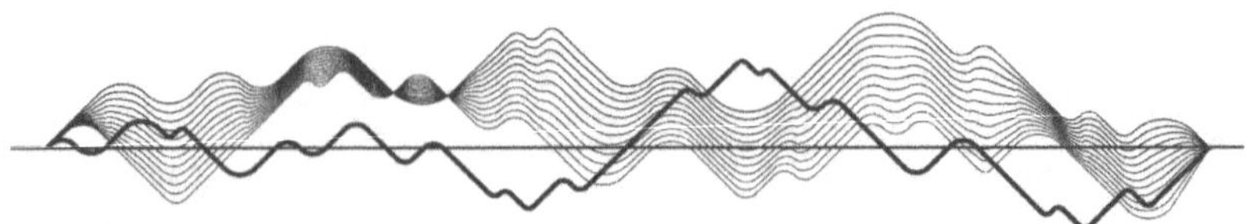

Chapter 32: Jory

"Someone messed with the feed on the cameras in your room and office." A short man hunched over a keyboard, tapping keys like a master pianist in the midst of a concerto. His concentration reminded her of days past, when the high streaming notes of Ryan's violin echoed through the house—his eyes closed as he moved with the music.

However, this man had none of Ryan's grace. His neck was almost nonexistent, and he gave Jory the impression of an old, fussy troll.

"Yes, Mike, I know. I've got it under control." Bram gestured toward Jory. "I want to hook her up."

Mike's fingers halted and twitched. He peaked over his shoulder, eyes bright. "Really?"

Bram nodded.

Jory flinched when Mike squealed with delight. "Just a moment, I have to get her ready."

For a moment, Jory thought he meant her, but instead of coming toward her, he shuffled over to a giant metal lounge chair.

Mike never left his stool, allowing the wheels and his pattering feet to glide him around the room.

"Who's this guy again?" Sebastian whispered in her ear.

"Bram's technician," she replied. "Apparently he used to work for the Bureau."

Sebastian was eyeing strange devices behind glass cupboards. "Why'd he come work for Bram?"

Jory shrugged. "Beats me."

"I don't like this," Sebastian said. They both grimaced at Mike's coos and hushed mutterings as he flipped switches and adjusted straps.

Jory grabbed his hand. "I know, but it's our best shot at taking on the Bureau."

He squeezed her hand, but his brows pinched down with worry. "Didn't Aiden say not to contact him again until you remembered everything?"

She looked at her feet. "Yes, but who knows how long that will take on my own? I need to get him and Dad out now."

"And Brinsley?"

"Brinsley's a dead man." The harshness in her voice caused Sebastain to take a step back.

"Jory, I don't think—"

"All right, she's ready." Mike caressed the chair, waving Jory over with an impatient hand.

Jory slid onto the black metal. It was as hard as it looked, and the cold bit into her thighs.

"Couldn't have put some cushions on her?" she asked with a half grin.

"They would interfere with the readings," Mike said dismissively.

He lifted a black circlet and slipped it over Jory's head, adjusting it until it fit snuggly. It hugged her temples, and a few hairs were pulled tight. She reached a hand up to fix them, but Mike swatted it away.

"Don't touch."

"I just—"

"Don't touch." Mike pushed her shoulders until she lay flush against the narrow back of the chair. Then he slipped a pair of thin black bracelets onto her wrists and pulled down two armrests. Pushing off the floor, he rolled across the room to where a monitor and keyboard were attached to an overhanging silver bar. Mike grabbed it and shuffled back over to Jory, pulling the computer along with him. The machine swung in a wide crescent until stopping a few feet away from her.

He jabbed a few keys, and Jory yelped when the bracelets and circlet clung to the armrests and headrest like they'd become powerfully magnetic.

"Hey, what just happened? Jory, you okay?" Sebastian reached out a hand.

"I'm fine, Seb. It just surprised me."

"Must the tall one be here?" Mike asked.

"He must," mumbled Sebastian.

Bram dragged a chair over and sat. He slipped a duplicate circlet onto his own head and leaned toward Jory.

Jory tried to shift away but was held firmly in place by the thing on her head. "Couldn't you do your thing on the other side of the room?"

"It's easier if I'm touching you." He rested his hand on hers, and Jory scowled.

"Fine, but if I sense you doing anything funny in there, don't think I won't fight back."

"Like you said, I'm not at the top of my game. I won't be trying anything."

"You'll honor our deal. I let you in on my conversation with Aiden, and you fix the mess you left inside my brain. You'll give him back to me."

He shrugged. "I'll do my best."

The muscles in her jaw tightened. "That's not good enough."

"That's all I can promise," he said, voice firm.

Her wrists jerked against the restraints. "You were able to set Amare straight."

"Amare is a child. He has a simple mind, and my work was easily undone. You are, as you said, a mess."

Jory let her frustration fester a moment longer before letting it go. This was the best she was going to get from him, so she should take it or leave it. Concentrating, she forced her muscles to relax.

"Fine," she said.

"Don't worry, I've got my eye on them," Sebastain said with a firm nod.

Not sure there's much you can really do, Seb, she thought. But it still made her feel better knowing he was there.

"Do you get seizures when exposed to strobe lights?" Mike asked suddenly.

"No. I don't know. Why?" Her muscles tensed all over again.

"Nothing to worry your fleshy head over, love."

My head's not fleshy...is it?

Jory and Sebastian exchanged a wary glance.

"So what now?" Jory asked.

"Now," Mike said as he began to type, "you access—what did you call it? The Tapestry?"

Jory nodded.

"You enter this Tapestry, and my darling should allow us to see, to some extent, what you see. Bram will be directly connected to your thoughts and should be able to communicate with you and your friend over in the Bureau."

Please don't be mad, Aiden.

"All right, so I'll just do that, then." Jory cleared her throat and let out a long breath. Overlapping the Tapestry with the real world had become relatively easy, but submersing herself completely into the realm of woven emotions took time. After long minutes of slow, concentrated breathing, she felt the shift and opened her eyes.

"This is quite remarkable."

"What the heck!" Jory turned to see Bram floating alongside her, examining his translucent fingers. He held them up before his face, looking through them to the intricate, pulsing weave around them. He reached for a thread, and Jory went to swat his hand away just as Mike had done.

"Calm down," Bram said with a grin. "I would be very much surprised if I could manipulate them as you do."

"Whatever, just keep your hands to yourself and don't wander off."

He grinned. "Wouldn't dream of it."

"I thought you'd just be able to speak to us, you know, like, mind to mind."

He floated over to another weave, bending to examine the various colors. "That's what we thought as well. What a happy development."

She rolled her eyes. "Ya, happy."

"It might have something to do with my ability. I can enter memories. So it does not seem so far-fetched to me that, with the help of Mike's equipment and your permission, I was able to come here."

"Well, you're awfully chatty," she said, then sighed. "I have a feeling I'm going to regret giving you 'permission.'"

He floated over to her. "Probably."

"Oh, shut up." She closed her eyes. She needed to concentrate. She also needed to block out his insufferable face for a moment.

There.

It was getting easier to find Aiden.

"Well isn't that a nasty set of strings."

Jory opened her eyes and followed Bram's gaze. She sucked in a breath and grabbed Bram's arm.

"We need to go."

"Who is it?"

"It's Ryan. Well, Ryan and not...Ryan." She tilted her head. "He actually looks a lot better."

It was true—the knots in his weave were loosening, and a good amount of the pressure was slowly releasing. For a moment, the dark, inky Ryan seemed to vanish, but then a shadowy head emerged and a hand reached out toward her.

"Yup! Time to go." Jory mentally latched onto Aiden's distant weave and pulled. When they rocketed away, she got the brief satisfaction of hearing Bram's sharp intake of breath. She grinned, gliding through the Tapestry like a figure skater over newly polished ice.

When they stopped, Bram bent over and gagged.

After regaining his composure, he glanced back the way they had come. "I take it Ryan's dark side doesn't like you much?"

Jory shook her head. "Not really. Apparently, to him, I'm the source of all Ryan's pain. I was hoping he'd be gone now that Ryan knows the truth about our past."

"Things like that don't go away so easily."

"Guess not." Jory turned back to Aiden's weave and took a steadying breath. Entering his consciousness was draining and painful. As much as she was looking forward to talking with him, she was afraid to feel it all again. All that pain and loneliness.

Wait, maybe I can bring him here...like Bram. It's not like he's leaving his body or anything.

Entering the Tapestry was simply a state of mind—her ability to see where and how everyone's emotions were connected. She'd still have to connect with him, though. The dull, ambient threads throbbed with sluggish luminosity.

They should be brighter.

Jory needed to get to him *now*. Her hands dove into the dimming light, fighting through the pain and loneliness trying to hook onto his consciousness. Aiden's heart leapt at her presence, and then he was there.

He pulled her toward him in a tight embrace, no longer holding back like he'd done in their shared dreams. She couldn't feel him like she would in real life. Here in the Tapestry, they had no warmth of flowing blood, but she could feel the strength of his emotions when he buried his face in her watercolor hair.

She clutched at his form, wishing she could hear the beat of his heart.

"Aiden, I'm sorry." Her tears spilled.

Aiden pulled away from her slightly, holding her face in his hands. A wide grin brightened his brown eyes. Wild bronze curls framed full, healthy cheeks. Here in this place, he looked healthy and whole, but she could feel the connection to the real Aiden and knew he was slipping away.

Aiden was dying.

New tears leaked from her eyes. Thumbs traced them as they fell into the lines of her face. No wetness remained, because they disappeared the moment they dripped from her skin.

"Say it again."

Jory tilted her head slightly. "What?"

"Say my name, Anna," he whispered.

"Aiden." His name tasted sweet on her tongue, and the boyish grin that erupted on his face made her heart twinge with guilt.

"I'm sorry," she said again, gently caressing the dimple in his right cheek.

"Why?"

She looked away, gritting her teeth to keep her eyes from filling with more tears.

"I still can't remember you fully." Frustration at her failure threatened to choke her into silence. "He targeted you specifically in my mind. The memories are locked away too deep."

Jory shook her head. "I don't have enough time. I have to get you and Dad out now."

Aiden pulled her into another firm hug. "It was selfish of me. I wanted to have one last moment with you remembering me...remembering us. I know you feel it, Anna. It won't be long now before—"

"No, I'm going to find you before that happens."

"And on that note." Bram stepped forward, orange eyes glinting. "Any tips on how we might do that?"

Aiden didn't spare him a glance.

"Don't waste your time on me. Once I'm gone, you'll have your chance. You can get everyone out while they're vulnerable."

His words were like tiny beads of ice trickling down the nape of her neck and sliding along the middle of her back.

"What do you mean? Why would *you* being gone weaken them in any way?"

Bram began to laugh. His building mirth made Aiden's eyebrow twitch. It was the first time he had acknowledged Bram's presence in any way.

"You're the new *me*!" Bram said when his laughter subsided. "Oh, I *am* sorry."

Jory glanced between the two. "What does he mean?"

Aiden pinched the bridge of his nose and let out a long breath. The action triggered her memory, and she placed her hand over his.

"You're angry," she said, quietly. "That doesn't happen often."

Aiden's eyes softened and, touching his forehead to hers, he breathed in deep.

"I miss how you smell." He sighed. "This is enough. Being in this moment. It's enough."

"Don't you dare," she growled. "Don't you dare give up. I will get you out, I promise."

His sad smile only stoked her anger.

He's giving up. He doesn't think I can do it. Why doesn't he think I can do it?

Aiden's eyes narrowed, nut-brown irises darkening to near black.

"Don't let her come until I'm gone," he said, finally addressing Bram.

"Wouldn't dream of it," Bram said. "How will I know when you're dead?"

He said it so casually, so callously, but Aiden wasn't fazed. He answered him like he was giving him directions to the corner market.

"Keep eyes on the building. When I die, you'll know."

Bram nodded.

No, no! What are they doing!

"Tell me how to get in now, Aiden! Tell me how to beat Brinsley."

Aiden shook his head, eyes grim. "It's too dangerous. You have to accept that I'm already gone."

She grabbed his face in her hands, entwining her fingers in his bronze curls, but her fingers found no purchase. His hair was like smoke, or swirling, floating water curling and sliding over her fingertips.

"You're right here," she insisted.

"I'm as good as dead," he said gently.

"I won't accept that."

He was slipping away, for real now. His form was fading—losing substance. Her hands fell through his image, grasping at air.

"I love you, Anna," he said, smiling softly.

He was gone.

"That self-sacrificing idiot!" She clenched her hands.

This isn't over.

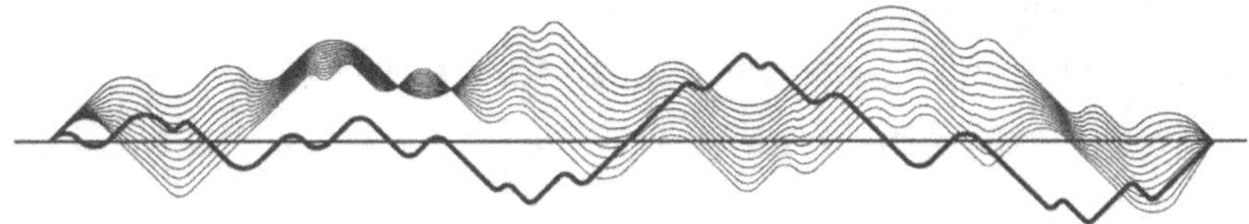

Chapter 33: Ryan

"This isn't over!" Ryan called after Krueger.

"Face it, kid. If this was real, you'd be dead five times over."

Ryan groaned. "I suck."

"Stop whining. You've only been doing this for a few weeks. It takes time and a lot of repetition. So keep punching the bag, and I'll be back in a bit with some burgers."

"Bacon?" Ryan asked, hope in his tone.

"And an extra patty." Krueger flexed his biceps and poked his muscle. "That's how you get beauts like these."

"Can I get in on that?" Rashida rolled her shoulders. A sheen of sweat coated her skin. She'd started coming to their training sessions regularly because apparently Krueger had terrible form, and she couldn't justify ignoring it.

Krueger tipped an imaginary hat. "Of course, love. Feel free to touch my biceps anytime."

"I *will* shoot you."

He gripped his heart. "You already have."

Rashida pulled out her nine-millimeter and rested her finger on the trigger.

Krueger grinned, a challenge in his eyes, before turning around and slowly strolling out.

Her eyebrow twitched, and she held the gun there a moment longer before letting out a long breath. "I *will* shoot him."

Ryan adjusted the gloves on his hands, pulling the Velcro back with a loud rip. He flexed his fingers and shrugged. "I know. I even think *he* knows. He's just crazy enough to think making you angry is worth the bullet in his butt."

"He better get my burger," she muttered.

Ryan lifted his fists, keeping his elbows close to his sides, and jabbed, landing a solid thwack onto the bag. Rashida caught his next punch then slapped his midsection, and his breath whooshed out with a dry cough.

She pinched his nose, turning his face to hers. "What am I going to tell you?"

"Breathe." His voice came out thick and nasally.

"And?"

"Drop my hips?"

She smacked his butt and he staggered forward, catching himself on the punching bag.

"Exactly. Ground yourself. You'll have more balance and control. Floating makes you vulnerable, easily pushed off. I know you want to feel taller, but you need to get over that."

Rashida fell into a boxing stance.

"Relax your hips as you exhale with the swing, then right on impact"—she landed a punch on the bag, and Ryan skidded backward—"you tighten your hips. Got it?"

He nodded, letting go of the bag.

A thud that was *not* Ryan's fist against the bag sounded in the makeshift gym.

"She's gone!" Sebastian had tripped in a mad dash, hitting his head against the low doorframe. His hands gripped his knees, chest heaving, and a trickle of blood trailed down his face.

Ryan rushed over to him, gripping his shoulder. "Geez, Seb, take it easy. Who's gone?"

"Jory."

The volume of Ryan's pulse increased substantially in his ears. Each beat surged through his brain. He tightened his grip on Sebastian's shoulder to keep from swaying.

"She ran off," Rashida said.

It wasn't a question.

Ryan cursed, swiping a hand through his hair. Taking a deep breath, he concentrated on releasing it slowly with his nose, forcing his emotions to halt in their typical spiral.

"Why would she go alone?" he asked.

Rashida shrugged. Her black ponytail swished to the side as she tilted her head. "I'm guessing her arrangements with Bram didn't go as planned."

Sebastian dragged an arm over his head and paled when a streak of blood smeared across his arm. "For the love of—*huuk*." He swallowed a gag. "I didn't realize I was leaking."

"Bigger problems, Seb," Ryan reminded him.

Sebastian nodded, then blinked. "I think that's the first time you've called me Seb."

Ryan arched a brow. "And?"

The man held up one long, slender finger. "Progress."

Sebastian flashed a grin, white teeth bright against his brown skin. But his smile disappeared a moment later, and his brows furrowed. "Why are you both so sure she left on her own? Couldn't she have been taken?"

Rashida waved a dismissive hand. "Bram's not Drake. We would know if anyone breached this place."

Burn. Wish douchepants could've heard that.

Ryan straightened, offering a hand to Sebastian. The lanky giant swallowed Ryan's hand in his and forcibly ignored the gore painting his forearm.

"I should've known," Sebastian said. "I could tell she was upset after entering the Tapestry with Bram."

"She what!"

"What do you mean 'get over it'?" Ryan slammed his hands on the table in front of him, and Bram sighed.

Bram's office was crowded since they'd gained a following. It took a ridiculous amount of effort not to Slice right through the nerves of Bram's vertebrae and leave him on the floor, limp as a dead fish and most likely crapping his pants as he lost control of almost every bodily function.

Why had he ever been afraid of this guy?

"Your sister is formidable. It really is a waste that she's jumping in now instead of waiting until that kid dies. Such a waste."

Bram looked weary. Smudgy gray shadows clung to the skin beneath his orange gaze. His shirt was wrinkled, collar askew, and he was slumped slightly in his chair, something

Ryan had never seen him do. He was like an old, crotchety panther yawning while a rabbit hopped on his back.

Tasha, the Psychic woman Ryan had helped take so long ago, stood behind Bram like a quiet shadow. Her pale hair was pulled back into a reserved ponytail, and her face remained void of emotion. Tasha would not look at Ryan. She'd never so much as met his gaze since he'd hurt her so badly two years ago. Tasha had faded since then, like a bird in a cage. He would have to rectify that. One day he would.

Unfortunately, not today.

What kid had Bram been referring to? Who was dying?

"Who's dying?" Sebastian hovered by the door.

Ryan glanced back at him and raised a brow at the open hostility showing in every tensed muscle on the beanpole.

Never seen him so angry.

Bram rubbed his fingers over his brow and sunk further into his chair. When Tasha rested a soft hand on his shoulder, he visibly relaxed. His brow smoothed out, he nodded, and Tasha immediately backed off.

"Who's dying, Bram?" Ryan repeated Sebastian's question, but he already had a pretty good idea of who it was.

No. No. No!

Bram smirked, tired eyes crinkling at the corners. "You know who. Pretty curls, cute little dimple when he smiles?"

Ryan spat a curse, running a hand through his hair.

"Ryan—"

Ryan cut Sebastian off. "It's Aiden, Seb."

I need to think.

Ryan chewed his lip in thought. "When was the last time you spoke to her?"

Sebastian pursed his lips. "Last night. She could have left anytime since then."

Ryan cursed. If she left right away, she could already be at the Bureau.

"How did she leave without you knowing?" Ryan asked Bram.

"Who said I didn't know?"

"You *let* her leave?"

"I feel like I'm beating a *very* dead horse." Bram rubbed his fingers over tired eyes. "Haven't we already established that your sister isn't someone any of us can stop now? She's remembered herself. She might actually put a dent in Brinsley's ranks before she gets killed. So let's take that as a win."

"I'm going after her. I just have to find a way to catch up with her. If only I could get ahead of her somehow, cut her off." As Ryan wracked his brain for an idea of how he could intercept her, a small hand tugged at his sleeve.

"Ryan."

Riri's hazel eyes crinkled at the sides as her wide mouth turned up slightly at the corners. "Remember me?"

"I can't let you do that, Ri. Besides, you can't go anywhere you haven't seen before."

"I've seen it," she whispered.

Ryan narrowed his eyes. "When?"

"My mom works there. She'd drive me and Calub to the entrance and tell us that if we were bad, she'd make us stay there. Marla found out and took us to Eileen."

"Marla?" Sebastian asked.

Riri shoved her hands deep into her pockets and looked at the floor. "Our nanny. Mom didn't know, but...she was Psychic too."

"So your mother isn't?" Sebastian prodded.

Riri shook her head.

Sebastian's brows pulled down in thought. "Then your dad?"

Riri shrugged. "Probably. I don't know who he is."

Ryan waved a hand. "Sorry, but this is beside the point. Ri, I don't know how Drake justifies using you, but I won't."

The Teleporter smirked. "And you'll stop me how?"

"Ri—"

"Jump us there and you go straight back," Kellry said to a nodding Riri.

"Wait a minute." Ryan grabbed Kellry's hand. "She's *my* sister."

Kellry grinned. "You're not my boyfriend. You can't tell me what to do."

"Like that would make a difference," Ryan grumbled.

"I'm going too," Drake said.

Ryan scrubbed his hands over his face. "Ugh, why?"

"Stop whining. If Kell's going, so am I," Drake spat.

"So am I!" Sebastian chirped, waving a hand.

"And me." Krueger lifted a finger, clapping his hand on Ryan's shoulder.

"Are we going on a trip?" A blond man stepped in, grinning. It was Hans, the Puppeteer. Ryan hadn't seen him this entire time.

Where the heck did he come from?

Momma J lifted a hand. "As will I—"

BAM!

Heads turned to Bram. He stood, fist planted on his desk where a crack split clean through the wood.

"Will you all just SHUT UP!" Bram's hands shook. Tasha inched forward with a trembling hand, and Ryan flinched, taking a step back.

"No one is going anywhere." Each word was barbed, stabbing into each of them in turn. Tasha placed her fingers over Bram's temples, and his signature calm returned. Bram straightened his collar when she retreated once more. Ryan hadn't realized how dependent on her Bram had become until now.

"Your sister made her choice," Bram said, his voice low and foreboding. "We will wait until our opportunity comes and strike then. We have worked for this too long."

Bram's uncharacteristic anger had sunk knife-sharp teeth into Ryan's belly. He peered through his lowered lashes at the man who had manipulated him, tortured him, held his mind captive for the past three years.

Why did I let him treat me that way? Why have I always been so afraid of him? I was terrified the moment I met him.

Sure, Bram had scary mind powers and arms that could choke out a hippo, but Ryan could incapacitate him with a wave of his hand. He could literally make him soil his pants right now.

Unless...that fear had been planted in him. Planted like the fake memories that still felt so tangible in his mind. Those nights Bram had snuck to his bedside and whispered doubt into his ear—he had been twisting his thoughts even then.

Ryan pushed, mentally throwing a shoulder against the point of fear. An opaque glass wall within Ryan's mind shattered, shards cutting through chains as the last of the doors flung wide open. Ryan staggered backward as the memory shifted to the surface, like a camera lens adjusting. Blurred images came into focus until they appeared clearly before his eyes.

It was dinnertime. Aiden was over as usual, holding Anna's hand beneath the table, his thumb brushing gently over hers. Ryan made a face after peeking under the tablecloth, and his sister kicked his shin.

"Your face will get stuck like that. Just wait," she said, grinning smugly.

"Will not," Ryan replied.

Aiden ruffled his hair, and Ryan couldn't help but grin.

"Why do you like her? She's gross. She plucks her nose hairs and leaves them in the sink."

"Ryan!" Anna reached over Aiden in a desperate attempt to pinch Ryan's nose, but Aiden came to his defense by intercepting the pinch and pulling her into a fierce hug.

"Let go. The twerp needs humbling!" she shouted.

Aiden wrestled with her, laughing.

"Would you three cool it? The food's getting cold!" Mom folded her thin arms, her no-nonsense glare zeroing in on them.

Aiden's head snapped back when a rubber band hit him in the middle of the forehead. They all looked at Dad, who was aiming his tiny rubber band gun. He lifted his arms in the air. "Score!"

Silence reigned for a full second before laughter erupted.

Mom shook her head. "What did I say about aiming that thing at people's heads? You're going to get him in the eye one of these d—"

Bang!

The front door crashed to the floor, ripped straight off its hinges. A whoosh of cold night air swept through the room, and gooseflesh erupted on the back of Ryan's neck and his arms, making his hair stand on end. A beast made of muscle Ryan identified right away as a Berserker clomped into the room. Appearing next to the giant was a hook-nosed man with burns racing up the side of his neck, face, and bare skull.

When the hook-nosed man lifted a gun, Ryan couldn't help but feel immediate déjà vu, comparing the moment to when Dad's rubber band gun had pointed at Aiden's head just moments earlier.

But this man's weapon wasn't pointed at Aiden. Instead, his line of sight was filled with his mom, and she slumped, blood pooling from the middle of her forehead—her pale eyes glassy. Only after registering these details did the deafening noise of the shot enter his consciousness. The sound screamed in Ryan's ears, and he clamped his hands over them. An acrid scent filled the air—bitter and smoky.

They all sat frozen, staring at Mom as viscous red liquid bloomed, slowly staining her blouse. When Dad stood, the lights flared to a blinding whiteness as his ability exploded to life. He yelled—a horrible, broken cry as pure energy shot toward the bald man. But it fizzled to nothing, sparks dancing and dying at the bent tip of the man's nose. Dad fell, followed by Aiden and Anna.

Fuzzy needles stuck out of their necks.

Their eyes darted around frantically, and Ryan realized they were still conscious but their bodies were paralyzed from whatever drug had been released into their system.

"Wait," Ryan said, his brain dragging. The giant pointed the needle-gun thing at him.

Ryan didn't think. He swiped a hand, and the Berserker collapsed, screaming.

"I can't feel them! I can't feel my arms, my legs!" The giant cursed multiple times, jerking his head around until the other man kicked him in the gut.

"Hush." The hook-nosed man locked his gaze on Ryan with a half-smile. "Interesting." His brows folded downward, but then his head jerked up. Ryan heard the familiar thud of the backdoor swinging shut and the blinds bouncing against the wood. Quiet, measured steps fell on the floor behind him until a large hand landed on his head.

Ryan looked up to see an orange-eyed man gripping his skull in a tight hold. The man held a dark, bitter hatred behind his gaze that turned Ryan's blood cold.

"Let's make a deal, Brinsley," the orange-eyed man said.

The pressure on his head increased, and a strange fog crept over Ryan's mind.

It was all there—the true memories that had lain beneath a false reality. Ryan gripped his head in his hands, pushing the memory down, away from the surface of his thoughts.

"Ryan, are you all right?" Kellry's voice was strained, cleaving a path through his blinding memories, and he realized he was squeezing her hand to the point of snapping her bones.

He nodded, then looked to Bram and inclined his head.

"I have to thank you, Bram. You kept my sister and me from being taken that day. We both know your reasons were completely self-serving, but—" Ryan shrugged.

Bram's eyes grew wary as he sized Ryan up and down. His lip curled.

"That's right, old man. Your hold on me is gone." Ryan smirked and winked. "Try not to wet your pants."

Krueger snorted out a laugh, and Kellry bit her lip.

"Watch yourself," Bram said.

Ryan released Kellry's hand and threw his arm around her shoulder, turning her toward the door. "I'm going, and whoever decides to follow, it's their choice."

He tilted his head back to Bram one last time. "I'll stop Jory before she gets there and bring her back."

"And if you fail?" Bram asked.

"Then I'll raise hell and make your goal that much easier," Ryan replied, smooth as stone.

"You will ruin everything, Ryan Zamora. Brinsley will capture and assimilate you into his facility without even having to lift a finger."

"Then I'll be out of your hair while you round up your little Psychic army all over again."

Krueger splayed out his fingers and bounced his hand in the air in a "drop the mic" sort of way.

"So we're not going with them?" Hans's voice piped up as the office door slammed, concealing Bram's smoldering glare.

Drake grabbed Ryan's arm, pulling him and Kellry to a halt in the darkened hallway.

"I have to speak with you." He looked at Kellry. "Alone."

"Dude, would you just leave her be?" Ryan asked.

Drake opened his mouth then shut it, the lines on his face creasing in irritation. "Not her, you cocky pissworm."

"Gross, man. Do worms piss?" Krueger asked, glancing over his shoulder at them.

Sebastian shook his head. "It isn't really pee. It's called vermicompost, and people make worm tea out of it to—"

"Tea!" Krueger pulled a face.

Sebastian shook his head vigorously. "Not to drink. You put it on—"

"Shut up, you two!" Ryan turned to Drake and lifted a brow. "Me? What—you gonna spray your dominance all over me? Put me in my place? Cause I'm really not in the mood."

Drake pulled in a long, slow breath through his nose. "Fine, fine. I'm the lovesick screwup that threw our efforts into chaos over jealousy. Can we all move past that now?"

"Can *you*?" Krueger quipped.

Drake ignored Krueger, eyes on Ryan. "I'm trying to help you, all right? Not many people know this, but when I worked at the Bureau—"

Ryan held up a hand. "Wait, you *worked* there? I thought you were a prisoner."

"He was," Kellry said.

"How does that work?"

"A story for another time, Ryan." Drake paused, clearly formulating his next words. "When I worked there, they would push Psychics past what they could mentally bear. Push them until they Fractured."

"You say that like it's a sickness or something," Ryan said.

Drake gave a slight nod. "In a way, it was. When a Psychic was pushed beyond their capabilities or beyond what their mind was able to bear, they did what the Bureau named Fracturing. With each ability, each person really, the results were different. Some would go mad, others would lose their powers completely. We had a few start hemorrhaging from the inside, or have a stroke. The list goes on."

He looked Ryan in the eyes then. "I think you've already had a bit of a Fracturing, Ryan."

An inky black shadow crouching within the recesses of Ryan's mind began to stir.

Drake shrugged. "I also believe Bram did, back when we escaped the Bureau. No one was able to break out of his memory wipes before then. No one. Now your sister, and you, apparently, have been able to. Somewhat."

"What I'm saying is to watch yourself, Ryan. I don't want to go on this crackpot mission and have you Fracture completely. You're unstable enough as it is, and I won't have you jeopardize our safety, Kell's safely, because you don't know when to pull back."

"Drake—" Kellry put a hand on the man's shoulder, and he stiffened.

Drake took her hand, and a low growl rumbled in Ryan's mind.

"All of this has been wrong," Drake said, thumb caressing the back of her hand.

Ryan gritted his teeth but stayed put. Kellry could handle herself. Besides, he gave up the right to be jealous when he rejected her.

"Everything that's happened, I never meant for you to find out. At least not until all this was over and you had a chance to grow up a bit more...had a chance to consider..." Drake bit his lip, perfect face forlorn.

Just kill me now, Ryan thought, groaning internally.

"I still can't help but hope that our paths will align one day," Drake continued. "But I'll do my best not to get in your way. I want you to be happy, Kell. *He* can't give that to you. So I'll wait until you realize that too."

She began to shake her head, but Drake placed a finger to her lips.

"I'll wait," he repeated.

Ryan couldn't help the gag reflex. It was just so stupid. Drake's words were so unnecessarily flowery. He exchanged a look with Krueger, who rolled his eyes and bent his neck, pulling at an imaginary noose.

"You are a bearded child, Krueger," Drake said, pursing his lips. He ignored Ryan, giving Kellry one more lingering glance before walking off.

Leaning in the shadow of a doorway, Lane pushed away from the wall, hair draping over her mangled face. She followed Drake.

Krueger shook his head as he watched her go. "She's like a bloody fly. Don't even know she's there unless she's buzzing in your ear."

"I'll be leaving in five minutes!" Ryan shouted after them. "Grab whatever you need and meet us by the entrance."

"That means if you need to take a dump, better do it now!" Krueger added.

Drake turned at the end of the hallway and jerked his head into a nod before heading left toward his room.

I'm coming, Jory. Don't you dare do anything stupid.

"Still got time for a burger?"

It was then that Ryan saw the bag and registered the scent of bacon. He glanced at Krueger ruefully.

"Sorry, man."

Krueger sighed.

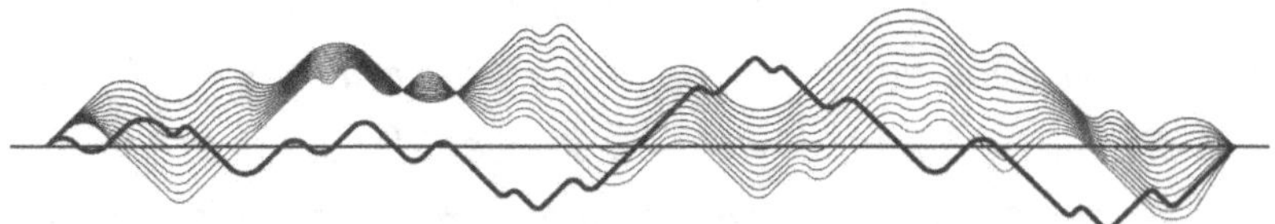

Chapter 34: Jory

Aiden clicked the timer and waved it in the air. "5:57. Nice!" Anna slapped her hands on her knees, head down, sweat dripping onto the track. The air was cloudy and humid. Her shirt was drenched and clung to her skin, and the anti-perspirant she wore wasn't living up to its name.

"Not good enough!" she shouted back, shaking her head. "Autumn Davis can run a 5:40."

"Autumn Davis has legs as long as stilts."

"Curses on the height-advantaged," Anna muttered.

Aiden tossed her a water bottle. She caught it, chugged half, then poured the rest over her head.

"You look like one of those girls from the shampoo commercials." A mischievous grin lit Aiden's features as he pushed wet strands of black hair out of her face.

"If those girls were sweating like linebackers, then sure."

Thunder rumbled in the distance as clouds darkened to a slate gray.

She studied him, admiring his bronze curls and broad shoulders. His ready smile that always gave her the urge to throw her arms around his neck. The musky scent of the cologne she gave him for his last birthday.

He wasn't tall by any means, but she still had to rise to her tiptoes to give him a peck on the cheek. She pulled away, but he threaded his fingers through her hair and leaned toward her, pressing his lips to her own. She could taste the tang of a sour-apple jolly rancher on his tongue. He placed his hand on her lower back, bringing her closer, but she broke away.

"I'm sweaty."

He shook his head and touched his mouth to hers again.

"I don't care," he whispered against her lips. Her heart stuttered, blood pumping as if she was racing around the track again.

Aiden had always been a gentle person. Kind and patient to a fault. But when it came to moments like these, all that patience flew out the door and a fierceness took over that left her dizzy.

He grabbed her arms and pushed her away. They were both a little breathless, and he laughed softly.

"We better stop or I'll toss you down and attack you right here," he said.

"You started it." Anna ran in place and shook out her arms, trying to burn off the nervous energy racing through her thrumming veins.

"Pffft." He lifted a hand to his mouth. "What are you doing?"

"You got me all riled up."

A fire danced in his eyes then, and he leaned toward her again. Anna's feet stopped bouncing, lips parting slightly.

"Gosh dang it." He scrubbed his hands through his curls and turned, cutting through the grass. Thunder rumbled in the distance.

"Hey, where are you going?" Anna shouted after him.

"Away from you, you temptress!"

"I did nothing!" Anna sprinted after him, overtaking him in moments. She tackled him, and they fell in a tangled heap. They rolled across the field and came to a stop, Aiden's weight pressed against her until he pushed himself up. He hovered over her with grass and dandelion fluff in his hair. The fresh scent of moist earth permeated the air as drops of rain began to fall. They stayed still and silent as the clouds released their gathered moisture.

Rain soaked them through, pounded the earth in that rhythmic way. Water glided down her face, tickling her ears, but she didn't move. Their eyes locked.

"Anna?" he whispered. Drops traced his jawline and fell from his chin.

"Yes?"

"Stay with me."

They were the same words Aiden had whispered all those years ago when they were kids and his dad was fading away on a hospital bed. His mom had left him shortly after Aiden was born, right after she found out his dad had cancer. His dad had battled it for seven long years after she left.

"Stay with me," he'd said then.

He'd said it again at his dad's funeral two weeks later.

It was moments like these that Anna knew just how much she meant to him. How much her family meant to him. They'd taken him in after that, and they'd never been apart since.

"Always," she whispered back.

It was like Bram had hijacked a rocket and crashed into a dam. The flood was merciless, drowning her heart in bittersweet memories. When Bram said he might be able to remove the walls burying Aiden, she'd grasped at the hope. He'd certainly delivered, demolishing them with the finesse of an elephant in a ballet recital. She'd come to herself, hours later, pillow drenched in sweat and tears.

It had worked, but everything was out of order, a time-line that looped and dipped like one of those roller coasters at an extreme theme park. No wonder she'd been a mess the past few years. Anger came, then. A white-hot rage that made her shake. Aiden was dying. Brinsley was *killing* him with whatever psycho experiments he was performing.

You're the new me.

What had Bram meant by that?

She didn't have time to unravel the hopeless mess within her mind. Almost immediately after she woke, Jory had thrown herself into the Tapestry and reached out, searching for Brinsley's threads. She could end him right then, snuff out his thread.

Kill him.

But she couldn't find him. The mass of pulsing, interwoven threads stretched on like a giant crystalline blanket. Colors refracted and undulated as far as the eye could see. Jory closed her eyes, reaching out for his individual threads, but it was like shoving her hands into a pot of oily noodles, her hands slipping and gliding over the strands. Was it because she wasn't familiar with his threads like she was with Aiden's or Ryan's? Or was he hiding his presence by some other means?

I have to get close to him. Overlap the Tapestry and sever his life-thread right then and there.

Giant trees stretched above them, their thick trunks sprouting long green branches. Dense brush and mossy stones littered the nonexistent path. Everything felt damp. It had been a misty day with no real rain, and now the scenery was blurred with a light fog.

"How can you tell where we're going?" Jory asked.

Ref stopped and closed his eyes, a black-and-orange helmet tucked under his arm.

"I can feel it."

Jory cocked her head, examining the guy in front of her. Ref was similar in height to Aiden, average, which meant he was still several inches taller than her and lean muscled where Aiden would get broad and bulky when he worked out.

Why did he come with me? Ref had been the only one she thought might not try to immediately stop her, but she'd still been surprised by his acquiescence.

"Can you tell me how to get to the Bureau?" she'd asked, after knocking on his door in the dark hours of the morning. He'd answered, hair mussed from sleep, wearing a white tank and charcoal-gray sweatpants. She realized then his hair wasn't black like she'd always thought, but a dark shade of brown. Stormy gray eyes met her own as his brows knit down in concern.

"Why?"

"If you can't tell me, I'll find someone else." She turned, but his hand shot out, grabbing her upper arm.

"Wait. Just give me two minutes." Ref pulled her into his room and shut the door. Putting a finger to his lips, he jerked his head to a snoring Krueger on the top bunk, then began throwing things into a bag.

"What are you doing?" Jory whispered as he shrugged into a black knit sweater.

"I'm coming with you."

"Why?"

He stopped a moment, then looked her in the eyes.

"You remind me of someone I used to know... He had that same look in his eyes that you have now." He shrugged his pack over his shoulder.

"Had?"

Ref pursed his lips. "Let's go."

Krueger stirred, slurred sleep speech rolling out of his mumbling lips. "Yesh, Rassshida, I do own...fleet ohv raptors. Would you...lerk to ride one?" He rolled over, and his blanket slipped down his bare back.

Ref turned her around, shoving her out the door.

"Hey!" she hissed.

"Do you wanna see a naked man?"

"Of course he sleeps in the nude."

Now, hours later, they hiked through the Northern California forest shrouded in shadow and thickening fog.

"How exactly does your ability work?" Jory asked.

He shoved his hands into the deep pockets of his sweatpants. "I'm what people call a Muffler. I can basically nullify any sort of tech within a certain radius."

He glanced at her face and seemed to take note of her confusion.

"You know, phones, computers, any type of electronic transmission."

Jory's eyes widened. "Wow."

He laughed softly, rubbing the back of his neck.

"Ya, it's not that amazing. I have absolutely no control over it. I have to wear this," he said, jerking his head toward the helmet under his arm, "if anyone wants to be able to use their phones, or watch TV, or do anything involving technology while I'm in the room."

"So if I took my phone out right now, I couldn't make a call?"

He shook his head.

Jory hardly ever took her phone out for anything, anyway. The only numbers saved on it were Sebastian's and Ryan's. She pulled it out now and saw that the screen was black.

"We're essentially invisible, which is why Drake was able to hide for so long. I make it impossible for anyone to track us electronically. Also, I can *sense* electronic waves and signals."

"Can you listen in on phone conversations or mentally track down emails and stuff?"

He shook his head. "But I've heard it's possible for some. It's not like it's common knowledge, though."

Jory nodded. Psychics were terrified of being found out. They couldn't exactly put out an ad and train with a mentor or go to some special school or anything.

Wouldn't that be nice.

She'd been lucky her mother knew how to help her.

"So you have to wear that"—she pointed to the helmet—"if you want to shut out all the...vibrations?"

He nodded. "It's more like static."

"How do you know we're heading toward the Bureau?"

"They have a massive energy signal. I don't know what kind of power source they're using, but trust me when I say we're definitely going in the right direction."

A massive energy signal.

A memory came then, her father crouched in front of her and Aiden, holding one light bulb in each hand. They'd gasped with delight when the filaments in each bulb lit up like miniature beacons.

"Your mom would never leave me," he'd said, grinning, "because then she'd have to pay the electric bill."

Jory cursed, and Ref lifted a brow.

"It's my dad. *He's* the energy signal."

"Your dad's a Generator? That's insane! No wonder the Bureau nabbed him. No offense, but why didn't you realize that before now?"

"My brains have been a bit of a wreck, remember? Dad hardly used his ability. He used to say we didn't have to pay for electricity, but I saw the bills. I know we did. He didn't want there to be any reason someone might find out any of us were Psychics."

Ref pushed a low-hanging branch out of their way, letting her step ahead before releasing it. "Smart man. I wonder how they found you."

He's right. How did *they find us?*

Jory was breathing hard. She hadn't gotten this much exercise in a long time. It was embarrassing, really, since she used to run miles every day.

"This was more of a hike than I realized." She swiped a hand over her brow. Despite it being cold outside, she'd worked up a sweat.

Pulling a hair tie off her wrist with her teeth, she raked her fingers through her thick black hair and wrangled the mass into a ponytail. She glanced at Ref and noted his gaze lingering on her hair a moment before glancing away.

Is there something wrong with it? She brushed a stray strand behind her ear self-consciously.

He cleared his throat. "Well, it's not like we can drive up to the front gate. Besides, we could only take the bus so far, and you can't even drive up the road without a pass," Ref said.

"Paranoid much?" Leaves crunched beneath her feet, and she threw out a hand when she stumbled over a thick tree root. Ref caught it, then immediately let go once she regained her balance. She mumbled her thanks.

"You would be too if you were secretly torturing people for the government," he said.

"I guess. With all those Psychics locked up in one place, you'd think they'd be able to overpower them. Bram...did he escape from there or something?"

Ref frowned. "Right, you wouldn't know about that. Ryan really didn't tell you anything."

"Obviously."

He cleared his throat. "Right, well, the Bureau forced Bram to use his abilities to alter the memories of almost everyone there, to trick them into thinking what they were doing was rehabilitating. Therapeutic-type stuff. Workers and Psychics alike."

You're the new me.

"Aren't there hundreds of people there? Wouldn't that cause a lot of strain?"

Ref shrugged. "Why do you think he's the way he is? The guy is brilliant, though, and still managed to get several of them to escape, even if it cost him."

Jory chewed on her lip, thinking.

You're the new me.

White walls, gloved hands, the mountain of minds altered. Bram's consciousness, his memories, were in shambles after what he had done at the Bureau. The countless memories he'd altered had threatened to overwrite his own.

She scanned the forest, nervous energy building. "They would have wanted to find someone to replace him."

"Good luck with that. Bram's ability is so rare, I don't even know if they have a name for it."

"What if they found someone better?" she asked softly.

Ref stopped and looked down at her, his brow lifted. "Better?"

Jory hugged herself, eyes on the dark earth at her feet. "An Illusionist...an Illusionist could do it."

Ref shook his head. "Illusionists are unreliable. Their abilities are always full of holes. Some can produce scents or noises to distract a person, but it's not often you find someone who can do anything visual. Drake is the only one I've known. He can make optic *and* auditory illusions, which is pretty rare."

Her eyes watered as frustration built inside. She knew so little.

"So someone..." She hugged herself tighter, hands balled into fists. "Someone who could manipulate all five senses would be unheard of."

"Well, ya—" Ref paused.

She felt the weight of his hand on her shoulder. "I'm sorry, Jory. Yes, someone like that would be perfect for the job."

Aiden's illusions had always been something out of a fairy tale. He'd create worlds around her, full of impossible things. Dragons and fairies. He'd take her places she couldn't go before she had a handle on her abilities, creating crowds of nameless people. Sitting in a concert hall, running down the beach, watching the circus...

Everything had always been so real. She could feel the vibrations of the music, taste the salt of the ocean, smell the popcorn.

"How long..." Her throat caught. "How long could someone keep using an ability like that? Just...constantly, without stopping, without breaking?"

Tears leaked out of her eyes. She brushed them away, but more came. How did Aiden have the presence of mind to even talk to her? How had he lasted this long? How much time did he have left?

"I don't know, but I don't think they'd want to waste someone like that. And I hate to say this, but if it was near impossible before, it definitely is now. There's no way we can get someone that important out. I don't know what your plan is or was, but I think when you see this place you'll understand."

Jory shrugged his hand off her shoulder and marched ahead. "Just show me where it is and then leave, Ref."

She heard him release a long breath and mumble some-thing. Crunching leaves followed her, and soon he trudged ahead, hands shoved in his pockets once more.

"I'm not going to leave you," he said.

Why do you care?

"Ref, I really think—"

Ref's arm flew up, finger to his lips. He closed his eyes, tilting his head slightly. Pulling his helmet over his head, he reached out and grabbed her hand, tugging her close.

"We're almost there," he said. "We'll be coming up on the first set of cameras soon. I don't wanna tip them off by shutting them down, and I'm not sure if they have audio, so just follow me and stay quiet."

She nodded and he released her hand. She followed him, taking a winding path while crouching low, creeping behind trees and bushes. After several long minutes, they reached a wall of solid concrete.

Ref tilted his head back. The top of the wall disappeared in the thickening fog. "What now?"

Jory placed her hand against the cold, hard surface. "How thick is it?"

Ref let out a breathy laugh. "You got a jackhammer hid-den in your, uh..."

Jory placed a hand on her hip. "In my what?"

He put up his hands, shaking his head. "Any way I thought about it, it sounded dirty. Figured I'd stop while I was ahead."

She lifted a brow. "Good choice."

Ref cleared his throat then crouched down to examine the wall. The moment he bent his knees, a whoosh whistled past Jory's ear, and Ref's head snapped forward.

Jory grabbed Ref's wrist and yanked him behind a tree.

She shook his shoulders. "Ref! Ref, are you okay?"

An arrow lay on the ground where they'd stood a moment before.

What the heck?

"What was that?" Voice shaky, Ref pawed at his helmet, fingers tracing over a deep groove on the top of it. If he hadn't bent down, it probably would have gone through his neck.

Jory cursed herself, pulling the Tapestry into view. She'd gotten too comfortable being separate from others' emotions, and she let her guard down. She should have connected to the Tapestry sooner. If she had, she would have felt the throbbing strands of the three people approaching them.

She noted Ref's strands beside her. Fear surged through his threads. But not for himself. For her? Why? She shook her head and concentrated on the three masses of threads. Three pale-green lifelines pulsed amongst each weave.

It would be so easy.

Those are three people. *They're not just a tangle of strings, Jory. Brinsley deserves to die, but do they?*

A soft twang and a moment later, an arrow burrowed itself in her thigh, tearing through flesh and muscle.

She collapsed with a gasp and stared down at her leg, where hot blood soaked through her pants. It burned, the pain flaring as colored dots danced across her vision. All she could think was, how? It had curved around the tree like a missile locked onto her position.

"Jory!" Ref was holding her, stroking loose strands of hair back from her face.

"Come on out, sweetheart," a voice called from behind them.

Ref cursed. "Not again," he whispered under his breath.

What is he talking about?

The pain was driving her mind in circles, but the Tapestry was still there. She could feel the cocky triumph of the jerk behind them, feel Ref's panic. She concentrated on her own threads and saw her own fear surging. She needed to think.

Looking at her threads now, it wasn't the first time she thought how her and Ryan's abilities overlapped in many areas. They had both seen the threads that day when Ryan had cut her off from Krueger. She was beginning to realize how much she could manipulate the emotions around her. What about her own?

She calmed herself, forcing the shock—the fear—to dim. Her hands stopped shaking, and as clarity came, so did a plan. She had no idea what abilities these three possessed. But she knew what *she* could do.

"We'll come with you!" she shouted.

"Jory!" Ref hissed, but she shook her head.

Trust me, she mouthed. She felt the apprehension, and then the resignation, within him. He nodded.

"Come on, then!" the voice shouted.

Ref took a deep breath, then lifted her up.

"You better know what you're doing," he whispered.

Two boys and a girl approached them. The girl held a crossbow reloaded and aimed straight at them. They were all in their late teens, perhaps early twenties. One of the guys tilted his chin, running his eyes along Jory's body, stopping at the arrow in her leg.

"Sorry, beautiful. I was aiming for Helmet-Head there." He was tall with light-brown hair and a nose that looked like it had been broken more than once.

Jory's brows knit together. *But she has the crossbow.*

"Your aim sucks," Ref said.

He shrugged, then held out his arms. "Hand her over."

Ref gripped her tight against his chest. "No."

Jory placed a hand on his chest, and he met her gaze with his stormy gray eyes. "It's okay, Ref."

The boy spread out his hands. "See? Your girlfriend likes me better already."

"She's bleeding a lot, Liam," the girl said. Golden waves brushed her shoulders, and she jerked her head to toss a few errant strands out of her eyes. "Let Oli take care of her first."

Liam nodded. "Good call, Leah. Come on, don't let her bleed out, you idiot."

Ref gritted his teeth, but Jory knew he had to feel the blood soaking his arm and dripping from his elbow to the forest floor.

The faint patter of hot crimson painting the leaves below them filled the silence. Ref laid her on the ground.

Liam was on Ref in a second, pulling out zip ties while planting a knee in the middle of his back.

Jory met his gaze.

Trust me.

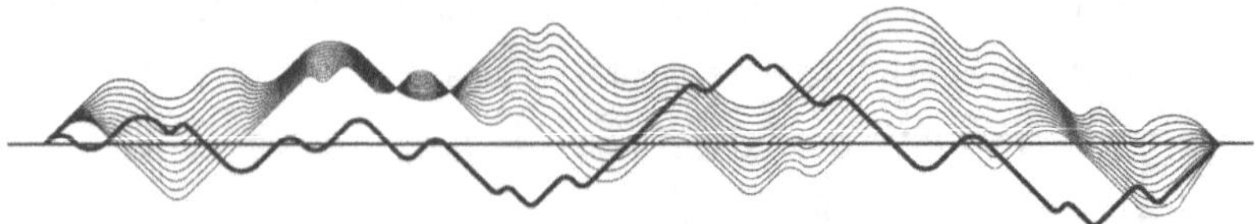

Chapter 35: Ryan

Tzzzzzzzzit!

Ryan's stomach lurched. He clenched Kellry's hand, pulling her with him as he stumbled forward. Teleportation was disorienting. His lungs bunched up into his throat, and it took a few seconds of garbled coughing to feel like they'd settled back in his chest where they belonged.

The trees around them grazed the sky. Ryan craned his neck back, trying to spot the topmost branches through the white mist.

How crazy would it be to fall from the top of one of those bad boys?

Ryan blinked. The thought wasn't suicidal, just curious. How long *had* it been since he'd fantasized about death? Days ago, he would have been picturing the long climb, the rush of the wind when he let go, and the satisfying splat at the end, his limbs splayed out in all sorts of wonky directions.

All that mattered then was Jory—keeping her from the truth, keeping her out of Bram's grasp. But now? Now Jory knew everything, and she was running toward someone even worse than Bram, like he always knew she would. *That* mattered, but other things mattered too. Like the slender, gloved hand wrapped in his own, and the man with the messy topknot striding ahead. Even grasshopper-legs mattered, Ryan thought as the man squirted a generous helping of hand sanitizer in his hands after holding Krueger's.

It was hard opening his heart again. What would happen if all this went south? With his luck, it probably would—

You can't think like that. You can do this. I can do this.

"We'll get her back," Kellry said. "And then, when we're ready, we'll get your dad."

Ryan smiled, squeezing her hand. "I know."

She blushed a little.

"What?" he asked.

"You should smile more," she said. "You have a good one."

Ryan's grin grew, and he leaned toward her ear. "And you look pretty when you blush," he whispered.

She grabbed the collar of his shirt, pulling him even closer.

"If you're gonna pull a stunt like that, then I'm not waiting." She pressed petal-soft lips against his, then pushed him away with a wink. "That's just a warning."

Ryan's heart lurched as that maddening scent of blossom-apple-whatever lingered in the air between them.

"Gross."

Kellry smirked, poking Riri in the cheek. "Shut up. Besides, shouldn't you have already teleported back?"

Riri cocked her hip, very Rashida-like. "Let me help. I'll stay until you grab her and whoever else, and we can all jump back."

"Go, Ri," Ryan said, voice firm.

"Fine." She hesitated, eyes looking beyond them, toward the Bureau. "If you happen to see my brother, tell him it's gonna be okay."

Riri glanced behind them. "Don't waste it all, Seb. What if the enemy sneezes on you?"

"Not funny, Ri." Sebastian pocketed the sanitizer. "C'mon, she could be there already."

"Seb's right," Ryan said with a nod. "Thanks Ri, you did great."

Riri narrowed her eyes.

"Nice-Ryan's weird." She shivered, took a deep breath, and with another *tzzzzzzit,* winked out of sight.

"Plan?" Drake asked.

Lane hovered beside him, salt-and-pepper hair draped over the unblemished side of her face. Her foggy eye became a mirror for the white mist around them, and the trees behind her appeared gray, blending into their surroundings.

"Stop Jory before she gets through the gate," Ryan said, answering Drake's question.

"And if she's already through?" Momma J asked, eyes grim.

Ryan scrubbed his hand through his hair, then cursed. He'd gone back and forth on this a million times.

"Then we go back," he said, finally. "Regroup. Save her and everyone else when we have the best chance."

Drake nodded. "Looks like you're not so stupid after all."

Ah man, did Drake just agree with me?

Ryan had thought hard about whether to go in guns blazing if Jory had made it past the gate somehow, but... He glanced at Kellry. Better safe than sorry.

Right?

Roman scoffed. "Pansy."

Hair rose on his neck, and his fists clenched at his sides. "She's *my* sister, and I won't have you all risk your lives when the timing isn't right. If she's in there, she's as good as captured."

"And Aiden?" Kellry asked softly.

Ryan pursed his lips. "He—"

Roman shoved a finger at Ryan's chest. "I came because I wanted to use your kamikaze Empath sister as an opportunity to punch a hole through this place and nab Eileen. If that's not happening, then I'm leaving."

The Berserker crossed his arms.

Are his fingers filled with iron? Doing his best to keep from wincing and spitting out a colorful curse, Ryan tried to play it cool. He gestured behind them.

"Then leave." Ryan jerked his head to the others. "C'mon, we're wasting time."

He nodded to Drake, who scowled but took the lead.

Falling into a quick jog, they followed Drake, Lane, and Kellry, who knew exactly where the building would be.

"I hate you." Lane's heated whisper to her sister was easy to catch.

"I'm aware" was Kellry's reply, coming out in a weary sigh.

"Are you? Do you really know how utterly, how thoroughly, I hate you?"

Kellry remained silent.

"You promised we'd never come back here. You promised me! Remember? The day you gave me this!" Lane pointed at her own face.

Nobody cares. Just shut up already.

It was a callous thought, but Ryan hated seeing the pinched skin between Kellry's brows, the guilt pulling down her confident shoulders.

"You didn't have to come," Kellry offered.

"Of course I did. Of course I did, you—"

"Jack, can you throw up a shield around us?" Ryan asked the larger man, shutting down Lane's rant. "I guarantee the closer we get the more company we'll have—meaning we should all shut our traps, if you didn't catch my drift."

Lane's face twisted into that nasty scowl as Momma J gave a sharp nod. Ryan couldn't say what changed in the air around him, only that he felt a little emptier, or perhaps blocked? However it worked, Ryan felt his ability dim as the protective sphere bubbled out around them.

They walked through the outer rim of trees, and Kellry whistled.

"Well that's new."

The wall was massive. Who knew how many pounds of concrete towered above them, going on for hundreds of feet on either side. An iron gate guarded by five people in charcoal uniforms seemed to be the only entrance on this side of the facility.

"Is this the only entrance?" Sebastian whispered.

Kellry narrowed her eyes. "As far as I know. It used to be a really long electric fence, but Bram kind of disintegrated it years ago."

Sebastian blinked a few times before opening his mouth to ask, "Disintegrated?"

She shrugged. "Long story. Let's just say his eyes weren't always orange."

Interesting.

"I'd assume if there were any other entrances, they'd be just as heavily guarded," Ryan said. "If she's going to try to force her way through, this is where she'll do it. And seeing that these guards are still standing, I'm thinking she hasn't gotten here yet. I'm going to step out of the shield and see if I can locate her nerve tree anywhere close."

"Roger that," Kellry said.

Krueger threw him a thumbs-up. "Lead the way, kiddo."

Right. She's probably not here yet—that's the best possible news. Now I just have to find her before she does something stupid.

The moment he stepped outside of the shield, Ryan blinked to activate his ability. He was surprised he didn't feel tempted to quell any of his emotions. Muscles retracted, tensing in preparation to fight the mental battle.

Maybe the day I'll get myself sorted isn't too far off.

Focusing outside himself, Ryan opened his eyes. Soft green luminosity left streaming afterimages in the white blanket of fog as he scanned the forest. Almost immediately, he saw four glowing nerve trees walking along the east side of the wall, rapidly approaching the gate.

Wait...scratch that, five. That one's carrying someone else.

Ryan darted forward, motioning the others to follow at a distance. Now that his vision was unhindered by the fog, he danced around the trees trying to get a closer look at the five glowing humanoid figures. The glow of his eyes streaked alongside him like two concentrated trails from twin jet planes.

Operating under his ability felt familiar and strange. It had been a while since he'd held it in place longer than it took to simply Slice through the nerves of a few people close to him. His eyes would be tired after the extended use.

The world around him had transformed into blackness—every tree and bush, every animal outlined in thin white lines. Transparent images overlapped themselves as far as the eye could see. It was chaotic, but it was *his* chaos. He concentrated, stretching his sight beyond that of a normal person.

Five gleaming, spindly nerve networks began jogging toward the entrance.

I can't tell if Jory's with them.

Honing in on the figures, the pulsating mass of branching nerves bunched up in the arms of the lead nerve tree felt all too familiar.

It's her. It has to be.

If he was fast enough, Ryan could cut them off before they got there. But he was running from the west side. He'd have to arc around the entrance to keep from being seen by the gate guards and incapacitate them the moment he was in range.

I'm not going to make it.

The realization hit him hard, and he flew into a sprint. But no matter how much Ryan dulled the pain of pushing his muscles, no matter how much adrenaline flooded his system, it wasn't going to be enough.

An image of his sister racing across the school track flashed in his mind—long black ponytail streaming behind her like the tail feathers of a raven. She'd been so fast, so free, so...alive. He had to give that back to her. Had to make it up.

No matter what.

Changing tactics, he swerved to the left, skidding and tripping over fallen leaves. His arms windmilled for only a moment, then he was off, sprinting again.

Straight toward the gate.

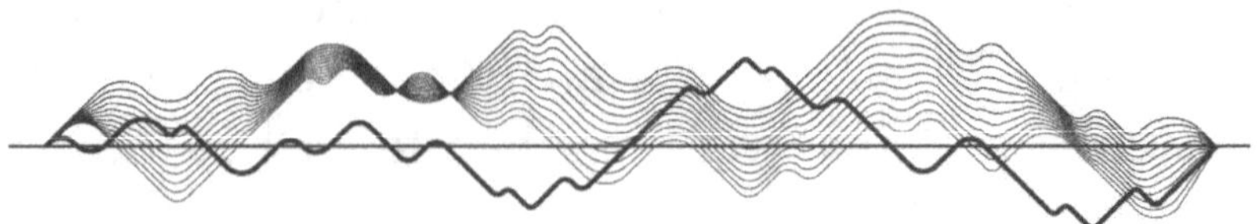

Chapter 36: Jory

"Anna, stop." Aiden's voice was even and cool, thanks to her calming his threads. Moments before, his eyes had been fiery with frustration, but now they were frozen over, something Anna had never seen before. He'd been angry before. This was different.

"But don't you feel better now?"

"You can't just play with the emotions of those around you. People have the right to feel, to react, to choose the way they live. If you mess with that, you're taking away their free will."

"But people are happier when I do this. I can tell what people need. I guide them, help them find the courage to say what they need to say, to calm down and think rationally."

"What happens when you're gone, Anna? What happens to these people when they aren't being 'guided' by you?"

Anna frowned and looked away. "I don't know. But they're better off."

He took her hand, smoothing his thumb over her skin. His voice was gentler now. "You can't know that. You're playing with fire, and it's wrong. People need to grow or not grow at their own pace."

He tipped her chin up, and she met his eyes. "They decide whether they are ready to share what's in their hearts. You don't have that right. Even if you are making that one moment better, ultimately it's not going to do any good. What you're creating is false."

"But —"

He frowned. "People aren't puppets, Anna."

It had been too easy.

Too easy to heighten the threads around her. All she had to do was play to the emotions that were most likely to get her what she wanted. It had only taken minutes to make them dance to her tune.

Three dancing mice to her pipe.

Oli had been first.

"It nicked your artery," Oli said, voice almost inaudible. He was a little short with black hair shaved close to his head and warm brown skin. "I'm going to have to pull out the arrow to repair it."

Liam laughed. "I thought that was obvious."

A thread of irritation flared within Oli, and Jory took the opportunity to feed it. The annoyance was an old one, buried beneath a timid exterior. Oli was not the confrontational type, and the amount of suppressed threads were like dry kindling waiting for Jory to drop the match. The thread swelled. Buried further was an ache, an adoration for the girl with the blonde waves and loaded crossbow. Jory tugged at it, slowly pulling it toward the surface. Easy to grab if she needed it later.

Oli yanked at the arrow, and white flashed over Jory's eyes. Jory gasped then whimpered softly as blood spurted out of the wound.

"Jory!" Ref was silenced by a solid kick to his midsection. His wild panic was distracting, so she calmed him, which took more effort than she thought it would. A twinge of guilt lit up among Liam's threads. She'd almost missed it while subduing Ref.

I can use that.

Liam's brows pulled down in deepening concern as she fed both the sympathy and the budding interest toward her.

"Would you hurry it up? Blood is squirting out like a freaking ketchup bottle." Liam glared at Oli.

Oli pointed an accusatory finger. "You're the one who shot her in the first place!"

Liam had already admitted this, but that was before his fleeting attraction was fanned into blind infatuation. His eyes darted to Jory then back to Oli.

"Leah shot the bow!"

"Of all the asinine things you could say." Oli gritted his teeth.

Patchy red blotches spread over Liam's neck and face. "Don't use stupid, smart words, Oli. You know how much I hate that."

Leah put up a calming hand. "Liam, let Oli work. The girl is bleeding, remember?"

Liam gritted his teeth but shut his mouth. Jory could have got him going again, but she waited, feeling woozy from the blood loss.

Sweat broke out on Oli's head as he took a deep breath.

"Sorry," he said.

Jory blinked in confusion, "For wha—"

Oli plunged a finger into the wound, and the blinding white slammed into her once more.

Mute the thread!

But it was so hard to think when someone was literally digging around inside her leg.

Pale and winded, he finished whatever the heck he was doing and sat back on his heels. Pulling out a water bottle, he rinsed his hands and her leg. Then he grabbed a length of gauze out of an army-green shoulder bag.

Jory glanced down. The wound was still completely open, but the bleeding had stopped.

"What did you do?"

He frowned, wrapping the white bandages tightly around her thigh. "I fixed the artery. Sorry I can't do more, but even that much takes it out of me."

He was a healer of some kind. Not like Damon, who had manipulated his abilities to his needs, but a true healer. Something Jory had never seen before.

"You're just weak," Liam said.

The anger within Oli was so easy to manipulate. Oli clenched his hands in response to her fattening the thread.

Arms cradled her as Liam lifted her to his chest. He jerked his head toward Leah.

"Grab hold of Helmet-Head. Oli doesn't have the balls to do anything if the guy tries something shady."

"Liam—" Leah glanced between the two, brow wrinkling with concern.

Liam began walking swiftly toward the gate.

"Sorry about the arrow," he said.

"That's all right," Jory answered, glancing at him from under her eyelashes. She felt ridiculous, but her efforts had the desired effect.

The boy's lips parted slightly in surprise, then a cocky grin split his face in two.

"Liam?" Jory did her best to make her voice sound fearful and innocent. "Where are you taking us? What did we do wrong?"

He tensed, and a thread of suspicion flared within him, but she quelled it. Shoulders relaxing, he gave her a reassuring smile.

"Don't you know what that wall is?"

She shook her head, eyes wide.

"You're at the Bureau." He ducked under a branch, and she took the opportunity to grip his shirt, turning the knob of his affection up another notch at the same time. He held her a little closer.

"The Bureau!" She sucked in a breath. "Liam, you can't take me there, I'm—"

She bit her lip and looked away, amping up the act.

"You're what?" he prompted with knowing eyes.

"I'm a Psychic," she whispered, close to his ear.

Liam was going to be her free pass to the top brass. There was no way they were going to get beyond those walls without being caught. She needed to give this boy a reason to take her straight to Brinsley. She'd sever the monster's thread, then find Dad and Aiden and incapacitate anyone else that got in her way.

I'll be able to see past Aiden's illusions. Heck, he'll probably sense my presence and make it easier for me.

It's a good plan.

It's going to work.

She glanced back at Ref, whom Oli had taken by the arm despite Liam's orders. He was tugging him along and saying something to Leah, who shook her head.

Ref met her eyes.

Trust me.

"Don't be scared," Liam said. "The Bureau isn't what you think. You'll be safe."

"Didn't you just try to kill us?" Jory hadn't wanted to say it, but hearing that word "safe" triggered her.

He had the decency to look sheepish. "You'll understand once you're there."

She made an effort to sound extra panicked. "You don't understand. My dad h-he was taken by the Bureau. He never came back. I can't go there."

She clutched his shirt a little tighter.

"Hey, hey, it's all right. Maybe I know your dad. I'm sure he's all right. Who is he?"

"His last name is Zamora. He's a Generator." Giving up this info was a gamble. But even if they knew who she was—knew she was an Empath—they shouldn't have their guard up too high. She'd never known of anyone strong enough to sever a life thread.

But then, I hadn't known Aiden's abilities were rare. They might know what I'm capable of.

She shoved the thought away. It was a risk she was willing to take.

Liam had stopped walking. "Zamora?"

He knows him. She'd expected that, no...more like hoped this boy would recognize the name. More proof that her father really waited beyond those walls. Liam could have spoken with him not long ago, maybe even today. Her heart lifted, sailing up her throat like a kite.

Jory nodded. "You know him?"

Liam's brows pulled down, his lips a grim line. One thread plumped up like a kinked hose.

Fear.

That's right, take me to Brinsley. At least...she hoped that's why he was spooked.

"Liam?" she prompted.

He blinked then glanced down at her, the threads of affection she'd fed glowing. "Maybe you should just go, forget about this."

For a moment, she cursed herself, realizing she might have spread the love butter a bit too thick. He glanced up, and Jory noted the glint reflecting off a black lens planted in one of the trees towering over them.

The fear inflated further, and pinpricks of pain stabbed her side as his fingers clenched tight around her.

An unnaturally strong thread of duty coiled around the fear, and they were walking again, then jogging.

Thank goodness.

Oli and Leah called out behind them, pumping their legs forward to match Liam's gait.

Her relief was short-lived when an all-too-familiar weave began to dash toward the guards waiting, un-knowing, at the gate.

Ryan, no!

Ryan leapt out of the tree line, arms out-stretched—jade-green eyes Slicing through the thickening white like huge fireflies. Three of the five men dropped like marionette dolls whose strings had been chopped with a bushwhacker.

The other two were invisible to her, like that girl Kala and Mateo had been.

Ryan halted in front of the other two guards, sizing them up.

Liam laid her on the grass. "Don't worry, I'll protect you."

"Wait, Liam. What are you doing?" Jory moved to stand, but Oli placed a hand on her shoulder.

"Don't undo all my good work."

"Leah." Liam's voice was soft, but the girl was already in front of them, and before Jory could register what was happening, she heard the soft twang of the crossbow releasing. Jory's head jerked toward her brother, but the arrow had missed. She sighed with relief until she heard her brother curse. The bolt had burrowed into his arm.

Ryan! She almost cried out his name, almost blew her cover. What had Liam done? How had he hurt her brother?

"Aww, I meant to get him in the kidney." Liam held up a quavering hand, the other resting firmly on his temple.

"You we're off by *that* much. Stop aiming for stupid stuff. Just brain him, Liam," Oli said, rolling his eyes.

He made it come back—changed its course.

"You're telekinetic," she said, her heart sinking.

He winked.

"You bet I am." Liam narrowed his eyes in concentration. "And this time, I won't miss."

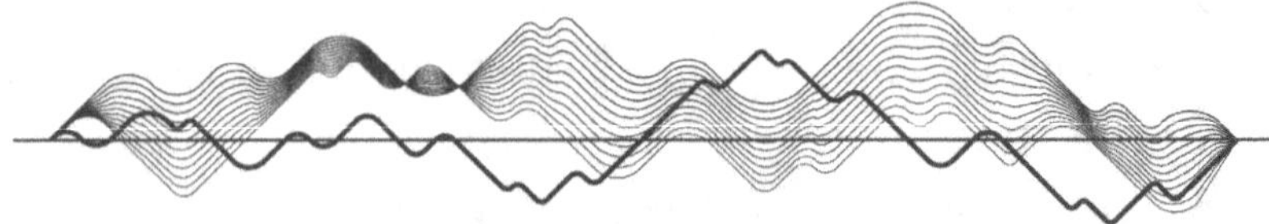

Chapter 37: Ryan

Of course two out of the five are Fortresses.

Ryan's left arm burned, so he went ahead and Sliced through his own nerves, letting his arm go limp at his side. He heard the soft release of a second bolt and lurched forward as it whistled past. When it missed, he scanned his surroundings to see if it would boomerang back like the one before. But it didn't. He took his eyes off the two guards and glanced Jory's way.

They were close now, and Ryan was able to identify not only Jory's nerve tree, but Ref's as well.

What is he doing here?

Arms tied behind his back, Ref had tackled another tangle of glowing lines with his body.

Jory's eyes glowed like icy globes hovering in front of the complex network that made up her brain. Lightning pulses of light coursed through her head. Even within the world of his ability, he could sense the venom in her gaze as those twin orbs of pale blue locked on him.

You're ruining everything! they screamed.

He was prepared for it, but it stung all the same. The sister he knew was gone. Replaced by...not Anna, but some hybrid of then and now with a nice big scoop of blind vengeance plopped on top.

The two guards he'd been unable to subdue spoke into radios strapped to their chests.

What do I do!

Ryan glanced around. Where was everybody? Turning his head back, he saw their wandering nerve trees some distance behind.

What the heck are they doing?

A thought hit him, and he turned off his abilities. Immediately, the world turned white. The fog was rapidly thickening, so he must have lost them in his mad dash toward the gate. Even now, Jory and the others were becoming ghostly shadows, shifting within the mist.

The two Fortresses charged forward as fog swirled around them. They ran like beefy versions of Mateo.

This is just great.

Ryan gritted his teeth and positioned his feet, but only one arm came up to guard his face. The other swung like a string of sausages with the arrow sticking out at an odd angle.

I'm so dead.

A burst of heat accompanied by a wall of flame left Ryan feeling like he'd toed the harsh, angled notes of Vivaldi's *Winter* and was catapulted backward into the racing, heated tones of *Summer*. The guards halted, skipping back as the tongues of crimson lashed out toward them. Kellry's hands moved with intricate motions, her fingers delicately arching in the air, but the fire shrunk when the moisture in the air choked the flames.

Muscles bulging, Roman released his Berserker abilities and barreled through the fire. Veins webbed around his neck and face, thick and ropey. He roared, a feral sound that left the hairs on Ryan's arms standing on end as he squared off with the closest Fortress.

Krueger strolled forward, cracking his neck from side to side.

"The cavalry has arrived!" Krueger gave a whoop and took a few bouncing steps while making a "come hither" motion with his hand. The other Fortress ignored him and charged Ryan instead of accepting the challenge.

Ryan braced himself, looking for some sort of opening where he could jab or duck away altogether. But this guy was so large. Every muscle was defined beneath his clothing, making Ryan acutely aware of all five-feet-three inches of himself.

I'm gonna be squashed like a bunch of grapes in a barrel. Like those wine-making ladies with their dancing bare feet, the fruit all wet and squelchy. I'll be mulch between their toes, juices flying, thin casings bursting with every step.

Toe jam.

A fist collided with his forearm like a sledgehammer against a pigeon bone. A loud snap rang loud in his ears. Ryan's pathetic attempt at a one-armed block had resulted in a broken radius. He could see the pale bone jutting out and the even paler exposed tissue.

He silenced the nerves mid-scream. Both of his arms hung limp now, blood trailing and dripping onto the forest floor. Heart hammering, body shaking, and stomach churning, frigid sweat coursed down his face. He was going into shock as the sight of his protruding interior caused his breath to come in panicked gasps. He numbed the panic, and immediately his breath slowed. His heart calmed to the gait of a racehorse instead of matching the pace of an ostrich with its tail on fire.

"RYAN!" Kellry's voice cut through the distance between them.

The guy cocked back another fist, but Krueger grabbed it, twisting and flipping the Fortress onto the ground. The guard's clothes burst into flames, but they were small, easily smothered.

Kellry cursed as the man hopped up once more with his white teeth bared. Charcoal streams of smoke billowed off his shirt.

Momma J stepped out of the tree line, appearing from the mist like a giant, angry poltergeist. He crept up behind the Fortress while Krueger let fly a barrage of punches. The guard blocked them all until a clasped pair of meaty fists came down on his head like Thor's hammer. The guy dropped hard, thudding to the earth in the ultimate K.O.

Momma J shook out his hands. Roman stood over the other Fortress, breathing heavily, knuckles dripping with the other guy's blood. His opponent's face was a pulpy mess.

"Well it's about time!" Krueger shook his head as Drake and Lane jogged into view.

"You had it covered," Lane said scornfully.

"We had it covered?" Krueger fisted his hands. "Look at the kid!" He gestured to Ryan. "He's freakin' armless! Hurry up and fix him."

Lane tsked. "I can't just wave a hand and put the doofus back together."

Ryan shook his head. "We don't have time for this. I guarantee more idiots are on their way. Let's grab Jory and get out of here."

Kellry was at his side, hands hovering over his mess of an arm. They shook slightly before she began ripping strips off the bottom of her shirt and tying them above his wounds, tight and efficient. The thin streams of blood slowed then trickled to meandering drips as she clamped the arteries shut.

"Can you see her in all of this?" Her voice was steady as she worked. Sweaty strands of red hair fell in disarray over her face. He wished he could brush them away, kiss her forehead, and tell her how amazing she was.

After all this, he would. Screw waiting.

Ryan nodded, activating his ability with a blink of his eyes.

"Crap in a basket," he muttered.

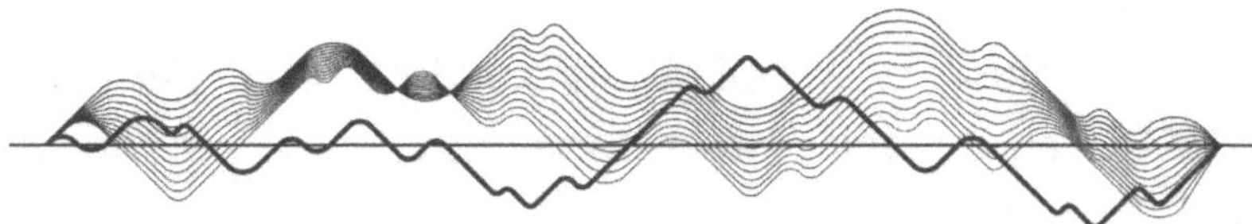

Chapter 38: Jory

Jory could see the weave amidst the fog, but now the white smothered anyone more than ten feet away. She couldn't quite make out what was happening on Ryan's end. A thread of pain burned white hot, but Ryan severed it almost immediately. His fading scream haunted her.

You shouldn't have come here.

"Get off me!" Liam pushed Ref off and kicked him hard in the stomach. "Freaking idiot! I thought I told you to hold him, Leah! I told you Oli was useless!"

Oli threw up his hands. "And you're a freaking headcase!"

"Oh ya?"

The two ranted at each other, and Jory used the distraction to edge over to Ref. He lay curled in on himself with his back toward her. She flicked open a small knife she'd swiped from Oli's medkit and carefully slipped it under the zipties then began cutting, calming the pain in Ref's belly before whispering in his ear.

"When you get the chance, run. I'm staying, so don't you dare look back." She closed the knife and slipped it into his hand. He clenched his fist over it.

She edged away from him once more.

Ref was angry—she could feel it.

Good. Get away from here, away from me. I'll only cause you trouble.

"Would you get a grip?" Leah stood between Liam and Oli. "There's enough testosterone between the two of you to fill an ocean."

Sunlight cut through the forest, clearing away some of the fog. About twenty people circled them, every last one invisible to the weave. Fortresses were dressed all in black, with helmets and bulletproof vests strapped over their chests. They held rifles and huge chunky handguns.

"Hand her over, Three-One-Four," one of them said, face hidden behind an opaque visor.

Liam flinched, the number clearly grating on him. His emotions were so strong now, others she hadn't even played with surfaced with a vengeance. She could almost read his thoughts.

Then memories. Memories and feelings forged into fleeting thoughts. A vague, cumulative picture was sketched out behind her eyes.

She felt Liam's doubt. Felt the utter boredom of walking around the facility day in and day out while holding meaningless conversations with smiling idiots. Felt that strange urge he had to follow instructions, an urge that battled with every rebellious bone in his body.

She felt his aching *need* to be free. It gnawed at his insides like termites through oak.

Jory saw the empty eyes of once-lively friends who came back out of "treatment." She shuddered at the indescribable fear he felt when it was his turn to go behind those white doors. Doors that slide shut without a sound, like a shroud dropped over a coffin. But then, nothing bad ever happened there...right? Liam was convinced of that, then the doubt would slowly creep in again and his treatments would escalate. Better not question—the Bureau was a safe haven, after all.

So Liam had turned his energy toward getting on the task force. He worked harder than anyone to become the perfect soldier, to harness his abilities so that he could step out of this cursed forest. Bring Psychics, like himself, back into the healing embrace of the Bureau. To protect them from the evil people outside who would hurt them—kill them.

Like his brother—shot down point-blank all those years ago.

But they never gave him a chance to prove himself. Just a string of false promises that fed his frustration day after day.

Now he had purpose. He had someone to protect again. Something inside him screamed that there was something wrong behind those gates and if he cared for this girl at all, he wouldn't take her through. What was this newfound love? This all-consuming desire to protect?

It was destiny.

Already she was opening his eyes to things he always knew deep down, things forcefully shoved so far that he'd lost them.

She was his destiny.

Jory pulled away from Liam's threads, gasping and shuddering. They'd held her as his mind screamed to be heard.

"That's an order," the man insisted.

"Yeah, yeah, okay." Liam's eyes remained distant as he lifted Jory in his arms. His grip and every muscle in his body tightened as he pulled her close to him. Every thread pulsed with the same purpose.

Fight.

Jory tried to calm his threads, but they bucked away from her like a wild stallion, slipping easily out of her fingers. Why had she fed them again? To get him to like her, to not question her? To get information from him? It all seemed so stupid now.

"Liam, don't," she whispered. "Just hand me over. I'll be fine."

He looked down at her and smiled, eyes tender.

"You're going to be all right."

Her stomach plummeted to her toes. *What have I done?*

People aren't puppets, Anna. Aiden's words were like nails hammered into her heart.

I'm so sorry.

Closing his eyes, Liam took in a long breath until every line on his face was smooth. Then his eyes snapped open. The air was vibrating, every pebble, every stone rising like gravity had become irrelevant, then shooting toward the men around them. Curses flew.

"Shoot him, Three-Zero-Zero!" A man shouted.

Leah lifted a shaking crossbow, but it jerked up and back, smacking her hard in the face.

Liam was shaking now, blood trailing down his nose and over his chin. He tilted his head back while the stones got larger, the barrage faster.

"WHAT ARE YOU DOING!" Oli screamed over the chaos. He lunged for Liam and was thrown back like a ragdoll, slamming hard into the trunk of a tree. Ref lay on the ground, curled into himself as debris threatened to impale him.

"Liam, stop!" Jory threw her arms around his neck. "It's okay, just stop. Stop!"

Why can't I calm his threads?

Blood was pouring out of his nose in earnest now, the veins on his neck and forehead straining against his skin. Red leaked out from the rims of his eyes.

"Liam, please! You're killing yourself!"

She'd known him for minutes, just minutes. How had this happened?

Some of the men sprawled on the ground got hold of their guns and started shooting. Thunderous bangs ensued that had Jory clamping her hands over her ears.

We're going to die. There's no way he can stop that.

Liam opened his mouth, a pained howl escaping his lips. The vibrations grew tenfold, bullets halting in their path, hovering in the air. One froze mere centimeters from Jory's face. Then, slowly, it turned and rocketed back the way it had come. Pockets of earth exploded around them, and men screamed as the bullets tore straight through their vests, burrowing into the flesh beneath.

Liam collapsed, taking Jory with him. She rolled off his body and lifted his head into her lap. His face was gray—eyes staring straight ahead. Veiny purple bruises spattered his skin where blood vessels had burst.

His gaze was glassy, and his threads were gone. Faded from the weave as if they'd never been.

Liam was dead.

Jory shook her head.

She held his head to her chest.

"Nononononononononono." The words spilled out in one continuous stream.

I drove him to this.

I killed him.

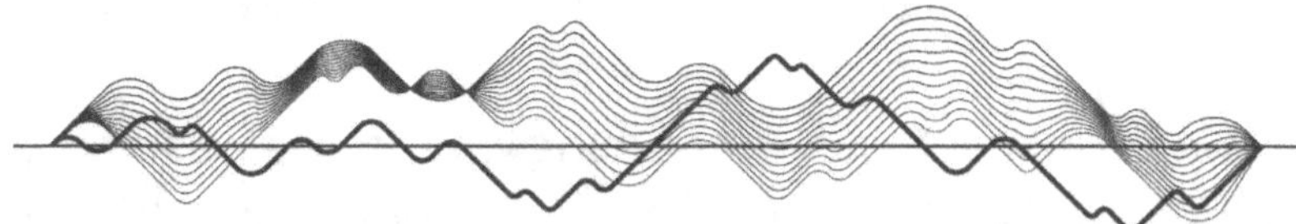

Chapter 39: Ryan

"What *was* that?" Krueger coughed, grimacing as he yanked a jagged stick out of his forearm with a shaking hand. "Does everybody still have their heads and or other essential limbs?"

"Is a head a limb?" Roman's gruff voice grumbled.

"I don't know, what else would it be?" Krueger asked, wrapping his arm with a ragged piece of cloth.

"A...well, a head, you idiot."

"Would you two just shut up? You're both idiots." Lane cursed, staggering to her feet.

"Ryan? Ryan, are you all right?" Kellry cupped his face in her hands, forcing him to focus on her.

Ryan had screamed for everyone to "hit the deck" just before an explosion of Psychic energy had torn through the air. He'd never seen anything like it. The boy carrying Jory...his nerves had lit up like a solar flare. A bright light that collapsed on itself within his body then whipped out in all directions like a neon-blue ring of raw telekinetic power. Ryan's eardrums had popped, and he could see blood trailing from everyone's ears.

A high-pitched noise hung above everything like one long, badly played note on a violin string, three octaves high.

Ryan couldn't focus. Something was off. He wasn't just being sluggish. It was like for a moment he didn't have control over his own limbs.

I can't feel my arms.

Wait. Of course he couldn't feel them. He'd cut them off. No, it was something else, some*one*.

"Ryan!"

Ryan hissed in a breath. "Yeah, sorry, yeah. I'm okay? I guess."

Kellry nodded, eyes wary as they coursed over the length of him. She had a nick above her left eye, and blood painted that side of her face.

"You're hurt." He went to touch her cheek, then mentally cursed himself when nothing happened. His arms were completely unresponsive, and for good reason.

Krueger, Roman, Lane, Kellry... Ryan ticked off all their names in the order he'd heard them. Who else? Momma J knelt on the ground while Drake wrapped torn cloths over his eyes. Blood bloomed through them, and Ryan pressed his lips together in a grim line, praying the gentle giant hadn't been blinded.

This was all falling apart faster than he had thought.

Wait. Someone's missing. He glanced over everyone again.

"Ryan, what's wrong?" Kellry asked.

"Where's Sebastian?"

Kellry's eyes widened, and she did a quick one-eighty search.

When was the last time I saw him? He couldn't remember. When he'd run off, maybe? Was he still lost in the mists? Ryan wouldn't put it past him.

"I don't see him," Kellry admitted.

He shook his head. Sebastian would have to wait. Ryan struggled to his feet, Kellry shouldering up under his armpit to help him.

I have to get Jory.

"C'mon," he said.

Kellry nodded, never moving from his side as they shuffled forward.

Ryan threw a glance over his shoulder. Momma J stood and began walking, and Drake was at his side, eyes glued on Kellry's back.

"You should stay," Ryan said to the Shield.

"I can see, if that's what you're worried about."

"How—"

"If I push my ability out a few feet around me, I can see. Not like I do normally, but...it is enough."

"Be careful."

Momma J smiled. "I'll do my best, Ryan."

Morning had come in earnest, sunlight bursting over the mountains. The fog was slowly dissipating, and gray, shifting shadows took the shapes of trees and brush.

Ryan stumbled, his foot hooking under a branch. Kellry caught him around his torso as his arms swung uselessly. The branch was soft, almost fleshy. He looked down.

Not a branch.

An arm.

Ryan fought down a surge of bile in his throat. The limb was bent at an awkward angle, a gun still clenched in its white-knuckled grip.

Peering into the dispersing mist, Ryan could see a multitude of black-clad guards lying, unmoving, their bodies impaled by rocks and debris of various sizes. They encircled his sister in a thick ring of groaning, writhing, and deathly-still bodies.

Ryan hadn't seen any of them with his ability.

Fortresses. All of them.

One man was peppered with a spray of pea-sized pebbles that had all gone straight through his torso. Another—struck by a boulder, the entire upper half of his...or her body crushed beneath it.

Ryan looked up from the carnage, zeroing in on Jory cradling a dead guy's head against her chest.

She mumbled something under her breath as she rocked slowly back and forth.

And then he saw him. Sebastian. He was tiptoeing around the bodies and wringing his hands when an arm sprung up and fingers grabbed at his pant leg. Sebastian squealed and kicked it away, his face twisted in a grimace of disgust.

"He lives!" Krueger gave an approving nod, and Sebastain returned the gesture with a wobbly smile.

He's coming from the opposite direction. Did he try to sneak around?

Sebastian was covered with tiny scrapes on both sides of his body as if a feral cat had been let loose upon him.

Sebastian's mouth flattened into a grim line as he watched Jory.

"...sorry, so sorry, I'm so sorry..." Her mumbles became clearer as she kept on.

Just get her and leave. We can't wait for her to snap out of it.

"Sebastian, grab her. Let's go. We don't have time."

He nodded. "Just let me wake up Ref. He's unconscious."

"Let Drake or Krueger get him. We need to leave. Now."

The hairs stood up on Ryan's neck. So slow—everyone was so slow. His arms felt like tube socks filled with rice, and each step was like walking through sludge. Gone were the speed and clarity that had focused every part of his mind and body mere moments before.

Sebastian placed a gentle hand on Jory's shoulder.

"Jor."

A stream of silent tears cut through the dirt on Jory's face, creating muddy trails. "Seb, he's dead, he—"

Ryan gritted his teeth. "Just grab her!"

Bang!

Sebastian glanced down at the hole in his shoulder. Dark, slick wetness blossomed on the plaid of his shirt like a black star. The shirt's pattern quickly disappeared beneath its rapid spread. One of the guards stood. She wore a tactical helmet with black-lensed goggles. But it was cracked and blood was leaking down her neck. She tore it off, and a mass of white braids unfurled. She bared her bright-white teeth and growled as she stepped toward Jory, one arm hanging limp at her side, the other aiming a gun straight at his sister's forehead.

Kala.

That couldn't be right. Kala might be rough around the edges, but she'd never do something like this.

A thin stream of smoke trailed from the barrel of her gun, disappearing into the lingering gray.

Too quick for thought, Kala fired again.

Ryan was ten feet away at most, but it was too far.

"JORY!" The scream tore from his throat as he lurched forward.

The bang shattered his insides as if it had torn through *his* flesh.

"SEBASTIAN, NO!" Jory's cry ripped through the morning like bone through flesh.

And that's when it registered. The lanky black man held the barrel of the gun, pressing it firmly up into his chest. He towered over Kala, and she screamed her fury into his face. When he flinched, Ryan saw the fear in his eyes. Not for the gun, not for the lifeblood soaking his clothing, but for the woman in front of him.

He was a giant before her, but his hands shook over the barrel.

Jory had told him. A long time ago—trying to get Ryan to sympathize with the guy who'd followed them out of Stark's Home and supported them. The guy who'd filled Jory's void as father, brother, and friend. The guy who had taken Ryan's place. Ryan had hated him for that, and at the time, it had only made him think less of Sebastian.

What guy was terrified of women?

A guy beaten by his own mother. But still, get over it, wuss.

That's what Ryan had thought at the time.

He'd been so heartless.

Sebastian coughed, blood spattering over Kala's face, flecks of red dusting her white hair.

"Sorry," he mumbled, before collapsing onto his knees. He didn't fall, just knelt there.

Head shaking, Jory reached out her hands, grasping at empty air.

Ryan could see Jory straining. A vein in her forehead pulsed, and her face was pale. It reminded him of another time. He switched on his ability. She was trying to feed Sebastian her life force—like she'd done with Krueger. A rope of multicolored threads connected Jory to Sebastian.

Sebastain's weakened heart pumped a little harder, but Lane wasn't there to stop the bleeding, wasn't there to close off the wound, and the blood just exited his body quicker. No, Lane was standing frozen behind him, useless. Like Ryan was useless.

Ryan severed the connection. Jory would die too at this rate, die for nothing. There was no way she could save him. Sebastian leaned and fell to the side, his body cradled by dead leaves.

"What a waste."

The last of the mist cleared away, burned off by the rising sun. Brinsley stood at the gate, surveying the bodies littering the forest floor. He stared down his beak of a nose at them all. Disapproving.

Then he smiled.

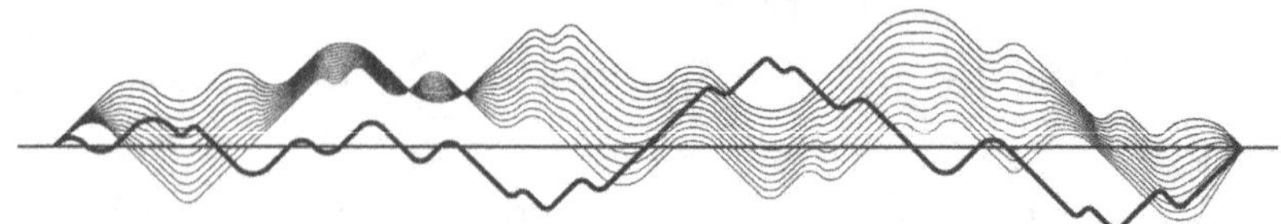

Chapter 40: Jory

"Love you, Jor," he'd whispered, as his eyes turned from warm brown to a dim, dark black.

Sebastian had become a void.

But...that was okay, because none of this was real. Not the boy still in her lap, his trusting, loving eyes still turned toward her. And not the body lying next to her, the skin turned an ashy gray from lack of blood.

But that man. That bald, pale thing standing before them, chin raised like he was king of the mountain—he was real.

And she was his personal reaper.

Kala grabbed Jory and yanked her up, making Liam's head thud unceremoniously against the earth. Then she hooked her arm around Jory's neck, pulling her close.

"Sir, what do I do with this one?" Kala asked.

"Diffuse her."

Jory flashed a feral grin, layering her world with the Tapestry. Brinsley's threads lay before her—bright, ripe, and ready for her to sever. She reached for the pale-green thread of life.

A sharp stab of pain in her throat made her gasp, and a cold rush flowed through her bloodstream.

The Tapestry disappeared—flickered out like a candlewick drowned in a puddle of wax.

Emptiness filled her, along with a cold dread.

Jory's abilities were gone.

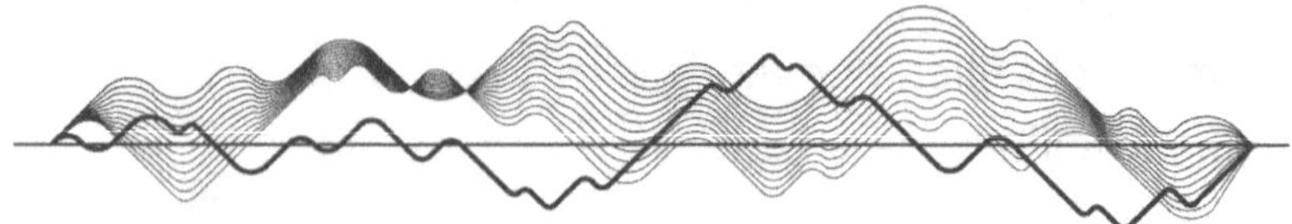

Chapter 41: Ryan

A dark, grisly silence squashed their lungs—bone-splitting grief choking out whatever oxygen remained. Brinsley stood, hardened and indifferent. Their loss was nothing to him.

Despite the momentary limbo, Ryan's brain was chaos. *O Fortuna* blasted through his mind, a chorus of dark fate forever at war within him.

Sebastian was dead.

Jory's limp body was being dragged off by Kala. Kala—who'd pumped lead into Sebastain's chest. What was she doing here? She was supposed to be long gone. Psychics and guards pooled out around Brinsley in an ever expanding semicircle.

It was over.

He'd failed.

Ryyy-aaan. His own voice spoke to him, calling out in a singsong tone. *I can help you, Ryan.* Black, inky tendrils stretched forward, offering relief, offering escape.

Go away!

I know our abilities better than you do.

Shut up!

I can give you your arms back.

Wha—

"I told you this was suicide," Lane said through gritted teeth.

"And I told you not to come," Drake shot back at her.

"I can't go back. I *won't* go back." Hysteria was laced through the quavering notes of Lane's voice. Her scars twisted and wrinkled as her brow knit downward in fear.

"Ah, my precious lambs are here at last." Brinsley lifted his arms in a gathering motion, beckoning them forward.

"You mean rats!" Kellry called back.

Brinsley shrugged. "Semantics."

"We aren't coming back, Brinsley," Drake said, jaw clenched.

Ryan had to give Drake props for not curling up into a sniveling ball. He actually looked a little imposing.

"Well that's unfortunate. Come, Calub." A little boy with glassy eyes stepped forward. It took a moment for Ryan to realize it was *their* Calub. Riri's Calub.

Riri's little brother stared up at Brinsley, his face blank and open.

What did they do to him?

"Just like I taught you, child, but leave the girls alive. Their kind is hard to come by."

Calub nodded, his irises shifting from brown to ghostly white. Ryan had seen that before, but it was impossible. Calub didn't have that ability. Calub was a Telekinetic, and a weak one at that, barely able to pick up a LEGO.

The only other person whose eyes bled out their color like that was Hans.

The Puppeteer.

And here they were, surrounded by a nice, fresh batch of dead guys.

Calub lifted his hands, fingers arching and falling like he was playing complex scales on a piano.

"Kellry, he's like Hans," Ryan hissed, loud enough for the others to hear him.

Immediately Kellry released her hold around Ryan's torso and swiped her hands together, her silver rings grating against each other. Heat roared to life, and this close, Ryan could feel a phantom breeze shaping the flames—something he'd never noticed before. The atmosphere was being sucked dry as the red fire swelled with life.

He could feel the others gearing up behind him. Grass and trees shriveled up as Lane continued to suck the moisture out. The water gathered around her in amorphous blobs. Krueger jacked guns off the bodies around them and cocked them back with a jerk of his arms. Drake copied the other man, pulling a pair of Glocks out of a guy's death grip.

Illusions didn't work against the dead, so Drake's meager Illusionist abilities were useless here. Momma J's eyes were still bound, but he placed his feet in a fighting stance, head cocked to the side, listening. Ryan wondered how well the Shield's *sight* would fare against the dead.

"They were Fortresses when they were alive, so maybe he won't be able to control them," Lane offered.

The bodies around them began to twitch then fling themselves upward.

"Sorry, Twoface," Krueger said, sighing. "The one time I wish you were right."

We're dead.

We don't have to be, Amadeus crooned.

I'm not talking to you!

Ryan locked eyes with Jory, held close at Brinsley's side. Her eyes were lifeless, just like they'd been after the night their mother died. After he'd let Bram take everything from her.

This wasn't supposed to happen.

We can get her back.

Ryan shoved Amadeus down, but he didn't budge. Instead, Amadeus stubbornly wedged himself into his consciousness.

Kala kneed Jory in the stomach, and his sister crumpled in a coughing heap.

All this time, Ryan had kept her safe the only way he knew how. He'd given up everything, everything! Including his sanity. And for what? They had her.

They had her.

"GIVE HER BACK!" Ryan's scream ripped from his throat, leaving him shaking.

Brinsley cocked his head. "And you are?"

Ryan blinked as the object of his hatred eyed him as if he were a fleck of mustard on his tie. Like the guy hadn't even had mustard on his sandwich, and there it was, yelling at him in bright-yellow fury. Why was it there? This lowly, disgusting, infinitesimal speck making pointless demands.

He doesn't remember me. I'm nothing to him. No one. He shot my mom, took my dad, and I'm just another face.

The Mindless surged forward. A mass of arms and legs, teeth and nails. Moaning, screaming, howling.

There was nothing for Ryan to cut through. This was just like in the sewage tunnels when he'd searched for the connecting thread amidst a sea of nerves flared to artificial life.

A Mindless leapt forward, hands reaching for his throat. The Mindless burst into flames but charged for him anyway. Ryan ducked, swiping his leg out and tripping it. Acrid fumes mingled in the air. Burnt flesh. It made him want to gag.

Bang! Bang! Bang!

"I hate these things!" Krueger unloaded the remaining bullets into the charging mass of bodies.

The shots tore through flesh and bone, some burrowing into skulls. But there were too many, and no matter how injured they were, they kept coming—crawling and clawing their way toward them. Some staggered aimlessly, disoriented by spheres of water encasing their heads. Others reached for Ryan, their bodies consumed in flame.

Magazines spent, Drake tossed his guns away and ducked down, searching for another weapon among the bodies that were still alive. One of the Mindless jumped on his back and bit into the tender flesh at his neck. His scream melded into the chaos. Water splashed to the ground as Lane rushed to Drake. Her hold on the enemy had shattered.

The Mindless who were once disoriented by her abilities regrouped, throwing themselves at them again.

Concentrate! You found the connection before. You can do it again.

I can see them. Let me help you, Ryan.

"JUST DIE ALREADY!" Kellry roared.

Her flames ate away at flesh, revealing the muscle and bone beneath. Desperation fueled her, and the wind picked up, feeding the flames into a rioting inferno and consuming the Mindless in red cocoons. Finally they began to fall, but fire spread from bodies to grass, then grass to trees now brittle and dry. The landscape lit like a wildfire at the peak of summer, and Kellry's hands fell to her sides as she stumbled backward in horror.

Like standing in the crumbling center of a hearth fire, the heat choked them. Smoke chased down their throats and filled their lungs. New screams erupted from the injured lying helpless on the forest floor. Momma J flung himself into the flames, appearing moments later with an unconscious Ref slung over his shoulder.

Still the Mindless came.

You're useless, Ryan. You can't protect them. You need me.

I can find it. I can find the connection! Just get out of my head so I can think!

"Ryan, get out of here!" Kellry shoved him.

"Can't you suck the flames back or something?"

She shook her head, the fire reflecting in her eyes. Her gaze leapt from him to her sister, who was fighting off the Mindless trying to kill Drake. Lane bashed its head with a rock over and over and over as it snarled.

"Enough!" Brinsley called out over the chaos.

Storm clouds gathered, forming in the treetops—swirling and unnatural. Lightning crackled and expanded, racing in an electric, net-like current through the charcoal clouds. The hair on Ryan's body stood on end as thunder boomed, drowning out the incessant ringing in his ears. Ryan had never seen clouds this low. Had never seen anything like this. The clouds released their moisture in a deluge that swallowed the flames and soaked them to the skin in an instant.

It ebbed into a drizzle almost as quickly as it had come. The scent of soggy, burnt hair mingled with the soft sizzle of misty rain steadily working to quench scorched skin. A girl stood at the forefront, the massive cement wall rising behind her. Bright sparks of static ran through her russet waves like a plasma globe. She looked so familiar, her tilted leaf-green eyes haughty and cold.

Treasa? But she's an Oculus. How is she controlling the weather? It reminded him of Lane's and Kellry's abilities. But it was something he'd never seen before.

Padraigin stood beside her, his orange curls plastered against his head.

What are they doing?

I know what it's like to be tied to another's will. To follow orders. Padraigin's words played through his mind. At the time, he'd thought he meant Bram.

He meant the Bureau. Him and Treasa both.

Brinsley patted Calub on the head, and the boy's ghostly gaze dimmed to brown once more. Immediately, the Mindless collapsed. Calub stumbled, eyes rolling back. A woman in pale-blue scrubs gathered him up in her arms, weaving back behind the guards.

Clap, clap, clap.

Brinsley's hands came together in a drawn-out applause.

"Look at you little rebels. So feisty."

"Cork it, Baldy." Krueger lifted a gun, arms straight and steady. Ryan could see his right index finger tighten on the trigger when the weapon simply fell apart. Each manufactured piece disconnected and tumbled out of Krueger's grasp.

"What the—" Krueger's jaw dropped, his eyes disbelieving.

Padraigin held up a quivering hand. His eyes blazed orange. Every gun left to their disposal fell apart, their pieces scattered across the forest floor.

You couldn't do anything. Useless. Always so freaking useless. Sitting there like someone just crapped you out on the grass.

They were taking them now, grabbing Ref and Momma J, zip-tying their wrists together.

"I won't go back. I'm not going back!" Lane kicked, spat, and bucked as they tore her off of Drake's limp form. "Drake, don't let them take me! DRAAAAAAKE!"

That deep, throaty hum poured out of her, and the people around her began to writhe as their blood boiled. Brinsley rolled his eyes and gestured to Treasa. When she nodded, a bolt of electricity shot from her outstretched hand. Lane shuddered as the yellow javelin of light hit her in the chest. Smoke steamed from the hole singed in her shirt, and her good eye rolled back as rain misted over her swaying body. She fell in a heap, feet and fingertips twitching. Ryan activated his ability for a moment, noting the live nerves. Lane wasn't dead. Not yet.

Kellry watched her sister, tears of frustration and hate brimming in her eyes.

I'm sorry. Ryan's heart ached for her.

You can still save her. At least just her, Amadeus whispered.

A hand landed on his shoulder. "Don't beat yourself up. We chose to come with you, kid."

Krueger's words pierced his gut one after the other—a fleet of arrows burrowing deep.

Brinsley nodded to Padraigin. "Round up the rest. I'm curious to see if any of them offer any promise."

Brinsley paused, considering something. "Is the one you told me about among them?"

Padraigin nodded, eyes flicking to Ryan.

Brinsley appraised him anew. "Ah, yes. Well he seems... formidable."

His brow lifted, a small smirk pulling at the corner of his mouth.

I'll bite your friggin' beak off your bald head. Ryan bit down on the words, wondering what Padraigin had told the director.

Brinsley narrowed his eyes, meeting Ryan's hostile gaze, then clasped his hands behind his back.

"Yes, well. Like I said, round them up. If any offer you any resistance, even that one," he nodded toward Ryan, "kill them. Except, of course, the Elementals."

Padraigin gave a firm nod, and Brinsley patted him on the shoulder before walking back through the gate with the majority of the Psychics in tow. Kala yanked Jory along. His sister followed, eyes distant.

I lost. She's gone. He wanted to punch something, to curse until his throat bled, but all he could do was stand there as the last of the guards surrounded them.

Kellry held out her wrists to the man approaching her, and he punched her across the face, sending her flying onto the wet earth.

"That's for your little firestorm, you freak."

Her gloved fingers dug into the ashy mud, but she stayed silent, standing and holding her wrists out once more, chin tilted up in defiance. The guard cursed and cocked his fist back again.

It was her silent defiance that tipped Ryan over the edge. Kellry would be her glorious self, and they would punish her for it. Punish her until the light dimmed from her eyes. Just like his sister.

"Don't touch her," Ryan growled. His ability flared to life.

This guy wasn't a Fortress. He wasn't anything. Just your run-of-the-mill meatbag. Ryan Sliced, cutting straight through the base of his skull. The guy crumbled like the ashen trees surrounding them.

"Ryan, there are too many. They'll kill you." Kellry held his face in her hands.

Her hair was soaking wet, tendrils crisscrossing over her face in a tangled web of silken, crimson threads. He wished again that he could tuck them out of the way. He wanted to trace his fingers along her jawline and press his thumb against her lips. He wanted to hear her laugh with her head back and eyes dancing. He wanted to laugh with her. Wanted to engage in snarky, sarcastic banter. Wanted to kiss her till their breath came out in short bursts, hearts pounding. Wanted to just hold her, feel her head pressed against his chest.

Everything that she was would be gone. If he let her walk through that gate, *this* Kellry would be gone forever.

I can't let that happen. Not now.

Sebastian was dead, Jory was taken.

I wasn't able to protect anyone. Not one single person.

He couldn't do it on his own. He'd failed at *everything* so far. Miserably. What was the point of fighting when everything he was trying to protect was gone? Why not hand it over to the one person who could actually do something?

"I'll be okay," she insisted.

Amadeus.

Yes.

Promise me you'll save her.

I promise.

Ryan let out a long sigh, relinquishing control to the encroaching blackness.

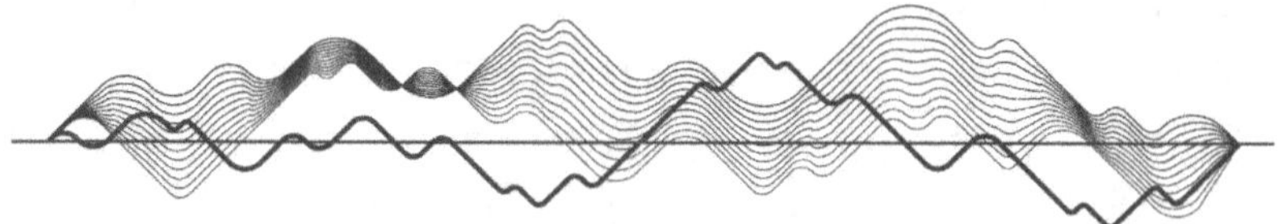

Chapter 42:
Amadeus

Amadeus rolled his shoulders.

His shoulders.

Finally. He'd missed this. Missed the feeling of control. Missed *feeling*.

Closing his eyes, he surrendered to the glowing network within. Most people misunderstood the structure of bones. They believed they were made up of dead tissue. When in fact, they were teeming with live cells and pain receptors.

Nerves.

Tiny hair-like strands branched out in great clusters that Amadeus played with. So many severed lines—his skin ripped open, his bones broken and tearing through tissue.

But that's all they were—severed nerves.

Amadeus connected them, pulling them together, letting them meet and meld. Bone sunk beneath skin, skin crawled over tissue, and soon his arms were whole once more. He was still a bit faint, for he could not replace the blood he'd lost.

Yanking off the cloth Kellry had tied to close off his arteries, he revived the muscle, felt the flow of blood down to his fingertips, and relished the lingering soreness. The arrow pattered to the ground as he forced it out. Amadeus flexed his hands and grinned.

Kellry was saying something to him, insisting on his response. He ignored her, looking instead at the guards around them—counting, calculating. Ryan loved this girl, and Amadeus had promised to save her. He would fulfill that promise.

Jory was out of reach, which was a good thing. He wasn't sure he would have kept a promise to save *her*. Ignorant idiot. That girl would forever be the source of Ryan's pain. Good riddance.

Padraigin's gaze honed in on him. Eyes questioning. He knew what Amadeus was capable of. But no one had quite seen what had happened with the limp guard. Not to mention Amadeus's body looked a mess—bloody, filthy, and swaying slightly, like he might faint at any moment.

"Ryan!" Kellry was being yanked away, and a ring of men and women surrounding Amadeus shot hesitant glances at the man he'd incapacitated.

Amadeus met Kellry's dark, almond eyes, and she blinked.

She knew. She knew right away that Ryan was gone. Her pale skin turned paler, and her lips twitched. He couldn't tell if she was angry or afraid. Maybe both. But she knew.

Smart girl.

He Sliced. Like a conductor's baton, thin and precise, he orchestrated their demise. Cutting through spines, watching as they fell, their bodies splayed out on the ground. Krueger whooped.

"Nice, kid!"

The hairs on the nape of his neck lifted, and Amadeus dove to the side as a blast of lightning crackled past him.

Treasa.

Adrenaline released.

This was the feeling. Heart beating, senses carved down to needlepoints of precision. He could smell the wet earth, taste the tang of electricity clinging to the rain as it fell in cool, misty swathes on his face. He'd been yearning for this for so long, watching in frustration as Ryan completely wasted it—took it for granted. Numbed it away.

Rolling to his feet, Amadeus ran toward Treasa. He needed to get in range to Slice through her nerves. Just a few more feet. With Padraigin and Treasa out of commission, they'd have a solid chance at running away.

Rocks and debris blasted toward him. A man thrust his hands forward as he manipulated the objects around him. Amadeus ducked and weaved, but a rock gouged through his cheek, and he hissed in pain as he Sliced through the Telekinetic's optic nerves. The guy stumbled forward, mentally chucking objects at random. Amadeus laughed as the blinded man's panic grew. A Berserker roared, muscles bulging as he charged, but it was easy to cut through his legs. He watched with a sneer as the guy pitched forward, eating mud.

The air hummed and Amadeus dropped to the earth, a spear of yellow light shooting over him. The air buzzed and cracked, and gooseflesh rippled over his skin.

Take care of Treasa, or you'll be dead.

Propelling himself forward, he ran, ducking low and zigzagging. Javelins of pure energy zipped past him, gouging out pockets of earth and creating mini craters in their wake. Out of the corner of his eye, metal flashed as Padraigin assembled an assault rifle out of the scattered parts lying around. Leftovers from his previous dismantling. Padraigin's eye settled into the scope.

Just a few more feet.

Amadeus grinned.

Gotcha.

Thick yellow strands of static laced around Treasa's body, branching out into the drizzling rain. Her tilted green eyes were bright and concentrated as she pointed at him. Amadeus swept out a hand, throwing as much mental force into the severing motion as he could muster.

Another spear of light shot toward him. The Psychic wave rammed through Treasa with the impact of an electromagnetic pulse. Her body was thrown back, producing an audible crack as it smacked against the cement wall. The lightning spear exploded into his side, and Amadeus arched his back, neck strained, fingers splayed, feeling as though he was being fried in a microwave with the dial set past ten. His teeth slammed together. He barely registered Treasa sinking to the ground with static still crackling over her.

Lightning propagated through the air, and he grunted as sharp white pain collided with his shoulder.

Ah yes...Padraigin. That's unfortunate.

When Amadeus fell, his world grew foggy as blackness collapsed at the corners of his vision. He was finished. They were finished.

I promised. I promised him.
Amadeus staggered to his feet.
Bang!
A great torrent of air rammed into them, dragging the bullet to the right. Another gale raged past, hurling Padraigin into the wall. Again and again, great gusts slammed his body against the cement until he lay as still as Treasa. Kellry was using wind? Amadeus groaned as a strong arm lifted him, tossing him up and over broad shoulders. A thick blanket of darkness swept over him, and he swore he could hear the slanted tones of *Lacrimosa*, the dark chorus whispering, creeping into his ears in scattered patches.

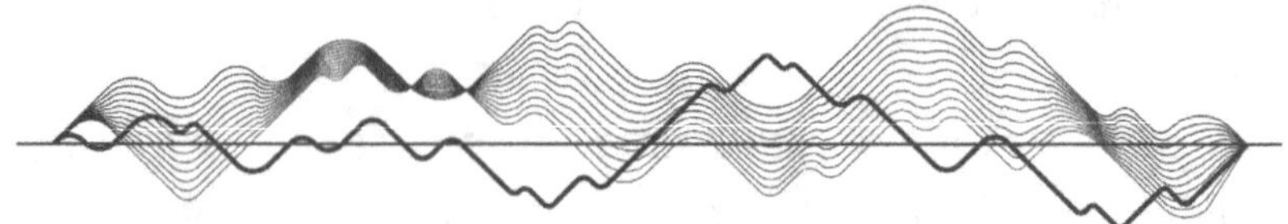

Chapter 43: Kellry

I've broken the covenant.

Again.

The first time was when she'd guided Ryan home with gentle pushes and nudges from her winds all those weeks ago—what felt like an eternity ago—when he'd been out of his ever loving mind.

Then again, to stop Roman from punching Ryan. But she'd never broken the covenant quite so flagrantly as now. That boy was trouble.

He's worth it, though.

Elementalist. What a stupid term. Kellry was a Gale Binder. A sacred oddity amongst her people. Her guise as a Fire Keeper had been a poor one, a distraction from what she really was. Only Lane knew, and if she found out what Kellry had done on multiple occasions—

Oh. Right. Lane was...

Heat burned in her chest, racing up her throat to choke her, smothering her in despair. She swallowed it, fisting her hands.

Face it. What's done is done.

Her mother's voice whispered softly. *Next steps, Kellriah-va. What is your next step?*

"Cheese whiz and rat piss!" Krueger growled. Damon Farrow, the Silvertongue, finished spraying antiseptic and began wrapping Krueger's bicep with fresh white linen.

"Couldn't you just sing some jaunty tune and make the bacteria jig away?"

Damon's deadpan stare made Krueger fidget slightly.

"No," he answered after a long moment. "I used too much of my energy coaxing Ryan's blood cells to multiply faster."

They all took that moment to glance at the slim boy lying on a faded blue cot. Washed and bandaged, a rust-red smear of drying blood stood out—stark against the white linen.

The lines of his face were smooth, the typical pinched skin between his brows relaxed for once. The angled lines of his face begged to be traced. Although he did not see it, Ryan was darkly handsome. A killer mix of warm beige skin, black, unruly hair, and brooding pale-green eyes. The kid could make a girl crumble into a million Fruity Pebble pieces from a mile away.

But now, the richness of his skin had been leached away, and his eyes sunk deeper into his skull than they ever had before. Shiny red burns spread over his right side like the branches of a slender tree or like that split-second flash of lightning as it sliced across the sky, bright, clawing fingers ravaging the night.

Somehow Treasa was able to use the abilities belonging to a Tempest Knight. Which did not bode well. It meant Brinsley had gotten his hands on yet another of her people.

Kellry reached out a hand, trailing her finger down one of the branches then over to his arm, where hours before his bone had been protruding through flesh.

How had it healed Ryan's wounds? That dark alter. She hated that thing.

What did it want?

It had risked its life, risked Ryan's life, to save her.

Why?

Krueger cursed, tearing his eyes away from Ryan's battered body. His fingers tangled into his hair as he hung his head.

Kellry pursed her lips.

Next step, Kellriahva, her mother's voice prompted.

It was time to go home.

That was, if she could find it.

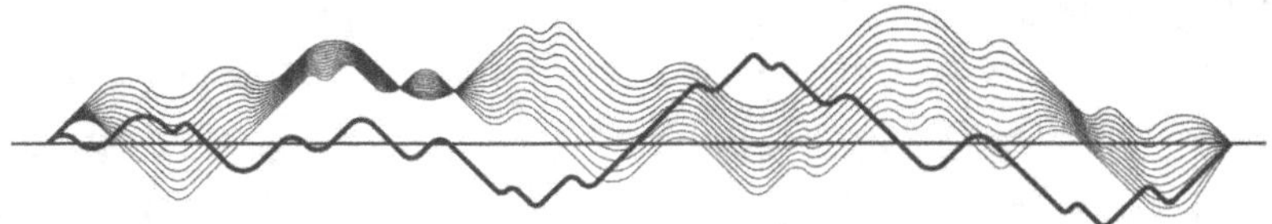

Psychic Abilities

Berserker- Releases muscle-enhancing chemicals within their body to become exponentially stronger.

Candor- Tricks others into telling their secrets and coaxing out their true feelings.

Empath- Feels the emotions of those around them as if they are their own, and in some cases, their physical pain. They can access the Tapestry, where people's feelings display as a great weave of colored threads. Strong Empaths can manipulate the threads while tapping into the Tapestry and use them as a portal to step into others' dreams.

Fortress- Immune to all other Psychic abilities.

Generator- Produces great amounts of sustained energy that can power anything that runs off electrical currents. They can also use that energy to shock those around them.

Healer- Heals physical wounds.

Huntsman- Pinpoints other Psychics within a certain radius.

Illusionist- Manipulates the senses by making others perceive things that are not real. Typically, they can only affect one or two of the five senses.

Infiltrator- Sees the world and objects around them as a massive 3D blueprint and can dismantle and reconstruct objects at will. Their eyes turn orange when accessing their ability.

Krueger's ability- Does not have a name. Krueger forces his victim into a dream state. Anything he does to someone in their dreams happens in real life. If Krueger kills his victim in the dream state, that person dies in the real world. Likewise, any injuries Krueger sustains comes back with him as well.

Mind Render- Rewrites memories, creating false realities. There is only one Psychic known with this ability.

Muffler- Nullifies any technology around them within a certain radius. They can sense electronic waves and signals. For some, it's even possible to mentally probe into phone conversations.

Oculus- Shares sight with another person. While activated, their eyes change to match the color of the person they are sharing sight with. They can also speak mind to mind while using shared sight.

Pacifist- Soothes others' emotions. Unlike an Empath, they can only sense and Soothe others' emotions and do not feel them as their own. They also cannot access the Tapestry.

Puppeteer- Controls the dead by reanimating dead bodies, creating Mindless. While enacting their powers, their eyes turn ghost white.

Rashida's Ability- Rashida is close to a type of Seer, except it's more intuition than seeing the future. Her ability allows her to sense attackers' moves before they land.

Seer- Sees glimpses of the future. Some people can only see a few minutes ahead while others can see years into the future. It is a rare ability that varies greatly from person to person.

Shield- Blocks other Psychic attacks weaker or on par with their own abilities. They send out a "bubble" of Psychic energy that makes anyone caught inside it unable to access their abilities.

Silvertongue- Convinces a person's mind to do things it normally wouldn't be able to do, like making a body heal faster. Incredibly rare.

Sleeper- Renders a person unconscious for an extended period of time with a mere "pinch." Abilities only work when making physical contact with a victim. Depending on how powerful the Sleeper is, a person could be put out for days or even months at a time.

Slicer- Sees glowing-white strands of light (called "nerve trees") that make up a person's nervous system and "cuts" through them, making limbs or organs limp or nonfunctioning. They can also see these "nerve trees" through walls. When this ability is enacted, the user's eyes glow. Rare.

Similar to an Empath, Ryan is able to see emotional threads as separate colored strands of light and can manipulate them.

Telekinetic- Moves or manipulates objects through thought.

Teleporter- Can travel from one point to another instantaneously.

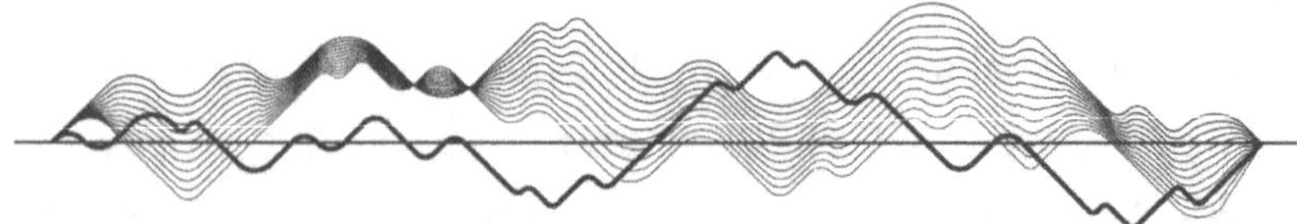

List of Characters

Aiden Ellis- Illusionist.

Amadeus- Ryan's alter.

Amare Johnson- Not Psychic. Kala's younger brother.

Anna/Jory- Empath. Ryan's older sister.

Bram- Mind Render. Escaped from the Bureau. Uses underhanded methods to capture Psychics with plans to ultimately fight against the Bureau.

Calub- Telekinetic. Riri's little brother.

Camden/Ref- Muffler. Works for Drake. He uses his ability to keep Drake's hideout off the grid so Bram and the Bureau can't find them.

Cormac O'Riley- Not Psychic. Head scientist and researcher at the Bureau.

Corwin- Seer. Taken in by Drake when Bram tries to capture him and his brother David.

Damon Farrow- Silvertongue. Escaped with Bram from the Bureau. He uses his abilities to heal fellow Psychics.

David- Sleeper. Taken in by Drake when Bram tries to capture him and his brother Corwin.

Director Brinsley- Not Psychic. Head of the Bureau. Leads the experiments on Psychics to find new ways to blend and harness Psychic abilities.

Drake Wesley- Illusionist. Formed a team of Psychics to save people from both Bram and the Bureau.

Eileen Kilpatrick- Huntsman. Works at Stark's Home to help find and take care of abandoned or orphaned Psychic children.

Hans Berkenstein- Puppeteer. Escaped with Bram from the Bureau and continues to work with him.

Jack Graydon/Momma J- Shield. Works for Drake.

Kala Johnson- Fortress. Amare's older sister. Works for Bram in order to get her brother back.

Kellry- Fire Abilities. Lane's younger sister. Escaped from the Bureau as a young girl and works with Drake to save Psychics from Bram and the Bureau.

Krueger- His ability has no name. Works for Drake.

Lane- Healing abilities. Kellry's older sister.

Liam- Telekinetic. Prisoner of the Bureau.

Leah- Illusionist. Prisoner of the Bureau.

Mateo- Fortress. Escaped with Bram from the Bureau and continues to work for him.

Mike- Not Psychic. Bram's guy for all things tech. Used to work as a researcher for Brinsley and the Bureau.

Oli- Healer. Prisoner of the Bureau.

Padraigin- Oculus. Works for Bram.

Rashida- Ability allows her to see attackers' moves before they land. Works for Bram.

Remy- Not Psychic. Works for Drake.

Riri- Teleporter. Calub's sister. Lives at Stark's Home with her brother. Uses her abilities to help Drake.

Roman- Berserker. Used to work for Bram, but switched to work for Drake after falling in love with Eileen.

Ryan Zamora- Slicer. Anna's brother.

Sebastian Davos- Sleeper. Met Anna and Ryan at Stark's Home.

Treasa- Oculus. Works for Drake.

Acknowledgements

When I first started devouring books, my mind itched to create new worlds both fantastic and meaningful. However, after reading over my first attempt at a story (where a girl gets whisked off into a fantasy world on a pegasus accompanied by two highly attractive elf boys), I realized I was better off reading stories than writing them.

But every now and then, a creative writing project would come along and words would spill from my fingertips like a freshly tapped tree.

Pure magic.

So (with a bit of trepidation) I took up the pen again, and here we are. Writing has saved me in more ways than one, and to sit here and be typing this at the end of my first published novel is a literal dream come true. So you bet I'm going to thank all the people who have made that dream a reality.

First and foremost, I'd like to thank my husband. Robert, thank you for the brainstorming sessions, and the six-hour car drives where every moment was spent fleshing out my latest idea. Thank you for your brilliant mind that helped me solve problems I'd deemed unsolvable. Ryan and Jory would definitely not have made it this far without you.

A big mamma hug to my kiddos: Alivia, Ryker, Rae, Airi, and little Kai, for giving me the space to be your mom *and* a writer. I love you. Each of you fill my world with joy.

A special thanks to my mom, for those almost daily trips to the library to sate my never-ending appetite for literature, for comforting me during all those query rejections, and for telling me not to give up.

To my dad, thank you for being so excited for me and for asking about my book every time you see me.

Hannah and Chantel. We all knew you'd be here. I couldn't have done this without either of you. Thank you for reading draft after draft, for combing over every word and correcting all those silly commas. You know you have a great critique group when you open up the document to find over 600 comments. The only reason I was praised for having such a clean manuscript was because of you crazy, talented ladies.

Ashley Bustamante, my talented author friend and cover artist extraordinaire. You swept in like a battle maiden of old and saved the day. Thank you for dropping everything at a moment's notice to read my work and answer my questions about the industry. You are simply stunning (also, thank your hubby for reading my book and loving it).

To my dear friend and cheerleader Elise George, thank you for reminding me of my worth and being ready to go full redhead on anyone who makes me feel otherwise. Bad reviewers beware.

To the beautiful Julie Spier, for listening to every book plot to every book I've read or written since we were seven, and never telling me to shut up. That's what best friends are made of.

Thank you to the Gordan Gang for being the best fans ever. Especially Melissa for being so angry with me that I hadn't written the sequel yet. The wait is almost over.

Thank you to my ultimate champion, the one and only Dennis Gaunt. I don't think I truly believed in my story before you messaged me that day.

To the lovely Lisa. Lisa Mangum, you are a word fairy. Thank you for taking me under your wing, for waving your magic writing wand over my head and filling it with all the writing tips and tricks a girl could ask for. (And thank you for slipping me your card at my first conference, that was totes smooth.)

To my dear Julie Wright. Thank you for being my first ever mentor, for being the absolute purest human being I've ever met, and for teaching me the importance of chasing my characters up a tree and lighting that tree on fire.

To my incredible publisher, AJ Skelly. Thank you for loving my writing, for fangirling over my characters and being so excited for every win along the way. I look forward to all the amazing things we'll do together.

To my first official beta reader and editor, Amanda Wright. Your comments made me snort with laughter. Thank you for always following up on me and for being my friend.

Thank you to my line editor Denica for making *Fractured* pretty and ready for printing, and to all my other editors and beta readers. And also to all the authors at Q&F, your stories are inspiring, and I love each and every one of you.

To my education teacher in college, thank you for telling me that I should pursue writing instead of teaching. You were right.

And most importantly, thank you to my Father in Heaven. For sending that undeniable prompting to pull *Fractured* back out from where I'd shelved it after all those rejections. It was nothing short of divine intervention.

www.ingramcontent.com/pod-product-compliance
Lightning Source LLC
Chambersburg PA
CBHW070305310726
48976CB00005B/1579